MARSHLIGHT

A totally enthralling psychological thriller
with a stunning ending

JOY ELLIS

Detective Matt Ballard Book 4

JOFFE
BOOKS

Joffe Books, London
www.joffebooks.com

First published in Great Britain in 2021

ISBN: 978-1-78931-852-4

This book is dedicated to Debbie Oldenhove.

You really have travelled a rough road in your battle with blood cancer. I, and so many others who care about you and admire your incredible courage, all wish you a return to good health in the very near future.

This one's for you, brave and special lady!

With love, Joy

PROLOGUE

Frances Morton sat towards the back of the small restaurant, well away from the window. She hated subterfuge, but it seemed that there were times when it was necessary. For the fifteen years of her marriage, she had been piggy in the middle between her husband and her sister. Neither seemed to realise that she had enough love for both, that their deprecating, sniping comments about each other hurt her terribly.

Jason was by far the worse of the two and that was why she was reduced to meeting Amy in secret, over a snatched lunch in a tiny backstreet restaurant. Frances regularly sneaked money from the housekeeping budget and saved it up to pay for these stolen hours with her sister, as Amy rarely had cash to spare. Not that she was mean or a sponger, it was just that money meant little to her and budgeting had never been her strong point.

She watched the door. Today she felt nervous. Their last meeting had been strange, to say the least, and now she was understandably apprehensive. Her sister, Amy Roberts, had always been a butterfly of a girl. Even in winter, she wore the brightest colours imaginable. Her clothes made people stop and stare, and she regarded every moment as a beautiful thing to be enjoyed at all costs. Like the butterfly, she never

1

settled for long: she flitted from friend to friend, lover to lover, and then flew away again. Not that she left a trail of broken hearts behind her. As far as Frances knew, there were no harsh words, just smiles, gratitude at having known her for a brief, colourful interlude. There was no doubt that she was an enigma.

Frances sighed. From childhood onward, the two of them had been like chalk and cheese. She was the "serious" one, the worrier, the one who married her first boyfriend after a suitably long engagement. He might be a pain where Amy was concerned but other than that, Jason was the perfect husband. Hard-working, conscientious and as serious about life as she was. Which probably explained his dislike of her hedonistic and unreliable sister.

She looked at her watch. Amy was late, but that meant little. She seemed to run to a different timetable from everyone else and was so easily sidetracked she was rarely punctual. Though that wasn't true of their last meeting a month ago. Amy had arrived on time and when she did, Frances had hardly recognised her. She had looked . . . well, ordinary. Plain clothes, flat shoes, no bright coloured streak in her hair. She was just not Amy. Frances's shock had been impossible to cover up. Amy had shrugged it off, saying she'd realised it was about time she grew up, then thrown in a comment about how dear Jason would probably approve of her seeing sense at last. Then she had told Frances that she had a regular job. At that, Frances had almost choked on her wine. As long as she could remember, Amy had never had a "regular" job.

Frances had left the restaurant feeling almost bereft. It was as if the real Amy had sent a very poor substitute in her place. This ersatz sister had no zest, no fun in her smile. Where had all her energy gone? All she could put it down to was Amy having met someone. Someone who had had a major effect on her. Amy had intimated as much, but said it was early days and she wasn't quite sure where this relationship was going. She had refused to say more, even though Frances had begged her to describe what this person was like.

The waiter interrupted her thoughts. Might she like to order now?

She knew then that Amy was not going to turn up. For the first time since they had started meeting in secret, Frances was going to eat alone.

An hour later, she left the restaurant, sad and ill at ease. Amy's phone was switched off and Frances suddenly realised that she had no other way of contacting her. She didn't even know where her sister was living, or who with.

Frances walked slowly home. Chalk and cheese they might be, but they had always had an unspoken bond, a connection, and in her heart Frances felt that somehow the gossamer thread that joined the two of them had been severed.

CHAPTER ONE

Liz Haynes stared miserably at her computer screen. After scrolling through the whole folder of pictures, marked up "Case Number Fourteen, Boyd Investigation," she shook her head. What the hell was she doing? The intimate photographs she had taken made her out to be some kind of voyeur. This was it, no more infidelity jobs. She felt a gentle squeeze on her shoulder.

'I know exactly what you're thinking.'

Hearing that familiar deep voice, she smiled. 'Well, Matt Ballard, you never mentioned you were related to Gypsy Rose Lee.'

He grinned at her. 'I don't need a crystal ball to understand what is going through your head. Our revered client, Mrs Thelma Boyd, is a sour-faced bitch and her husband, the faithless Mr William Boyd, is a likeable, friendly sort of man. You feel pretty grubby taking pictures of him in the works car park with his personal assistant.'

'*And* I can recognise love when I see it.' She closed the file and turned to face Matt. 'If only he'd had the courage to tell his wife, gone down the painful but ultimately safest and fairest route, and divorced her. He'd have saved us all this horrible sordid mess.' She sighed. 'Oh, Matt. I love our PI business, really I do, but—'

He held up his hands. 'But no more spying on cheating spouses?'

'I know it's what private investigators are supposed to do, but we can afford to cherry-pick, can't we?' She looked at him hopefully.

'We can and I'm fine with it. It'll be a bit of a relief, actually.'

Liz exhaled. Thank goodness. The last two infidelity cases had really got to her. Matt, on the other hand, was more detached. And since they were usually quite simple and lucrative jobs, she had wondered how he would take it. 'You're an angel. Thank you.'

Before he could reply, she noticed a new email in her inbox.

'Hey, it's from Christie. I wonder what exotic location she's in now.'

Matt laughed. 'That cousin of yours must have the cushiest job in the world.'

'It's certainly original and perfect for her, although last time we spoke she said it won't be going on too much longer. Auden believes this will be his last book — his health is failing, apparently.'

Poor Christie. What would she do now, Liz wondered. For the past ten years, her cousin had been a researcher for a bestselling author called Auden Meeres. He wrote mysteries, all of which had intense characters and intricate, convoluted plots. Tremendously popular, each new book of his was eagerly awaited by readers all around the world. They were always set in different locations, which was where Christie came in. Auden could no longer travel, so Christie was sent off to the latest setting and tasked with producing an in-depth description of the place and its inhabitants. She recorded dialects and listened to local stories from the past. She also took quantities of photographs and brought back little souvenirs, but these were for her own benefit, to jog her memories of the place and help her relay her impressions to her employer. Auden was blind. Christie was his eyes, and the research she did enabled him to continue filling his books with authentic characters and detailed descriptions.

'So? What does she say?' asked Matt.

Liz skimmed through the long message. 'Oh! She's coming here. His latest book is set in the Fens.'

'And there was me thinking she was on her way to sunny Barbuda.'

'She says she'll stay in a Premier Inn, as she has no idea how long it will take her to complete the assignment.' She looked up at Matt and raised her eyebrows.

'For heaven's sake,' he said. 'We have a perfectly good and hardly used guest room. Tell her she has a home in Cannon Farm for as long as she needs it. That is, if she can cope with the remoteness of Tanners Fen.'

Dear Matt. Some partners would balk at taking in a relative they'd barely met on an open-ended visit, but not him. He knew how fond she was of Christie. It would be good for her to have her cousin around.

She jumped up and hugged him. 'Thank you, Mattie. You really are the best.'

He looked smug. 'Yeah, well, it has been mentioned before.' He kissed her lightly. 'So, when's she arriving?'

'In two days,' Liz said. 'She's driving down on Monday, leaving early to avoid the traffic.'

'Good idea. Well, we'd better tie up what we have running so you can take some quality time out with her and show her the Fens.' He pointed to the computer. 'I'm guessing from those photos you had on the screen that the Boyd investigation is well and truly concluded?'

'Poor sod. I'm afraid it is, although I'm glad we won't have to deal with the obnoxious Mrs Boyd anymore. I shall take great delight in saying goodbye to that woman.'

'So, apart from our greatest failure so far, I guess we are up to date.' Matt looked at her ruefully.

'We are, and as I've run out of ideas regarding our missing person, maybe it's time to ring our client and tell her we've exhausted all avenues.' Liz sighed. 'I hate to admit defeat — in fact it goes against everything we believe in — but we've done all we can.'

Matt nodded. 'Do you want to talk to her, or shall I?'

'I'll do it. In fact, I'll do it now or I'll put it off for ever.'

Frances Morton was an old school friend of hers, so it was a bit of a stretch to call her a client. Frances had very little money of her own and Haynes and Ballard Private Investigators had offered their services pro bono. Liz liked to think that if something went terribly wrong in her life, someone would lend a hand without whacking in a massive great bill at the end of it.

It wasn't an easy call to make. She felt she was letting her old friend down, but finding a missing person, an adult, wasn't easy, especially if that person didn't want to be found, which was so often the case. She finished by saying that she'd call in and see Frances in the morning, to explain exactly what they had done over the last few months. At least it would save her covering the same ground, should she decide to continue the search herself. But the truth remained: after four months of enquiries, they had found no trace whatsoever of Amy Roberts.

'What does your gut feeling tell you about Frances's sister?' she asked Matt.

'I think one of the most difficult people to trace is a free spirit,' he said, after some thought. 'Everyone who knew Amy said she was mercurial, unpredictable and totally independent, one of those people who march to the beat of their own drum. Amy always had faith in her own abilities, built her own world and thrived in it.'

Matt walked over to a wooden filing cabinet, opened it and took out a file. '"Free spirits know when to be selfish in order to follow their passions. They put themselves first and, if something matters deeply to them, they pursue it. If something makes them feel trapped, whether it be a job, friends or even close family, they will cut those ties and set themselves free.'" He pushed the folder back into the drawer and closed it. 'I think she cut her ties and followed whatever dream she was following.'

'What about that radical change of appearance the last time Frances saw her? That really bothers me, Matt. It was so out of character.'

'I have no answer for that. What does your gut tell you, my love?'

'That something happened to her. Free spirit or not, she loved Frances. Amy would have told her if she was going away, I know she would.' Liz felt just as Frances did. Amy was impulsive and she did float between relationships, but she kept in touch with her sister. She had never, ever disappeared for six months without contacting her. 'I'll go and talk to Frances tomorrow, Mattie, and go over what we've done, but let's not close the book on her. We might hear something, or maybe think of some channel of enquiry that we'd overlooked. Is that okay with you?'

'Sure. Believe me, I hate to be beaten too, but I still think she'll turn up one day wondering what all the fuss is about.' He smiled. 'Now, forget that for a while and email your cousin. Tell her she has a comfortable bed waiting for her on Tanners Fen.'

* * *

Christie McFerran couldn't have been more delighted when Auden told her that his latest book was to be set in the very place where her cousin Liz lived. It would make things so much easier for her, having a guide, someone with contacts and first-hand knowledge of that strange, watery world.

She stood back and surveyed her luggage. She had everything she thought she would need for a trip to the Fens. Walking boots and waterproofs featured predominantly. In a separate carry case she had her laptop and everything else she would need for her work. That part was easy, she had done this so many times before. However, today's packing ritual was tinged with poignancy because this could be her final research trip for her wonderful employer. She sighed. Auden had become a dear friend as well as her boss, and for his sake she was sad that his health was becoming a serious problem.

Christie sat down on the edge of her bed and thought back to the first time they met. She'd had a job in one of Yorkshire's major libraries and knew that Auden Meeres often used it, though she had never actually seen him there. The senior librarian always helped the author when he required assistance, but on this particularly hot day in June, sixteen years ago, she had broken her ankle stepping down from a Kick Step fifteen minutes before he was due to arrive, and the job had fallen to Christie.

He was an imposing figure whose age it was impossible to guess. Tall, dignified, impeccably dressed and sporting a piratical black patch. It was to be three years before she discovered that the patch was for show. His overpowering presence almost made one forget his blindness. He was delivered to the door by his chauffeur, carer and right-hand man, expecting to be met by the librarian, who would guide him around.

She would have been nervous but for the grip on her arm and the slight tremor in the deep, well-articulated voice that betrayed his own hesitancy.

Auden Meeres was an eccentric who shunned all things technical. He insisted that his books be based on research conducted on location, immersing oneself in the atmosphere, tasting particular foods and drinks and listening to the local dialect.

'I need to know about Agatha Christie. I am making a reference to her in my work in progress and I need to know about her disappearance in 1926 — exactly how long she was missing for, where her abandoned vehicle was found and its make. Do you have something that might help me?'

Christie sat perched on the edge of her bed, surrounded by all the paraphernalia of travel, and heard her young self say, 'Oh, it was a Morris Cowley, sir. She abandoned it near Newlands Corner in Surrey.' And then she had blushed. Even now she could feel the heat on her cheeks.

Her words had been followed by a silence that felt interminable. By the time it was broken, she had already written her resignation, hunted for a new job and started selling copies of the *Big Issue* on the streets of Scarborough. When it came, the revered author's hearty belly laugh brought horrified looks from every corner of the reading room.

'Well. Reference books be damned. Next time I'll just ask you, Miss . . .?'

She had told him her name and explained its origin. Her grandfather had been one of the police constables in Guildford who had been commandeered to dredge the Silent Pool in the search for the missing author, and her mother had been intrigued by the mystery of the eleven-day-long disappearance. Christie was eternally grateful that her mother had picked the great literary figure's surname and not her first to call her baby by.

She shook her head and laughed softly, still, after all this time, amazed that he should hunt her down five years later and request — no, demand — that she work for him as his researcher. Now it seemed that chapter in her life would be shortly coming to an end. She wasn't sure if she was frightened at the prospect of change or excited by it.

Christie stood up abruptly and shook off the memories. She had plenty to organise over the coming two days as she had no idea when she'd be back. First, she had to ask her lovely old neighbour to look after her house yet again, and then call on Auden to receive detailed instructions as to exactly what he wanted her to research. Tomorrow she would clean the house, empty the fridge and make sure all was safe. She would pack what she could into the car tomorrow night and hit the road at around five thirty in the morning. She calculated that it would take her about three and half hours to get to the Fens from where she lived on the outskirts of Scarborough, so she would arrive at around nine on Monday morning. She'd never been to Liz and Matt's home before and was pleased that she would be staying with them rather than living out of her suitcase in a hotel room. Not that she ever minded that, but she was looking forward to spending time with her cousin again. It had been far too long.

She felt bad that she hadn't been there for Liz during her recovery from the horrific incident that led to her quitting the police force, but she had been globe-trotting for Auden in some far-flung spot, and Liz had chosen not to burden her with the seriousness of her injuries until much later. Now, at last, they could catch up properly.

Christie finished packing, closed her case and carried it down to the hall. She never left it until the last day to pack, as an extra twenty-four hours allowed her time to remember any small item that she might have forgotten. A trip to the Fenlands didn't mean travelling to the ends of the earth but in the past, she had been far from any shops in some very inhospitable places, and it didn't do to forget essentials.

Christie unlocked her door and went out into the sunshine. As she walked across to her neighbour's house, she decided that if this was to be her final trip, she would be sure to make it a memorable one.

CHAPTER TWO

When Liz arrived at Frances's home, she was surprised to find her husband Jason's car still in the drive.

'It's his day off and he insisted on speaking to you, Liz.' Frances spoke in little more than a whisper. She sounded apprehensive, as if she wasn't sure exactly what her husband was going to say and was afraid she wouldn't like it.

'No problem, honestly,' Liz whispered back. 'I know how he feels about Amy, so I'll tread warily.'

Frances went to put the kettle on, and Liz found Jason in the lounge, cleaning out the ashes from the fireplace. She had always liked Jason, thought him a down-to-earth, "tell it how it is" kind of guy, and it was obvious that he loved Frances to bits. All the more surprising, then, was his reluctance to build bridges where Frances's sister, Amy, was concerned.

He nodded at Liz and asked how she was getting on now. Frances had told him about what had happened to her, Liz knew, and he seemed slightly surprised to see her looking as fit as she did.

'You know me, Jason, I just bounce back.' The cockiness faded. 'Well, I guess I'm about as recovered as I'm going to be, not quite the old Liz, but a fair to middling replica.'

She grinned at him, somewhat ruefully. 'It could have had a much worse outcome, so I'm lucky as hell really.'

'Well, you look great, I'm glad to say. When Frances told me how long you'd been in hospital, I was really worried for you, no word of a lie.'

Liz had no doubt of his sincerity, but she'd gone over the attempt on her life far too often. 'Right now, I'm more worried about that wife of yours, Jason. Frances looks wrung out. She's taken her sister's disappearance really badly, hasn't she?'

His smiling face closed down like a shutter. 'Oh, the *disappearance*.' He pointed to an armchair and Liz sat down. 'I want to talk to you about that, Liz.'

She waited.

'Now, please don't take offence at this because there's none intended. I know that you and Matt have been trying to help Frances find her sister, but I want you to give up.'

His voice was controlled, but she could sense the anger behind it. Liz said nothing.

'I believe that taking Frances's theory that something terrible has happened to Amy seriously is just feeding the misguided image she has of her sister. Amy is selfish and unreliable, always has been. She thinks only of herself. She's just gone off somewhere, probably with yet another man. She hasn't disappeared, mark my words. She'll be back when she gets bored.'

'You seem very sure about this, Jason,' Liz said calmly. 'If it's any consolation, I'm here today to tell Frances that we can't find any trace of her sister. We've done all we can, but we've got nowhere. I didn't want to keep giving her false hope.'

'I see. Well, I can't say I'm surprised and, frankly, I'm glad to hear it.' His face was still stony, but he seemed a little pacified. 'Maybe she'll start to see reason now and admit that her no-good sister has just gone off without giving my poor wife a second thought.'

'It's not like that, Jason Morton!' Frances was standing in the doorway with a tray in her hands. 'And perhaps it's time *you* saw reason, not me.' She placed the tray on a coffee table and looked directly at her husband. 'What you and she think of each other is immaterial right now. I love you both and I always have. But like it or not, I've been close to my little sister from the day she was born. I *know* something has happened to her. Right here.' She laid her hand on her heart. 'And if you can't get that into your thick skull, then—' her voice broke — 'then there's no hope.'

Jason stood up, went to his wife and held her tightly in his big arms, 'Shh. I'm sorry, all right? But, oh, Frances, you know what she's like. You can't blame me for getting upset because I believe she's done what she's done a dozen times before. Amy uses you, she always has, and I hate to see you hurt.'

'But can't you see, Jason, that I don't mind! I've accepted that Amy isn't like other people since she was a toddler. She loves me in her own way. I'm her safe place, her constant, the one she runs to if the world tries to make her conform and be something she isn't.'

Liz watched, wondering if she should slip quietly away and let them talk this through alone. Then she decided that the conversation probably wouldn't have happened if she hadn't been there. And maybe she would hear the truth. So she stayed.

'I don't know how you can be so . . .' Jason struggled for words, 'so *accepting* of the way she neglects you. You don't see or hear from her for months at a time. She floats in and out of your life only when she needs something. Can't you see how that hurts me?'

Frances freed herself from his arms and sank down on the sofa. She patted the seat next to her and he sat down. 'Then I know this will hurt you too, but I'm going to say it anyway. I just hope you'll forgive me.'

Jason's brow furrowed. He looked puzzled. 'Forgive you? What for?'

'I *have* seen Amy. She's always told me what she's up to and where she's going. We've met up every month for years,

14

without fail.' She gave a great, heaving sigh. 'I never told you because I knew how you'd react and what you'd say. I can't bear the fact that the two people I love most in the world can't even be civil to each other. You spoke about being hurt — well, I've been torn apart by this damned struggle between you for more years than I can count.'

Liz saw various emotions compete for dominance in Jason's expression. Then he seemed to deflate.

'You lied to me. All these years, you've been lying.'

The words hung in the air. Now Liz knew why she was here. She leaned forward and met his eyes. 'Jason, in my work I saw every kind of lie, believe me. Treacherous lies, malicious lies, some very dangerous, but there are also lies that come from a place of love. Frances loves you. All she wanted was to put a stop to the friction and keep some harmony in her home.' She looked from one to the other and her gaze settled on Frances. 'And I'm betting she lied to Amy, too, about you.'

Frances nodded slowly. 'All the time. I'd say you were happy for us to meet. I'd even say you'd treated us to a coffee and a sandwich.' She shrugged. 'I so wanted you to like each other, just a little. Well, at least tolerate each other and make life bearable. I wanted you to see her for the strong, courageous girl that she was, someone who defied convention, who wasn't afraid to be her own person and be true to herself. Not like me, who meekly accepted what life threw my way and never thought to question it.'

Jason sighed. 'But what you didn't see was that I believed, and still do, that *you* are the strong, courageous one — seeing life as it really is and tackling the world head on. In my eyes, it's Amy who's the weak one, chasing dreams and running from them when they don't go her way. Using and possibly being used by people. Hurting them with no thought for their feelings.'

Neither spoke again for a moment, so Liz ventured, 'Let's set recriminations aside and move on to what's happening now. Frances, I think it's time you told Jason about the last time you saw Amy.' She turned to Jason. 'This is why Matt and I offered to help find her.'

Frances drew in a deep breath and nodded. 'I couldn't believe it when I saw her, Jason. The bright colours had gone. She wore a dark coat, a simple plain sweater in a sort of oatmeal shade, with a white blouse underneath and a brown straight skirt. She had flat slip-on shoes, and her hair had been cut in kind of straggly, uneven layers, the bright streaks gone.'

Liz saw the pain in her friend's face, and that Jason was beginning to register surprise.

'Why?' he asked.

'I have no idea, other than a brief aside about some relationship she was still unsure of. When she mentioned it, her face clouded over with an expression I've never seen on Amy before. There was a kind of excitement, but it was overshadowed by doubt, indecision and uncertainty. It wasn't my Amy. None of it.' Tears filled her eyes. 'After that, I never saw her again.'

Jason patted her leg and murmured a few words of comfort. It must have been an effort for him, Liz knew, but he seemed willing to revise his opinion, stand down. She'd always liked him; now he was really going up in her estimation.

After a while, he looked up at her. 'I'm beginning to understand why you helped my wife. But you say you've come up with nothing?'

Liz sighed in her turn. 'Zilch. And we've hit a blank in every area that we've tried to investigate. Because she moved around so much, had no fixed abode and no regular job, it's been all but impossible to find recent friends or acquaintances, or to chart her movements.' She pulled out a clear plastic folder from the bag that lay at her feet. 'This is a list of organisations and people we've contacted. You'll see that it's pretty comprehensive.' She laid it on the coffee table. 'We aren't drawing a line underneath this, Frances, but for the time being, there's nowhere else to go. If we hear anything, or think of something else, we'll follow it up and tell you about it, I promise.'

Jason thanked her. 'Don't worry. I'll help Frances in whatever she wants to do. Now I know the facts, I'll do my best to support her.'

As Liz left, she heard husband and wife apologising profusely. They were both in tears. It would take a while, but now the air had been cleared, she had a feeling that the healing process had already begun. She got back into her car, drained but relieved. It was time for her to forget mysteries and crime for a while and prepare for her cousin's arrival tomorrow. Everything would have been perfect, but for the nagging question of Amy Roberts. Where was she?

* * *

After a day spent preparing the house and shopping for their guest, Matt and Liz turned in early. They talked for a while as they always did, then, aware of how thin the walls were, they took full advantage of the empty house to make as much noise as they wished.

Now, Matt lay exhausted and happy next to a sleeping Liz, marvelling at the intensity of their lovemaking after all this time together. He knew it couldn't last — the passion of the euphoric early stages would mellow into companionship, become comfortable as the years passed by, but the journey was a glorious one so far.

A siren echoed across the fen as a police car hurtled through the dark night towards some incident. Matt experienced a pang of nostalgia. He missed the job he had spent the greater part of his life doing, missed the adrenalin rushes, the camaraderie, the sense of being part of something special that made a difference. He had never been able to confess his longing for the old days to Liz.

He sighed into the darkness, knowing he couldn't go back, even if he wanted to. He had made a terrible mistake in the past, one that haunted him and gave him nightmares still.

Add that to the horror of the investigation that had almost ended Liz's life and did indeed end the life of his closest friend, then going back was not an option.

He drew closer to Liz, the love of his life. They had made a new start together and it was working well for both of them. He stroked her smooth, warm skin. He envied the way Liz had managed to walk away from the force. She had returned to the station once to visit but said she felt nothing other than a wish to escape as soon as she could. After that, she sometimes met a few of her old colleagues for a coffee or a drink but always well away from the nick. Perhaps it was because she knew that her health had suffered so badly that in any case, she wouldn't have passed a fitness test. Yet she had been such a damned good detective. He envied her stoicism.

Listening to another siren call across the marsh, Matt knew he still hadn't reached that level of acceptance.

* * *

On a different part of the coastline, along another stretch of eerie marsh, two women walked the high sea defence — a sort of levee they called the sea bank. One was sure-footed and strode out confidently. The other was nervous, uncertain of the terrain and fearful at the prospect of being out on the edge of Sly Fen at night.

'Come on, keep up.' The older woman, Gina, sounded impatient. 'You are aware that this is entirely for your benefit, aren't you?'

'Yes, and I appreciate it.' Delphi, the younger woman, was slightly out of breath. This was not her idea of fun. 'It's just that I've grown up with the old stories and they've made me too scared to ever venture near the marsh at night.' She sounded apologetic. 'I'm sorry, but my grandfather swore he met the black dog out here one night on Sly Fen — "Hairy Jack" he called it. Said it was the herald of death, and Grandad was no liar.'

A derisory laugh floated back to her on the breeze from the Wash. 'Oh, Delphi, do grow up! You're not a child anymore! Those are old wives' tales. The Fens are awash with them. We probably have more superstitions here than any other county in England. All fuelled by ignorance.'

Delphi had loved her grandfather and felt a little hurt at those words. 'My grandad said his brother died just a few days after he saw Hairy Jack, so surely that proves something, don't you think?'

'Of course it does. Proves he was gullible and completely taken in by those superstitions. It was a coincidence, nothing more.'

It was getting harder to walk. Delphi only had a small torch and the uneven ground, churned up by the cows that used it to walk to their grazing areas, was hazardous. Her friend was moving away and she struggled to keep up.

'Think about it,' Gina called back. 'You were only told to keep off the marsh because of the mists and the tides. This place is prone to flood very quickly when the tide turns, and it can move faster than you can run. The old ones tell their children all those stories so they'll be just like you were — terrified of the marsh.'

Thankfully, her companion stopped, and Delphi caught up with her. She felt jittery and uncomfortable. It would take a lot more than a few scoffing remarks to make her doubt what her family had instilled in her from birth. Delphi was a "Yeller-belly." She had been born and grown up here, and just maybe she knew a bit more about this marsh than her friend. But she wasn't going to say this to Gina, who was trying to improve her mind, show her there were rational explanations for everything that happened. Gina was very intelligent — had been to university and everything. Delphi had never left Lincolnshire.

'Right. Now, look out over Sly Fen and tell me what you see.' Gina had adopted her lecturing tone, which made Delphi feel like a small child in a schoolroom.

She stared down into the darkness. 'Er, the marsh. The night sky. Some stars. And that's about it.'

'All right . . .'

Delphi felt deflated. 'So, what am I supposed to be seeing, then?'

'One of the few remaining areas of mature saltmarsh, home to all manner of plants, birds and invertebrates.' Gina flung out an arm in an all-encompassing gesture. 'These tidal mudflats are feeding grounds for amazing waders. You can find grey plovers, whimbrels, curlews, godwits and greenshanks. It's a wonderland, Delphi, not just a marsh.'

'But it's night. I could appreciate all that in daylight, but not in the pitch dark.' She hoped she sounded reasonable. She didn't mean to whine, though all she really wanted was for this lesson to be over and to get back to the safety of Gina's home.

'True, but you can't experience the sight of phosphines and methane escaping into the air from the marshes in daylight, can you?' Gina's eyes sparkled in the torchlight. 'Or maybe it's bioluminescence? What do you think?' she asked.

'I don't know what that is,' Delphi said flatly.

'I forgot, you didn't study much science, did you? Oh well, no matter. It's just a natural glow caused by something like fireflies or honey fungus.'

Hearing the word *glow*, Delphi started to feel even more uncomfortable. 'Is that what we're looking for, Gina? Lights out here on the marsh? Because if it is, I'd like to go home now.'

Gina laughed heartily. 'Dear girl. Please don't tell me you are frightened of a little marsh gas burning off. Think it might be the spirits of the dead luring you into a watery grave? It's a natural phenomenon, Delphi. It has science behind it. Come on, agree with me. You know I'm right.'

Delphi nodded slowly. 'I'm sure you are, Gina. You're far too smart to not understand all that. But I've never seen it and I've spent my whole life listening to the folklore of this fen. I'm sorry but it still scares me.'

Suddenly there was an arm around her. 'Silly girl. There's nothing to be afraid of here. Well, except for the tides, and you could get lost if you ventured onto the marsh itself and a haar — a sea fret — came rolling in off the Wash. But you're hardly going to do that, are you?'

Suddenly Delphi felt ashamed of her superstitiousness. She gave a little laugh. 'No, I'll not be going out onto the marsh, and you're right, I am silly.'

They stood together staring out across the dark expanse of marsh, but there were no lights, natural or supernatural.

'They aren't playing ball tonight, scaredy-cat, so let's give them a few more minutes and if nothing happens, we'll go back for a stiff drink. We can try again another night.'

Delphi nodded, silently counting down the minutes. In her ear, her grandfather's voice was whispering to her to get the hell off Sly Fen.

CHAPTER THREE

It was an emotional reunion for both Liz and Christie. As children, she and her cousin had been particularly close. Both had one sibling and neither got on well with her own sister.

Liz's sister Sarah had been a restless sort of girl, needing constant stimulation and what she termed "adventures." It had been no surprise when she started travelling, finally settling in a remote part of New Zealand. Liz believed she had inherited this from their parents, who also felt the occasional need to answer the call of the wild. Even now, in their mid-seventies, they still spent their holidays exploring little-known places that were way off the tourist track. On the other hand, Christie's sister Emily had been a shy, retiring girl, scared of her own shadow and unable to make friends, even with her own sibling. The cousins, however, got on brilliantly and soon became surrogate sisters.

Liz watched Christie step from her car and was flooded with memories of their childhood, back in their home county of Hampshire. She was delighted to see her looking so well. Christie hadn't had the best start — rheumatic fever had scuppered her plans of becoming an investigative journalist. It was rare these days, but a simple throat infection and a glitch in her immune system, undetected in childhood, had permanently damaged her heart. The research job was perfect for her, as she could do it at her own pace and it allowed a lot of time for study, both in Auden's beloved books and on the internet. It was a win-win situation for Christie, providing interesting and sometimes exciting travel to unusual locations as well as time immersed in books.

Christie hugged her tightly. 'You look amazing.'

'I was going to say the same,' said Liz, grinning from ear to ear. She held her cousin at arm's length to take a good look at her. 'You look better than I've ever seen you!'

'At this point in the mutual admiration society's annual meeting, I shall go and put the kettle on,' laughed Matt.

Christie turned and hugged him too. 'The gorgeous Matt Ballard. Handsome as ever. How could we leave you out?'

'Ah, a rather more mature, faded kind of handsome these days,' he replied with mock sadness.

After they had given Christie time to settle into the guest room and shown her where everything was, they took their tea into the conservatory.

'So, what does Auden need from you and this trip to the Fenlands?' asked Matt. 'I'm sure Liz and I'll be able to help with some things.'

Christie opened a leather-bound notebook. 'There are dozens of specifics here, but in general, I need to get out into the terrain itself and record what I see, hear, smell and even sense. His mysteries are full of descriptions of each location. He aims to make the reader feel like they know the place, maybe even like they might want to visit it.'

'I read one not so long ago when I was recovering. It was called *From Distant Shores*, I think,' mused Liz. 'It was so evocative of the west coast of Ireland that I could almost hear the uilleann pipes. I realised that it was you who had seen that wonderful landscape. It felt quite strange to know that.'

Christie looked suddenly sad. 'We have a kind of connection. We aren't sure how it happens but I manage to convey the essence of the places I visit and he's able to pick it up and put it into words. It works beautifully.' She sighed. 'But he is far from well now. This really will be his last book. That's why it has to be the very best I can make it for him.' The smile returned. 'Anyway, there's plenty here to source and research, like local history and folklore.'

'Matt will help you there,' said Liz. 'His family were descended from real old web-foot fenmen, and if he's not sure about something, he'll point out some old Yeller-belly who does.'

Christie turned the beam of her smile on each of them in turn. 'That's brilliant. I'm betting you sat around the fireside with your mum and dad filling your head with mysterious tales, didn't you, Matt?'

Matt's face darkened. 'Not exactly. I'm afraid I didn't have the best childhood. My dad was wonderful, but he died when I was still at school and we won't even speak about my mother. Most of my knowledge came from my grandparents and just being here.'

Liz changed the subject quickly, aware of how stormy Matt's relationship with his mother had been and the hurt she had done him. 'You told us that Auden doesn't like to get his information from the internet, but surely that's the first port of call for all research now?'

'He's very much old-school, Liz. He wants first-hand experience wherever possible. For the rest, he trusts books, but not the web. He suspects that the information found on those sites is inaccurate, never peer-reviewed or verified.' She placed her empty mug on the coffee table. 'Auden has a very particular way of producing his novels. When he passes away there will be a fascinating legacy for someone. He has no family, so I'm not exactly sure who that will be, although maybe Richard, his friend who looks after him. Each of his twenty-five novels has its own large document box containing a pristine first edition, along with all his recorded notes and plans for the manuscript. There is a list of all publications used in the research and a guide to the location of the relevant books in his vast library. There are agents' letters and editorial comments from the publishers, together with newspaper articles and reviews. With his later books, the ones I've been involved in, there are photographs I have taken, and endless descriptions of the locations used, both written and recorded. He is terribly methodical.' She laughed. 'I thought I was organised, but I'm a mess compared to him. Anyway, that's why I have to buy and use books. Then they go into his collection in Yorkshire.'

'Well, if you want books, you've come to the right place,' Liz exclaimed.

'Oh?'

'The one thing Fenfleet can boast of is its bookshop. It's quite something. Plus, I happen to know the manager really well. Once you're settled and organised, I'll take you there and introduce you. You'll love it.'

Christie smiled. 'Better and better. Can we go today?'

'Of course, if you'd like to. We'll take you for a walk along the sea bank here, just to see the marsh, then we'll have lunch and go into town,' Liz suggested. 'That is, if you want to jump straight into your research?'

'I feel I must. This book is so important to Auden and, with his illness, I can't afford to hang about.'

'It really is severe?' Matt asked her.

Christie nodded. 'I spoke to Richard before I left. Every week shows a marked decline. Apparently, Auden's been meaning to write this book for years. I think the Fens have special significance for him, but he's never said why. In any case, I need to get him exactly what he needs so he can at least make a start.'

'Then I'm totally at your disposal,' said Liz. 'We're between cases, and Matt has volunteered to take on anything that needs urgent attention.'

'This is really so good of you both,' said Christie. 'But please, if you have work come in, don't refuse it on my behalf. I'm used to finding my way around places, honestly.'

'This will be a welcome break, believe me.' Liz meant it. Their recent cases had not been particularly arduous but they had come in one after the other without let-up. Spending time with her cousin on an interesting project would be a lot more fun than tracking unfaithful spouses.

'Then lead on to the sea bank and my first look at your marsh.'

* * *

When they reached the top of the sea bank, Christie stopped in her tracks and just stared. The long, straight path ran on for ever — or it seemed that way, because she could see no end to it. It simply disappeared into the horizon.

To her right, hummocks of coarse grass formed islands in murky little seas of dark water in the boggy, muddy brown marsh. What seemed like miles further off lay a glittering, pewter ribbon that she assumed to be the Wash. She looked back along the path. The vegetation on the slopes of the bank was lush and deep, and a mixture of lacy white cow parsley, tall hogweed, scarlet poppies, purple vetch and pinky mauve mallow created bright specks of colour dotted about the long grass, complemented by a necklace of yellow dandelions that grew along the path itself.

Away to the left stretched acres and acres of farmland. She wasn't sure what the crop was exactly — the bright green of young growth could have been anything.

'You look a bit mesmerised,' said Matt, a hint of amusement in his voice.

'I'll say!' Christie started taking photographs. 'This is incredible. And I don't think I've ever been anywhere with 360 degrees of uninterrupted sky.'

'Bit special that, no high ground,' he said. 'If you stop and slowly turn right round, sometimes you can see at the same time banks of iron-grey thunderclouds, fluffy white cotton-balls of clouds and a pure blue cloudless sky, depending on which way you face.'

'And the sunsets and sunrises are spectacular,' added Liz. 'I never tire of coming up here at sunset, it's breathtaking.'

'We saw an aurora borealis from this very spot once, didn't we, Liz?' said Matt. 'It's the only one I've ever seen here, and I was totally gobsmacked.'

They walked on for a while, Christie asking questions and taking more photographs. Then they turned and retraced their steps. 'I can see why there's so much folklore here,' she said, gazing out at the marsh. 'This is a beautiful day, but if it were misty or dark, I could imagine things getting pretty spooky.'

'But not as creepy as Whisper Fen,' Liz said, 'just a bit further along the coast. Or Sly Fen, for that matter. That one is even worse.'

Christie caught a pained expression on Matt's face when Liz mentioned Whisper Fen, but she decided not to ask. Well, not right now. She suspected that something about that place had affected Matt very badly at some point. 'So, Matt, will you be able to tell me some of the old tales and superstitions that are peculiar to this part of the coast?'

He walked on, staring at the ground. 'I can tell you what I was told as a kid, but if you want some proper folklore I suggest we introduce you to Dominic Campion and his wife, Pip.'

'Oh yes,' Liz said. 'Good idea. Dom knows all the old tales.' She nudged Matt. 'And I'm betting it wouldn't take much to convince him to take Christie on a ghost walk.'

'Dead right! Any excuse to drag some unsuspecting soul out onto the marsh after nightfall!' Matt laughed. 'But I'll not be joining you on that one.'

'Not a fan of folklore?' Christie asked.

'It's not that, but as a copper I did enough night shifts to last me a lifetime, thank you. Traipsing around in the dark has lost its appeal.'

'Tell you what, we'll go into Fenfleet and check out the bookshop, and on the way back, we can call in to Dom and Pip's place.' Liz slipped her arm through Christie's. 'They run a B&B on the outskirts of Fenfleet, not that far from Sly Fen. Pip is a fantastic cook and Dominic is a brilliant host. I think you'll like them.'

Christie had met some wonderful people as she had travelled around gathering information for Auden. She loved listening to their stories and watching as they interacted with those around them. People fascinated her, and she was already relishing meeting Pip and Dom. 'I'm sure I will,' she said warmly.

* * *

'You are going to love this.' Liz locked the car and grinned at her. 'It's the best bookshop I've ever come across. Mind you, I expect you've seen dozens in your travels?'

Christie nodded. 'Some quite surprising ones. I love the people who work in bookshops too, they're so passionate about books and writing and always willing to help with research.'

'Bit like you as a librarian,' said Liz. 'I remember how excited you were back when you first met Auden Meeres and were able to help him.'

All at once, Christie remembered that this was going to be her final research trip. Soon, she would be looking for a new job, whatever that might be. She hauled her thoughts back to the present. 'Okay, let's go and inspect this literary treasure trove.'

Liz had been right. The moment she stepped through the doors of the Reading Room, Christie beamed with pleasure. This was the kind of place she would have chosen if she could have owned or had to design a bookshop.

She wandered from section to section, her admiration growing as she noted the way the books were displayed. It was a rambling hotchpotch of "rooms," each housing a different category and including both literature and reference works. Over time, the owners had obviously bought several of the adjoining properties along the cobbled street and allowed the shop to spread from one to the other like ground elder. Christie entered the travel section to find it demarcated by the colourful flags of different nations and, looking up above the shelves, she noted huge poster-sized photographs of African sunsets, Brazilian rainforests, Venetian waterways and other beautiful scenes.

Without even realising that Liz was no longer with her, she left the room and entered the next. This was devoted to poetry and classic literature, the various sections being separated by five-foot-high sepia photos of poets and writers. Rupert Brooke, Alfred Lord Tennyson, Robert Louis Stevenson and Charles Dickens adorned one wall, while George Eliot, Oscar Wilde, Seamus Heaney and Elizabeth Barrett Browning stared at her from the opposite side of the room.

She was just moving on to see what the other rooms had to offer when she smelled the aroma of fresh coffee. A rather splendid staircase led up to a small café that advertised hot beverages, a selection of Danish pastries and other snacks.

'Ah, you found the café!' Liz said. Behind her stood a tall man, smiling down at Christie.

'I'm Tom Parrish, the manager. Liz tells me you're working for Auden Meeres. Wow! We are honoured. He's one of our bestselling authors, his books walk off the shelves. Whatever we can do to help, we'll be happy to assist.' His grip when he shook her hand was firm and welcoming.

Christie occasionally found herself taking an instant liking to someone. It was like coming across an old friend again after many years. As often in such moments, she had to remind herself that this was their first meeting.

It was like this for her with Tom Parrish, who had a slightly lopsided smile in a studious, bespectacled face. 'So, where can I direct you first?'

'Local history section if you have one, please. I need some basic information on the draining of the Fens and then as much about Fenland folklore as I can gather.'

'Ah, boggarts, bogles and the like. Great stuff.' He grinned mischievously. 'I have to tell you, though, that if you're planning on selling your granny to the Tiddy People, they seem to have disappeared of late.'

She looked at him bemused for a second, then laughed and told him that Granny was already quite safe on the Other Side, thank you, and it was the will-o'-the-wisp she was looking for in particular. 'Auden is writing a tale of murder and treachery that's set in modern times but incorporates ancient myths and ghostly happenings, mainly here but also in Cornwall. I spent most of last month down in the West Country, digging up tales of the wreckers.'

'From here we're going on to see Dominic Campion,' added Liz. 'Hopefully to get him to take Christie out on one of his famous after-dark marsh walks.'

'Oh, Dom. Yes, he's the guy for local folklore all right.' He turned back to Christie. 'Incidentally, we had wreckers up the coast here too, but they lured ships into the sandbars and the shallows rather than onto rocks. But come and see what we have here first, then you can get genned up before hunting the boggarts.'

He indicated towards an arch-topped door, obviously reclaimed from some old chapel or ancient building, which led into a reconstructed crypt. There had been an original stone wall along one side of the room, with deep inset windows with metal grills. The designer had used these to best advantage and turned the room into a copy of a small Lady chapel. The higher walls were covered in historical maps and plans of the surrounding countryside, while lower down were old bookshelves and hymnbook cupboards containing a wealth of material on Fenfleet and Lincolnshire. In one corner was a lectern in the shape of an eagle, which sported an antiquated tome on the history of the industrial archaeology of the county. A carved pew, probably rescued from a disused church, ran down the centre of the room, providing a place to sit and browse. Already, a dozen or more titles were calling to her from the shelves.

Christie was totally in awe. What a gem of a shop! It was far superior to anything she had expected to find in this small market town.

'Told you you'd like it,' Liz said smugly. 'Now, can I leave you with my friend Tom for a little while, Christie? I need to pop along to the bank while we're in town.'

'Liz, I'd be quite happy if you left me here for days.' How lucky she was that this last project was set in a place where she was being offered so much help! With luck, she'd be able to tie it up in record time.

Tom soon reappeared with another book in his hand. 'This one is kept in the children's section for some reason. God knows why, it would scare the pants off most kids, but I suppose they like all that. Have a look anyway.' He handed her a book with a spooky cover on the ghosts and ghoulies of the Fenlands. 'You can take anything you like the look of up to the café if you want. We can check them out over a coffee.'

'You're trusting,' she said, raising an eyebrow at him.

'You don't look the shoplifting type to me.'

'Ah, you haven't noticed the big inside pockets in my jacket, have you?'

He smiled. 'You aren't wearing a jacket.'

'Rats! There goes my career in crime.'

His laugh was spontaneous. 'I don't wish to lose us business, but we do have a fairly good library in town. You've only been in here five minutes and you seem to have six or seven books there.'

'Relax, Tom. I get paid for buying these. My boss is rather generous when it comes to reference books for his work.'

'In which case, I like him even more. Let me take those upstairs for you. Come up when you're ready.'

She watched him skip away and head for the stairs with a stab of envy. Her heart had not been desperately damaged by the rheumatic fever but taking a flight of stairs two at a time was a definite no-no, and she certainly didn't possess unlimited energy, something that Tom exuded with every step.

Christie realised that she was staring and dragged herself back to the books. *Concentrate, McFerran! You are here to work, not admire the locals.*

She gathered a couple more titles and made her way upstairs, where Tom beckoned her over to a table close to the counter. 'Come and meet Delphi. I've told her all about you. She's a massive fan of Auden Meeres and she's dying to meet you.'

A small, frothy-haired blonde woman appeared from behind the café bar, smiling broadly. 'Ooh, I've read all of his books. I love them. Especially the one set in the Hebrides, that was awesome.'

Christie smiled back, wondering how old Delphi was She had a very childlike appearance, but was probably much older than she looked. 'Ah, yes, *To the Darkest Dawn*. Boy, did I freeze my assets doing the groundwork on that one!'

Delphi smiled broadly. 'So he's actually going to set his next book here in the Fens? How exciting!' Her soft blue eyes sparkled.

'Certainly is,' Christie said. 'I obviously can't give away the storyline, but the area around the Wash is one of the main locations featured in it.'

Delphi grinned at Tom. 'Wait until Gina hears about this, Tom! She'll love it.'

'Gina?' Christie asked.

'Gina Spearman,' Tom said. 'She owns the Reading Room. I'd introduce you, but she's at a book fair today. Maybe you'll meet her before you leave.'

'Love to.' Though Christie had to admit she was perfectly happy dealing with the rather attractive manager.

A few minutes later, Liz returned, and Tom and Delphi went back to their work.

Christie bought five books and took a free bookmark with the Reading Room telephone number on it.

'Next stop, Stone House,' Liz said in the car. 'I rang ahead, and Dom and Pip are both at home. I'm confident you'll like them just as much as the lovely Tom.'

Christie smiled to herself. Personally, she wasn't quite so sure about that.

Stone House was located in a largish village between Fenfleet and Tanners Fen. It was an old red-brick farmhouse that had been sympathetically restored and extended to accommodate three suites that made up a guest area while retaining the owners' privacy.

The kitchen, where they now sat, smelled of ground coffee and home baking and from the look of the large golden-topped pie on the table, Liz had not exaggerated Pip's culinary skills.

Phillipa Campion couldn't have been more welcoming, and when Dominic hurried in, full of apologies for missing their arrival, Christie immediately saw why Liz had been so sure she would like these people. In all her wanderings, Christie could not recall ever having been made to feel so welcome. It seemed as if her last assignment for Auden was going to be charmed.

When Liz broached the possibility of Christie joining one of Dom's ghost walks, Pip gave her a nudge. 'Be prepared. Once he gets started on his favourite subject, you'll need more than one notebook.'

They all laughed. Christie then explained the kind of thing her boss was after.

'Well, I've got a parish council meeting this evening, but if you want to join us after dinner tomorrow night, we'll drive over to Sly Fen after dusk and, if the weather's right, you might actually get a sight of your will-o'-the-wisp!'

'Really? I thought they were just a legend,' she said.

'Oh no,' said Pip, as if they were discussing a sighting of some not very rare bird. 'We often see them. It depends on the weather, the temperature, atmospheric pressure and the like.'

'One thing you'll realise, though,' added Dominic, 'is why the old 'uns believed they were supernatural. Even to the most scientific mind, they are something of a revelation.' He shrugged. 'Some locals still believe what their ancestors did, that the science is wrong.'

'Really? I would have thought that with recent advances in communications, TV and the like, such opinions would have been a thing of the past.'

Pip and Dom laughed.

'Sorry, but this is the Fens,' Dom said. 'We might have computerised tractors that can navigate and plough a field to within a couple of centimetres' accuracy, but superstition still stalks the backwaters and the marsh paths, believe me!'

Well, she certainly hadn't expected to be able to witness the lights for herself, so this was a real bonus. Christie hoped that conditions would be right on the night.

'We might have company, if that's okay, Christie?' said Pip. 'We have a long-term resident staying this week and he asked to join us if we went out while he was here.'

'Fine by me,' she said. 'Is he another folklore addict?'

'Well, he's a reverend,' Dom shrugged, 'but don't be put off by the title. Ian Hardy is a grand character, though sadly a little subdued at present. His sister, who lives not far from here, is unwell and he's terribly worried about her. The outing and someone new to talk to will do him the world of good. Now, apart from baking a pie for tonight's dinner, I'm reliably told there are home-made chocolate brownies, so any takers?'

As she enjoyed the delicious cake, Christie decided that if ever she came this way again and couldn't stay with her cousin, she would be sure to book a guest room at Stone House.

CHAPTER FOUR

Having settled some bills and sent out the last remaining invoices, Matt drove into Fenfleet. He intended to catch up with Liz and Christie before they went to the Campions', and parked close to the police station. Far too close. Before he knew it, he was through the door and in the foyer.

He looked around, hoping to see his old friend, Jack "Swifty" Fleet, or possibly DC Bryn Owen. It seemed that every time he visited, he saw more new faces and fewer familiar ones. It was inevitable, he supposed, but it served to accentuate his feeling of no longer belonging.

Both Swifty and Bryn were out.

'Excuse me, sir?'

He looked around to see PC Debbie Hume, who had worked on a case that involved two of Matt's dearest friends.

'Debbie, how are you?'

'Okay, DCI Ballard, thank you.'

'It's just Matt now, by the way.'

'You'll always be DCI Ballard in this place, sir,' she said with a smile. 'If you have a few minutes to spare, DCI Anders said she wanted a word with you if any of us saw you around.'

'Of course. Do you know if she's free now?'

Debbie turned towards the front desk. 'I'll ring up for you.'

Anders was free, so Matt made his way slowly up the familiar staircase, a little sadder with every step.

'Matt! Come on in and grab a chair. Coffee? Oh, of course you do.' She picked up her phone and asked her office manager to arrange the drinks. 'How are you doing out there in the land of the free?'

He smiled, but Charlotte Anders saw through it immediately.

'Not exactly what you expected, huh?' She grimaced. 'I guess this job takes a lot of getting over.'

He sighed. 'You're right there, Charley. Oh, I'm as happy as I could be with Liz. She's coping brilliantly, the business is doing well, and I should be on top of the world, but . . .' He sighed.

'Say no more, Matt. I didn't rise to these dizzy heights because I couldn't see beneath the skin.'

He stared down at his feet. 'It's hard to explain, though . . . anyway, forget all that. What did you want to see me for?'

'Actually, this might help to lift that mood a little. How do you feel about doing a little bit of undercover sleuthing for me, on an unofficial basis?'

He sat up straighter. 'Tell me more.'

'Well, I'm under a bit of pressure to try to lay to rest an old case that's haunted us for about four years. You never had anything to do with it — in fact it was mainly handled by Saltern-le-Fen — but we had some involvement because it happened right on the divisional borderline. Now they've dropped the whole thing into my lap.' She took a sheet of paper from a file and passed it to him. 'Recall seeing this in a newspaper clipping dated Christmas 2017?'

The Fenland Constabulary still have no new leads on the murder of Lindsay Harrison earlier this month.

Twenty-three-year-old Lindsay, of Calthorp Village, was found brutally murdered in an alleyway at the back of the nursery where she was working. Her wages, mobile phone and a ring had been stolen, and her empty purse was found nearby.

A young man who was helping police with their enquiries has been released without charge.

Her father and mother have given an impassioned plea for help, both on the television and on local radio. It is understood that an anonymous benefactor has offered to put up a reward for anyone giving information that results in an arrest.

If you saw anything, or have any knowledge that may help the police with their enquiries, please contact . . .

Matt looked up from the paper. 'Yes, I remember it, but as you say, it wasn't anything I was involved in. We were up to our necks ourselves at the time and I just recall hearing that Saltern had taken the lead on it.'

'It was one of those cases that seemed so clear-cut. A bungled robbery. A thief who didn't expect a little snip of a thing like Lindsay to put up a fight and killed his victim, accidentally maybe, but in any case, she died of asphyxiation.' Charlotte Anders sat back in her chair and folded her arms. 'It all got off to a flying start, we even had a suspect, a boyfriend that she'd recently jilted, then it all collapsed. He had a solid alibi and was obviously really cut up about her death. And that was that.'

'It was never closed, though — the case, I mean.' That wouldn't happen, especially not with a young woman's death.

'Oh no, but Saltern are run ragged at present and out of the blue, some young contemporary of Lindsay's has kicked off a social media enquiry of his own into exactly how and where the police failed her. It has to be stopped, which is why I've inherited it. I've got Bryn working with me but the others have another high-profile case on their hands.' She looked at him hopefully. 'Because of intense pressure from above, I wondered how you'd feel about checking a few people out for me? As I said, unofficially. How's your workload at present?'

Matt grinned. 'It just got busier. But it'll be me on my own to start with. Liz has her cousin staying with us, and she's helping her with a work project. She'll join me if things get interesting. Is that acceptable?'

'Very. Now.' She leaned forward, her elbows on the desk. 'I don't have to tell you that even though you are still bound by the Official Secrets Act, there's a lot I can't tell you. I'm just going to give you some names and you find out all you can about them for me. It will fall well within the remit of a registered PI, but I'd prefer to consider you as my own personal snout.' She gave a dry laugh. 'If you're up for it. Liaise either directly with me, or with Bryn if I'm tied up, on our mobile numbers and tell us everything you find out. I'll update you wherever possible if anything new occurs. Can you live with that, Matt?'

'As long as it doesn't cause problems for you, Charley, I'm happy to help. Most happy.' It wouldn't exactly be doing what he had loved, but it was the next best thing.

Charlotte opened a drawer and took out a large sealed brown envelope. 'Maybe I shouldn't have assumed, but I did. There's nothing in here that you couldn't obtain from outside sources — the media and so on — but I've prepared this to save you time. The first thing I want you to do is see how the original suspect is doing and what he's up to now, four years down the line. Okay? Details enclosed.'

He thanked her and stood up, feeling a lot happier than when he had entered the office that had once been his. 'You'll be hearing from me.'

'Thank you, DCI Ballard. I appreciate it.' She winked at him. 'Good luck, Matt.'

Downstairs, Matt stuck his head around the CID room door and saw Bryn taking his jacket off. 'Hey, boss! Good to see you. Have you seen the DCI?'

He nodded and grinned wryly. 'And accepted her challenge,' he said under his breath.

Bryn smiled broadly. 'Not quite the old team back together, but it'll do. Does the sarge know yet?'

'Hold on, son. I've only just left the DCI's office! And Liz's busy for a few days anyway. I'm sure she'll chip in as soon as our house guest leaves.' He went on to tell Bryn about Christie and her mission.

'Interesting stuff. I've even read one or two of Meeres's books myself. For an old guy, he's bloody good, I have to admit.' He lowered his voice. 'I'll update you as and when, boss — within the guidelines, of course.'

He winked, rather like Charlotte Anders had done, giving Matt that old warm feeling of being part of something again. As he drove home, the Manila envelope next to him on the passenger seat, he wondered what Liz would make of it.

* * *

Christie had taken herself off back up onto the sea bank to record some observations on her phone and Liz was getting supper together. It was a simple affair tonight, as Liz was tired after the excitement of seeing her cousin again and introducing her to her friends. It was at times like these that she knew she could never have gone back into the force, not even as a civilian, as some of her old colleagues had suggested. Fatigue brought with it a variety of different, sometimes mild, but nevertheless irritating side-effects. Today it was a thumping headache. Another day, it would be lapses in memory and concentration, or sometimes even hand tremors or difficulty forming words. Still, after a sleep and some painkillers, the symptoms did subside with no lasting ill effects.

Matt had rung her earlier and said he'd planned to meet them in town but had been sidetracked. He'd explain why later. He had sounded excited, which cheered her up. He had seemed rather low recently and, even though he was clearly enjoying having Christie to stay, there was an underlying shadow. All was not well with him, she could tell.

She prepared a salad, covered it and put it in the fridge, wondering what the problem was. It couldn't be the business. Apart from their one missing girl, every case had been brought to a satisfactory conclusion and work showed no signs of slackening off. Maybe it *was* the disappearance of Amy Roberts. Matt hated to be beaten, and having to admit defeat was galling. Maybe that's what was eating away at him. As she checked through the fridge to make sure she hadn't forgotten anything for their supper, she decided to go ahead and ask him when they were alone. As long as this headache lifted.

Liz heard her phone ringing.

'Liz, it's Pip here. Listen, Dom's meeting tonight has been cancelled. We've checked the weather and thought tonight might be good for the trip to Sly Fen. Would Christie be up for it?'

'I'm sure she will. We're only having a simple meal tonight, so supper won't take long. What time should she be with you?' Liz asked.

'Sometime around darklins,' Pip replied.

Liz smiled. Blind man's holiday. Old Lincolnshire for twilight. 'Okay. She's out on the sea bank at the moment, but I'll tell her as soon as she returns. I'll ring if she's not up to it, but I'm pretty sure she'll be there like a shot.'

'Tell her to wear strong walking boots and a warm jacket. It gets chilly up there at night, even in summer.'

Pip rang off and, just as she did, Christie walked in the back door. 'Great sky up there at present, got lots of pictures.' Her smile faded. 'Are you okay, Liz?'

Liz forced a smile. 'Headache, that's all. Happens every so often. I call them my mini migraines, but this one is being a bit of a bugger.' She sat down on a kitchen chair. 'Now, before I forget, Pip phoned and brought the marsh walk forward to this evening around twilight, if you're agreeable? I did say I thought you'd be fine with that. I'll have to give it a miss, I'm afraid.'

'Absolutely, if it's no trouble to you,' Christie said enthusiastically. 'I can remember my way to Stone House, so I'll drive myself over and you can get a rest.'

'We'll give you a key.' She stood up. 'In fact, I'll give you the spare right now. Keep it until you leave.' She took a key from a tin in a kitchen drawer and handed it to Christie. 'It's the front door. We'll make sure we don't leave the key in the lock when we go to bed.'

Matt's car pulled in with a crunch of gravel. Thank goodness. She could leave Christie with Matt and sneak off for some more painkillers and half an hour's lie down. The headache was starting to become unbearable.

Matt recognised what was happening the moment he entered, and bundled Liz upstairs amid assurances that he would sort supper for himself and Christie and then get hers when she felt up to it. Liz didn't argue. She swallowed two of her strongest painkillers, pulled the curtains, lay on the bed and closed her eyes.

* * *

Gina Spearman looked out from her bedroom window and gazed across the marsh to where the sun was setting. Most would have marvelled at the glorious light show and maybe even regretted the loss of the bright day, but Gina simply noted the herald of nightfall, which she loved because it was the precursor to darkness. She put her preference for the later hours down to being born at ten o'clock in the evening. She always felt most alive as the day drew to a close.

She lived in the farthest outskirts of the village, and her garden extended to the very edge of the marsh. Her home had once been a prestigious farmhouse belonging to a rich family of potato farmers called Ashton. When the family dwindled away, the last remaining Ashton placed the house on the market. It was difficult to sell, being probably one of the biggest properties in the area, so, anxious to move on, he accepted Gina's offer, a bargain for her. It was far too big for one woman, but she didn't give a damn. It was everything she'd ever wanted. It had class, history and made a statement. A statement about *her*.

She glanced at her watch. Her guests would be here shortly. She was an excellent cook. She could have been a top chef — she certainly had the temperament for it, though keeping staff might have been tricky.

Gina never dressed for dinner. She wore what her mood dictated, and if that happened to be jeans and a T-shirt, so be it. It was her table, and she was providing top-quality food. She went into the dining room and checked that everything was as she wanted it. All perfect. Flowers, candles, sparkling glasses and soft music.

Tonight was a small, carefully calculated step towards a new business venture that she had in mind, and her three guests were about to be charmed into believing that she was the best investment they had ever come across. The two men, brothers, were first-class prats and the woman — well, what a disaster. But they were nothing to her but a means to an end.

Gina had just completed her final preparations, ensuring that the wine was the right temperature and casting a swift and professional eye over the food, when the doorbell rang.

She threw open the front door. 'James, Lucas and dear Abigail! Come in. Come in. Welcome to Tadema House.'

Oh, this was going to be such fun.

* * *

Matt sat on the side of the bed, holding Liz's hand. 'You look much better now, sweetheart. Can I get you something to eat?'

Liz smiled up at him. 'Not just yet, Mattie, but yes, the headache is backing off. The sleep and the tablets helped. What time is it?'

'Almost nine o'clock.'

She blinked a few times. 'And did Christie get off for her ghost hunt okay?'

'Oh yes.' He grinned at her. 'Very excited about it.' He shook his head, 'And I bet Dominic is in his element with a new pair of ears to bend with his ghosties and ghoulies and long-legged beasties.'

'I'm sure he is. But at least she's in safe hands. He and Pip know that area blindfold. Not that I think they'll see any lights, but she'll get a good feel for the place and how the old-timers viewed it.' She sat up and stretched. 'Now, what was it you wanted to tell me about? Why you got held up in town, I think.'

His eyes shining, he told her about his conversation with DCI Anders. 'Charley says it's quite kosher, but she wants us to keep a low profile, find out certain things for her without drawing attention to our enquiries. I think it'll be mainly surveillance and checking up on people who were involved with the original investigation. Bryn is our contact and he's chuffed as little apples to have us working in the background.'

Liz had some instinctive reservations about actually assisting the police but saw how much Matt's mood had improved and decided not to rock the boat. 'Interesting, if somewhat irregular. So, we are now working as snouts — that's a turn-up for the books! Still, I suppose there are more civilians working in the old station now than there are regular police officers.'

'She needs to get this case cleared up and closed in double-quick time. This young man who has taken up a crusade against the police is apparently starting to collect a massive following on social media. Gold Braid want results and detectives are thin on the ground. She's pretty desperate, Liz.'

Liz gave him a tired smile. 'Then we'd better help her out, hadn't we? I guess Christie's used to doing her research on her own, and she did say not to turn down any work that comes up.'

'Spend a few days with her, sweetheart. Have a bit of downtime and enjoy her company, then join me when I've worked out a plan of action, checked out backgrounds, addresses and so on. There's plenty I can get on with.'

Liz was pleased to hear him speak with renewed determination. She decided to put off asking what had been bothering him — for a while at least. 'If you're sure, that would be perfect, but if it hots up, rope me in. Christie will understand.'

'Absolutely.' He squeezed her hand. 'Thank you.'

'What for?'

'You know very well what for.' He kissed her forehead. 'Now, how about some food before it gets too late?'

'Something light would be perfect, darling.' At times like this, his concern for her, his care for her needs, made her feel like the luckiest woman on the planet.

CHAPTER FIVE

Unsure of exactly what Dominic and Pip meant by twilight, Christie arrived too early. She'd expected the guest house to be full and was surprised to hear that the only guest was the Reverend Ian Hardy.

'We should have been on holiday ourselves,' said Pip ruefully, 'but the holiday company collapsed and the whole thing fell through at the last minute. Ian's a regular, more like family really, and no trouble, so when he rang, we were happy to accommodate him. We've decided to have a bit of a break at home.'

Pip brushed aside Christie's commiserations, saying that, actually, it was nice to get down to those jobs she'd been putting off and have a bit of time for herself. 'Come on through and I'll introduce you to Ian.'

Christie's first thought was that Reverend Hardy must have been terribly handsome when he was a young man. Even now, in his late seventies, he was quite striking, with chiselled features offset by warm brown eyes. His hair, though almost white, was still thick, and he wore it slightly long. Christie wondered what attendance at his sermons was like, and imagined a church packed with women, all competing to join the choir, the bell-ringers, the Mothers' Union, the flower arranging roster, the church cleaning group and the rest.

'Pip here tells me you work for Auden Meeres,' he said. 'I met him once, many years ago. He was charming, eloquent and funny. I liked him a lot.'

'Really?' Christie was intrigued. 'Not many people have met him, Reverend. He is something of a hermit, especially now his health is so poor.' Most people had heard of Auden, but with only two exceptions, she had never before come across anyone who had actually made his acquaintance.

'We were in the same hospital for a while, both of us bored silly. It was a delight to find a fellow inmate with whom you could hold a decent, intelligent conversation.'

'Oh, you'd certainly get that from Auden. He is one of the most fascinating raconteurs I've ever met and a gentle, kind man, as well. I am very fond of him.'

'That's so nice to hear.' Ian Hardy smiled. 'One so often finds that one's heroes have feet of clay. Fame can damage, there is no doubt about it.'

'Luckily, not in his case.'

'All set, intrepid explorers?' Dominic strode into the room, his black Labrador, Jessie, close at his heels.

'Excited,' said the reverend. 'I once saw St Elmo's fire around the mast of a ship, but I've certainly never seen the will-o'-the-wisp.'

'I can't promise that we definitely will tonight, but the conditions are good, we may be lucky.' He flopped down into a chair. 'Pip's bringing in a tray of hot drinks to fortify us.' He glanced at his watch. 'We'll set off in about twenty minutes. Meantime, I'll fill you in on a little local history.'

'So where exactly are we going?' asked Ian.

'Sly Fen. It's a little-known stretch of marsh that's rarely visited, even by our more ardent bird-watchers. There's no doubt that it's a dangerous place to venture if you don't know the terrain, but it was my playground as a kid and I know every inch of it. Just follow my instructions, and we'll be fine.'

Ian's excitement infected Christie. This was exactly the kind of thing that Auden craved to hear.

Pip handed out steaming mugs of tea and Dom began his account, Christie and Ian listening like wide-eyed children round a campfire. 'There are many tales of hauntings and strange occurrences in this area. It is a big county, but nevertheless Lincolnshire has forty-seven individual "Black Dog" ghosts. They are said to haunt lonely places and are often harbingers of death. Throughout the years our particular bit of marsh has been the site of numerous assorted phenomena. Both Pip and I have seen your will-o'-the-wisp on numerous occasions. When I've been out on the marsh, I have also witnessed some, how can I put it, inexplicable happenings. By the way, we call the lights the "hobby lantern," although the most well-known term is the one you used. There are actually dozens of different regional names — Will the Smith, hinkypunk, Kit-in-the-Candlestick, pinket, foxfire, Jenny-burnt-tail, jack-o'-lantern, the Welsh pwca and the Cornish Joan the Wad. The list is endless, but its most common name — other than will-o'-the-wisp — is *ignis fatuus*, or foolish fire, and I expect you have heard of corpse candles.'

'Ah yes, they were supposed to be seen around houses or places where a death was soon to occur. A large light for an adult, and a small, pale candle for an infant, I believe.'

'You seem familiar with those, Ian,' said Dom, with a grin.

'I lived in a rather remote part of Wales for a time. The *canwll corfe* was regularly sighted, bringing terror upon the somewhat naive community. Strangely, they were often correct.'

'Mmm, I can't say that surprises me. I'm not particularly superstitious myself, but I never dismiss what I don't understand.' Dom paused for a moment and scratched his chin thoughtfully. 'Well, back to Sly Fen. There are several tales of disappearances. The last one occurred during the Second World War, but mainly they stem from the Victorian era. They all involve folk being lured from the safety of the path and into the treacherous marshes. The light we have seen is bluish in colour and resembles a cold flame, sometimes with a misty halo around it. Don't be deceived into thinking this one is a death omen, though — I've seen it more times than I can count, and it's never yet coincided with a death. Now, the popular belief is that it's methane, or marsh gas, which can ignite spontaneously and form flames over boggy ground. Others believe it has something to do with phosphorus and chemical reactions. I'll leave it for you to decide once you have seen it for yourselves. Hopefully the conditions are right tonight.' Christie shivered — excitement mixed with a hint of trepidation.

Dom told them a few more tales of deaths and disappearances, and then looked at his watch and announced it was time to start. 'It's a ten-minute walk from the place where I park the Land Rover. The tides will be well out and we should be able to stay out there for about half an hour, all being well.' He stood up.

Dominic's old Land Rover bounced and ground its way down the uneven track, away from the village and out towards the marsh. There was an unseasonal chill to the evening, which Christie didn't know whether to put down to the temperature or the vague unease that clung to her like a slightly unpleasant smell.

The reverend was quiet too. All the "campfire" excitement had dissipated like smoke from dying embers. The only one of them who seemed unaffected was Pip, who sat making a shopping list for the next few days' meals by the light of her torch.

'Nearly there. It'll be a bit bumpy from now on, I'm afraid, but I'm going to drive the old girl up to the top of the sea bank, so hang onto your hats. Here we go!' Dominic dropped a gear and motored the old vehicle hard up a steep incline. They came to rest staring out across the salt marsh. It was not quite "darklins," and a meandering path out towards the Wash could still clearly be seen, twisting and turning through the sedge and rushes. The light was not going to hold for very long, however, and Christie felt another shiver, this time of pure apprehension. Earlier in the day she had been impatient for this moment, relishing the thought of a glimpse of the "foolish fire," but now, as she stood breathing in the salty ozone, she longed to be anywhere but here.

'Now, I'm going to put this,' Dominic was manhandling a large battery-powered lamp up onto the roof rack of the Land Rover, 'up here. It will act a bit like a beacon. You'll be able to keep your bearings from it. But don't worry, we'll be staying together in any case. I'll go in front and Pip will be "tail-end Charlie." You tread where I tread, and we'll have no accidents. Oh, and don't panic — we don't have quicksand here. If your foot should go in the mud, it won't suck you down. It's the tides that catch people out and the pools of deep water, it's not a swamp, okay? It's just a fen. They even graze cattle here in certain parts, so we aren't in any danger, if we're sensible. We're heading for that cluster of low bushes over to the right. See them?'

They nodded.

'There is a dry spot there where we can all sit and get a good view right across the marsh. The lights are usually seen about three hundred yards out. By the time we get there, it should be just about dark enough to see them clearly. The sky and the weather look just about perfect, don't they, Pip?'

His wife lifted her pale eyes up to the scudding clouds and the almost black line on the horizon. 'As good a night as any. Let's go.'

The going was much firmer than Christie had feared, although silvery lagoons and pools glistened dully in the twilight, reminding her of exactly where she was and not to take the apparently easy path for granted. Birds that made this boggy terrain their home grumbled and fussed as the "expedition" made its way across their nesting ground.

Christie concentrated hard on stepping in Ian's footprints.

The reverend was stalking Dominic, Christie followed Ian and Pip scampered lightly behind her, softly humming some familiar but irritatingly unrecognisable tune.

They reached their destination. Christie glanced back to find the beam of their home-made lighthouse coming from a totally unexpected direction. They seemed to have travelled in a loop, even though she could have sworn they'd walked in a fairly straight line.

'Okay, make yourselves comfortable and keep your eyes peeled.' Dom swung his arm out over the fen. 'That's the general direction to watch. It will be low to the ground and it will move, so the first one to spot it, tell the others. Don't shout, I've known it to disappear if there's too much noise, although heaven knows why.'

They settled down on the dry grassy hillock with a cluster of small stunted, windblown bushes behind them. It was almost night. They turned off their torches and strained their eyes into the darkness. Every so often, Christie turned to check that the beacon was still there, but her earlier excitement had returned.

As she peered into the gloom, she made copious mental notes for Auden Meeres.

It was certainly eerie out here on the marsh. There were noises that defied explanation and shadowy movements that caused her skin to prickle.

It must have been about ten minutes before Christie felt an urgent tug on her sleeve. Pip whispered into her ear, 'Look! Straight ahead. About two hundred yards out towards the Wash. There's the shadow of two large hummocks of sedge, then a bit to the left . . . tell Reverend Hardy.'

'Got it!' The reverend had seen it.

Christie's eyes darted about the skyline, then she saw it — a flickering light, dancing slowly in the dark.

Her heart pounded. She was sure the others must hear the thundering coming from her chest. Was she really looking at the same light that had held generations of country folk in awe? She needed to be clear-headed if she were to describe this for her employer, but the sheer mystery of the thing made it hard to be objective.

It was indeed a kind of phosphorescence — bluish, she thought — with, as Dominic had said, a misty sort of corona around it. It hovered for a moment then moved off slowly across the marsh. For a while, she lost it, and almost cried out. Then it was back, closer now, dancing along an invisible path. It moved slowly away, then flickered for a while in one spot, just like a cold, blue candle flame.

'Look!' This time the hushed word came from Dominic. 'Look to the left of it. There's another one!'

To Christie's surprise, another light was swaying and weaving across the boggy ground. This one had no mist surrounding it and looked for all the world like common lamplight. For a moment she thought she saw a hunched and indistinct shape behind it. Someone or something carrying a lantern? She grasped Pip's arm and, in a hoarse whisper, described what she thought she'd seen.

'It's shadow, Christie. The light moves over the uneven earth and throws back solid-looking shapes, but it's only the rough ground thrown into relief.' Christie imagined her smiling. 'But you can certainly see why poor travellers were fooled by these, can't you?'

The lights were about ten yards from each other when they started to move away, each taking its own invisible path through the mire. After about five minutes, all they could see were two hazy, glimmering patches low on the horizon.

'Time to go, friends,' said Dom. 'I would say our *ignis fatuus* put on a bit of a star performance tonight. You don't usually see two together, do you, Pip?'

'Quite a rarity. You've both been highly honoured this evening. Now, let's get home. The tide turns rather fast here and I don't want to get caught napping.'

Dominic moved to the front again and they made their single-file way off the Sly Fen. There was no late glow of fading evening light to guide them this time, just the bobbing beams of their torches cutting sharp lines through the inky blackness.

Christie finally saw the outline of the vehicle, with its welcoming ray shining from the roof. She heaved a sigh of relief.

Then Dominic suddenly stopped. 'Hold it a minute. Quiet!'

They all stood, silent.

'Stand still. Hold on to each other and turn off your torches, quickly!'

Christie did as she was told, though she hated to lose the light. Her hand gripped Ian's shoulder and she felt Pip's arm slide through hers.

Out on the fen another light bobbed.

They remained motionless, staring. 'I could be wrong, but I think that's some bloody idiot out there, and the tide will be on its way in. It comes in fast here.'

She heard the intake of his breath.

'Pip, see the others safely back to the Land Rover. I'm going to take a look.'

'Like hell you are!' Pip said angrily. 'If someone is foolish enough to wander out here, then it's up to them! But you are not going to walk into danger because of their stupidity. Get back to the vehicle and turn the main headlights on. We can call out to them. But you know our rule. Neither of us goes wandering off alone, ever!'

The reverend and Christie backed her up, so Dominic hustled them all into the Land Rover and turned on the engine.

They stood on the bank and shouted in the direction of the light, but still it moved further out towards the estuary and the incoming tide.

Dominic manoeuvred the Land Rover until its headlights pointed towards where they had seen the mysterious sight, but no one showed up in the beam. He switched them off again and a few moments later the bobbing light was back, making straight for the Wash.

'Had you considered that it might be another will-o'-the-wisp?' Ian's voice was calm. 'I do not think we have some drunken idiot blundering about out there. In fact, I don't think that's a human being at all.'

Dominic Campion stood very still and gazed out over the salt marsh. 'If it is, then it's the first time it's ever fooled me in thirty-something years of wandering this area. If it isn't, then tonight someone will be very lucky to get out of the marsh alive.'

By now, the light had gone completely and in silence, they stared into the dark, empty space. They were all terribly uncertain.

Pip spoke softly to her husband. 'I think the reverend is right, Dom. Let's go home. I'm certain that tomorrow we won't be hearing any news about a missing person. What we just saw was another manifestation of the hobby lantern — different to the others, but still just a phenomenon, and one that nearly had you rushing off after it. Come on. We all need a drink.'

They drove back to Stone House in almost total silence. When they got there, Philippa poured them all generous shots of brandy. Dominic lit the imitation gas "log" fire, and they pulled their chairs up to its comforting flame.

'I seem to have got a bit more than I bargained for tonight.' Christie felt somewhat responsible for the dramatic end to the evening. After all, if she hadn't been so keen to go out there, they would never have seen that last, disconcerting light.

Dom swilled his brandy around in his glass and stared at his wife. He shook his head and scratched absentmindedly at his brown wavy hair. 'I still can't believe I was taken in by a hobby lantern. I'm sure you're right . . .' His voice trailed off.

'You're not the first Fenlander to be misled by the lights, my darling. And at least you're here to tell the tale.'

Dom looked sadly into his glass. 'But I was going to go after it, wasn't I? I nearly broke our first commandment, to never go off on your own at night. I was so sure it was a torch I saw, but now I don't know what to think. One thing's for sure, that light was very different to all the others we've seen, wasn't it, darling?'

'Absolutely. But it moved too quickly after we started hollering. Even if it had been a local up to no good, rabbit-trapping or the like, no one moves that fast on the marsh in the dark. And if it was a local, they know the tides better than anyone, they simply wouldn't be there in the first place. I think it proves that you should never get complacent about the Fens, not even when you've spent most of your life on them.'

The reverend sat back in his chair and smiled at them over the rim of his glass. 'So, it looks as if we've been privy to no less than three separate phenomena. Am I right?'

'It looks that way,' said Dom.

'Anyone got any theories?' Ian Hardy looked at Christie and raised an eyebrow.

'It has to be marsh gases, surely? Or a natural earth energy, maybe even some kind of electromagnetic force. I have no idea what exactly, but surely it must be a kind of spontaneous episode sparked off by the nature of the marshy ground?'

Ian's gaze passed on to Pip. 'And you, my dear? What are your thoughts?'

'I don't know, Reverend Hardy, and that's the honest truth. I don't come from here like Dominic, but I grew up with them on the Cambridge fenlands, a right water-world. As a child, I was warned of the ghost lights and given all the folklore and the tales of witchery — enough to scare a bairn half to death. But sense dictates that Christie is probably right. It's just methane leaking from old rotting organic matter, or atmospheric conditions. I really don't know.'

'Dominic?' The cleric moved his gaze to the serious face of the fen man.

He brushed a stray dog hair from his khaki chinos and reached down to stroke the sleek black head of Jessie, the Labrador, who'd forgiven him for leaving her at home. 'I first saw the lights when I was small, and firmly believed they were the will-o'-the-wisp, a malevolent spirit that roamed the marshes and lured unsuspecting travellers, especially children, to a watery grave. Then, when I became a teenager, I scoffed at the old tales and adhered to the theories of my school science teacher, a man I liked and respected enormously.'

'So, given how much you admired him, if he'd said that they were caused by little green men from the planet Zorg, you'd have gone along with that?' Pip smiled affectionately at her husband.

'Probably.' He grinned sheepishly. 'He was my hero at the time. Anyway, I've been seeing the lights on and off ever since then, and I've speculated on their origin every time. I still do. Like Pip, I'm torn between folklore and chemistry, superstition and science. What about you, Reverend? You have a religious background, but I get the feeling you don't dismiss the ideas of ghostly manifestations out of hand?'

The old man stared into the fire and sighed. 'I have lived long enough and seen enough strange things to accept that not everything has a logical explanation. I do believe in science. I am constantly amazed at man's scientific ability — discovering DNA, calculating the distance between the stars and the planets, brain surgery and now artificial intelligence. I am in awe of the minds that can understand these things. But I also believe that not everything is black and white, good or evil. Life's grey areas can be confusing but most interesting. Tell me, Dominic, if you had to decide one way or the other, which side would you come down on? If forced to choose between alternatives, there is usually one tiny doubt that gnaws away at your gut and that sways you in the end, rational or not.'

'With apologies to my science teacher, I suppose that if someone really twisted my arm it would have to be superstition that won out.'

'Why?' Christie hadn't expected him to answer that way.

'Because there's one small thing that no one has ever been able to explain to me — the lights move about the marsh, you saw that for yourselves tonight. Now, if the lights were caused by gas emissions, they wouldn't dance all over the place, would they? Why do they always move away from you when you approach or make a noise? I have tried countless times to get closer, but they are like timid creatures that retreat into hiding when confronted by humans. That is the one thing I have never understood.'

'And if you can't get close to the little beggars, how can you study them?' Pip said.

There was no simple answer to Dominic Campion's question, although Christie did wonder. If it really was a gas, surely it *would* move away if you approached it, simply because of the air displaced by your approaching body. She decided to say nothing. She was still going with the science.

They sipped their brandy and fell into a ruminative silence, no doubt each of them pondering on the reasons for the strange movements of the will-o'-the-wisp. After a while, Christie had a thought. 'Ian, you never actually gave us your opinion of tonight's display.'

There was a long pause while the old gentleman settled himself in the winged armchair he was occupying. He coughed. 'Apologies to my worthy bishop and to those who would condemn my beliefs, but I would have to agree with Dominic. I do not know what those lights that we witnessed tonight are, but I had a distinct feeling that they were not benevolent. I was happy to get well away from Sly Fen — I was feeling most uncomfortable out there, most uncomfortable.'

Christie was quite shocked at the reverend's words, but again decided to keep her thoughts to herself. Perhaps they weren't so strange after all. The Bible was full of otherworldly happenings — resurrection from the dead for one — and if the church could uphold exorcism, maybe a belief in spirits was not so unthinkable.

There was another long silence. Pip got to her feet. 'So, who fancies a toasted sandwich for supper? You'll have one before you leave, won't you, Christie? There's cheese, ham, tuna, whatever you want.'

Christie quietly thanked heaven for the Pips of this world.

CHAPTER SIX

Christie didn't see Matt and Liz until breakfast the following morning. She had stayed up quite late with the Campions and it wasn't until Ian Hardy had said that he had to be up early that they realised how the time had flown.

'I cannot believe that you saw the hobby lantern!' exclaimed Liz. 'And not one, but three of them! It's extraordinarily lucky. I've never seen one yet.'

Christie was delighted to see that Liz was much recovered, though she still looked a little pale and tired. 'Auden is going to be thrilled to bits. I sat up for over an hour last night, just putting down all my thoughts and feelings about them.'

'I bet Dom was cock-a-hoop, wasn't he?' said Matt, passing her more toast.

'Not exactly. Actually, he was pretty upset.'

Matt and Liz gave each other a puzzled look. 'Why?' asked Liz.

She told them about his belief that there was someone out on the marsh who was in danger, and how he'd almost broken his promise to Pip never to go onto the marsh alone at night. 'He was convinced it was a human out there. Now he's gutted that the lights had him fooled for the first time in his life.'

'I bet he is!' Matt said emphatically. 'He's the local expert on the marsh and its history and superstitions. If the lights fooled him, there's little hope for the uninitiated.' He grinned at her. 'Oh, and injured pride will have come into it too.'

'I'm sure.' Christie shook her head. 'But to be fair, I think he was more disappointed in himself for almost breaking their code of safety.'

'He'll get over it,' Liz reassured them. 'Now, what's on the cards for today?'

Christie looked at the dark rings under Liz's eyes. 'I'm going to suggest that you have a slow start today, Liz. There were some other books in the Reading Room I'd like to buy, so I'll go into town and sort that out, then we can decide when I get back.' She noted the relief that crossed her cousin's face.

Three-quarters of an hour later, she was back in the bookshop. Tom seemed genuinely pleased to see her again, but he wasn't quite the man of yesterday. He smiled in greeting but he seemed distant.

She browsed for a while, found one of the books that she wanted and saw an interesting volume that would make a great gift for Richard. She always took him a memento of her travels, and this was perfect for him. It was a book of paintings inspired by the shipping forecast. Apparently, his father had spent much of his boyhood on Lundy Island where the shipping forecast was sacred, being the only way to tell whether they could expect the *Lundy Gannet* to call with their provisions and mail from the mainland. Christie took the book to the counter along with one on the Lincolnshire dialect.

Tom came over, still looking preoccupied. 'I'm glad you've come in. I found something you might like.' He looked anxiously over his shoulder to the half-closed office door behind the cash desk. 'I'm afraid I won't be free for a coffee right now. Gina has thrown a wobbler at one of the staff, and I'd better hang around to pick up the pieces.'

The half-muffled sound of someone very angry and trying to keep the volume down came from the back room. Christie thought she caught the sound of a stifled sob beneath the onslaught.

She must have looked concerned because Tom touched her arm and gave her one of his lopsided smiles. 'Don't worry, we're used to it by now. Our Gina has a bit of a short fuse, I'm afraid, and Delphi, bless her, is somewhat prone to histrionics. It's a pretty explosive mix sometimes.'

'That's Delphi?' She recalled the smiling young woman of yesterday. 'Oh dear. Hardly good for staff relations, I imagine.'

'Oh, Gina is a great boss really, Christie. She calms down as quickly as she flares up. She's very highly strung, I suppose. Very "artistic" and extremely well educated.' He gave a sigh. 'She can't help being frustrated with us mere mortals.'

Christie didn't miss the slightly wistful note.

He pushed his glasses further up onto the bridge of his nose and readjusted his smile. 'Anyway, let me show you what I found.'

The disagreement backstage had subsided by now. Tom ferreted around on some shelves behind the desk and reappeared with an art book. 'Blow them,' he said suddenly, 'they can sort themselves out. Come on, up to the café.'

Christie followed him up the stairs and decided that she really must get a look at this talented and wrathful employer before she left.

Tom got the coffees and Christie twisted his arm into letting her buy him a bun to go with it. 'So? What do you have for me?' she asked eagerly.

'It might be of no use at all, but I remembered seeing this painting somewhere, it just took a little while to locate it. Look.' He opened the book and pointed to a large plate in colour. The text beside it gave a short history of the artist and his work.

She drew in a breath and held it, immediately transported back to the previous night on the marsh. The lantern-lit, night-time scene seemed to depict exactly what she had witnessed, and what Auden Meeres was trying to conjure in words.

'Tom! That's perfect. It represents the whole essence of what I'm trying to capture for Auden's book.' The painting was called *Jack O'Lantern,* and was made in 1872 to illustrate a book of poetry. The artist was Arthur Hughes, whose work she already knew and loved. A copy of his painting, *April Love,* had hung on her grandmother's sitting-room wall when she was a child. She could easily recall the tearful girl in the exquisite blue dress standing in shadowy woodland and wondered absently what had become of it.

'How much is the book, Tom?'

'I'm not asking you to purchase it, Christie. I'll happily photocopy that page for you.'

From Tom's anxious look she realised that he thought she'd assumed he was chasing a sale. Which she didn't think at all, she just wanted the book. How complicated the simplest interactions were sometimes.

He looked on the back cover and told her that the price was thirty-five pounds.

'Great. I'll take it. Don't feel bad. I didn't think you just wanted to sell it. You've done me a real favour, finding this. Perhaps you could do me a photocopy as well, if you don't mind?'

'I'd be pleased to. It might help ease my conscience a little.'

As they drank their coffee and ate their buns, Tom told her about his elderly mother, Margaret. 'Hey, she'd love to meet you! She's an Audenaholic! How about calling in for tea on my day off? Better still, why not come to supper one evening? I can do a mean steak and Caesar salad — mind you, that's about all I can do. I only live five minutes from here. You'd be very welcome.'

Christie accepted his invitation with alacrity, hoping she wasn't treading on anyone's toes. He hadn't mentioned a wife or girlfriend, but that wasn't to say there wasn't one.

Tom was attractive in a nerdy kind of way — surely someone had snapped him up by now. She decided not to ask any questions. After all, if his mother was like most, she would probably give her his entire life history almost as soon as she walked in the door.

She was adding a note of his address and telephone number to her contacts when a loud sniff behind them heralded the arrival of Delphi. On catching sight of Christie, she blew her nose and hurried off to the kitchen.

Tom jumped up. 'Back in a jiff.' He went after her and was gone for only a minute or two before emerging from behind the café counter with a rueful smile on his face. 'She says she's sorry and she'll see you next time you come in.'

'Poor Delphi. She looked really upset.'

'Don't worry, honestly. She'll be back to her old self in no time.' He paused. 'This happens quite often, but after all, if she was that unhappy, she'd leave, wouldn't she?'

Christie thought that would depend entirely on the girl's circumstances. What chance would there be, realistically, of another job in Fenfleet? She said, 'I suppose so. Well, I'd better pay for these books. I have to get back to Liz. We're thinking of heading down to Friars Shore to soak up a bit more local colour.'

'If it's solitude you're looking for, you might be unlucky. You could well find some twitchers out there today. There has been a sighting. One of our customers was all excited about some rare migrant that he'd read about on the internet. They issue Recent Bird Reports for this part of the county. It's a real bird-watcher's haven around—'

'So, this is the redoubtable Miss McFerran. Tom, an introduction please.'

Tom jumped up, almost knocking his chair to the floor, and Christie took an instant dislike to Gina Spearman.

The strength of it surprised her. Christie was a mild-mannered, even-tempered person. She had been told on several occasions that she possessed the irritating ability to see both sides of every argument or situation. She lost her temper perhaps once every seven years. On this occasion, however, she took one look at the elfin features, the almost black hair cut in a short, angular cut, the quizzical smile and icy-blue eyes and found herself calculating when her last outburst had been.

Gina Spearman was just a little too polite, too exaggeratedly affable. She enunciated each word as if the recipient might not understand her, and was patronising towards Tom. But at the same time, she left you wondering if you were being too judgemental. You caught a disparaging comment here and there, but always couched in a backhanded compliment.

Christie found that she was being very cautious in her responses. It came out as formal, rather stilted, most unlike her open, easy-going self. As they spoke, she discovered that she was being made to feel important one minute and an embarrassing irritation the next.

Deciding to drop the cat and mouse game, Christie made her excuses, paid for her books and, graciously refusing Gina's offer of a small discount, left the Reading Room.

Outside, she sat in her car, wondering at her reaction to the woman she'd just met. It was completely irrational. She didn't even know Gina Spearman and she would probably never see her again. Yet, in that brief exchange of pleasantries, this woman had rattled Christie beyond belief.

It was also most unlike her to make instant judgements of people, and if she did, she usually revised her opinion pretty quickly. But this one, she had a feeling, was going to stick with her. With a grunt, she started the engine and pulled away. Best forget about Gina and make sure that their paths didn't cross again. That should be easy enough, shouldn't it?

* * *

Liz was grateful to Christie for her consideration in allowing her a little more time to recover. Now, after a hot shower, two cups of tea and some breakfast, she felt fine again.

She wandered into the dining room, where Matt was engrossed in his laptop, scrolling through reams of paperwork that had arrived from Charlotte Anders. 'Interesting?' she asked, sitting at the table and watching him. He looked up and she saw a light in his eyes that she'd often seen when they were still "real detectives," a spark of enthusiasm that meant he was fully committing to a new case.

'Very interesting indeed.' He beamed at her. 'You're going to enjoy this. It's like being back on home territory.'

Liz's chest felt tight with anxiety. She managed to utter a flat 'That's good.'

Matt didn't seem to notice. 'I've rarely seen so many dead ends. This case must have been really exasperating to work on. It's either terribly simple — a bungled mugging, end of story — or there was something else behind it, some very clever and complex plot.' He sat back and folded his arms. 'My money's on the latter. I think there is a lot more to the death of Lindsay Harrison than has ever come to light.'

He sounded so engaged that Liz began to feel a little warmed by the flame. 'You mean a deliberate and premeditated murder?'

'I'm sure of it. And before I get on to Charley's first request — checking out the boyfriend — I want to find out all I can about whoever's behind the social media posts about police inefficiency. I want to know who he is, what he was to Lindsay and exactly what his agenda is.'

'Mmm,' said Liz thoughtfully. 'As in, is this "justice for Lindsay," or an attempt to cause trouble for the police?'

'Exactly. And that's my mission for today.' He sat forward again. 'How long before you can join me, do you think?'

Liz weighed up how much she could reasonably be of help to Christie and how long a break she needed before pitching back into work. 'Three or four days, most like.'

'Okay, that's good. I'll collate everything and by that time, I should have a handle on how to play it.' He looked at her. 'But Christie's free to stay as long as she needs — no problem there, we can still feed and water her. It's not like being back at the station and never knowing when you'll be called on to work overtime. This is down to us, and we work according to our own timetable.'

'I like the sound of that, darling. It's what we planned, after all.' She stood up. 'I'm going to make a few phone calls and get ready for when Christie gets back. I was thinking she might like to talk to our old colleague, PC Jack Fleet. He's a local, as were his parents, and I seem to vaguely remember him telling me he had a relative who knew everything about the history of this area. It could help Christie's research.'

Matt nodded and murmured something, his eyes back on his screen. Oh well, she thought, at least he's a hell of a lot happier.

* * *

Christie was on her way back towards her cousin's place when she reached the road that led to the Campions' guest house. On an impulse, she pulled off and headed towards Sly Fen. She felt a sudden need to rid herself of the shadows that still clung to her from the night before. Seeing the place in sunlight should help to dispel some of the malevolent atmosphere. As she approached the lane, she saw someone who looked familiar walking slowly along the edge of one of the vast arable fields. She slowed down and called out, 'Reverend! Where are you off to out here?'

Ian Hardy turned, surprised, then his solemn face broke into a smile. 'Christie, how nice! I'm just walking, my dear, trying to make sense of things.'

That makes two of us, thought Christie. 'I was just going down to the marsh. I felt I needed to lay some ghosts to rest.'

'Would you like some company?' the reverend suggested. 'It might do both of us some good.'

She parked where Dominic had left the Land Rover. The two of them got out and stood staring across the desolate marsh. Christie let out a sigh of relief. Sly Fen looked like a completely different place — less vast, less threatening. Of course, the tide was further in now, covering the sepia pools. She could make out all manner of birds, busy flying in and out, feeding, squabbling noisily and strutting around. She had almost expected to see policemen in wellington boots, strung out across the boggy terrain, looking for a missing person last seen heading out into the marsh at night. She berated herself for being so silly. Still, it had given her some great material for Auden. It had also made her realise how these superstitions could take hold in an isolated community.

Ian Hardy broke the silence. 'Actually, my reason for being out here this morning has nothing to do with last night. It was concern for my sister that brought me, seeking solace in the big skies and the empty paths.'

Christie was brought back into the present moment with a jolt. So she was wrong. She had assumed that he too was feeling confused about their late-night excursion. 'I'm so sorry. Can you talk about it? I'm told I'm a good listener.'

Ian stared out towards the wide band of silver water formed by the incoming tide. 'I think I'm losing her.' He gave a long sigh that seemed to melt into the air and drift out into the lonely marshland. 'The doctors have told me that she probably won't be able to cope with another bout of infection. They are doing their best, but she has an immune deficiency caused by an old illness and she is in her seventies now.'

Christie hadn't known that she was actually in hospital. For some reason, she had believed his sister was still at home and he was visiting her there.

'She never married, you know,' he went on. 'A shame, really, she is such a good soul, and when you are sick you need someone of your own around you, other than a doddering old fool of a brother.'

Christie really couldn't put Ian Hardy into that category, and told him so.

With a laugh, he said he wasn't so sure about that. He went on to tell her something about their childhood. Even in their early years, he and his sister had shared a deep bond. Losing her would affect him terribly. His sadness when he spoke about her coming death reminded Christie of Richard's when he told her Auden might not finish the book she was researching. Richard loved Auden.

'You must come and visit her cottage, Christie. I'd love you to see it. Then you'll appreciate why a big lummox of a man like me stays in a guest house.' He gave a chuckle.

Christie didn't quite know what he meant by this, but he didn't elaborate.

After a while they lapsed into a comfortable silence, then, out of nowhere, Christie began to tell Ian about her earlier uncharacteristic reaction to Gina Spearman, a complete stranger.

Ian gazed out across the sedge and reeds and sea lavender, the lagoons of dark water. 'The situation you describe sounds like a simple clash of personalities. I am a firm believer in personality types. Certain folk just don't get along, and that's it. Sometimes it's a form of survival instinct. You pick up some characteristic that your mind doesn't like or cannot cope with and you react instinctively to it, but without conscious thought. I really wouldn't worry about it too much. If you stay away from her, you can't get riled, can you?' He smiled thoughtfully. 'One thing is for sure, some people love to see the effect they have on others, and the greater the reaction, the better they like it. They engineer situations so as to watch their victims squirm. So, if you think this Ms Spearman might be that particular type, either steer well clear, or if you can't avoid her, don't react at all.'

'Avoiding her is something I'll gladly do,' Christie said with feeling.

Ian's gaze was still on Sly Fen. 'Watching people interact has always fascinated me. My sister used to tell me off whenever we went out. She'd say I was the worst "people-watcher" imaginable, often completely ignoring her while following a conversation between two perfect strangers.'

Christie laughed. 'I know what she meant. I had a friend like that. I used to ask why she even bothered to invite me along.'

'I'm sure it's annoying, but it's something you just can't resist. If a snippet of overheard conversation or some unusual body language attracts your attention, you're sunk.' He tried to look apologetic and failed.

'I think in Gina Spearman's case, it's the intensity of the anger I felt towards her that upset me. It was over an hour ago now and I'm still seething. Maybe it was because I'd heard her berating a member of staff who seemed like a sweet, innocent soul. Or was it Tom's protective attitude? This woman clearly didn't need it.' Frankly, she thought there was very little Gina would need protection from. 'I just don't understand it.'

'You'd have to know a lot more about the dynamic in that shop before coming to any conclusions, Christie. Maybe Tom is in awe of her? She's obviously an extremely good businesswoman.' He frowned. 'We all allow others to influence us. Sometimes we don't even know why another human being's opinion should be important to us — maybe we need their blessing because we're unsure of ourselves. We are afraid of making decisions in case we make a mistake, so we turn to a "stronger" character for their approval. Usually, though, that stronger one is nothing of the kind. A lot of people who appear tough, outspoken and dominant are insecure and weak on the inside, the last person you should be placing your trust in. Listen to me, preaching away as usual and there's not a pulpit in sight! Forgive me, Christie, I'm being an idiot.'

She assured him he was far from that. They walked back to her car, Christie still thinking about what he'd said.

Ian patted her arm affectionately. 'Keep honest people in your life, my dear. Nice, open, friendly souls who nurture you, not the leeches, the ones who drain you or play games. They're a vexation to the spirit.'

Suddenly it came to her. Games, that was it. Gina Spearman was a game-player. Those tempers that flared then miraculously subsided, the accusations and put-downs that were followed by compliments and accolades. They were all a game.

Christie drove them back towards the Campions' house wondering why. What possible end could Gina's games be serving?

She waved goodbye to Ian, the question going round and round in her head.

CHAPTER SEVEN

It wasn't until about ten that evening that Matt finally shut down his laptop. Liz was in the kitchen going over what she and Christie had achieved that afternoon. From what they told him at supper, they'd been out on a most productive expedition together. Christie had already sent Richard several assorted files to read or play to Auden.

Matt made them hot drinks and declared he would shortly be turning in. He was no longer used to such intensive homework. It really was like having a police investigation running, a far cry from spending days proving something everyone already knew about, like a misbehaving spouse. Thank goodness they had had only had one missing pet to find, or he'd have dismissed the PI business as definitely not for him. He smiled to himself. Actually, that case — if you could call it that — had been rather satisfying, resulting in one very lucky and, he had to admit, beautiful dog rescued from being shipped out of the country. When they returned it, the look on the owners' faces, especially their young son, had made doing the job worthwhile. But Matt Ballard didn't see himself spending his days retrieving lost dogs. All credit to Ace Ventura, but Matt preferred hunting for people. The photo Frances Morton had given them of her sister Amy flashed into his mind. Hunting for people. Sometimes even that wasn't easy. He had been convinced that Amy had gone off of her own volition, following some new dream, but he had to admit that the sudden change in her that Frances had described at their last meeting was way out of character.

'You really are away with the fairies, Matt Ballard!'

He looked up to see both Liz and Christie laughing at him.

Liz shook her head. 'Christie was just telling you that we met Jack Fleet this afternoon.'

'Oh, sorry,' Matt said, 'I was miles away. Jack? Perfect, he'll have a whole list of people who can tell you about local history.'

'He's offered to take me to see where they used an old beam engine to drain the fen. His cousin is the curator of a museum there.' Christie was clearly delighted at the prospect. 'People are so helpful and friendly here, aren't they?'

'In the main, yes,' said Matt, remembering all the people who'd been far from helpful, often downright aggressive. But that was when he worked as a policeman. 'So, what do you think of Bomber County so far, Christie?'

'I'm amazed at how much I like it here. I've travelled a lot and seen many different places, all of which you'd think had more to offer than these flatlands, if you'll excuse me saying so. But there's a strange airy beauty here that has started to work its magic on me. There is no breathtaking drama unfolding, no roaring waterfalls, no deep green pine forest, no snow-topped peaks, but maybe that's the whole point. The bleak, never-ending droves and river paths don't take your breath away at all, they actually give you room to breathe. Nothing towers over you, nothing confines you and nothing closes in on you.' She shrugged. 'It's hard to put into words, but if I had to live under these big skies, I think I'd be very happy.'

Liz nudged him. 'She's clearly been bitten by the Fenland bug, hasn't she?'

He grinned at her. 'It certainly seems that way. But I'm not sure she'll feel the same when they're harvesting and there's wall-to-wall mud across the lanes, or when that snide east wind comes in on a January morning and bites through to your bones.'

'I'd cope, I'm sure,' said Christie. 'I've suffered worse.'

'By the way, my friend Tom from the Reading Room has invited Christie to dinner with him and his mother,' said Liz. 'Do you remember Margaret, Matt?'

'Of course I do, a very nice woman. She's another one who'll be able to assist you, Christie. I hope you said yes?'

'I did and I'm looking forward to it.' Christie pulled a face. 'At least it won't be as scary as my last evening trip out. Dinner with an elderly lady sounds a much safer bet!'

They all laughed. 'You'll like Margaret,' Matt said. 'They're both great company and the old lady is a real laugh if you get her onto the subject of village life a few decades ago. She adores Tom, and he takes his responsibility for her very seriously. He told me that he's actually perfectly happy for her to live with him, so he can keep a close eye on her as she gets older.'

'Not many men of his age would want that sort of dependency,' Christie mused.

'Very true,' Liz said. 'But his father died young, and Tom rather slipped into the role of the man about the house. Plus, he loves her to bits, and she's very independent, not at all demanding. It just seems to work for them.'

'Is he married? Engaged?' Christie asked, thinking it might be good to know this before she arrived on his doorstep. 'Long-time girlfriend?'

'Tom? Oh no!' exclaimed Liz. 'In fact, I don't think he has ever had a really serious relationship. He has certainly gone out with quite a few women, but none have lasted. I used to go on at him about settling down, but he just shrugged it off, saying he's happy as he is.' She paused. 'However, I think he *is* carrying a torch for someone. Don't ask me who, because I've no idea. It's just a hunch, a woman thing, you know?'

'Uh oh, here we go. Time for me to say goodnight,' said Matt, standing up. 'I'll leave you two to discuss woman things. Sleep well, Christie. See you up there, sweetheart.'

By the time he got to the top of the stairs, he had forgotten all about Tom's marital status and was back with DCI Charley Anders and the four-year-old murder of a young woman. He had no idea why, but he was convinced that when they came to the end of this unusual assignment they would know the truth and Charley would have her murderer.

As he hung up his jacket and folded his trousers, he wondered where that thought had come from. All he had been assigned to do was follow up a few names and so far, he had seen nothing other than dead ends in a carefully investigated case. Even so, he and Liz were going to give the DCI her killer, and that was that.

* * *

As she finished her cup of tea, Christie was considering who Tom might be lusting after. Delphi? But hadn't Delphi been wearing a wedding ring? She sincerely hoped it wasn't the dreaded Gina. That would be horrible. No, hopefully it would be some other woman, someone she hadn't met.

'What do you know about his boss, Liz?' she asked, trying to sound casual.

'Not a lot. I've met her a few times in passing. I know that the bookshop was her brainchild, but other than that and the fact that she lives in some gorgeous old house out on the edge of the marsh and has a valuable art collection, I know nothing about her as a person.'

Christie decided against telling Liz about her extraordinary antipathy towards Gina Spearman. There was a good chance she'd never even see the woman again. After all, she had plenty of work to do, and there were enough really nice people around here to compensate for this one nasty woman.

'Well, I'm off to type up a few more observations about those acres of fields we saw this afternoon with the chains of pylons marching into the distance, and then get some sleep.' She gave her cousin a warm smile. 'You've been brilliant, Liz. I've got far more work done than usual already, and all because you guys know so many helpful people. I'm going through Auden's requests at a rate of knots. I do appreciate it.'

Liz smiled back. 'It's no trouble, honestly. I'm enjoying showing off my home county. Now, where would you like to go tomorrow?'

Christie glanced at her notebook. 'If it's not too much trouble, I'd like to go to Greenborough and speak to some of the fishermen who moor their boats in the tidal river. Auden wants to know about the seasonal patterns of their catches, which I'm led to believe are cockles, mussels and brown shrimp — oh, and any special knowledge required to navigate those particular waters.'

'Sure thing,' Liz said. 'We can check the tides to make sure the boats are in. Greenborough is only around three-quarters of an hour from here.'

'Great, and if we have time, I'd quite like to take a stroll through Fenfleet, but down the back streets and alleyways this time, and did you mention somewhere called Whisper Fen?' Christie asked.

Liz suddenly looked serious. 'I'll take you to Whisper Fen anytime you like, but if you don't mind, don't make too much of it in front of Matt. He went through a bad experience there which involved a close mate of his. It's not his favourite place, and since his friend sold up and moved away, we don't go there unless we have to.'

'I understand.' Christie recalled the look on Matt's face when the place had been mentioned before. 'We don't have to — it was only that you said it was quite eerie.'

'No, we'll go. It's certainly worth seeing. It's only ten minutes up the road from here. If you want deep, dark Fenland stories, that's the place to visit all right.' Liz collected up the mugs. 'I'll tell you some of them when we get there, especially the story of Holland House. I still shiver when I think about it.'

Christie didn't press her. She was sure Liz would tell her what had upset Matt if she wanted to, but she wasn't going to pry.

Upstairs in her room, she typed out her recollections of what they had seen that day, hoping she had done justice to the vista of massive arable fields and the long straight roads that went on forever. She sent the files to Richard, along with a few images so that at least he could see what she was talking about if Auden could not. To her surprise she had an email straight back.

Is it too late, or can I ring your mobile? Richard.

With a frown, Christie called him back. 'Is everything okay?'

'Not really, Christie. I'm afraid that even though the book is going well, Auden is very poorly. We had to have the doctor round again today. I'm not too sure how long his health is going to hold out. If he has another serious setback — and the doc said it's quite possible he will —I'm scared that his last and best may never be completed. He has given me a list of extra things for you to check on for him, nothing too complicated, but when you're through, I suggest you get back up here. I'm sure you can help him just as much from memory. I've read and listened to everything you've sent us. The place certainly seems to have made a deep impression on you. It sounds very atmospheric.'

Christie felt a stab of regret. She didn't want to leave yet. In a mere couple of days this strange county had captivated her. But work was work and if Auden needed her, she would go. She assured Richard that she'd complete her tasks as soon as possible and then return immediately to Yorkshire. From what he'd said, she thought the work would take her three days at the most. Richard said that would be perfect, if she could manage it.

They ended the call on a rather sombre note, both aware that their dear friend might not be with them for much longer. With a sigh, Christie scribbled a reminder to contact Tom in the morning. If she was to have dinner with him, it would have to be within the next couple of days.

She lay in bed wondering why this particular trip had stirred up such strong emotions in her. It was odd, but she felt as if she'd forged new and lasting friendships in a matter of days. Ian Hardy, the Campions, Tom and Delphi, even PC Jack Fleet, Liz's old workmate, they had all made their mark on her and she wanted to know them better.

She determined that when this assignment was over, whether she still had a job or not, she would come back to the Fens and spend some time here. She wouldn't take advantage of Liz and Matt's kindness, even though she would probably be very welcome, but would stay at Stone House with Pip and Dom.

In other words, she told herself, leaving now didn't mean turning her back on the place forever. With that thought, she drifted off to sleep.

She woke again at around two in the morning, this time not feeling quite so upbeat. What would she do when her work for Auden came to an end? She wasn't exactly penniless, she reminded herself. *Thank God.* Her grandparents had left her a small inheritance and a three-bedroom terraced house in a pleasant tree-lined street in Scarborough, but she needed work, needed stimulation to keep her enquiring mind active. It would be very easy to allow her illness to take over and become a semi-invalid, and she didn't want that. Her job with Auden had been perfect, but she'd never find another like that. How many blind authors needed someone else to be their eyes?

This led her thoughts to Richard. He'd been so much more than just a pair of eyes — he'd been mother, nurse, cook, secretary, companion and confidante to Auden for years. Whatever would become of him?

She shifted about in the soft bed, trying to find a comfortable position. She hoped that when their friend passed away, he would see that Richard was well-looked-after. He deserved it. Richard had given a great part of his life to the blind writer. He loved him. Neither of them spoke of it, but she had seen the look on Richard's face when Auden became ill. It was much more than simple compassion. When Auden hurt, so did Richard.

As she slipped down into the warm womb of sleep, she felt a deep pang of sorrow for both men.

* * *

Gina sat at her computer in her upstairs study at Tadema House. The fact that it was two thirty in the morning meant little to her. She required very little sleep and a short nap was usually sufficient to refresh her active brain. For over an hour now, she had been trawling the various social media platforms — Twitter, LinkedIn, Facebook and the rest — but could find very little on the woman who seemed to have caught the attention of her dear Thomas Parrish.

She sat back in her expensive office chair and stared at a picture on the screen. Like her employer, the reclusive Auden Meeres, Christie McFerran avoided the limelight. She didn't even have a Facebook page. Of course, Gina didn't either, but she was surprised that the younger woman eschewed the site. Everything that Gina had learned about Christie came from brief biographical notes issued by Auden's publishing house, and from press notices and editorials about the author and the amount of detail that went into what he wrote. She herself preferred deeper, more demanding fiction but she admired his working method. Gina loved books with a passion, and Tadema House had an extensive library, something she was sure would impress Auden Meeres's little helper.

She smiled coldly. That was something to remember if she ever needed bait to tempt the elusive Ms McFerran into visiting. She fancied that there might actually be a brain lurking in that rather attractive head. The little research assistant might prove a welcome distraction for a while.

She glanced down at the open notebook beside her and went over what she had learned so far. Christie McFerran was currently living in Scarborough, where her employer also lived and worked. Single, aged thirty-three, for the last six years she had worked as a researcher for Meeres. Her job was to obtain information regarding the landscapes and customs of the places where he set his mystery novels. And that was all she'd found. Except that dear Thomas had told her that she was at present staying with her cousin in Tanners Fen. She gave a soft laugh. Liz Haynes was at the other end of the spectrum as far as being well-known went. Everyone in the Fenfleet area had heard about the police detective whom a killer had left for dead. The grapevine also said that she was living with her old boss, the recently retired DCI Matt Ballard. Which meant Gina knew that Christie was staying at remote old Cannon Farm, on the edge of the sea bank.

Of course, dear little Thomas and Delphi would fill her in on whatever they gleaned from the researcher themselves. How very satisfying. She stretched. There was little more to be done here, so she might as well grab a few hours' sleep before another day dawned. 'And I wonder what delights that will bring?' she whispered to the heavy drapes, the oak panelling and the richly coloured carpet. 'I wonder . . .'

CHAPTER EIGHT

Time passed quickly. Christie and Liz had talked to fishermen, traipsed the backstreets of Fenfleet and the much larger
market town of Greenborough, and finished the day gazing
across the marshes at the strangely named Whisper Fen.

Now Christie was on her way into Fenfleet again, this
time to see Tom and have dinner with him and his mother,
her thoughts drifting back to the empty shell of Holland
House and its probable decline. Apparently, it had belonged
to two dear friends of Matt and Liz. Liz had said little about
it, except that Matt's friend Will had sold it and moved away
after a tragedy occurred there. Then the people who had
bought it had a change of heart and put it up for sale again.
A property developer took it, his plans fell through and now
it was empty. Liz said that the house had known too many
deaths in its lifetime. The place had had a profound effect on
Christie, although she had no idea why. It seemed desperate
to be lived in again, to be cherished and cared for, but there
seemed little chance of that. Liz had told her that each year
storms and unnaturally high tides were encroaching, and she
believed its days were numbered.

Christie told herself off. Ever since she'd arrived on the
Fens, she seemed to have been oversensitive. Everything she

encountered seemed to give rise to some intense emotion. She put it down to Auden's illness and anxiety over her impending lack of employment.

She turned into the road Tom had indicated and wondered if she'd made a mistake. The area seemed rather run-down, not quite what she had expected from an address like "The Courtyard." There seemed to be no actual residential dwellings here and she couldn't work out the purpose of the buildings that she passed. They seemed to be very old. Maybe they were the back entrances to some of the shops along the High Street.

At the bottom of the road she took a sharp right-hand turn into a tiny cul-de-sac. Christie found herself in a single Georgian terrace of six three-storey dwellings, each with a small garden fronted by wrought-iron railings and an ornate iron gate with the house number woven into the metalwork. The gardens were well tended and full of summer colour. There were no buildings opposite, just an old red-brick wall that stretched the length of Friary Terrace. When, later, she looked out from an upstairs window, she saw that there was a broad waterway on the other side.

The Courtyard was the end house, it turned out, with a slightly larger triangular area in front, walled in on two sides. Each house seemed to have an allotted parking space alongside the wall.

Christie was early — she usually was — and didn't think they'd mind too much. She reached across to the passenger seat and picked up the bottle of red wine and the posy of cream freesias that she had bought for Mrs Parrish, got out of the car and made for the front door.

Tom kissed her lightly on the cheek, took her jacket and hurried her through to the lounge to meet his mother, all in a stream of enthusiastic chatter.

'Oh, great choice!' he said, admiring the wine. 'Just right for the steak. Mother, meet Christie McFerran.'

Her arthritis obviously made it difficult, but despite Christie's protests, Margaret got to her feet to greet her.

She appeared to be a smaller, feminine version of her son. She had the same lovely thick dark hair, although hers was streaked with silver, and the same studious features adorned with glasses. She even had the same habit of pushing them higher onto the bridge of her nose. Her handshake was firm, notwithstanding the knotted finger and knuckle joints. She sat down again with a sigh of relief and beamed at Christie. 'I am so very pleased you could make it to see us before you leave, Miss McFerran.'

Christie asked her to please use her first name, at which the old lady smiled warmly, saying that was a relief and to call her Margaret.

After asking her how she liked her steak, Tom left them to continue his preparations in the kitchen. Christie soon found that the old lady was as easy to talk to as her son.

Margaret was touched by the little posy of flowers and declared that they had always been her favourites. She had Christie put them beside a framed photograph of a handsome and upright man whom she said was Tom's father.

Looking more closely, Christie thought to herself that she would never have known. The man in the photo had short, straight blond hair and fine, almost delicate features. Only the eyes were similar, a different colour but with the same direct gaze. They were honest eyes.

Tom came in, an oven glove on one hand, and told them to make their way to the dining room, as the meal was ready.

The house was beautifully decorated, though Christie wasn't sure which Parrish was the designer, mother or son. It had a certain classical, artistic flair that made her think it had to be Tom, but some aspects were homely and old-fashioned, which she thought must be Margaret's doing. Whoever the designer was, it worked, and notwithstanding the antiques and quality furniture, the house was most definitely a home and not a showplace.

Tom had prepared a delicious smoked salmon starter and they chatted comfortably while they ate. His mother turned out to be something of an Auden Meeres buff. She had read every one of his novels and clearly recalled all the plots and characters. Christie had remembered to bring one of his signed photographs but had refrained from giving it to her at first in case she wasn't the sort of person who would appreciate that kind of thing. She now presented it with a smile, and Margaret propped it up against a jug of water so she could admire it while she ate.

They were about halfway through their succulent steak when the doorbell rang. Mother and son looked at each other. Evidently, they hadn't been expecting a visitor.

Christie heard voices in the hall and Gina Spearman strode in, shattering the happy atmosphere.

'Look, Mother, Gina has brought you a bottle of champagne.'

Not just champagne, Christie noted. Bollinger, no less.

'Oh, it's nothing. Thomas told me your arthritis had flared up badly, and there's no better medicine for it than champagne.' She regarded Christie in mock surprise. 'Why, it's Christie! Oh, I had no idea. I'm so sorry. I'm interrupting, I'll be on my way.'

She glanced at Tom from beneath her long lashes. He began to flap around her, insisting she stay, and making much of drawing up another chair to the table.

'I'm sorry, Gina, I can't offer you supper, we've nearly finished, but will you have some wine?' He indicated Christie's bottle of claret.

The wrinkle of disdain was almost imperceptible, but Christie caught it, as she was intended to, and so did Margaret.

Gina uttered a long drawn-out 'Nooo, I don't think so, thank you, and I really can't stay. I'm on my way round to see Jane. She seems to have yet another disaster for me to sort out for her. How she keeps that art gallery running I have no idea. Well, must dash. Enjoy.' She indicated the Bollinger and swept out of the room.

Tom escorted her out. Christie and Margaret exchanged a look.

'How very refreshing.' Margaret's eye had a mischievous twinkle.

'Sorry?'

'My dear, you're the first person I've met who hasn't been taken in by her.'

'Oh, I've only met her once. I barely know her,' Christie said.

'Know her? You never will.' Margaret gave a sardonic laugh. 'I just wish my son had your perspicacity.'

Christie looked gratefully at the old lady, relieved to find that she wasn't the only person who disliked Gina.

Margaret indicated a card on the mantelpiece. 'Quick, before he comes back. That's the kind of thing that has him entrapped.'

While they were still talking out in the hall, Christie got out of her seat and picked up the card. It was expensive, handmade and with an unusual, ornate design. The script had so many flourishes and scrolls that she had trouble reading it. She squinted at it:

'Thomas. My right arm. My strong and faithful friend. My Maxfield Parrish. Whatever would I do without you? Just to say thank you for being such a wonderful manager and for putting up with me and my ways. Gina.'

'It came with a cheque for a hundred pounds.' Margaret spoke through gritted teeth.

Christie put the card back and returned to the table. 'Why?'

'There was yet another row at the shop and as per usual, Tom poured oil on troubled waters and prevented a valued member of staff from walking out. It's the way she deals with every problem — throw money at it. Trouble is, she gets away with it.'

'Is Tom really that taken in by her? He seems so straightforward, so honest. Surely he has his reservations about her?'

'*Besotted*, Christie. He's obsessed with the bloody woman. The silly boy will believe that tonight was a genuine spur-of-the-moment visit. He won't realise that it was cleverly engineered to spoil our meal. And it won't have spoiled his evening at all. He'll be thrilled that she called by.' She shook her head. 'You wait and see. He'll be full of it. By the way, she can do no wrong in his eyes, so don't bother to criticise her.'

'What was that in the card about "My Maxfield Parrish," Margaret? Is Maxfield his real name?'

'Oh, please,' Margaret said. 'Do I look like the kind of woman who'd call her son Maxfield? He's not even Thomas. *I* christened him Tom. No, it's *her* again. She likes to think she's an expert on art. Have you heard of the American artist, Maxfield Parrish?'

The name vaguely rang a bell. She seemed to recall the "common man's Rembrandt," but couldn't bring to mind any of his paintings.

'He was all the rage in the 1920s,' Margaret went on. 'He painted dreamscapes. The fact is, Gina is pig-sick that Tom has an artist's surname. Her so-called "friend," the Jane she mentioned, is a Waterhouse, and Gina's specialist subject is the Pre-Raphaelites. She idolises the Victorian painter, John William Waterhouse.'

'Ah, that would explain why the Reading Room has such a splendid art section.'

'Exactly. As far as I know, there aren't any famous painters with the surname Spearman. Must be very galling for her.'

Tom returned, smiling broadly. 'What a kind gesture, Mother.' He picked up the bottle and looked at it appreciatively. 'I bet that cost a bomb. I'll put it in the fridge for you, or maybe we should all share it tonight? What do you think?'

Christie thought that she'd rather drink neat bleach but smiled sweetly and reminded him that she was driving. Margaret said that she had been enjoying the delicious red and didn't want to spoil it, so he duly took the revered bottle to the kitchen.

'If I could bring myself to do it, I'd tip it down the sink when he's at work,' Margaret whispered to her with a fiendish expression. 'Fortunately, the vicar is collecting for the church fund at present. He's calling tomorrow for any items we might want to get rid of. Need I say more?'

Christie stifled a giggle. *Nice one, Margaret.*

The evening continued, Tom blissfully unaware that his mother and their guest had somewhat lost their sparkle.

At nine o'clock, Margaret "left them to it," and retired to bed.

Delighted to have met this lovely lady, Christie gave her a farewell hug. Margaret gave her a long look, thanked her for everything and said something rather strange: 'I wish . . .' Her eyes were suddenly full of sadness, but she said no more. She made her way slowly and painfully out of the room.

'Let's go into my snug, shall we? I'll make some coffee.' Tom led her into a tiny book-lined room at the back of the house. A fire was already laid in the fireplace, with two big armchairs facing towards it and little else but a couple of side tables and a standard lamp to read by.

Christie gazed at the countless books. No leather-bound volumes these, they came in all conditions and sizes, from first editions to scruffy old orange-and-white Penguin paperbacks.

'I just love books, don't you?' Tom said.

'Totally. What a fantastic room!' Christie stepped forward to look more closely at his collection.

'Have a browse while I get the coffee.'

Christie noticed all the art books but resisted jumping to conclusions. His taste in art seemed to extend from wispy watercolours to H R Giger.

'Pretty diverse collection, eh?' Tom set their cups down on the tables with a smile. 'I wish I had time to read them all. It's dangerous working in a bookshop. Sometimes I think I spend more than my wages. Gina does pretty well out of her staff, even if we do get a discount.'

By the sound of it, you earn it, putting up with her moods every day. 'So who is Jane?'

'Jane Waterhouse. You'd like her, Christie. It's a pity you have to leave so soon, I could have introduced you.'

Considering how much she "liked" his friend Gina, missing Jane came as something of a relief.

Tom stirred his coffee and gazed at his shelves. 'She's an artist and has a gallery in Herring Lane. She lives in the flat over the shop, where she has her studio, right up in the attic with one of those big skylight windows set in the roof. She used to come to the Reading Room quite a lot. Gina sort of took her under her wing. Jane is a great painter, but not too hot on the business side of it — actually, she's useless with money. Gina is a really good businesswoman, so she has ironed out a lot of problems for Jane.'

At what cost? Christie couldn't help but wonder.

'That's where she was going tonight. To avert another disaster, it seems,' he said.

Yeah, let's hear it for Gina Spearman. Between clenched teeth, she managed to say, 'That's very good of her.'

'Gina's like that, Christie. True, she has her difficult side, but she has such a kind heart. She comes from a very sad background.'

Badly needing a bucket at this stage, Christie settled for a long sip of strong coffee. *Change the subject, quick.* 'So, you like Giger?'

'Amazing man! Didn't you just love *Alien*?'

'Well, I wouldn't say "love" exactly,' she said. In truth, the Swiss surrealist's biomechanical life forms had frightened the life out of her. 'And Turner? Bit of a contrast with Giger.'

'I find beauty in so many different things, don't you? Now, Gina has tunnel vision when it comes to the Pre-Raphaelites.'

Oh God, she's back again.

'She was at Keble College,' Tom went on. 'She has a Masters, you know. She wrote a fascinating paper on the formation of the Pre-Raphaelite Brotherhood in 1848.'

Again, that hint of wistfulness that Christie had noticed before. But this time she understood. 'Your father died before you had the chance to go to university, didn't he?'

Tom looked surprised. 'Yes, he did. But I would never have left Mother. Even if Father hadn't passed away so young, I would have thought twice about leaving her.'

'You get on very well together — you and your mother, I mean.'

'I adore her. I'm so lucky. She has never been a drain on me. Never once, in all the years since my dad died, has she demanded anything of me. That's probably why she is such a pleasure to do things for. When I hear some of the others talk about their families, I go cold.'

'You know, some people would think you have a bit of a rough deal having an elderly mother to look after.' She spoke gently.

'I'd rather have Margaret Edith Parrish any day than screaming kids or an unfaithful wife.' He meant it too, she could tell.

'Don't you ever want to settle down? What if you met someone special?' she asked, curious now.

There was a strange look on his face, a yearning, a desperate lovesickness that might have come straight from one of Gina's Pre-Raphaelites. Then it was gone. 'I'm quite happy as I am, thank you. I'm too self-centred to change now, anyway. It would have to be a very special person to get me to share my life with them. I really do like my own company, you know.'

Liar. Self-centred indeed. You are one of the most unselfish people I've met. My cousin was dead right, you are holding a torch and you are going to get burned, Thomas Maxfield Parrish.

They talked on for another hour or so before Christie took her leave, promising to call into the shop, or at least ring, before she set off for Scarborough. He gave her an affectionate hug and once more lightly brushed her cheek with his lips.

Christie sat in the car for a moment, beset by a maelstrom of emotions. She pushed them away roughly and switched on the ignition. It had been a lovely evening with a single blemish. A bloody great big one.

Once she was in bed, Christie lay in the darkness and tried to sort out why she was so confused. She thought she'd got to the bottom of it just before she drifted off to sleep. She hated to see people being taken in, used, or played, like pieces on a chessboard.

Tom was a human being, not an expendable pawn in Gina's game. She yawned and sighed. Although maybe she was wrong. Maybe that was exactly what he was. A pawn.

Once again, Christie woke with a start at 2 a.m., this time from a nightmare. Sweating, she sat up, put on her bedside light and drank some water. As she did, she noticed the photocopy of the will-o'-the-wisp that Tom had printed off for her, propped up against the dressing table mirror.

So that's what had sparked off her dream. She recalled it vividly. She had been out there, on Whisper Fen, that cold and eerie stretch of marsh they had visited earlier. It was frightening, a bad place to be, but that was fine because she herself was the jack-o'-lantern, the will-o'-the-wisp, the foolish fire. And she was hunting for prey. She recalled her sheer malevolent delight when she had seen the travellers enter the fen. It was a game, with only one winner. After a while they came closer, drawn to her unearthly glow, and the game reached its conclusion.

She felt sick, sick at herself for what the dream-Christie had done, contemplated, wanted. Needed.

Christie got up, took the picture down and put it away in her folder. She left the light on when she went back to bed.

CHAPTER NINE

Matt woke early and went downstairs to make tea for himself and Liz. As he passed the door to the guest room, he heard movement inside. 'Ready for an early morning cuppa, Christie?' he called out.

'Am I ever!' came back the answer. 'I'll be ready in five.'

He smiled and continued down to the kitchen. He knew that Christie was on a tight schedule, needing to get finished and back to Yorkshire, so she was obviously geared up for an early start.

He was just getting the milk from the fridge when she arrived in the kitchen, fully dressed but with dark circles around her eyes. He held out a mug of tea to her. 'Boozy night at the Parrish residence, was it?'

'Could have been if I wasn't driving.' Christie took the tea and thanked him. 'It was a lovely evening.'

Matt had not been a copper for nothing. 'But?'

'Am I that transparent?'

'Like a pane of glass.'

She flopped down in a kitchen chair and grunted. 'I think I'm turning into a grumpy old woman.'

'At thirty-three?' Matt laughed. 'I don't think so.'

'Well, I'm leaving tomorrow or first thing the day after anyway, so never mind.'

'It doesn't work like that with policemen, Christie, even retired ones. Come on, tell me all.'

She exhaled. 'Okay, well, I've taken a dislike to Tom's boss. It's irrational and stupid. I mean, I've only met the woman twice. Last night, she turned up unannounced in the middle of a very pleasant dinner and,' she gave a hopeless little shrug, 'and kind of ruined everything.'

Matt sat down opposite her. 'Some people have that effect on you. It just happens without rhyme or reason. I wouldn't stress over it.'

'Margaret feels the same about her. In fact, she's desperate for her son to see Gina Spearman for what she is.'

'And that is?'

'A user, a manipulator. And that came from Margaret, even if I do wholeheartedly agree with her,' Christie said.

Matt frowned. He knew Margaret to be easy-going yet of extremely sound judgement, and such harsh words weren't like her at all. 'Then you're probably both right. Sadly, people have to find out these things for themselves, don't they?'

'I just don't want to see Tom hurt, that's all.'

Hmm. He could have understood that comment if Christie and Tom had been friends for years, but three days? Three brief meetings? That was pretty intense in anyone's book.

'Room for a little one?' Liz stood in the doorway.

Matt was heartily glad to see her. He passed her a mug of tea and pointed to the other kitchen chair. 'Christie's just telling me about last night and a certain unwanted visitor.'

On hearing the story, Liz frowned. 'So that's who Tom has been mooning over! I'd never have guessed.'

'Talk to Margaret if you get the chance, Liz,' said Christie. 'I think she could do with a listening ear after I've gone. She's seriously worried about him.'

Matt was about to comment that sons never make the right choices as far as their mothers are concerned but stopped himself. It made him think of his own mother, and he really didn't want to go down that road. Liz said she'd make a point of dropping in on Margaret after Christie had gone, then asked what she had on the cards for that day.

Christie pulled a face. 'I've got a full itinerary, and if you have other things to do, Liz, they aren't the most exciting tasks.' She glanced at her notebook. 'The town library, possibly some parish records, the drainage museum and, if there's time, a quick visit to one of Margaret's friends who is an expert on the ecology of the area.'

'Oh my, we are down to the nitty-gritty now, aren't we?' said Liz. 'But I'm happy to tag along if you'd like me to.'

Christie smiled at her. 'What if I get the boring stuff sorted this morning, then you come with me this afternoon to see the museum and Margaret's friend, Rebecca?'

'Okay,' Liz said. 'Sounds like a plan. I can get some jobs done before lunch. Back here for a snack? One to one thirty?'

Christie stood up. 'Perfect. I'll go and get ready and make an early start.'

'Don't forget breakfast!' Liz called after her.

'I'll grab something in town, Liz, don't worry. I want this out of the way as soon as possible, now I know I haven't much time.'

Matt didn't miss the hint of regret. When she had left, he said, 'Someone doesn't want to go. I wonder if it's our scintillating company, our mysterious fenlands, or someone else?' He raised an eyebrow.

'Mmm, I wonder,' said Liz thoughtfully. 'Although maybe it's all three.' Her expression brightened. 'I guarantee she'll be back when this assignment is finished. Now, breakfast?'

He stood up. 'I'll do it. Then it's back to work.'

'Anything interesting shown up yet?' Liz asked.

Matt took some cereal bowls from the cupboard. 'I spent all afternoon yesterday trying to get a handle on the person behind the media campaign. It's a man called Duncan Hartland. He has a massive online following — I reckon he tweets as much as Donald Trump before he got banned. He's clever about it though, no pictures of himself on Facebook and he doesn't seem to have been involved in any other campaigns against the police. He's clearly completely obsessed with Lindsay and the mishandling of her case.'

'There was no mishandling,' Liz said firmly.

'*We* know that, but as they never found her killer, people like Hartland are just waiting to point the finger at police inefficiency.' He passed her the cereal. 'I have found someone who does know this Duncan Hartland, or professes to. Luckily, he's local, so I'm going to see him this morning. His name is Barry, and he works in a timber yard just outside Fenfleet, on that long road that runs along the waterway. I tracked him down after seeing his messages on Facebook, which were pretty antagonistic to Hartland's posts. I wondered why, so I messaged him and after a couple of interesting chats, found out that Barry had a big falling out with Hartland about a month ago. If he's still at odds with the guy, I could be in luck.'

'Sounds promising,' said Liz, pouring milk onto her cereal. 'Did he give you any clue as to why he dislikes Hartland?'

Matt shook his head. 'He's said nothing specific yet, but his replies to Hartland's posts and to my messages seemed considered, unlike some of the rants you get on social media. He sounds intelligent. You need to read some of the posts and tweets that Hartland has put out on social media. There's an edge to them that I really don't like. They smack of obsession.'

'Scary,' Liz said softly. 'We know exactly where that can lead.'

'Don't we just,' Matt said with feeling. 'At the very least, it's unhealthy and tends to attract all sorts of weirdos and cranks to the "cause." I'm really looking forward to talking to this Barry fellow. Hopefully, he'll know quite a bit about our friend Hartland.'

Liz gave him a long look which he couldn't interpret, then it was gone. She said she would scan through the posts after she'd done the chores, as she wasn't going out with Christie until later.

He ate his breakfast and soon forgot her strange, searching look. It was good to be doing something with a more fulfilling potential outcome than dropping an unfaithful husband or wife in the slurry. After all, finding a killer was the ultimate aim of every detective in the world. Retired he might be, but Matt Ballard still had aspirations, and right now, finding Lindsay Harrison's killer was number one.

* * *

Liz watched him drive away from Cannon Farm full of mixed emotions. Of course, it was good to see the old enthusiasm back. Nothing pleased her more than to see Matt happy, but on the other hand it was very worrying that their own cases didn't hold the same appeal for him. She was totally committed to their small detective agency, even if she did hate the infidelity investigations. Matt had started out full of drive, but over the months it had waned. He never admitted it, but he obviously missed his old job. The way he had jumped at this crumb the new DCI had thrown him made it abundantly clear. What really worried her was her feeling that he didn't quite appreciate that this wasn't *his* murder investigation. He was just a pair of eyes and ears on the streets, filling in a few gaps because everyone else was busy.

Liz went upstairs and began sorting out the laundry. She hoped that Matt wouldn't be disappointed. She had the distinct feeling that being involved in this case would only serve to make matters worse for him in the end.

* * *

Christie's morning started well and by ten, she had managed to get a fair bit of the information she required. She was now heading for the parish church of St Benedict. It was her hope that she'd find someone there who could talk to her about how and where the parish records were stored before they were automated.

As she walked down the aisle of the lovely old church, she saw a hunched figure sitting in one of the front pews, deep in prayer. It wasn't until she got closer that she recognised Reverend Ian Hardy.

He looked up as she approached, and she saw that he had been crying.

Christie sat down next to him and asked him what the matter was.

'It's Evie. She took poorly after supper yesterday evening. It was touch-and-go all night. I've been with her at the hospital, and she has rallied.' He shook his head slowly. 'What a fighter! She is now "comfortable," as they say, and sleeping. I've come in here to light a candle for her and to have a few quiet words with my boss.' He raised his eyes.

Once again, Christie found herself resenting the fact that she'd be leaving so soon. She really wanted to spend some time with the reverend and, by the look of him, he could do with a friend right now. 'Is there anything I can do?' she asked.

'Bless you, but you've got work to do and you have worries of your own with your Auden Meeres being ill too.'

This was true. Her priority had to be Auden, but the parish records could wait. Half an hour wouldn't make any difference. 'Come and have a coffee with me, Ian, and a bite to eat. I missed breakfast and I'm starving. Then you can tell me all about your sister. I'd love to hear more, honestly.'

He nodded and got to his feet.

They found a small café in a back street. She ordered drinks and some pastries, and they took them to a secluded corner table.

As soon as he sat down, every ounce of energy seemed to drain out of him. 'I'm going to lose her.' The simple statement contained a world of grief and sorrow.

Christie reached across the table and held his hands in hers. He must have done this for others countless times. 'Tell me about her. Were you close as children?'

His face assumed a little more of its usual cheerfulness. 'Oh, thick as thieves, as our mother always said. Evelyn and

I were the best of friends. I am older than her in years, but she has always been much older in terms of knowledge and common sense. She was a vivacious girl and had scores of admirers, but she never settled down.'

'It bothers you, that, doesn't it? You mentioned the other day that she never married.'

'It always seemed such a waste. She was so bright, so intelligent, and she definitely had the looks in our family.'

'Nonsense,' exclaimed Christie. 'You're handsome now, so you must have been quite something at twenty-one.'

He laughed. 'Ah, but you never saw Evelyn.'

He took his wallet from his jacket pocket and began to sort through credit cards and various folded pieces of paper. 'Here. It's very old.' He passed her a black-and-white photograph. It was sepia with age and spotted with tiny brown marks.

The girl was probably about eighteen. She sat cross-legged on a wall, wearing white tennis shorts with a cap-sleeved blouse. Her tennis racquet and a knitted cardigan lay casually at her feet. The front wheel of an old "sit-up-and-beg" bicycle was visible to one side of the picture. She was stunningly beautiful. 'I see what you mean!'

Christie let Ian talk on, listening to his tales of their childhood days and his reminiscences of his sister as she grew up. 'Evie could have been a film star if she'd wanted. But she chose nursing. Her working life was a constant struggle. She was too good-looking, no one took her seriously and she had to prove herself, day after day. Then, of course, some of her fellow students were jealous, she had beauty *and* brains. But she persevered and spent her whole life in hospitals, dedicated to tending the sick, bless her.' He sighed. 'Now she's being nursed in her turn.'

'So, what are you going to do now?' Christie asked. 'Go back to the hospital?'

'I must go and grab a shower and a change of clothes, then I need to fetch a clean nightdress and toiletries from Evelyn's cottage. The doctor thought she would probably sleep through the morning but they have my mobile number, just in case. I'll go back and sit with her until I know which way things are going.'

Christie produced a card from her shoulder bag. 'Here's my mobile number. I'm not here for much longer, but if you ever want to just talk, please do ring me.' She thought quickly, then glanced at her watch. 'Listen, I'm pretty well ahead of my morning schedule. Would you like me to come to the hospital with you? At least you'll have someone to go and get you a coffee and play I Spy with if Evelyn's asleep.'

Ian squeezed her hand.

'You go and do what you have to,' she said firmly. 'I'll finish up here, then ring me and I'll meet you in the hospital car park.'

As soon as he had gone, Christie rang Liz and told her she'd be late for lunch and about her arrangement to sit with the reverend. Liz said not to worry, she'd see her later.

That done, she hurried down the narrow, cobbled street back to St Benedict's church. On her way, she glanced into a shop window opposite. On an easel facing out to the street was a painting of the Fens. She crossed the road and peered into the window.

It came to her that rarely had she been as drawn to paintings as she had been on this particular trip. The picture Tom had discovered of the travellers crossing the fen at night had made a deep and lasting impression on her — so much so that she'd even dreamed about it. But this one was different. Somehow, this watercolour expressed everything she had lived through since arriving in this marshy county.

The subject was a derelict and decaying boat, leaning slightly to one side, half in and half out of the murky water. Reeds surrounded it and the river it stood in melted into an aqueous sky. On the far side of the bank stood a heron, staring into the gently flowing depths, its beady black eye trained on the water in search of fish. The surrounding terrain was marshy with the great clumps of coarse grass that she had become accustomed to seeing out on the marshland. The sky was cloudless but changed subtly in tone from one side of the canvas to the other. It was clearly dawn — the colours had that morning hint of green.

She peered at the price ticket. Two hundred and twenty-five pounds, framed.

She didn't give it a second thought. This was special.

It was not until she opened the door that Christie saw the name *Waterhouse* engraved in the glass. So, this was the famous Jane's gallery. She cursed silently but managed a smile and a good morning. 'I'm interested in the painting in the window.'

The woman flowed rather than walked across the gallery floor. She was tall and willowy, with long, straight, ash-blonde hair that fell to below her shoulders. She had a strange, otherworldly smile. Her fingers were long and slender, and she wore no jewellery. Christie was mesmerised by her eyes, which were an arresting violet blue. She had no doubt that this was Jane Waterhouse; the talented artist that Tom had told her about, the woman with no head for business. She couldn't imagine what this delicate, ethereal creature might have in common with the sharp-edged, calculating Ms Spearman.

'What can I tell you about the painting?' she mused, almost as if she were talking to herself. 'Well, it was originally sketched about five miles from here, at a place called Cassons Marsh, a pleasant enough sounding name, except that a "casson" in old Lincolnshire history was a lump of dried cow dung that the poor folk used for fuel.' Her blue eyes sparkled. 'I hope that doesn't put you off? Anyway, it was painted early in the morning, just before the mists lifted. It is true to life — the heron really was there, as was the boat. I sometimes use a bit of artistic license to introduce some local atmosphere, but not in this case.'

Christie took to Jane immediately, just as she had taken to Tom and Ian.

She paid for the picture and was prepared to take it as it was, but Jane offered to frame it for her and have it ready for early the following morning. She showed her a selection of frames and mounting boards, and they settled for a plain dark wood surround with a gilt inset and a mossy green mounting board.

'I'd like to give you longer to frame it but unfortunately I'm leaving tomorrow.'

'No problem,' said Jane. 'I'll do it this afternoon and you can collect it when we open in the morning.'

Christie lingered awhile in the gallery, admiring Jane's work and listening to her slow, languid voice telling her about the various paintings.

'This is the river, down near Haven Bank. I recall that the heavens opened just as I was completing my initial sketches for this one. Oh, and that is an evening picture, looking across the fen to the church spire close to Allen's Gowt, with the setting sun just bidding the world goodnight. I'm not really happy with that one, though. I didn't do the evening justice.'

Her chosen medium was watercolour, but the works were nevertheless powerful evocations of atmosphere, climate and weather conditions. Christie thought of Turner, even though Jane's work was more ethereal.

'That was made in the orchard of a friend of mine who lives down near the marsh. I have another here of her house.'

She took Christie into an alcove — a dark room, but the few pieces were carefully lit. The painting of Tadema House was magnificent. It could only be Gina Spearman's. Who else would think to name their house after the scholarly Victorian painter, Sir Lawrence Alma-Tadema?

She was tempted to ask Jane about Gina but held her tongue, afraid of hearing her praises sung as Tom had done. But as seemed to be the way with her disciples, Jane just couldn't help talking about her.

'I had actually painted it as a gift — she was good to me when I underwent a rough patch a while ago but,' she added, sounding slightly hurt, 'watercolours aren't really to her taste. I should have thought about it, I suppose. After all, I do work in other mediums sometimes. I mean, someone who's an expert on the Pre-Raphaelites is always going to prefer oils.'

Surely anyone with a decent bone in their body would have been deeply moved to be given such a gift! The care Jane must have given this excellent piece was evident in every brushstroke. How devastated the artist must have felt to have her gift refused. And how would Gina have phrased her refusal? Christie would have loved to have been a fly on the wall on that occasion.

The more she looked at the painting, the more she realised that the loser had been Gina. The words "nose," "spite" and "face" came to mind. This was a superb painting. The light, the textures, the perspective, everything about it was perfect. Although she had never seen the real Tadema House, she was certain that no one could have done it greater justice. Christie pushed back the urge to buy it, because she didn't like her reasons for wanting to. It would make her no better than Gina — playing games. Besides, she had no wish to be reminded of bloody Gina Spearman each time she looked at it.

Returning to the main gallery, she took one last look at her new acquisition. For a moment she actually breathed in the salty ozone. Jane Waterhouse was a truly great artist.

CHAPTER TEN

Barry, Matt's new Facebook friend, turned out to be the transport and logistics manager of the massive timber yard, Breslow and Wright. Matt wondered how such a young man — he didn't look more than twenty-five — could have achieved such status. Then he saw the ID badge hanging at his neck. *Barry Breslow.*

'Family business?' Matt asked.

Barry nodded. 'We've been here since the 1800s, used to make pit props and railway sleepers. Actually, sleepers are still our main product, along with telegraph and timber poles.'

Barry Breslow's angular face was dominated by a pair of designer glasses with thick black frames that looked huge beneath his cropped hair. He wore skinny jeans and his black fleece jacket bore a logo depicting the letters "B&W" entwined around the trunk of a tree.

They sat in an office at the rear of the transport yard. Several massive trucks with lifting gear on the back were parked outside. 'This is much bigger than it looks from the road,' Matt observed.

'I've got a fleet of ten wagons on the move at present,' Barry said nonchalantly, 'and we deliver nationally and internationally. Timber is big business, I'm glad to say.' He crossed his slim legs. 'So, you want to know about Duncan Hartland.'

Matt went to reach for his warrant card, then remembered. 'Yes. I'm a private detective, but at present I'm working with the police. What can you tell us about Hartland?'

'Well for a start, he's a bastard.' Barry's casual air disappeared. He got up and began to pace his office.

'Anything a little more explicit, Barry?' Matt tilted his head. 'Like, how you came to know him.'

'He worked here for a while. Idiot that I was, it was me that hired him.' He grunted. 'Learned my lesson there all right. Never take anyone at face value.' Barry flopped back into his chair. 'We had a mass of work on and then we got hit by a stomach bug. I had four drivers off and was pretty desperate. Hartland dropped in out of the blue, asking if we had any vacancies. He had a clean HGV licence, looked smart and seemed intelligent. He said he could supply references and only lost his last job because the haulage company went into liquidation. He gave me their name and I knew they had folded about a month before, so I believed him.' He groaned. 'What a mug! I hired him on the spot, never took up a single reference.'

'What was he driving?' asked Matt, glancing at the big trucks outside.

'Oh, not one of those, the wagons with the cranes attached, he hadn't had the training to operate one of those babies. We have smaller trucks for fencing and gates and the like. He drove one of them.'

Matt wanted to hurry this up a bit. Background was essential, of course, but he wanted to know about the man himself and why he'd upset Barry Breslow so much. 'So he didn't work out. What did he do exactly?'

Barry exhaled. 'I had no idea when I took him on that he'd come here for a reason. And that reason was Paula Harrison, who works in our stores. He was infatuated with her but wasn't making any headway, so he got the idea that if he was working in the same company, he'd get to see more of her and strike up a closer relationship. He became such a nuisance that I let him go after six weeks.' He gave another grunt. 'He was crap at the job anyway. We're a good team here, but Hartland didn't do teamwork.'

Matt was puzzled. 'Surely this kind of thing happens, doesn't it? I don't mean harassment, but not every new employee works out. You were pretty vindictive about him on social media.'

Barry looked rattled. 'He really upset Paula, Matt. I mean scared her badly, and—' he paused — 'er, well, I'm pretty fond of her myself, actually.' He stared down at his desk. 'I knew she'd had a rough time in the last few years because of her sister. She told me there was some guy practically stalking her, but I had no idea it was Hartland. If I'd known, I'd never have hired him.'

The penny dropped. Matt could have kicked himself. Paula Harrison! The dead girl Lindsay Harrison's sister. He was losing his edge; the surname hadn't even registered. 'Ah, I see why you were so angry.'

'Yeah, this whole campaign of his is a crafty fucking scheme. He wants to look like a hero, fighting to get Lindsay justice, but he dreamed the whole thing up just to get into Paula's knickers. I'm telling you, Matt, there's nothing he won't do.'

Did that include murder? Matt asked himself. Would he go that far to get Paula's attention?

Barry was still staring at the desk. 'I know I shouldn't answer posts on Facebook and the like, and I never tell anyone what I know about him, but I feel compelled to say something when he starts spouting that sanctimonious crap.'

'Do you have his address, Barry?' asked Matt.

'Sure, I'll give you what details I have, although he's changed his mobile number and I don't have the new one.' He turned to his computer and Matt heard a printer whir.

Matt read the paper Barry handed him and saw that Hartland lived just outside Fenfleet, on the Saltern Road. He'd drive past on his way home and take a look at the place. He thanked Barry Breslow for his time and stood up to leave.

'What's he done, Matt?' Barry asked.

'Probably nothing. He's of interest simply because of his anti-police stance. Just because a case isn't solved, it doesn't mean that people haven't sweated blood and tears over it.'

'Ex-copper?' Barry raised an eyebrow.

'Retired copper, there's a difference.' He handed Barry his card. 'If he tries anything else, or if you hear anything about him, will you ring me?'

'Willingly. I'd like nothing better than to assist in getting him shut up.' Barry held the door open for him. 'And if you ever want a nice bit of feather-edged fencing or a five-bar gate, give me a shout. I'll even throw in the ironwork for free.'

* * *

Christie had just spent a fruitful twenty minutes with St Benedict's verger when she received the call from Ian. He was on his way to the hospital. It was only five minutes away on the edge of town and she hoped to get there and park before Ian arrived.

She had achieved a lot this morning, and it wasn't yet midday. Her appointment with Jack Fleet's relative at the drainage museum wasn't until four, so she thought she could afford this diversion.

The hospital was small, and it was difficult to find a parking space, but she managed eventually. She locked the car and went to the main door. Ian arrived five minutes later. His grave expression told her that his sister's condition hadn't improved.

At the door to Evelyn's room, she stood back and let Ian go in first. After a few minutes, he beckoned her forward.

Evelyn, looking almost doll-like in the bed, was asleep, her breathing uneven and ragged.

'They don't think it will be long now.' His voice was a whisper. 'It could be today, maybe tonight, they don't know. They want me to try and get some sleep, but how can I leave her?'

'Do they have a restroom anywhere, Ian?' Christie asked.

'Yes, it's right next door, with a bed and everything.'

'Then you go and lie down. I'll stay here, and if there's any change for the worse, I'll get you immediately.'

'It's a terrible imposition. It's not fair on you,' he protested.

'You'll be good for nothing if you don't get some sleep. Go and rest, even for a little while. It's best you do it while I'm here. Your sister might need you later.'

He finally agreed, squeezed her shoulder and left the room.

For an hour, Christie sat holding this stranger's hand in hers, the room silent but for the patient's uneven breaths. Christie's mind wandered back over everything that had happened during her short stay in the Fens. It was just a pity that Gina Spearman always seemed to seep into her thoughts like a nasty smell, spoiling her memories of what had been quite a momentous few days. She was deep in an imagined conversation with Gina when she felt the hand exert a slight pressure.

'Could I have drink, please?' The corners of Evelyn's mouth turned slightly upwards.

Gently, Christie placed the straw between the dry lips and held the cup while she sipped.

'Oh, that's so much better. Hello, you're a lovely young thing, aren't you? Do I know you?'

Christie smiled. 'I'm Christie, a friend of Ian's. I'm sitting with you for a while so he can have a nap, nurses' orders. He was here all night.'

'I know, my dear. I've drifted a bit, but I knew he was here. How long have you known my brother?'

'Only a few days, but I feel as if I've known him for ever. He's a wonderful man, isn't he?'

She sighed. 'Oh yes. Handsome, too, in his younger days. You should have seen him then.'

'He said the same about you. He showed me a picture of you, Evelyn. Sitting on a wall, in tennis shorts?'

'That tatty old thing. Not my best, but Ian loved it for some reason. I'm surprised it hasn't fallen to bits by now.'

She closed her eyes. Christie was afraid the talking might have tired her too much.

'It's all right, my dear, I'm just resting. I'll tell you if I am planning to depart.' She gave a soft laugh. 'I know it won't be long before I have to give in. I'll try not to drag it out for my brother's sake.' Her weary eyes slowly opened. 'You know, my dear, it doesn't seem five minutes since I was a young thing like you and look at me now. Where did the years go?'

Her eyes closed, and she continued to speak. 'You seem like a good friend to him. You wouldn't be here if that wasn't the case. So, if I should not get the chance, please tell Ian he was the best brother I could have had and I love him dearly.' Her grip tightened. 'Would you be kind enough to fetch him for me now, my dear? I am so weary and if I sleep now, I might never want to wake up.'

Christie ran from the room to call Ian. Evelyn's brother took her hand in his, told her how much he loved her, was graced with one last loving smile, and his beautiful sister slipped away.

While Ian spoke with the doctor about what would happen next, Christie went downstairs and called Liz, dangerously close to tears herself. 'I'm so sorry but I can't face chatting to Jack's relative about drainage systems, or Margaret's friend either, and Ian needs some support right now.'

'You stay with him. I'll ring Swifty's cousin and explain. He'll understand. Ring when you've seen Ian safely back to Pip's place. Just do whatever you think best, and we'll expect you when we see you.'

'Thank you, you're a star.' She sighed. 'I just wish I didn't have to rush off like this. So much seems to be happening around me at present.'

'I hate to add to the pressure,' Liz said, 'but before you do anything, would you ring Richard? He tried your mobile but it was switched off and he needs to talk to you urgently.'

Christie felt like she was heading for overload. Had Auden . . . ? *Please, no, not him as well.* She told Liz she would and rang off.

Richard sounded relieved to hear her voice. 'There is good and bad news, Christie, and it could affect your return. Auden was rushed into hospital this morning. I feared the worst, but it turned out that it wasn't at all life-threatening. The doctors think that with a small operation, which will make things easier for him, plus the right treatment in a specialist care centre along with plenty of rest, his quality of life could be much improved, for a little while at least. He won't be back to work again for two or three weeks.'

Christie heaved a sigh of relief. 'So he's not in any danger?'

'Not at all. He's suggested that you stay put and don't rush what you're doing. You can send all your latest research by email or post. Then he thought you might like to take some time out, have a holiday before returning, since there won't be anything to do here until he gets home again.'

A tear slid down her cheek. Auden was okay and the pressure was off. She wiped away the tear, not knowing whether to laugh or cry. She assured Richard that she'd complete her research over the next few days and get it off to him. She ended the call feeling as if a massive weight had been lifted from her shoulders.

As she waited for the lift back up to the third floor, she tried to decide what to do once her research was complete. It didn't seem fair to stay too long with Matt and Liz, but she didn't want to leave the Fens. She'd take her unexpected holiday right here. There were things she wanted to do, people she wanted to get to know better and . . . she realised that she had already made the decision. She acknowledged that she might move here permanently when her job finally came to an end. Property here was much cheaper, so it wouldn't be so urgent to find work immediately. As the lift doors opened, Christie's sprits soared. Big changes were coming.

CHAPTER ELEVEN

Seeing Ian's distress, Christie offered to stay with him for the rest of the day. She had more time to offer him after Richard's news.

'I have to go to my sister's house,' said Ian. 'There is some paperwork there that I need to pick up and then I have to register the death, and also talk to her solicitor.'

'How about you drive back to Pip and Dom's,' Christie suggested. 'I'll follow you, then I'll take you wherever you want to go. You shouldn't be driving at a time like this but you can't leave your car at the hospital.'

Ian accepted her offer and twenty minutes later, they were both in her car and driving towards Evelyn's house.

It was situated on the outskirts of the village where the Campions had their guest house. It was the last of five properties in a winding lane that meandered off into the farmlands. It was obviously very old, built of stone and flint, not the brick of most Lincolnshire houses. It had tiny lattice windows and a wooden porch over the front door with bench seats on either side. On one, a trug basket containing some old gardening gloves, a ball of green string and a trowel. The other had a couple of ancient cushions on it and from the covering of hairs, Christie guessed that Evelyn had owned a cat.

They went inside. Ian stood in the centre of the sitting room and looked around him as if he had never seen the place before. His gaze roamed over the open fire in the inglenook, ready laid with paper, kindling, logs and coal. He picked up silver photo frames and set them down again, ran his fingers gently over a scarlet glass paperweight on her desk. He wandered aimlessly about the room, as if trying to commit every object in it to memory. After a while, he sat down on an old chair that had been given a new lease of life by a colourful patchwork throw and gazed out of the French doors into the garden.

Christie didn't quite know what to do. She felt like an intruder on his grief. She had offered to wait in the car, but he'd said he'd appreciate her company, so here she was, awkward, her heart going out to this lost and lonely man.

She followed his gaze into the back garden and nearly gasped aloud. It was vibrant with colour, a shimmering tapestry of hundreds of flowers all tumbling over each other.

'She always insisted she wasn't much of a gardener, but everything she planted grew to amazing proportions. I used to tease her, ask her what she was feeding them — had she stolen something from the hospital pharmacy — chrysanthemum steroids, for instance? She would laugh. The garden liked her, she said, plants grew as if they were happy to be there.' He rubbed at his forehead. 'Me, I can't even keep a houseplant alive for longer than a week, so green fingers didn't exactly run in the family.' He got up and opened the door. 'Go outside and look around, Christie. It's worth a stroll, it's such a pretty garden.'

Like so many properties in the Fens, the house was surrounded on at least three sides by conifers and high fencing to provide a barrier against the powerful east wind. As you looked across the fields you could see little homesteads dotted here and there, islands of domesticity in the great sea of potatoes, beans, peas and grain.

Christie walked around the garden, enchanted. Evelyn had followed no plan when she planted: a great curtain of orange-flowered runner beans grew intertwined with clematis and sweet peas. A row of potatoes was backed by a row of vivid dahlias, and herbs jostled for space between lavender and sweet-smelling dianthus. An old sundial fought for recognition above a cluster of bright red geraniums and purple petunias. She followed a brick and gravel path that led past a shed and a small greenhouse, through a rickety gate and into a tiny orchard. There, among the fruit trees, she found a magnificent mulberry, heavy with the delicious magenta fruit. Christie reached up to touch one. The feel of the fruit evoked a childhood memory of her mother holding the basket, while Christie climbed the tree and dropped the berries. Afterwards, they would make a wonderful syrup that her mother poured over vanilla ice cream. Christie hadn't seen or tasted a mulberry in years.

She had noticed the house name — The Mulberries — but she hadn't expected to see a real one. After all, people called their houses all sorts of things. Her neighbours back in Scarborough lived in Honeysuckle Lodge, where there was not a sprig of sweet blossom in sight.

She wandered under an arbour covered in tiny, creamy, yellow-flowered banksia roses, to find what appeared to be a pump. She couldn't resist trying it out and moved the black iron handle up and down a few times until a gradually increasing flow of water started to pour into the waiting bucket.

Christie sat on a mossy stone bench overlooking a small pond with a backdrop of overgrown rockery, covered in cascading alpines and miniature conifers. She pictured Evelyn, lovingly tending to her small piece of paradise, much as she tended her patients, with care and attention.

She returned to the cottage and found Ian sitting where she had left him, gazing into the distance. 'Lovely, isn't it?' he said.

'It's a dream, Ian. She must have been very happy here. An awful lot of love was poured into that garden.'

'Oh, no doubt about that. She loved this village, the people and this cottage.' He stood up slowly and stretched. 'Let me show you the rest of The Mulberries.'

The tiny cottage had been left unmarred by added modernisations. The front door opened directly into the living room. There were original beams across the ceiling and the fireplace still had its firedogs and kettle hob. There were windows looking out on three aspects and a door at the side of the inglenook led through to a surprisingly spacious kitchen. Ian told her that it had once been four poky rooms — a kitchen, scullery, coal hole and walk-in pantry. It had been opened up to form one big room with a larder without doing away with any of its original character.

Looking around, Christie took in an old Belfast sink, solid pine cupboards and a farmhouse table with drawers at either end and two pine chairs with arms and colourful seat cushions. The only recent addition was an electric cooker and hob, but even this had been designed along the lines of an old-style range. The fridge-freezer had been concealed behind one of the pine doors.

Ian pointed through a window. 'There's an old red-brick outbuilding out back that used to be a laundry. Evie had electricity laid on and it serves as a utility room.'

A steep flight of stairs led up from the kitchen and into the bedroom. When Christie ducked beneath the lintel, she saw why Ian would have found it difficult to stay here. There must have been two bedrooms when the house had been built, but Evie had converted the smallest into a bathroom.

She wasn't sure what she had expected of the bedroom itself, probably something Laura Ashley — flowery and a bit chintzy. Instead, she found a highly polished dark wood floor with a single cross-beam of the same rich oak crossing the room from one end to the other. A pair of dormer windows looked out over the fields, both with mahogany poles supporting curtains in a William Morris design. A matching throw was laid across the iron-frame bedstead and one wall displayed a woven tapestry panel, so rich and detailed that it had to be genuine.

'Her one treasure,' Ian said behind her. 'It's been in the family for years. As a child, Evelyn would sit and stare at it for hours. I think she knew every stitch. It's a Morris, of course, woven at Merton Abbey, in the late 1880s we think. She designed the whole room around it.'

'It's quite the most beautiful thing I've ever seen. I can totally understand her love for it.' Greens and blues predominated, with here and there a touch of golden yellow and a flash of burnt orange. Christie picked out acanthus, along with other flowers, animals and birds all entwined together throughout the design. The detail was minute. She spotted tiny insects on the leaves and delicate stamens in the blossoms. Christie found it hard to drag her eyes away from it.

Besides the bed, the room was furnished with a heavy, eight-drawer tallboy with a single photograph on top, a solitary bedside table with a Tiffany lamp and a carriage clock, two window seats and an ancient oak chest. A scattering of soft rugs and an ornate wrought-iron candleholder completed the picture. There was no mirror, no wardrobe, no paintings on the walls, no central light and no radio or TV.

'Evie loved nature, adored her garden and respected the artists whose themes were plants and flowers, like William Morris.' He indicated the tapestry. 'She had little time for artifice and no time at all for television. For entertainment, she read, and listened to audio recordings, radio plays and discussions. Oh, and she did enjoy seeing a good theatre production whenever she visited me in London, which was once every two months, without fail.' He opened the door to the bathroom. 'Now, here was the one place she allowed herself the luxury of a real pampering.'

Christie stepped in past him and gave a little gasp of amazement.

The room centred around a pure white enamel bath, resplendent on claw feet and fitted with Victorian design taps. White marble tiles with a greenish vein in them ran up to the ceiling and at hip height, a dado rail, a barley-sugar twist of deepest holly-green ceramic, ran around the walls. There was a huge, Gothic arch-topped mirror and wall lights that were old gas mantles converted to run on electricity. White painted base cupboards ran the length of one wall, with various size shelves above, holding piles of fluffy towels and fancy green bottles of perfumed bath oils. In one corner was a shower cubicle, and even there the glass was Victorian, etched with climbing ivy and honeysuckle. She saw a handbasin, a toilet and a partly concealed cupboard door that led across the top of the landing to the bedroom and formed a long, narrow walk-in wardrobe. So that was where she kept her clothes!

Ian looked around. 'This would have been the second bedroom, so you can see why I had to stay at the Coach House.'

'What will you do with it, Ian?'

'Nothing at present. I need to come to terms with her death before I can think of disposing of it. I expect it will have to be sold at some point, but not yet. Meanwhile, I'll sort her things out. I see no reason to delay on that. But now, if it's all right with you, we really should get into town. There are arrangements to be made, and I want it all dealt with as swiftly as possible.'

It was mid-afternoon and although they hadn't eaten, neither was hungry, so they gathered up the documentation Ian had come for, locked up again and climbed back into Christie's car.

She dropped Ian at the solicitor's and parked nearby. He said he would probably be a while, so she decided to walk round to the Reading Room and tell Tom that she'd be staying on after all. She left her spare car key with Ian in case he got through earlier than expected.

To her dismay, on entering the bookshop, she was greeted by a tall young woman with an earring through her eyebrow and a stud through her nose, who told her in a gentle tone belying the metalwork on her face that Tom had taken a day off. He would be in tomorrow and could she pass on a message? Christie said she'd ring him at home.

'Oh, I don't think he's at home today. He mentioned going out with a friend, shopping in Peterborough, I think.'

Christie thanked her for her help and went up to the coffee bar in the hope of seeing Delphi. The café was almost empty and Delphi was wiping down shelves behind the counter.

'Oh, hello! How are you? I hope you aren't looking for Tom. He's gone off with Gina for the day.'

She sounded almost grudging. The news was as unwelcome to Christie as it obviously had been for Delphi. What was Gina up to? She had to be up to something.

Delphi poured Christie a coffee, refused payment and sat down with her. 'Dead quiet this afternoon, Christie. A short break won't hurt and there's no one to yell at me either. You off tomorrow, then?'

Christie told her about her change of plan and asked her if she'd let Tom know, in case she got held up with Ian. Delphi promised to pass on the message as soon as she saw him.

'They may call in later. Gina likes to check the order before it gets put through. She is very hot on sticking to the budget, doesn't trust the undermanager to get it right. She doesn't really trust anyone, not even Tom. She's always going on about over-ordering. Still, it's her money, I suppose. I wish I had what she's got. I'd buy my Denis a top-of-the-range car and we'd go on holiday somewhere hot and expensive.'

'Denis is your husband?' Christie enquired.

'Oh yes. We've been married for almost six years now and I love him to bits. We haven't had a holiday since our honeymoon, and that was two years after the wedding!'

'What does he do?'

'Like most around here, he's in the food industry. Works for a big onion grower. Money's rubbish but they keep promising him a step up the ladder. He might even make management if he hangs on with them.'

Christie had a feeling that Denis would be standing on the bottom rung for a long time. 'Any kids?'

'No. Well, Denis has a girl from his first marriage, but she is in Australia and we don't hear much about her. It was what they call a mucky divorce. He was in a right state when I met him, now he reckons she did him a big favour. At least he knows I'd never mess around with other men. You're not married then?'

'No. I've not been exactly lucky in that area.' Christie didn't elaborate.

'You poor thing! Still, I'm sure your knight in shining armour will arrive one day and whisk you off your feet and carry you into the sunset.'

Christie decided that at her age, the armour might be slightly rusty, and the horse would probably have arthritis. And the mere thought of being whisked gave her vertigo. 'Oh, I am quite happy as I am. By the way, where did you get that lovely name? Is it short for something?'

'My mother is an armchair traveller. She reads about travelling the world and drools over all those holiday programmes on the box, though in reality she's too frightened to even go on the river trip from the Greenborough Marina. She gets seasick as hell, and she wouldn't dream of getting on a plane in a million years. Anyway, she watched *Shirley Valentine* about ten times and fell in love with Greece. She bought loads of travel magazines and finished up renaming the house Athena. The dog had to learn to answer to Artemis and the cat got called Hecate. I think I'm quite fortunate to be named after the Oracle's birthplace. My brother wasn't so lucky — she'd been watching a thing on canals, so he's called Corinth, Corrie for short.'

Christie said that considering some Greek names, it could have been a lot worse. She checked her watch and decided she should get back to the car.

She left the shop wondering about Tom and Gina. She wished she'd had the courage to ask Delphi more about their trip, but she was afraid of sounding like a busybody.

She had just unlocked the car when Ian arrived at her side. He looked tired and grey.

'I've helped so many of my parishioners through their bereavements and I've buried both of our parents, but this . . . this is hard.'

She felt a stab of pity for him. 'Is there anyone you could call? Someone you are close to, who could come and stay with you for a while?'

He shook his head sadly. 'My clerical friends are only acquaintances, really. They're the sort of people I can call for a good theological debate but not to cry on their shoulders. I do have friends, it's just that very few of them knew Evelyn. They don't really belong to this part of my life somehow.'

Christie slipped her arm through his. They stood beside her car in silence. After a while, she said, 'Let's walk down to St Benedict's and light a candle for her.'

He clasped her hand tightly and nodded.

Fifteen minutes later, they were walking out of the churchyard when suddenly Ian stopped. 'Christie, I'm going to ask a favour of you. Please, if it's not what you want, just say so, all right?'

She looked at him, rather mystified. 'Of course. What is it?'

'You mentioned not wanting to outstay your welcome at your cousin's. Well, I was wondering if you'd like to move into The Mulberries for a while?'

Christie's first impulse was to say yes. 'But you need to sort out Evelyn's things, I'd be in your way.'

'Far from it. I'd appreciate the company and perhaps you would help me? It would be a relief to know that someone was living there. I can't bear to think of it sitting empty.'

'Wouldn't you like to stay there yourself, instead of with the Campions?' she asked.

'Frankly, I've become used to being looked after, and Pip and Dom are like family. No, Christie, I'm not ready for my own company just yet.'

It didn't take long for her to make up her mind. 'I'll talk to Liz and Matt as soon as I get back, Ian, and as long as it doesn't offend them, I'd absolutely love to stay there. I'll look after it, never fear.' The tension left his face, and she knew she had made the right decision.

* * *

After supper, Matt, Liz and Christie sat around the kitchen table, drinking wine and discussing the coming fortnight.

'Please don't feel you have to go,' said Liz, with an anxious smile. 'We love having you here.'

'And I love being here,' Christie assured them. 'But if I stay at The Mulberries, I'll be taking a big weight off Ian's mind. I can help him sort Evelyn's things and I won't feel so guilty about imposing on you. I'll still see you and we can meet in town for lunch, can't we, Liz?'

'It's up to you entirely, Christie,' said Matt. 'But your room is still here should you change your mind, or if living alone in someone else's past gets too much for you. Tell you what, hang onto the spare key. If things get a bit heavy, what with all the grieving, just come back, okay?'

'You're an absolute diamond, Matt Ballard!'

Liz groaned softly. 'Oh Lord, don't tell him that! There'll be no living with him.'

Christie was too excited to sleep. She'd led such an unusual lifestyle working for Auden, never knowing where she'd be going next, that the thought of actually putting down roots and making lasting friendships was positively intoxicating. Yes, it was sad the way it had come about, but right now, she felt strong enough to cope with anything. She finally fell asleep to a dream of eating mulberry syrup on vanilla ice cream in a garden full of flowers.

CHAPTER TWELVE

Still in his dressing gown and holding a mug of morning tea, Matt stood in the garden of Cannon Farm. He stared into space, his mind on the Lindsay Harrison case. Last night he had had a word on the phone with Bryn Owen, who said Duncan Hartland had never cropped up as a person of interest in the enquiry. As soon as he had done what Charley Anders had asked and checked out Lindsay's ex-boyfriend, Matt planned to make some enquiries about Hartland.

He kicked a stray pebble off the lawn, considering what he knew about men who developed a fixation on a certain woman. Such obsessions could be dangerous. They had an insidious habit of turning bad and could suddenly escalate at an alarming rate. He'd seen it before and found it frightening. Matt determined to go and talk to Paula Harrison and ascertain exactly how much of a nuisance Hartland had made of himself. He'd also be interested to see what she thought of Barry Breslow and how accurate she believed his opinion of Hartland to be. Barry had admitted to being fond of Paula himself, so maybe jealousy was a major factor. He had been vitriolic enough about Hartland.

Matt started to wonder what kind of beauty Paula Harrison was to have men vying for her attentions like this.

He turned around. Talking about beauties, Liz was coming across the lawn, smiling.

'Taking the morning air, my darling, or are those little grey cells on overtime? Planning your next move?'

He smiled back. 'Bit of each, but mainly thinking about obsession — not mine, I hasten to add, but that of a certain Duncan Hartland.'

'Well, maybe you'd like to take your obsessions into the shower, as I'm about to do a cooked breakfast.'

They strolled back to the house. 'So, what are Christie's plans for today?' he asked.

'She's going into town early to collect a painting she bought, then Jack Fleet's cousin is going to see her at the drainage museum. She's coming back for lunch, and then I'll help her take her things to her new temporary home.' She squeezed his arm. 'She doesn't really need help, she hasn't got much, but I want to get a look at this cottage she keeps raving about.'

'She certainly seems to like it,' he said. 'Boy, did she wax lyrical about the garden. She seems very impressionable. Her take on things is sort of emotional, and the language she uses is quite flowery, isn't it? She often comes across as old-fashioned. It could be irritating if you didn't know that she's just a thoroughly good and honest person, and very sensitive.'

'I know what you mean. I suppose it's her job. I guess she's developed such an outlook because of having to make a blind man — someone from an older generation — see the world through her eyes.' Liz pushed open the back door. 'We, on the other hand, deal in plain facts, the nitty-gritty side of life.'

'Don't we just! Even Christie couldn't be poetic about a holding cell!'

They both laughed.

'When we were kids,' mused Liz, 'Christie excelled in English and literature and the creative subjects like art and drama and music. Whereas I loved maths and science, and you couldn't get me off the sports field. We were complete opposites, yet for some reason we thought along the same lines and appreciated the other's point of view. Neither of us had a thing in common with our biological sisters.'

'And your bond has lasted into adulthood. That's pretty special.' Matt kissed her lightly. 'I'll leave you with your memories and have that shower. I've got a full day ahead.'

'Oh?'

'The ex-boyfriend,' he said. 'The young guy who was in the frame for a while until his alibi checked out. Charley needs to know what he's up to these days. So that's me set for the day.' He gave her another kiss. 'See you in ten minutes. I must say, I'm looking forward to having one of your breakfasts!'

* * *

Christie arrived at Jane Waterhouse's gallery just as she was opening up for the day.

'Now that's what I call eager. Not everyone is so enthusiastic about collecting their purchases.'

She glided back to the counter, as if on castors. Her movements were so effortless that at any moment Christie half expected her to drift through a wall or dematerialise in front of her eyes.

'I haven't wrapped it yet, I thought you should see it first.'

The picture was propped up behind the cash desk. If possible, the frame had even enhanced the painting's subtle tones. Christie expressed her delight and waited as Jane carefully encased it in bubble wrap and thick brown paper. She was just placing the parcel in a carrier bag when a familiar voice called out from the floor above.

Christie looked towards the spiral staircase that could only lead up to Jane's flat and studio. As she had feared, the person looking down upon her was Gina.

'Well, well. Miss McFerran. Don't tell me you've stooped to buying one of my little friend's artistic efforts, have you?'

The woman looked slightly dishevelled, not quite the sharp-edged businesswoman of their previous encounters. Her dark hair was damp, clearly from a recent shower, and she was dressed casually in faded jeans and a sweatshirt. She ran a hand through her short, unbrushed hair and, dropping a half-open grab bag on the floor at her feet, smiled broadly at Christie.

'Actually, I have just purchased a most beautiful watercolour.' Christie's hackles were up already. From the corner of her eye, she caught a glimpse of the painting of Tadema House in the alcove. The spurned gift.

'Each to her own, Miss McFerran. For my part I prefer something with a little more *body*.' She cast an unreadable glance at Jane, who was trying unsuccessfully to unravel a knot in her ball of parcel string. She seemed to have shrunk in stature.

'Sorry I can't stay and talk. I don't take many days off and I plan to make the most of this one. At least it started well, didn't it, Jane?' Another knowing look. She hefted her bag over her shoulder and was gone.

Christie wasn't sure which of them was the more disconcerted by Gina's barely veiled innuendos, her or Jane. She decided to help poor Jane by acting as if the exchange had completely passed over her head. She thanked her for doing the framing so promptly and said she hoped to see her again soon. She left as soon as she politely could and was relieved to get outside into the air.

There was now a slight rain falling and the moisture on her skin was refreshing. She wished for a downpour, a drenching rain to wash away the negative emotions the encounter had aroused.

She put the precious picture in the boot of her car and covered it with blankets. As she drove to her meeting with Jack Fleet's cousin, she kept telling herself not to make assumptions. Gina could well have been trying to deceive her into thinking there was something between her and Jane when in fact there was nothing. That grab bag didn't have to be an overnight bag, did it? And what if she *had* stayed. It was perfectly acceptable if she had been working till late. Maybe she'd had a few drinks and didn't want to drive. Maybe.

Yeah, and maybe they were lovers. 'Christie!' she said out loud to herself. 'For heaven's sake, get a grip. What does it matter anyway?'

A little further on, she asked herself where Tom fitted into it all. Poor Tom. What a mess. Again, she admonished herself. She didn't know the facts and she didn't even know the people concerned. Not everything is as it appears. She tried to think pump houses, drainage ditches. Her job. Couldn't she just leave bloody Gina to play her sodding games?

* * *

Jack's cousin was a mine of information and was able to tell Christie everything Auden had asked her to find out about the history of the draining of the Fens. He said that in his opinion, even though serious large-scale draining first started in 1631, only now were people really reaping the benefits in terms of the rich arable soil. It was all very interesting, but Christie couldn't stop her mind wandering back to Jane Waterhouse and her gallery. She was glad to be finished and on the road back to Cannon Farm, though she was sorry to be leaving her cousin.

It had been really good to catch up with Liz again, and the thought that she might move here permanently meant they'd be able to rekindle the close friendship of their youth. She hadn't yet told Liz of her idea. She hadn't told anyone, just in case it didn't work out. But Liz would be the first to know.

Then, while they were putting Christie's things in the car, Liz said, 'I can see you settling here, you know. You appreciate things about this county that others don't.'

Christie was tempted to spill the beans there and then, but said instead, 'There is something about this place, I don't know what, it's certainly not St Mary Mead. For a start, you're at risk of getting your car dented by cauliflowers or potatoes flying off a passing tractor. Yet . . .' She shrugged.

'Hang around a village roundabout when they're bringing the harvest in off the fields and you'll pick up enough fresh vegetables to last you a month. It is a great place. It's smelly when they harvest the brassicas, worse when they pick the spring onions, stifling when they treat the fields with silage and no more than two chocolate-box houses are allowed per village, unless you live in that snobby little one close to Sly Fen, of course.' Liz laughed.

There it was again. Somehow Gina had crept into even that conversation. "That" village was where Tadema House was located. No matter how much she tried, Christie couldn't get away from her. Well, she was looking forward to staying in The Mulberries, and she was determined not to let Gina Spearman ruin it.

She hurried up to her room one last time to check that she hadn't left anything behind. They were due to meet Ian in half an hour. Liz was going to follow her in her own car, have a quick look at the cottage and then return home.

When they arrived, Ian was already there. The rain had cleared, and the garden glistened in the sunlight. Christie introduced them, and Liz offered her condolences.

'Thankfully, I finished all the arrangements this morning,' Ian told them. 'A post-mortem wasn't necessary since it wasn't a sudden death. Evelyn had already secured a plot in the village churchyard. I've spoken to the vicar and the undertakers, and we can have the service on Thursday next week. Pip, bless her, has offered to lay on a buffet at Stone House.'

Christie was pleased it had all come together so quickly. He probably had commitments in London and would be wanting to get back as soon as he could.

Inside, Liz said that Evelyn's cottage was just as Christie had described it. She thought it delightful, especially the garden. Liz helped her bring her things in and then said she should be getting back, as she didn't want to be in the way. 'I'm sure you have a lot to do and now I can picture where you are, I'm happy.' Liz gave her a hug, whispering, 'Don't be lonely, Christie. You know where we are if you want some company.'

Christie waved her off and returned to where Ian was looking through the contents of a sideboard.

'I had no idea she'd kept these!' He held up a small, engraved silver trophy. 'I won that when I was fifteen, came in first in my school's annual cross-country run. Evelyn was there, clapping and cheering as I gasped my way across the finishing line. I assumed it had been thrown away years ago.' Ian was pulling out item after item, alternately laughing and sighing. 'Well, I never guessed my sister was such a sentimental old squirrel. She's kept a whole hoard of keepsakes from our past. Isn't that wonderful?' He looked up at Christie. 'Dominic let me have a lot of packing boxes from Stone House. If I put aside the things I'd like to keep, would you be kind enough to pack them up for me? Dom said I can store them in his garage until I go back to London.'

'I'd be happy to, I'm good at packing,' said Christie, relieved to have something useful to do. 'If you like, I could take what you don't want to one of the charity shops in town.'

'Excellent idea.' He smiled at her. 'Do you know, I've been dreading this, but now we are finally here, it's quite, well, releasing somehow. I feel we are taking care of things for her as she would have wished.' He looked around the room and sighed. 'How can someone so vital suddenly cease to be? It seems wrong, somehow, that perishable things like a vase of flowers or a houseplant can outlive the human being that tended them.'

He didn't sound sad, just philosophical. Christie was forced to agree with him. 'I keep trying to imagine Auden's home without Auden in it. It's full to bursting with books, Auden's whole world in one place, spent amid his literature. We know it's going to happen, but the thought of him not being there with a novel unfinished seems unthinkable, somehow.'

'Death really is the greatest mystery,' mused Ian. Then he gave a little laugh. 'I've presided over more funerals than you've had hot dinners, my dear, but death still mystifies me. No matter how strong one's faith, I defy anyone to say they don't wonder about it.'

They sorted and packed for over an hour and a half, then Christie made tea. They took it out into the garden. She wondered how many times Ian had sat here drinking tea with his sister, and from the faraway look on his face, he appeared to be thinking the same thing.

Her phone rang, interrupting the peace. She saw the caller was Richard, stood up and wandered down to the orchard.

'Christie! Thank God! It's Auden. He's in a coma.'

'But . . . Whatever has happened? I thought it was just a minor operation.'

'It was. Something went wrong, a complication, probably due to his illness. Christie, he's on a respirator.' There was a catch in his voice. 'He's stable but they have no idea what his chances are.'

She was torn. He would need her. She should go to him. She and Richard had been friends for a long time and she hardly knew Ian, but he needed her too. She saw Richard in her mind's eye. Although he must be approaching fifty, he still retained a boyish charm. His hair was dark and wavy, and he had deep, expressive eyes, always full of understanding and compassion. Richard was one of life's truly unselfish people.

'Oh, I'm so sorry, Richard. Do you want me to come back? Can I help in any way?'

His reply came as a relief. 'Thank you, my dear. But there's little point at present. I have plenty to keep me busy here. You stay on. I'll keep you informed. You needed to know, that's all. Auden wanted you to have a break, he sent you off immediately after your trip to Cornwall and he felt bad about that. Let's see what happens. I'll call you if his condition deteriorates.'

She made her way slowly back to Ian. All at once, death was everywhere. It was strange. She decided not to pass on what she had heard to Ian, he had enough to cope with. So she told him only that Auden was holding his own. And she had a strong feeling that Auden would do just that. He would hold onto life until he could write the final chapter of his book and set down his pen with the words "The End."

At four o'clock, Ian declared it was time he got back to Stone House. He thanked Christie for her help and wished her a good night's sleep in the Morris room. He had even thought to change the bed linen.

He gave her a set of keys and squeezed her arm in parting. 'I appreciate this, Christie, more than you'll ever know.'

Needing to get out and shake off the veil of sadness that had descended upon her, Christie locked up the cottage and drove into the town. There, she went to the florist and ordered a spray of flowers for the funeral, in the brightest colours they had, to reflect Evelyn's garden. Having done that, she headed for the Reading Room. She wanted to see Tom before the shop closed.

Staff were dusting the shelves and generally clearing up for the night. Tom stood at the till, a strange, lost expression on his face. He didn't even notice her walk in.

'Penny for them.'

'Oh, Christie. I'm so sorry, I was miles away.'

'I came to tell you that I'm staying on for a while.'

'Delphi told me. I'm so pleased.'

But the words lacked conviction.

'I also wanted to thank you for the other evening. It was really kind of you to invite me, and I thought your mother was a gem.'

An odd look passed over his face. Irritation? Surely not.

'Yes. As I said, she's the best.'

There was none of his usual animation. Something was obviously wrong, either here or in the Parrish household.

'Thomas! A word, please.'

He stiffened like a rabbit caught in the headlights, stammered an apology and asked her to hang on.

Bristling with annoyance, Christie pretended to browse the new titles while remaining within earshot of the back office. The Reading Room's owner was evidently in another of her "Let's Nail a Member of Staff to a Large Lump of Wood" moods. It appeared that Thomas Maxfield was the one being crucified today.

The humiliating diatribe continued for some five minutes. It sounded as though it concerned the work experience girl's extended lunch break, but Christie couldn't be certain. If it hadn't been so cruel and hurtful, it might have been funny. Why ever did Tom put up with it?

Suddenly she was overcome with exasperation at the whole situation. She almost felt like walking into the office and challenging Madame Spearman. Then she saw Delphi hurrying down the stairs from the café, jacket and handbag over her arm.

Christie asked Delphi to apologise to Tom for her. She had to leave, but she'd call him later. She had some news for him.

Delphi's face was a picture of despair. 'Oh, Christie,' she blurted, 'it's not always like this. Poor Gina, she's had a really bad time of late. I know it looks awful, but you don't know her. She can be really nice.'

Poor Gina? Christie held back her retort. 'It's none of my business, Delphi. It's just that I need to get back and I can't wait right now. Don't worry, I'll ring him.'

Delphi looked the picture of misery. 'You will come in again, won't you?'

She relented. 'I'll try and get back for a coffee and a Danish tomorrow.'

She would, too. Someone needed to try and instil some sense into Tom before he had a nervous breakdown over Little Miss I've-Got-a-Degree-in-Harassment. Plus, she couldn't wait to tell him that she'd met Jane Waterhouse and even bought one of her paintings.

An image of the dimly lit alcove and the painting of Tadema House rose into her mind. What a fool Gina had been! It was a masterful study of light and shadow. What's more, it had been painted with love, as a special gift. Then it hit her. Gina's rejection of that gift, and thus of the artist's skill and talent, was all about controlling her "friend."

Christie swallowed hard. My God. What a bitch. Maybe she should buy it, just to show Jane that someone appreciated her talent. And, of course, to give Gina the finger.

* * *

Matt drove slowly through the trading estate until he spotted the firm he wanted. He steered through the impressive gateway, smiling as he recalled the original set-up of "David Watkins Fenland Glass," a dilapidated Portakabin and an old barn. Now Watkins was producing glass for all the local double-glazing companies and exclusive, fancy glasswork for architectural designers.

Matt sat in the car and watched the staff, who were just leaving for the day. He was interested in a man named Paul Redman, Lindsay Harrison's ex-boyfriend.

After fifteen minutes, only a handful of stragglers were left, and the shutters were coming down over the doors to the factory section of the building. There had been no sign of his mark, but he did see a familiar face making for a nearby car.

'Jim! Jim Smith!'

The man started and turned. 'Matt Ballard! Bloody hell! How are you, mate?'

Matt got out and approached the smiling man. They shook hands warmly. 'I'm fine, thanks. How's life treating you, lad?'

'Fair to middlin'. My goodness, I haven't seen you in years. You're looking good, mate.' Jim Smith had an expressive face that looked as if it had been remodelled several times over. Which wasn't far from the truth, as he had been an amateur boxer in his youth and then went on to play rugby, which he swore did much more damage than his brief career in the ring had ever done.

'You in a hurry, Jim? Stand you a pint? The Wild Goose is only five minutes away.' Looking at his old teammate he realised how long it had been since he, Matt, had been near a rugby pitch.

'Since me and Denise split up, me time's me own. See you there.'

Matt climbed back in the car, glad that his trip hadn't been entirely wasted.

Ten minutes later, he and Jim were both sitting at a small table in the Wild Goose beer garden, with glasses of Sleeping Beauty, Matt's favourite local brew. Having brought each other up to date on the last five years, Matt decided it was time to broach the reason for his visit to Watkins Glass.

'Know Paul Redman, then, do you?'

Jim's grin resembled a dent in a well-used rugby ball. Then it faded. 'Poor bloke. First his girlfriend gets topped, an' then you lot bang him up. He's never been the same since.'

Matt chuckled. 'He wasn't ever banged up, Jim. Just held for questioning. It wasn't my case, but it's come up again. I'm looking for background on it now.'

Jim frowned. 'Not planning on hitting him with more of the same, are you? Cause I reckon that'd just about finish him off.'

'No, nothing like that. I'm just checking out where everyone involved is now and trying to spot anything that might have been missed first time around. Paul's not going to be in the spotlight for her murder again, his alibi proved to be watertight.' He paused. 'I thought they'd split up, Paul and Lindsay? You just said girlfriend, not ex.'

'He swears it was a temporary thing and all down to her. As far as he was concerned, they'd have sorted it all out. He wanted to marry her.'

Since Jim seemed so much in the know, Matt dug deeper. 'What can you tell me about Paul, Jim? Like, how has it affected him?'

Jim pulled a face. 'If you ask me, he's badly damaged by what happened. I used to have a drink with him sometimes, but I kind of dropped it.' He shook his head. 'I feel bad about it sometimes, cause I know he's lonely, but it was the same thing every time, over and over, and it started to do my head in.'

Matt frowned. 'What was he on about?'

'Paul's got a bee in his bonnet about some mystery admirer, some bloke who was after her who filled her head with fancy ideas. He said she changed. He was certain there was another man in her life.' Jim took a long swallow and wiped his mouth with the back of his hand. 'And he's dead certain it was this man killed her.'

There had been no mention of this in the notes Charley had given him, and certainly no hint of a "mystery man" in the newspaper reports. Matt sat forward. 'Anything else?'

'Other than the fact that Paul was talking about hunting him down? Nothing.'

Was he, indeed? Not a smart move. 'As I said, it wasn't my case, but I never heard anything about that.'

'Because he never spoke about it to the police, mate. He reckoned they'd think he was guilty, trying to swing the blame from himself and onto some non-existent mystery guy. Can't really blame him, can you?'

Matt was forced to agree. 'I'm guessing he's pretty anti-police now?'

'And how! Wary as hell.'

Matt thought fast. 'Reckon he'd talk to me? Since I'm a private detective who's only looking for the truth.'

Jim's answer surprised him.

'Like a shot. He's rattled on for ages about trying to get the money together to hire a private dick to find the stranger who turned Lindsay against him. If you took it on, it'd be the best thing that's happened to him in years. If you've got the patience to cut through all the shit — the conspiracy theories, the fantasies and whatever else his bruised mind has conjured up, that is. If you have, well, go for it.'

'I've been sifting through lies and bullshit all my working life, Jim. I'm happy to give it a try,' Matt said.

'Well, he was off today, so he'll be back in tomorrow for the weekend shift. Want me to talk to him? Kind of pave the way for you?'

Matt nodded. 'Absolutely. You talk to him and I'll call back at the factory same time tomorrow and have a chat with him.'

Jim downed the last of his pint and sighed. 'Thanks, Matt. That was very tasty. I'd get another round in, but your mates are hot as mustard on the old drink-driving, so, do it another time?'

Matt smiled. 'Another drink would be great. I'm just sorry it's been so long. We had some good times knocking the hell out of the Greenborough front row, didn't we?'

Jim rubbed at a cauliflower ear and gave him that face-splitting grin. 'Bloody marvellous!'

As Matt headed back over the fields to his home, he felt the embers of his old excitement begin to smoulder. The spark might extinguish, of course, turn out to be a story that Paul had invented to help him cope with Lindsay's death. He'd just have to see.

CHAPTER THIRTEEN

Over a week passed. Ian had taken from the cottage all the precious keepsakes he wanted, and they were now packed and stored at Stone House. He'd told her he might take more, should he sell the property, but for now, Christie had everything she could possibly need for her comfort. She was enjoying her time at The Mulberries. She had seen Tom and Delphi twice since his dressing-down by Gina and, although he always seemed pleased to see her, there was a certain detachment in him now. Christie had made a flying visit to Yorkshire and managed to see Richard, visit Auden — who was still in a coma, collect more clothes and check her own house.

Now, Evelyn was being committed to the earth in the midst of a squally shower. It was difficult to distinguish between the windblown raindrops and the tears in some of the mourners' eyes.

It was a quiet affair, the majority of the attendees being neighbours and friends from the village, along with a few old friends from her nursing days. Ian had refused the offer to conduct the service in person, opting instead to read the eulogy, followed by a prayer for her.

Christie thought it very sensible of him. Although he hid it well, she knew he was taking Evelyn's passing badly, and she feared that even the reading might be too much for him. But when he stood at the pulpit, his voice rang out. He spoke of her youth, her vitality, her beauty and her diligent work throughout a lifetime spent caring for others. He told a sweet story from her childhood and finished with her love of nature and her cherished garden at The Mulberries. He then quoted a poem by William Morris, which spoke of the beauty of his own garden at the Red House in Kent. He said that Evelyn had always loved it and had embroidered it on a sampler that hung in her kitchen.

I know a little garden-close
Set thick with lily and red rose,
Where I would wander if I might
From dewy morn to dewy night,
And have one with me wandering.

He concluded with the words that it had ever been his sadness that she had always wandered the garden alone, with no one with her.

Christie glanced up to the vaulted ceiling and thought about Auden, still in his long unnatural slumber, and of Richard, silently mourning a love he had never been able to realise.

After the interment, they all moved on to the Coach House. Evelyn's closest neighbours and some old working colleagues who had remained in touch with her came along, and a handful of the clergy who were down from London in support of Ian.

Christie made herself useful, taking platters of food around and refilling glasses, while Evelyn's friends recounted anecdotes from her life.

In a corner of the room, dressed in black, a plate balanced precariously on her lap and a glass of sherry in one hand, Margaret Parrish sat quietly. Christie hadn't noticed her at the funeral.

Margaret smiled at her and patted the seat next to her. 'Such a lovely service, dear. You know I much prefer a less formal ceremony, with poetry and the departed person's favourite music. I think one should celebrate the passing of a life, not have to suffer through long, cold, "official" sermons and prayers.'

Christie agreed wholeheartedly.

'I had no idea you knew Evelyn,' said Margaret. 'We were old friends, you know. After she retired from nursing, we used to help run the League of Friends shop up at the hospital, until my arthritis got too bad, then we met for coffee every week. I shall miss her.' Margaret was silent, lost in a reverie. Christie touched her hand lightly. 'Tom tells me you're staying on for a while. It would be lovely if you could call in for tea one afternoon, if you have time.'

Christie assured her that she would. She asked after Tom, whom she hadn't seen much of lately.

Margaret frowned, and her lips tightened. 'Oh, I don't know what the matter is with him. He is becoming moody and irritable. Worse than a teenager. In fact, he was much nicer back then.'

This unexpected outburst caught Christie by surprise.

'Sorry, my dear. Simply the ranting of a selfish old woman who didn't manage to get her own way for once.'

Christie was even more puzzled.

Margaret smiled ruefully. 'The fact is, my son has ruined me. He's spoiled me unmercifully and now that for once in my life I am not his number one, I am having trouble handling the situation.'

Although she hated to say the name, Christie felt compelled to ask about his relationship with Gina.

Margaret set down her empty glass. 'There is no relationship. It's all in his head. That scheming woman plays him along, then drops him like a hot potato. And he can't see that she's doing it.'

Hoping she wouldn't upset Margaret even further, Christie said, 'I called into the bookshop a week or so ago and Delphi said they had gone off together for the day. Is that usual? Do they often spend time together?'

Margaret sighed heavily. 'I belong to a club, you know, one of those townswomen's things. There was a guest speaker that day that I particularly wanted to hear. Tom always runs me down to the meeting hall in his lunch hour. You saw how close we live to his shop, five minutes at the most. He would walk home, drive me to the other side of town, then go back to work. I used to get one of the others to drop me home afterwards or get a taxi. More often than not, Tom would slip out of work for ten minutes and collect me himself — his idea, mind you. I never asked him to take me anywhere. He did it because he was happy to. Anyway, he went to work that morning and at ten thirty, in comes Gina Spearman. She insists that the others can manage without him for the day, and that she's taking him down to Peterborough to see an art exhibition that was being held in the Cathedral. She was going to treat him to lunch at Dante's, her favourite restaurant, and then they would go shopping together. He rang me to let me know that he might be late home. I reminded him about my meeting, and he told me to get a taxi. Well, I couldn't. By the time he rang me it was nearly eleven, the talk started at midday and there was some fair or other on in the town and there were no taxis available.' She looked down at her shiny black shoes. 'I know how petty it sounds, but I felt really hurt. It was not the fact that he told me to go by cab, it was the way he said it.'

It did sound petty, but Christie thought the way he dismissed her must have come as a shock to Margaret.

'But if I thought *I* was upset,' Margaret continued, 'it was nothing to how Tom felt later that day. Gina decided that they should have lunch first and in the restaurant bar, they happened to meet up with an old university friend of hers. Tom doesn't believe this was anything other than coincidence. I think otherwise. So anyhow, Gina asked this chap if he wanted to go to the exhibition with them, and then, knowing full well that Tom had to get home for me, decided to make an evening of it and stay on in the city until late. They had taken her car, so, in front of this other man, Gina hands my Tom a twenty-pound note and tells him to get the train home.'

What a cow. Christie could imagine how mortified Tom must have been.

'Next day he arrives at work to find another of her slimy cards, full of apologies, and saying she knew he wouldn't have wanted to leave his dear old ailing mama. "Do forgive me, Maxfield."' Margaret pulled a face. 'Ugh, how I hate that name! "I'll make it up to you, Maxfield." It was attached to an envelope containing two tickets for a concert in Lincoln next month that Tom has been desperate to go and see. I have no idea how she got those tickets. I've been trying for nearly a month to get him one, they're like gold dust.'

Christie glanced around, looking for Ian. He had held up remarkably well, but she still worried about him. He was engrossed in conversation with another elderly cleric and didn't appear to be in imminent need of rescuing. She returned her attention to Margaret.

'Have you met Evelyn's brother, the Reverend Ian Hardy?'

Margaret's eyes lit up. 'Oh yes! What a handsome man. I first saw him at Evie's retirement garden party. I was bowled over, but sadly there's no hope for me.'

Christie was amused to see this elderly lady confess to a yearning for an attractive man. She laughed and said that Margaret shouldn't let age stand in her way.

'Age be damned! It's the bloody arthritis that's holding me back.'

They giggled like a pair of naughty schoolgirls. Christie offered to bring Ian with her to tea, if the offer still stood.

Margaret nodded furiously, not daring to speak for laughter.

They sat together, chatting, until Tom arrived to collect his mother.

Christie smiled and hugged him affectionately. He was polite and attempted a cheerful smile, but there was a lassitude about him that she hadn't seen before. He refused a drink on the grounds that he was driving and silently escorted his now equally silent mother to his car.

By the time the last mourners had left, it was early evening.

Ian looked gaunt. Though the service had taken its toll on him, he was reluctant to retire to bed. 'I'll never sleep. I'm far too strung out. I need to do something to stop my mind constantly going over the funeral. I still can't believe my little sister is gone.'

Christie suggested a walk and Dominic volunteered to accompany them. Jessie had been shut in for the major part of the day and deserved a good run. They piled into Dom's four-wheel drive and drove down to a spot on the sea bank that she'd visited on her very first day in the Fens. It seemed like a long, long time ago now.

The conditions were perfect for blowing unwanted thoughts from their heads. The rain had stopped but a strong wind whistled along the high causeway. It wasn't cold but up on that open stretch of marshland, the strength of the gale obliged them to shout in order to hear each other.

The dog raced back and forth like a mad thing, barking furiously, putting up marsh birds. They walked along the river's edge for about twenty minutes, then turned and retraced their footsteps. The vehicle was a tiny spot in the distance. They were all amazed at how far they had walked. Ian had rallied, blaming his earlier fatigue on the stress of the day. Now he strode along so purposefully that Christie had trouble keeping up with him.

Suddenly really struggling, she asked the two men if they minded if she sat down for a few minutes while she got her breath back, assuring them it was nothing to worry about.

Dominic produced a rather grubby rubber ball from his pocket and began to throw it for Jessie. Ian sat beside her on the low wall, looking concerned. 'How are you doing?'

'I'll be right as rain in a bit,' Christie gasped. 'It creeps up on me sometimes. It's just a weakness.'

'I recall you saying it was rheumatic fever. Is that right?' She nodded.

'You don't hear of that so much these days, especially in people your age.'

She nodded again and they watched Dominic Campion play with his tireless dog.

Her breathlessness subsided, but they sat a little longer, gazing at the sky as it changed with the approach of dusk. Christie told Ian that she had caught a bad streptococcal throat infection when she was in Africa with her parents. Back home she had become really ill, with painful, swollen joints and a fever. Luckily, it had been diagnosed fairly quickly. The disease is no longer as virulent as it was sixty years ago, so she'd got away pretty lightly. 'There is a slight stenosis of one of my heart valves, but I have regular check-ups and I've been able to live a more or less normal life, as long as I don't overdo things.'

'I do hope I haven't put too much strain on you over the past week. You have been a rock, driving me around and helping me sort out Evelyn's belongings.'

'Certainly not, Ian,' she said. 'It's just a combination of the funeral, Auden's condition and walking into a strong wind. I should have thought about it and not gone so far.'

'What were you doing in Africa, if I may ask?'

'Dad was an ornithologist. Not a bird-watcher, it was his job. He provided information about the movement and migration of birds all around the world. When I was at school and we had to write about what we did in the summer holidays, my compositions made slightly different reading to those of the other kids, I must say. While they were describing the beach donkeys at Morecambe, I was expatiating on the mysteries of the souk, or the majesty of the fjords. By the age of ten, I had probably seen more of the world's wilder places than most adults ever would.'

'Sounds like you had a good childhood.'

'The best.'

'And your parents now?'

She threw up her hands. 'I have no idea! Dad's retirement didn't stop them travelling. The last I heard they were

136

looking for a crofter's cottage somewhere in the Hebrides. He wants to write the definitive article on the Arctic skua. I haven't seen them for over a year.'

'Okay to start back? If you're up to it, Christie,' said Dominic. 'We are losing the light.' He called Jessie to heel, and they made their way to the vehicle.

'Thanks,' Ian said softly, smiling at her.

Christie tilted her head. 'What for?'

'It was a good idea to get out this evening. I feel much restored. I think I will sleep now.' She slipped her arm through his. It was time for him to draw a line under today and begin a new chapter in his life.

When they got back to Stone House, Ian said goodnight and went up to his room, but Dom took Christie's arm. 'Let's walk down to the pub. I'll buy you a brandy. It's a great restorative after you've had a little wobble.'

'Just a small one, Dom. I still have to get back to The Mulberries.'

'Leave your car here and I'll walk home with you. It's only ten minutes from here.' He grinned. 'Personally, I think you've earned a large one.'

Christie didn't argue.

The bar was busy, but Dom found them a small table tucked away in an alcove, then went to get the drinks. Christie was just settling back and enjoying the welcoming, comfortable atmosphere, when she heard a familiar voice.

At the other side of the bar, on a seat facing out towards the gardens, was Delphi. Christie couldn't see her companion, as their seat was obscured by the bar. Delphi was speaking in a stage whisper, gesturing theatrically.

Christie strained to hear what was being said. It was most frustrating that she only caught one side of the conversation. Then she clearly heard Delphi whine, 'It's a wonderful gesture and I'd love it more than anything, but how can I?'

There was another gap in which her unknown partner had obviously worsened Delphi's dilemma.

'Oh, that's not really true. He would if he could, but it's so difficult. There are other things that have to take precedence.'

Delphi had swung round and was now facing the bar.

Wishing to continue eavesdropping unseen, Christie sat further back in her seat and turned away from them. After a while, the contentious topic must have been dropped because Delphi's voice resumed a conversational tone, and Christie only caught the odd word after that.

Whoever this man was, it wasn't Denis, the husband. Yet Delphi had seemed so sincere when she'd said she'd never mess around that Christie was totally intrigued. She didn't even consider that this other person might be a woman. Delphi's tone betrayed intimacy, a sharing of secrets, clandestine gossip. So it came as something of a shock when Gina Spearman stood up and went to the bar to pay and collect Delphi's jacket from the coat rack.

She passed Christie's table without noticing her. Sunk low in her chair, Christie saw a look on her face that combined amusement, concentration and malice. It didn't make for a nice expression.

Gina returned with the jackets, now charming and benevolent once more. She bestowed a radiant, friendly smile on Delphi, held the door open for her and followed her out into the night.

'You okay?' Dominic was standing in front of her, placing their glasses on the table.

She hadn't heard him arrive.

'You look as if you've seen a ghost. You haven't been reading more accounts of devilish lights on the Fens, have you?' He grinned.

She laughed. 'I'm not sure what I've seen, but it's none of my business anyway. I must stop being so nosy.'

Dom phoned Pip and asked her to join them, but she said that she was cooking for the next day and they should not worry, just enjoy themselves. They sat drinking until late.

Dom walked her home and laughed as she fumbled with her key. Christie told herself she really shouldn't drink so much.

Inside, she made her way very carefully up the stairs and sank into bed. But when she thought of Gina's face as she passed in front of her, she became stone-cold sober in an instant. After that, sleep was a long time coming.

CHAPTER FOURTEEN

Life at Cannon Farm had returned to normal now that Christie was no longer there. Liz had turned to assisting Matt in his search on behalf of Charley Anders, and had to admit that she was starting to feel the buzz herself. They had already produced a report on Paul Redman, detailing his activities and behaviour patterns from the time of Lindsay's death up to the present day. Liz was surprised he even managed to function, let alone go to work each day. He was a mess. He remained eaten up by his belief in the existence of another man in Lindsay's life and that this man had killed her. So far, they had found no actual evidence to support his claim. On more than one occasion, she and Matt had discussed Paul Redman well into the night, but they could never arrive at a conclusion. Had Paul conjured up this fictional figure to justify Lindsay's departure? It was possible that this unknown man was real, but equally possible that Paul couldn't face the truth that she didn't love him anymore and had invented him.

Liz closed the site she had been looking at and accessed Duncan Hartland's "Justice for Lindsay" page. She skimmed through it, as she did on a daily basis. He certainly wasn't giving up. New posts appeared with monotonous regularity, each one yet another string of vitriolic accusations against the police for their incompetence. He was a pain in the arse, but so far they'd not managed to find anything actually criminal about his activities on or off the web. She was anxious to have a talk with Paula Harrison, Lindsay's sister, whom Duncan Hartland apparently lusted after, but Paula was away on a course and wasn't due back for another two days.

Fed up with reading through the endless stream of insults, she closed the site and stood up. Matt would be home soon, after another "chat" with the unfortunate Paul Redman. The young man now spent every spare moment trying to find proof that Lindsay had been seeing someone else. Then, even if a "lead" he discovered was highly improbable, he would ring Matt and beg to see him. It was wearing, but she and Matt had agreed to follow up even the most tenuous tip-off, because any one of them could produce a murder suspect.

She wandered into the kitchen and filled the kettle. She had been pounding the keyboard for two hours and needed a shot of caffeine. As she got out the coffee, her mobile phone rang. It was Christie.

'They've taken Auden off the respirator. He's breathing!'

'Oh, that's fantastic news!' Liz said. 'You must be so relieved.'

'Oh, am I just!' Christie sounded absolutely delighted. 'Richard has been at the hospital with him. He said there've been brief moments of consciousness and, best of all, he responded to Richard's voice at one point. He said the doctors are now "cautiously optimistic" that Auden will make a pretty good recovery. The downside is that it will take time, a long time.'

'So, are you off up to Yorkshire?' Liz asked.

'Not immediately. I'll go when Auden's a bit better. My old neighbour is keeping an eye on my house for me. I dropped in on her last week, and she's happy to keep it aired and to forward my post.' Christie laughed. 'She's been doing it for years now, ever since I started working for Auden, so it's nothing new. She's in her eighties and says it gives her life a bit of purpose.'

'How is Richard coping?' Liz asked.

'He's over the moon that Auden recognised him. Richard doesn't care how long it takes, just so long as he has Auden back. He'll always be there for him. At least the house is already equipped for disabled living and the hospital are going to arrange nursing assistance for Richard. He's confident that he'll cope.'

'So we'll have you for a bit longer,' Liz was pleased. It was good to have her cousin close by.

'My job is on hold, Liz, and it could be for quite a while. Ian is happy for me to stay here for as long as it takes, so, yes, I'm a temporary fixture on the Fens, if you know what I mean.'

'Good! Then come to supper tomorrow night. We'll celebrate.'

'Well, actually, I was wondering if you and Matt would like to come here for dinner. Matt hasn't seen the cottage yet and I'd love to cook for the two of you — you've been so kind to me.' Christie sounded quite excited at the prospect of entertaining guests.

'Matt will be back any minute and, as long as he hasn't planned any work, we'd love to. You're really happy there, aren't you?'

There was a pause, then Christie said, 'It's strange, but I feel more at home here than I've ever felt in my own place. This tiny cottage and that glorious garden feel, well, so positive. The house and garden both seem to draw every ounce of negativity out of me. I feel totally at peace.'

Liz giggled. 'Have you been on the wacky baccy? Don't get too chilled, you'll fall over!'

'I know I'm going to miss this place when I do leave. Still, I've had a bit of a reprieve and I can stop worrying that I'll never see Auden again, so all is good. Seven o'clock tomorrow suit you?' Christie asked.

'Sounds great. If anything changes, I'll ring immediately after Matt gets in. Otherwise, see you then.' She ended the call and finished making her coffee, but before she could drink it, the house phone rang.

'Can I speak to Matt Ballard, please?'

'He'll be back shortly. Can I take a message?'

'Tell him it's his mate, Jim Smith. He's got my number. I've got a bit of info for him.'

Liz wrote the name down. 'Is it about Paul Redman, by any chance?' she asked. 'I'm Matt's partner, Liz. Matt told me about you and how you played rugby together.'

'Oh, right. Well, yes, it is. Could you tell him I reckon flaky Paul was right about his bird seeing another bloke? I'm only part-time at David Watkins Glass. The rest of the week I work for a big houseplant importer over Spalding way. Well, I was delivering a vanload of plants to this garden centre earlier today and it turned out to be the one that Lindsay Harrison used to work in.'

Liz wondered what was coming next. They had already visited the garden centre but had had no joy. 'Go on.'

'I've got a friend who works there, so I had a bit of a word. He gave me a name, a girl who also worked there but left just after Lindsay was murdered. My mate reckons she knew more than she let on to the police.' Jim gave a little sniff. 'Could be a red herring, Liz, but my mate was certain this lass was frightened because of what she knew. Worth a check, in't it?'

'Absolutely. I'll pass all this on to Matt and get him to ring you straightaway. And thanks, Jim, this could be the lead we've been looking for.'

Matt arrived home ten minutes later, looking grim following another less than productive conversation with Paul Redman. Considerably cheered by her news, he grabbed the phone and called Jim back. Soon, they had the name. No address, but Jim was able to tell him where she worked.

'Sandy Giles,' said Matt, with a grin. 'Works for Lucas and Sons Garden Centre on the Saltern Road, about three miles outside Fenfleet. Fancy a trip to choose a new plant for the garden?'

'Why not? And they have a nice restaurant, so you can buy me lunch,' she said.

'Deal. Get your bonnet on.'

* * *

Christie's earlier upbeat mood rather evaporated when she noticed Evelyn's appointments calendar still up on the kitchen wall. It was one of those long narrow ones, showing a month a page.

It seemed so sad. She ran her finger down the days and their activities. The dentist. Tea with MP. Coffee morning at the church, change the water filter, mobile library . . . Tasks she would never attend to, rendezvous she would never keep.

Her phone rang, breaking into her sad thoughts. She was surprised to hear Jane Waterhouse's voice, asking if she happened to have lost a rather nice fountain pen. Christie checked her bag. No pen.

'Jane, yes, it seems I have mislaid mine. It's a vintage pen, dark green with a gold nib and has black ink in it.'

'That's a relief. It's definitely yours, then. I found it underneath the counter and had no idea when or how it got there. If you are passing, do call in and collect it.'

'It would be a pleasure, Jane. In fact, I'll drive over right now. I can't believe I hadn't missed it before.' Christie was cross with herself. The pen had been a present from Auden after her first completed research assignment. It was precious to her and she used it whenever she could. It was over a fortnight since she'd bought the picture, but a lot had happened in that time. She decided that was probably the reason, and not early onset Alzheimer's.

Jane welcomed her in and went to fetch the pen. While she waited, Christie noticed some new pictures on the walls and went over to take a closer look.

She stood contemplating a study of moss, ivy and lichen on an ancient, crumbling stone wall. If she stayed here too long, she thought, she was in danger of spending an awful lot of money. Every painting spoke to her, and she wanted them all.

Jane floated back to her carrying the treasured Parker. Christie put it in her bag and thanked the artist for taking the trouble to call her. She then asked if she could have another look at the painting in the alcove.

It seemed to take Jane a moment to think which one she was referring to. With a slightly uncomfortable look, she told Christie it had gone.

Her sense of almost profound loss took Christie by surprise. She recalled thinking of making Jane an offer for it, and then dismissing the thought. She congratulated Jane on the sale, saying it was a wonderful piece of work and deserved to be sold.

Jane looked embarrassed. 'Well, er, I didn't actually sell it. Gina Spearman — remember her? Well, she asked me for it.' She shrugged. 'It was intended for her in the first place, and she does own Tadema House. She collected it yesterday.'

This sounded a little defensive to Christie, who now felt angry as well as disappointed. The disappointment she could understand, but the anger was something else.

'I told her how much you liked it,' Jane was saying, 'and how you'd mentioned that watercolour was the perfect medium for the subject and the light. She seemed to see it with different eyes after that. She apologised to me and said she shouldn't be so blinkered about her preferences so, if it was still on offer, she would love to have it. So, at last it's gone where I intended it to. I should thank you. She obviously hadn't seen its worth until I told her what you'd said.'

What a load of bullshit. Christie hastily thanked her again for the pen, made her excuses and turned to leave.

Jane asked where she was staying. When Christie told her, she exclaimed, 'I can't believe it! Then you have to see this before you go.'

Jane pulled a cloth off an easel to reveal . . . the garden at The Mulberries. Her anger forgotten, Christie stood with her mouth open, gazing at the painting. A blaze of different

145

colours lit in shafts of evening sunlight. The black iron pump, the sundial, the profusion of mismatched plants. She thought of Ian and immediately told Jane that she had to have it. He had spent the last week committing the place and his shared past with his sister to memory. This painting was perfect for him. Jane had captured more than a pretty garden lit by the last rays of the sun. She had captured the essence of the woman herself, the creator of the original work of art — the garden.

Jane reached out and laid her soft, slender fingers on Christie's arm. Perhaps she had seen the moisture in her eyes. 'Were you a close friend of Miss Hardy's?'

Christie didn't know what to say. How could she say that she had met her once, briefly, but felt a strange affinity with her because of her brother and her cottage? She gathered herself and said, 'I'm a friend of her brother, Ian Hardy's. That's why I'm staying at The Mulberries.'

'I see. Then I'd love you to buy the picture, but can I ask you a favour? I am having an exhibition here next Wednesday. May I keep it until then? It was my main exhibit. Oh, and please come along, won't you? You can take it at the end of the evening. You're becoming one of my best clients!'

Christie had an urge to grab it and run to her car with it. She wanted Ian to have it now, today. Instead, she said that of course she'd love to attend the show and take it with her afterwards.

Christie left the studio. Outside, she realised that she hadn't even asked the price.

* * *

Sandy Giles worked in the gift section of the garden centre. It hadn't taken too much detecting to work that one out, as all the staff wore name badges. Matt let Liz take the lead. She was to try a friendly opener, reveal that they were private detectives — not the police — and ask for her help.

When they got to the counter, a couple of the other staff were talking animatedly but Sandy wasn't joining in the general banter. She was a thin, mousy-haired young woman, who appeared to be a quiet sort, unassuming and rather serious.

Liz had chosen a box containing a William Morris design china mug and coaster that she thought would look lovely in Christie's bedroom at The Mulberries.

'That will be £14.99, please,' said Sandy Giles.

Liz took out her credit card, then looked at her curiously. 'I know you from somewhere, don't I?' she asked casually.

Sandy stared at her blankly. 'Sorry, but I don't . . .'

'Oh yes! You were at Rowantrees, weren't you? In the garden centre. I used to go there a lot before we moved. So, do you like it here?'

Sandy looked anxious. 'I'm sorry I didn't recognise you but I, er, wasn't there long.' She gave a dismissive shrug, almost shoved the box into a bag and pushed it towards Liz. 'Put your card into the machine, please, or use contactless.'

'The thing is, Sandy,' Liz pushed her card into the reader and tapped in her PIN number, 'we need to talk to you about Lindsay Harrison.' She handed the girl her business card, which stated that she was a registered private investigator.

Sandy Giles looked horrified.

'It's okay,' said Liz softly. 'Nothing heavy, just a chat. Can you take a few minutes to talk to us? We'll buy you a coffee if you like?'

The girl shook her head vehemently. 'No, no, I can't! I don't want to talk to you at all. Please, take your purchase and go. I've nothing to say to you.'

Matt leaned forward and whispered, 'Have you any idea how bad this looks, Sandy? People who protest as much as you usually have something to hide, wouldn't you say?'

She threw him an icy glare. 'Just leave.' She pushed Liz's receipt into the bag, thrust it at her and turned away.

'That went well,' he murmured to Liz.

'Think about it, Sandy,' said Liz, in a loud voice. 'Because we'll be back.' As they left, she glanced back and saw Sandy standing at the rear of the till area talking urgently on her mobile. Her face was twisted in anxiety. 'Not quite the reception I visualised.'

Matt shook his head. 'It's at times like this that I miss my warrant card. It would be nice to be able to assert a little pressure and suggest a trip to the station.'

'Since that's no longer an option, we need to be canny. Suppose we come back at closing time? Maybe she'll be inclined to be reasonable away from her workmates. She was getting a few funny looks while we were speaking to her.'

They wandered around for a while and then went to the restaurant for lunch. It was tempting to go back and try to reason with Sandy, but the last thing they wanted to do was cause a scene. They decided instead to go home and regroup.

Matt unlocked the car. Just as they were getting in, a battered-looking van squealed to a halt, blocking their exit.

'What the . . . ?' exclaimed Matt.

The driver threw open his door and strode up to Matt, stopping inches away from him. 'Dunno what your game is, pal, but I suggest you leave my sister alone.'

Matt stood his ground. He remained silent, seeming to grow in height.

'D'you hear me?' The young man took a step forward, but Matt laid his hand on his chest.

'I hear you all right, son. Now, you listen to me. We are private investigators, working with the Fenland Constabulary on the murder of Lindsay Harrison. We are interviewing anyone who knew or worked with Lindsay at the time of her death. Your sister falls into that category. You got a problem with that?'

'She's got nothing to tell you. Just leave her alone, will you?' He took a step back.

Liz moved around the car and stood next to the man. 'I'm sorry if you're worried about your sister, but it would be better if she talked to us, because otherwise the police will have to do it. Formally. Understand?'

'But she's got nothing to say. Can't you just talk to someone else?'

'She does have something to say, and you bloody well know it,' Matt retorted, then added, a little more gently, 'What's your name, lad?'

'Tony. Tony Giles.' He seemed to relent. 'All right. She *can't* say. All right? And that's all I'm saying.'

Matt glanced at Liz. 'Someone threatened her?'

Tony looked thoroughly miserable. 'What do you think? Look, for God's sake don't tell her I told you this. She's kept it secret since it happened, but she's getting ill over it, it's eating away at her. Tell you what, if I can convince her to talk to you — just you two, not the rozzers, understand —if, and I only say if, I can get her to let it all go, can you keep it to yourselves?'

It would be their best chance of getting to the truth. 'We aren't with the police,' Liz said carefully. 'We're helping them. We'll treat whatever you tell us with respect, I swear.' This was suitably vague, she hoped.

Tony couldn't seem to decide. He looked down, shuffled his feet, muttered to himself. Finally, he said, 'Look, I'm picking her up when she finishes. I'll talk to her and ring you if I manage to talk her round.' He looked at Liz, his gaze now imploring, almost humble. 'I'm really worried about her. Do you think speaking to you will help? Or will it make it worse?'

'I can't say, Tony. We don't know the circumstances. But I reckon the best thing for her would be to talk about it.' She reached out and touched his arm. 'I think you'll be doing the right thing.'

He sighed. 'Okay, I'll do my best.'

She handed him a card. 'Here's our number, Tony. We live on Tanners Fen, you can bring her to us or we'll come to you, or we'll meet you somewhere, whatever Sandy prefers. It's her choice.'

He took the card and nodded. 'I'll ring you if she agrees.' He turned and climbed back into his van, suddenly looking much older.

'Poor guy,' said Matt. 'He's in a real dilemma, isn't he?'

'Let's just hope he gets through to her. That girl and what she knows could be the key to this whole case, couldn't it?'

Matt nodded slowly. 'It certainly could. Now we just have to wait.'

CHAPTER FIFTEEN

Having finished lunch, Christie wondered what to do with the rest of her day. In the blink of an eye, she seemed to have gone from being frantically busy to having time, lots of it, on her hands. Her research was done, Ian was sorted, all the moving and packing was finished. Christie wasn't used to having so many empty hours. She thumbed through the local free paper and saw that there was an open-air art exhibition in the market square that afternoon. She had never been a person who visited art galleries, but since seeing Jane Waterhouse's work, she had begun to take an interest. She decided to go. It would be something to pass the time.

In the sunshine the market square resembled the streets of Montmartre, though the exhibitors were rather more restrained. Christie strolled around for half an hour or so but saw nothing that approached the quality of Jane Waterhouse's work.

'So, nothing tempted you? Not quite up to the standard of our Jane's efforts, eh?'

Christie waved her holiday mood goodbye. 'Well, there's nothing here that's in her league, yes.'

Gina kicked at a tuft of grass that had fought its way through a broken paving slab. 'True, she *is* good, though I find her paintings can be a bit like her — wispy and a bit insipid.'

'Not everyone wants powerful paintings — or powerful people, for that matter. A hint, an allusion, a suggestion, can be just as effective as a blow on the head.'

Surprisingly, Gina made no comment. She continued flattening the presumptuous clump of grass.

Christie was about to invent an imminent appointment when she was favoured with a wide smile. An arm linked through hers.

'Come on, I'll buy you a coffee. I know a place that does a wicked espresso,' Gina said. 'We haven't had a chance to have a proper talk yet.'

Before she could open her mouth, Christie was whisked into a rather plush lounge bar, propelled towards a thickly upholstered chair and left sitting, somewhat breathless, while Gina went to the bar to order coffee.

Thrusting a handful of notes and change into the back pocket of her jeans, Gina flopped into a chair opposite Christie and treated her to another puckish smile. She wore a rugby shirt, denims and soft leather boat shoes. Her hair was done in its usual chic, boyish style. The whole ensemble looked costly. It suited her.

Christie wanted to be anywhere else but here. She kept thinking about Gina's sudden change of heart concerning the painting of Tadema House. The coffee arrived and Christie drank it quickly, planning on making a swift exit.

'I think Tom fancies you.'

Christie choked.

The ghost of a smile briefly flickered across Gina's expression, to be replaced by consternation. 'Dear me! I am sorry. Was that my fault?'

Still coughing, Christie was unable to respond.

'No, really,' Gina said. 'He's always talking about you at work. I think he'd like to ask you out but he's very shy, you know.'

Christie was finding it hard to breathe. How dare she! Poor Tom was eating his heart out over Gina, and well she knew it.

But she wasn't going to give Gina the benefit of seeing that her barb had struck home, so she merely said — once she could speak again — that she was sure Gina was mistaken.

Gina gave Christie one of her *Oh, have it your way, but I know better* smiles and changed the subject.

She enquired about Christie's work and what it entailed. Despite herself, Christie found she had become engaged in an intense discussion about literature. Gina proved to be well educated and very well read, and Christie became totally absorbed.

Then, Gina began to shift around in her chair, tear tiny pieces from the edge of a beer mat and pick at a fingernail. Like the jack-o'-lantern, her enthusiasm seemed to flare, burn brightly for a brief spell and fade equally as quickly. Seeing how bored she so suddenly appeared to be, Christie made her excuses and left.

As she walked back to the square, she glanced back and saw Gina standing motionless at the door to the café, staring after her. She neither waved, nor acknowledged her look. She remained standing for a few moments and then turned on her heel and strode off in the direction of the Reading Room.

Christie returned to her car and sat behind the wheel, going over the last hour. She had been treated to an insight as to why Tom, Delphi and Jane all behaved as they did toward Gina. Christie had always considered herself to be independent and strong-minded, yet she had been forced to act according to Gina's whim three times in less than an hour.

She counted those times. Gina had instigated an exchange of words when Christie hadn't even wanted to speak to her. Gina had shepherded her into a pub when she'd had no intention of drinking coffee with her. And finally, Gina had engaged her fully in a conversation that she hadn't wanted to have.

Christie McFerran had been manipulated, picked up and dropped like the toys they all seemed to be. She swore that next time, she'd be ready for her.

But wait. Wasn't she entering into the game? It would make her no better than Gina. She thought of Evelyn, of Auden. Neither would have stooped to such behaviour. They would have considered it trivial. Which it was.

She drove slowly back to The Mulberries, where she went into the sitting room, fished behind the couch and brought out Jane Waterhouse's painting of the fen. It was still carefully wrapped. She had intended to leave it that way until she got it safely home. Now, she decided to hang it where she could appreciate it until her return to Scarborough.

She looked around and saw, on the wall facing the window, a picture-hook. It had been painted over in an attempt to conceal it without removing it in case the old plaster crumbled. It seemed firm when she tested it and the space and light were perfect.

Doing her best to save the packaging, she unwrapped her prize and carefully hooked it onto the pin. The peace of the scene, its watery tranquillity, suited the room. How on earth could Gina belittle the work of such an observant and sensitive artist? So she didn't use oils. She thought again of Turner's watercolours.

She had to stop thinking of Gina. She stared out of the French window and saw at once how to clear her mind. She had promised Ian she would care for the cottage, which should mean caring for Evelyn's precious plants as well. A couple of hours with her hands in the rich Lincolnshire soil was the perfect solution.

Absorbed in her labours, she stayed out well into the evening. After a hearty meal, she sat on the garden bench with a large glass of cold Sancerre and waited for the moment Jane Waterhouse had captured so well, that last burst of golden sunlight that picks out each individual tone and hue and imbues it with brilliance. A final surge of strength that flares up and blinds you with its radiance before the evening brings the shades and subtleties that steal and fade the colours, turning them eventually to grey.

It never came. As so often happens in that part of the county, the turning tides brought nothing but cloud. As if mocking her, they deprived the moment of its glory. Still, Jane's picture remained.

Cheated of her glorious finale, Christie went inside and poured herself another drink.

She started at the sound of the doorbell. Who could be calling on her tonight? Ian?

To her surprise and delight, Tom stood on the doorstep, grinning broadly.

'I see you've embraced rural life to the full.'

She suddenly realised that she was still wearing her oldest jeans and T-shirt, both smeared with muddy soil. Her mud-caked wellington boots stood beside the door. She was not looking her best, to say the least. She threw the door open. 'Would you like a glass of wine?' At the back of her mind, she heard Gina saying, "I think Tom fancies you."

She hurried through to the kitchen to find another glass. When she returned, he was wandering around the sitting room, looking appreciatively at the contents.

'It's ages since I've been here. I used to bring Mother over to play Scrabble or cribbage with Evelyn but I always left her at the door. It's a beautiful little place, isn't it? Did you know it's over two hundred years old?'

'Yes, Ian told me a bit about it. It has a very good atmosphere.' Despite the chat, she felt constrained in his presence, which she hadn't before. Christie found herself watching him, noting his reactions to what she said and asking herself, what if . . . ? No matter how often she told herself not to be so bloody stupid, Gina had planted an idea in her head, and she couldn't get rid of it.

She handed him a glass of wine and asked whether he had just called by to make fun of her new rural wardrobe, or whether there'd been a particular reason for his visit.

He laughed and said that despite indeed enjoying the sight of Miss McFerran in wellies, he had actually been sent by his mother to invite her and the Reverend Hardy, if he were free, to tea on Thursday.

Christie was pleased. Her social calendar was filling up nicely.

She noted that Tom seemed so much more relaxed than he had at the funeral and she was relieved to hear him once again speaking fondly of his mother.

'Word of warning, though. Should there be coconut pyramids in the selection of dainty cakes, avoid them like the plague. I don't know what she does to them, but good manners aren't worth the indigestion. They sit in your stomach like a breeze block and probably have about as much flavour.'

She burst out laughing. 'So which of the home-baked goodies is safest?'

'Oh, all the rest are delicious, it's just those coconut things that never work out.'

She promised to give them a miss and said she would love to see his mother again. She was sure Ian would also be delighted to come but she would ask him tomorrow and ring Tom at the shop to confirm.

'Great. Mother will be delighted. Hey, I hear you're going to Jane's exhibition on Wednesday. I'll go along as soon as the shop shuts, so I'll see you there.' He glanced up at the newly hung picture. 'Oh yes. Very nice indeed. I thought it must be this one. Gina told me you'd bought it.'

With a jolt of irritation at the sound of that name, she said, 'Jane is very talented. If I had a lot of money, I would fill my home with her work.'

'Gina believes you're heading that way already. First this one, then the main exhibit at her show. Mind you, she painted that here, didn't she? I've not seen it yet. Is it good?'

'It's beautiful, Tom. I've bought it for Ian, as a memento of his sister's beloved garden.'

'That's a generous gesture, Christie. You really like Ian, don't you?'

Was there a hint of jealousy in his voice? *For God's sake, woman.* She replied that she was very fond of him, he reminded her of her grandfather and he was excellent company. Plus, since he had allowed her to stay in The Mulberries at no charge, it was the least she could do to say thank you.

'It's still a lovely thought. I'm sure he'll be absolutely delighted with it.'

'Well, it is remarkable.'

She was very close to telling Tom about her meeting with his boss that morning and what she'd said about him, but sensibly held back. She knew that whatever she said, Gina was more than capable of twisting every word.

To change the subject, she told him a bit about the garden and was surprised to find that he was extremely knowledgeable about plants — he even knew their Latin names. When she commented on this, he laughed and said, 'I have Mother to thank for that. While other kids were saying "A for apple, B for bear, C for cat," I was being taught "A for aster, B for begonia, C for clematis."' He glanced at his watch. 'Oops! I have to go, Christie. I promised Mother I'd be back in time to record some old film for her. Thanks for the wine. Mother will be really pleased about Thursday.' He stood up. 'And I'll see you in Herring Lane on Wednesday evening, if not before. You never know, you might develop a yen for a seedy novel or a copy of *Whitaker's Almanac*.'

'Or one of Delphi's Bath buns,' Christie added.

'Exactly!' He waved as he got into his car and called back, 'And warn the vicar about the coconut pyramids!'

The engine of his shiny blue Peugeot purred into life and he drove away, carefully negotiating the potholes and tyre tracks along the lane.

She watched him until the rear lights of his car disappeared into the night. For Margaret's sake, she was mighty relieved to see the old Tom resurrected. Happy for herself too. She liked his friendly company and was glad he was back to normal. With a goodnight to the garden, she closed the door. The day had ended well, after all.

CHAPTER SIXTEEN

Somehow, Tony Giles had talked his reluctant sister into meeting with Matt and Liz. He rang, as promised, and they arranged to go to his small terraced house in Fenfleet.

The street was narrow, flanked with cramped houses with tiny front gardens and no garages. There was nowhere to park.

'Bet it's a right bun fight when everyone gets home,' muttered Matt, hunting for a space.

'I'd pull into Gibbs Lane if I were you,' suggested Liz. 'We can walk from there. There's usually spaces along by the recreation ground.' They finally found a gap in a long line of cars parked up for the night.

The sparsely furnished house was obviously a rental property, with the usual lack of maintenance. Matt's eyes kept being drawn to a large damp patch in the corner of the living room ceiling that must get to twice that size in wet weather.

Initially, Sandy Giles was taciturn and suspicious but after a while — and considerable effort on both their parts — she began to relax a little. Her brother was supportive and surprisingly gentle with her, calmly encouraging her to open up about what had occurred.

'We were friends, Lindsay and me,' she began. 'We worked in different departments but we met up in our breaks and sometimes had a drink together after work.'

Sandy directed all this to her feet, not once looking up. Matt decided that this made it easier for her, as if she was telling the story to herself.

'She was a lively girl, very pretty and well-liked. Lots of the lads at Rowantrees asked her out but she was happy with her boyfriend. Not that they all gave up.' Sandy sighed loudly. 'Then, about a month before she died, she told me she was feeling trapped in her relationship with her boyfriend, Paul Redman.'

For the first time, she looked up and her gaze fell upon her brother. 'I just didn't understand it. For months she had talked of nothing but how happy she was and how they hoped to marry as soon as Paul had saved a bit more money. She adored him. She'd even chosen a wedding dress, though she hadn't told Paul.'

She lapsed into silence.

'But you did find out why, didn't you, Sandy?' coaxed Tony.

She lowered her head again. 'We were having a coffee in the cafeteria and she accidentally kicked her bag over. Everything fell out. I helped her pick it all up and something had slid under my chair. It was a card, with hearts and flowers on it. It had fallen open, and I saw it just had a large X on it and underneath, another name, not Paul's. She grabbed it from me before I could make out what it said. She said it was just Paul, trying to make up after a row, but although I couldn't see the name clearly, I knew it wasn't his.'

She was silent again. Tony came to the rescue. 'That was the first of several things, wasn't it, sis? And then she told you she was going to split up with him.'

Sandy nodded.

'What else happened, Sandy?' asked Liz softly.

'Flowers arrived. Then chocolates and other gifts. She hid everything away so quickly that no one except me really noticed.' She gave a bitter laugh, the first time she'd shown any sort of emotion. 'She tried to tell me it was Paul, desperate to get her to change her mind. The others all believed her, but I knew she had a secret admirer, I just knew it. Then one evening, just as I was leaving, I saw her in the car park, sitting in a strange car with another man. They were sitting close and laughing. I sneaked away, hoping they hadn't seen me, but I think he did, because suddenly, he drove off, really fast.' She stared directly at Liz. 'The next night she was murdered.'

Matt was puzzled. 'That's awful, Sandy. It must have been a terrible time for you. But why didn't you tell the police? There was nothing to be frightened of, surely? You hadn't done anything wrong.'

She looked at him, her eyes huge, her expression scared. 'Because the day after the murder, I had the first phone call. It was on my mobile. They said that if I told anyone what I knew about Lindsay, the same thing would happen to me.'

The words hung in the air. So that was it, the reason for her four-year-long silence.

'And the calls continued?' asked Liz.

'Oh yes, regularly. In the end I changed my mobile number, but the calls started to come in on the house phone.' She swallowed. 'I had a nice little flat at the time. I had the phone cut off.' Tears welled up in her eyes. 'Then they came by letter, to Rowantrees.' She shook her head and wiped her eyes with the back of her hand. 'So I left the job that I loved, but they still didn't stop. They came through the door at home, nasty little notes. In the end, I couldn't cope anymore, so I moved in here with Tony.'

'And they finally stopped,' Tony finished. 'But by then the damage was done.'

Matt could believe it. No wonder the girl hadn't spoken out all these years.

For a long moment, no one spoke. Liz said, 'Did you keep any of the notes, Sandy?'

The girl shook her head. 'I destroyed them as soon as I got them.'

Matt understood that too. Sandy Giles was being terrorised by a killer. She would not have been capable of trying to plan any counter-attack or defend herself against this dangerous individual. 'Was it always a man's voice, on the phone?' he asked.

'Yes, I'm sure it was. But it was kind of soft. He didn't shout or be gruff but I think that was worse, because he sounded, like, really quiet and intimidating.'

Matt saw that her hands were shaking. He was suddenly concerned about the psychological damage this had done to the girl. She needed professional help. But would he be turning this interview, which might have been cathartic for her, into even more of a problem? He glanced at Liz. The girl had had enough.

Liz smiled gently at Sandy. 'You've been very brave, Sandy. We'll leave it there. Thank you for talking to us.' She turned to Tony. 'You have our number. Please, just ring if we can help or if anything else comes to mind that might be important.'

They stood up, thanked them both again and left. They walked in silence back to the car and, once inside, Liz said, 'So, there really was another man. Paul Redman was right.'

'And from those threats, it sounds like he's also right about him being her killer.'

* * *

Christie was ready for bed, happily tired after her gardening efforts. She had the feeling that Evelyn would approve, even if her skills were somewhat limited.

She went downstairs to check that all the windows and doors were locked. It was probably unnecessary here, but she felt responsible for the place. As she approached the front door, there was a gentle tap on it, and someone called her name.

'Christie! It's me, Tom.'

She opened the door to find a worried-looking Tom with a tear-stained Delphi clinging to him.

161

She ushered the pair into the sitting room and sat Delphi down on the couch. She offered them both a brandy. Delphi nodded furiously but Tom declined, waving his car keys at her. 'I daren't. Look, I'm really sorry about this, Christie, but I couldn't think of where else to go. Mother is a light sleeper, and I didn't want her to start asking questions. Jane is out. We went to the shop — I have the keys, I thought we could talk there, but we could see a light on in Gina's office. You were the only other person I could think of.'

She assured him that it wasn't a problem. Delphi was sobbing. Christie offered Tom a hot drink and pressed a glass of brandy into the shaking girl's hands.

When she came back with the coffee, Tom said quietly, 'She's had a barney with Denis. He's told her to bugger off and not to go home until she's back to the Delphi he married.'

'Whatever did she do? She told me she loves him to pieces.'

'She does. It's just that, well, it's difficult . . .'

Christie recalled Delphi and Gina's conversation at the Coach House bar, and was convinced that it was his wife's employer that had upset Denis so badly.

Tom sat on the couch and put a reassuring arm round Delphi's shoulder. Christie pulled up a chair and waited. It took a while and much blowing of the nose and swallowing, but finally, she emitted a plaintive wail. 'We never argue, never! But he . . . he's been so unfair! So,' she swallowed again, 'so awful to me!'

Apparently, it all started when Delphi had complained that she hadn't had a proper holiday in years. It hadn't bothered her until recently. She knew Denis couldn't afford more than a few days at Skeggie and that he would have taken her anywhere she wanted if he only had the resources, but it didn't make any difference. Gina had just had a glorious vacation somewhere tropical and had returned with exotic gifts for the staff. Her accounts of the glorious weather, the clear blue seas, the lavish hotels and fabulous food unsettled them all for weeks.

Delphi had been more upset than anyone. Poor Delphi dreamed of Greece. She had been named after a sacred site once considered to be the centre of the world, and she badly wanted to see it. Obsessed with the place, she pestered Denis to do more and more overtime and even took on an extra evening job herself, cleaning for a local dental surgery.

'It wasn't one-sided. I worked as hard as him. I deserved a good holiday, didn't I?' She looked imploringly from Christie to Tom.

'Everyone deserves a holiday once in a while,' Christie said cautiously. 'But if money is a problem, there are other things that have to come first.' She thought of her globe-trotting childhood and felt guilty.

'Well, this time money isn't a problem. I've been offered a free holiday — all I needed was my spending money. But Denis has gone ballistic.'

So that was what the meeting in the bar had been about. Gina undermining Denis. She was providing the holiday for Delphi that he couldn't. But why? Was she really prepared to spend all that cash on taking Delphi away just to get at her husband? Delphi was sweet, but hardly a match for the whip-smart Gina. The thought of the two of them alone together for a fortnight made for an interesting picture. Christie could only think that Gina would be bored out of her skull within the first few hours and probably be at Delphi's throat by nightfall.

'How can he deny me the chance of a lifetime? It was so generous of Gina. She was going anyway, of course, but the friend who was supposed to join her dropped out. She's taking a flight to Athens, having a few days in central Greece to see Mount Parnassus, the site of the Delphic Oracle, then on to an island for the rest of the holiday. Oh . . .' Her voice trailed away into a sigh. 'I'll never forgive him if he won't let me go.'

Christie laid a hand on Delphi's and tried to get her to see the situation from Denis's point of view.

'You know what men are like — sorry, Tom. He probably feels that he has failed as a husband and a provider. I'm sure he does his best for you, he's probably just very hurt. His pride will have taken a nasty knock, especially if he's been working all hours to save up for something nice for you.'

'Oh, sure! And then the car will go wrong again, or the roof will need attention, or the telly will need replacing. There's always something. It'll be another bloody weekend at sodding Skegness, I know it.' She took a slurp of her brandy.

At least Gina wasn't able to see the fruit of her actions, Christie told herself. She'd have loved this scene. Christie asked Tom what he thought.

After a moment, he said, 'Well, Denis told me that in another six months he'd have saved enough money for a "good couple of weeks in the sun," so I imagine he would be pretty miffed. But I feel sorry for Gina too.'

Christie bit her tongue.

'She was so pleased about it. When her original travelling companion backed out, the first person she thought of was Delphi. She was looking forward to giving her a special treat.'

'Gina was the only person who really understood what going to Greece meant to me.' Delphi had stopped crying and her lips were puckered in a childish pout.

Tom concluded with, 'So it seems that through no fault of her own, Gina's gesture has resulted in an almighty mess.'

Christie reminded herself that she too had been taken in by Gina's manoeuvrings earlier that day. After a few moments' thought, she suggested Delphi ring Denis. He'd be worried about his wife, and no matter how angry he was, he wouldn't want to think of her wandering the streets at night.

Delphi declared that he could worry all he liked. She was never going home again. Tom raised his eyebrows at Christie, as if to say, "now, what?"

'Come on, Delphi. You don't mean that. You just need to talk this through sensibly with him.'

It took another fifteen minutes of cajoling before Delphi agreed to phone her husband. From what Christie overheard, he was upset and sorry for his harsh words. He immediately offered to come and pick her up. He duly arrived and they hugged each other tightly. Denis shook his head disbelievingly and said, like her, 'We never argue.'

Christie waved them off, both relieved and angry. Tom thanked her profusely, and wearily left The Mulberries for the second time that day.

Christie trudged up the stairs with a heavy heart. Oh, why couldn't Gina Spearman just go and settle on some Greek island and never be seen again?

CHAPTER SEVENTEEN

The following two days passed peacefully. Delphi apologised for inflicting her troubles on her, and Christie immersed herself in preparations for the meal with Liz and Matt. The evening was a great success. Matt was very impressed with the cottage and admired Jane's painting of the Fens. The more time she spent here, the more she realised that this was where she wanted to be. Tom called to rearrange their tea, as his mother had an unexpected hospital appointment. Fired by the success of her evening with Matt and Liz, she suggested that he bring Margaret to dinner at The Mulberries that evening with her and Ian. He sounded pleased, adding that it would spare them all from having to face the infamous coconut pyramids.

Now, on Wednesday evening, she was standing outside Jane Waterhouse's gallery, trying to muster the courage to walk in. It was only seven o'clock, but looming thunderclouds had made the evening prematurely dark. The narrow, dim cobblestone walkway of Herring Lane was lit up with bright lights, and soft music emanated from Waterhouse Gallery. Through the window, she saw smartly dressed viewers browsing the paintings, glasses in their hands. Christie noted the expensive crystal, took a deep breath and went in.

Jane floated between the guests. Red stickers were applied as paintings found buyers.

The painting of The Mulberries stood raised on a dais, dominating the room. Christie couldn't wait for the exhibition to close so that she could take it home for Ian.

She accepted a glass of white wine and saw Jane heading towards her, smiling warmly. 'I'm so glad you could make it.' She walked with a swish, in a full-length caftan in a deep, rich crimson made of some fine material that Christie couldn't identify. It complemented her long blonde hair. She resembled a magical creature, a high priestess or a fairy queen.

Christie thanked Jane for inviting her and said how excited she was to be taking possession of the painting of Evelyn's garden.

'I am delighted that it is going back to the place where it originated, even if only for a while. It seems right, don't you think?'

A young man in a smart suit and a ponytail was beckoning frantically from the other side of the room. Jane said that Gary, her assistant, was helping her with prospective buyers and must be close to a sale.

Christie made her way around the gallery, looking carefully at the paintings. The more she saw of Jane's work, the more it spoke to the way Christie herself saw the Fenlands but was unable to express.

She was lost in a study of poppies and feverfew growing in tangled profusion around a discarded tractor wheel when Gina and Tom arrived. For some reason, it hadn't even entered her head that Gina would be at the show.

Tom came over, smiling broadly. He helped himself to a glass of wine, saying he'd come on foot. 'Thank God! I thought we'd never get away from the shop. The till went wrong just as we were cashing up, then the computer failed to send my late order to the book wholesaler. Nightmare!' He took a long swallow and raised his glass to Jane who waved from across the gallery.

Gina had homed in on two rather elegant, middle-aged men and an overdressed woman, whom she obviously knew. They were enthusing over a dramatic skyscape.

'The Hammond brothers,' Tom whispered in Christie's ear. 'James and Lucas Hammond. And the woman, who frankly needs dressing before she leaves home, is James's wife, Abigail. Stinking rich. They own a huge country club on the outskirts of town, and rumour has it they are building an even bigger one out Spalding way. I have no idea where they get their members from. Most folk round here can barely afford to clothe themselves, let alone play squash and drink cocktails.'

Christie commented that they seemed very interested in Jane's larger watercolours. She decided to be polite to Gina if she ran into her, friendly and impersonal. She would not rise to her snide comments. She was just going over how else she would conduct herself when Tom decided they had to see the star of the show, the painting of Evelyn's garden.

'I think it is probably her best work yet. You were right about it, Christie. It is a beauty. He's a lucky vicar.' Tom paused. 'Oh, good, there's Sophie and Lars. Come and meet my neighbours from Friary Terrace.'

In the course of the next hour, he introduced her to a number of other people. She hadn't yet spoken to Gina.

The red stickers multiplied. Gary and Jane were apparently doing good business. By now, the conversation in the room had risen in volume, discreet laughter having given way to loud guffaws. Jane drifted around, apparently in a daze. Maybe she couldn't quite believe the reception her work was getting.

Christie looked again at the clock. Only another thirty minutes and she could claim Ian's gift and make her getaway.

Tom went to get a taxi for someone, and Christie found herself alone. Suddenly she was very tired. She found a seat and decided to sit the remainder of the evening out.

She heard one of the Hammond brothers laughing. Then there seemed to be a scuffle in the far corner of the room, followed by a shout of distress. Christie didn't know why, but she was suddenly terribly afraid. She knew she really ought to go and see what had happened but she couldn't summon the energy.

She heard people calling to one another amid the disorganised melee. Christie made out, 'Is she all right?' 'Whatever happened?' 'Oh, how awful!' 'Look!'

Her body weighed her down. She hauled herself from her seat and made her way across the room as if she were wading through molasses. Somehow, she knew what she was going to find.

Tom was pushing through the spectators to where Gina lay. She was "coming to," waving a feeble hand, asking what had happened. Beneath her lay Christie's painting. The frame was smashed and the picture . . . Beyond salvation. Red wine flowed across the flower beds. A shard of broken glass protruded from the sundial . . . Christie turned away.

But not before seeing a scene that would remain etched in her memory: Jane, her mouth open in a silent "o," her slender hands to her face. Gary staring with unconcealed horror at the destruction. Tom perched on one knee, as if he were proposing to Gina. And Gina herself. One hand raised to her forehead, the other reaching out to Tom. Most deeply engraved was the flash of triumph that passed across the prone Gina Spearman's face.

Christie drove home like an automaton. She unlocked the door and let herself in. That night even the cottage failed to work its magic.

She lay in bed and listened to the voice in her head. "A blackout, so unfortunate. Desperately sorry. Just collapsed, no warning whatsoever. Dreadful pity. It was such a wonderful painting. No, no, not the drink, just passed out, it was very warm, and I'm probably overworked or stressed. There was nothing I could do, you see, everything just went black, and I woke up on the floor . . ."

She knew it had been no accident. But how could someone be so vindictive? Why go to such lengths to hurt her?

And why did Gina hate her so much? They didn't even know each other. There was no history between them.

* * *

Thursday morning, Christie woke early. She took her tea and toast to the seat overlooking the garden and pondered the previous evening's tragic denouement in the cold light of day. Was it really not an accident? And why her visceral dislike of Gina, right from their first meeting? She, who had always prided herself on her ability to see the good in people.

And how had she become so involved so quickly with a collection of perfect strangers? Why the excessive interest in these people's lives?

Christie stared gloomily into the garden. And then there was the way she had left the gallery. Normally she would have stayed, found out exactly what had occurred, done all she could to help, brushed off the fact that the painting had been damaged and generally been considerate and practical. Instead, she had stormed out without a word to her hostess, or Tom, or anyone. Why was she acting so out of character?

There was nothing for it but to ring Jane as soon as the art gallery opened, though God alone knew what she was going to say.

Pouring herself another mug of tea, she thought of Gina running down those stairs. She suddenly remembered that she had invited Ian, Tom and Margaret to supper tonight. She must apologise to Tom.

Tom, who had kept her company all evening, introduced her to his friends and entertained her, and she'd paid him back by marching off without so much as a word. And what of Gina? For all Christie knew, she really had been ill.

So much for the idyllic, peaceful life. She heard a car drawing up outside and looked at her watch. It was eight o'clock. Maybe it was Tom, come to give her a bollocking on his way to work.

She went to the door and flung it open. Standing on the doorstep, she saw a slender young woman with long blonde hair in a ponytail. It took her a second or two to recognise Jane Waterhouse. A Jane with her hair pulled tightly back, wearing a T-shirt and cut-off chinos.

'I do hope I'm not disturbing you. I know it's early but I wanted to see you before the gallery opens.'

Christie assured her that she was delighted to see her, invited her in and offered tea.

Jane declined the tea, saying she had something in the car for her. She went to her beat-up Ford, returning with a square, flat package wrapped in a blanket. She carried it into the sitting room, unwrapped it and stood it against the wall.

It was Christie's painting. She gasped. 'How . . . ? But it was ruined!'

'Not as badly damaged as it first looked, actually. The frame was good for nothing but kindling and there was a slight tear towards the centre of the picture, luckily not severe. It was the stain that took rather a lot of work, but as you can see . . .'

Christie shook her head, amazed. 'How did you get this repaired so quickly and so well? You must have been up all night!'

'Yes, that's why I look like I do. I'm an art restorer by trade. I've rescued far worse than this one, I can tell you!'

'Jane, I don't know what to say. You're a genius! But listen, about last night—'

'Please, I have to apologise to you.'

Christie stared at her, confused.

'Gina was distraught when she saw the picture. She insisted I restore and reframe it immediately. She said that if it was beyond repair, she would commission me to paint you another — the same subject, same view over the garden. She really was terribly upset.'

Hmm. Another game? 'How is she?'

'Well, I had her to stay with me last night. She often does anyway, I've more or less given my spare room over to her.' Jane looked down at her sandals. 'Gina has a bit of a, er, problem living alone in that big house. Sometimes she just can't cope. She mostly crashes out with me, or occasionally with other friends. It's a bit of a phobia, I think. She is very highly strung, very intelligent, but not good on her own. Heaven knows what happened last night. One minute she was fine, doing a massive deal for me with the Hammond brothers, then — bang! She's better now. She has no recollection of fainting and she won't see a doctor, she's so damned stubborn!'

Christie's mind was racing. Had she made a totally incorrect assumption about Jane and Gina's relationship? Then perhaps she was wrong about other things as well.

They both looked at the picture. Whatever damage Gina Spearman had done was not visible now. Jane certainly knew her job. 'You really didn't have to go to all that trouble. You must be exhausted.'

'When Gina says she wants something done, you do it. And I have Gary working in the shop today, so I'll probably slope off if it's quiet and take a nap. Oh, I forgot to ask. Are you feeling better yourself? Gary saw you sit down, he said you didn't look well at all. I was just about to come over to you when Gina hit the deck. I knew when you left so suddenly that you must have been ill.' Jane sounded perfectly sincere. She really did think she'd been poorly.

'It was nothing, really. I often get episodes where I go rather weak. It's left over from a childhood illness, nothing to worry about. It soon passed when I got home.'

'Well, that's a relief,' Jane said. 'Well, I must go. I have to get ready for work. Glad you're better now.'

She walked out into the morning. A shaft of sunlight caught her pale hair. Even in T-shirt and chinos she retained her regal, mystical demeanour.

Back in the cottage, Christie took the painting into the light and looked at it closely. If you'd never seen it before, you would never have known it had been damaged. Jane had worked a miracle. But Christie knew. There were shadows where there had been none, slight changes to the brush-strokes, almost imperceptible alterations. It was still perfect for a gift, but to her it was tainted, and she was glad to be giving it away. Gina had managed to poison it for her.

She put the picture behind the couch. Ian would still love it, which was what counted. In the meantime, Christie didn't want to look at it.

She busied herself with chores, putting off the moment when she must contact Tom. Not only did she feel bad about how she'd treated him, she hated lying to him. Then, just as she was running out of things to do, there was a knock on the door.

From amid the rustle of cellophane paper, someone asked, 'Miss McFerran? Flowers for you. Hope you've got plenty of vases!' He thrust the huge bouquet of flowers towards her.

She took them through to the kitchen and tore off the greeting card, already knowing who the sender was. On the front, the word "sorry," with a cartoon of a rather misera-ble-looking teddy bear. The card read, "*I hope you will forgive me? Gina.*" She stared at the bouquet, which she'd thrust into the deep butler sink. It must have cost a fortune. Among the roses, carnations, delphiniums, lilies and gypsophila were at least six other exotic varieties that she'd never even seen before. What to do with them? Her impulse was to throw the whole lot away — or boil it in oil.

She went into the garden and found a bucket, filled it with water and stood it and the flowers in the outside laundry room. She wanted to look at them about as much as she had wanted to look at the painting.

Yet another dilemma. Bugger! Now she'd have to acknowledge them, and she wasn't sure how. She should just call the Reading Room, but the thought of being polite to Gina made her want to throw up. She sighed miserably. Well, she couldn't just ignore the gesture. She picked up her phone. She would tackle both problems with one call. She took a deep breath and dialled.

It rang for some time before a slightly harassed-sounding voice asked if she could help. She was told that Gina was off sick, and Tom had driven over to take her some lunch and see how she was. She sighed with relief. The only thing she could do was leave a message for Gina, since she didn't have her home number. She hung up, frowning.

Jane had said that Gina was fine this morning and was staying with her in Herring Lane. The shop said she was sick and at home in Tadema House. So which one of them was telling the truth? She thought about it. The answer was probably both. She had spent the night at Jane's, then gone home and rung in sick. Oh well, she had tried. Christie stared at her phone. Should she? Tom's mother was her one ally when it came to Ms Spearman, and about as fond of her as Christie. She had the excuse of their dinner party that night.

Margaret answered almost immediately. She greeted Christie warmly. Good. So Tom hadn't told her how selfish and uncompassionate she had been. Margaret assured Christie that she was eagerly looking forward to their meal that evening.

They chatted for a while until Christie asked how Tom was. Margaret said he was fine. 'Now, my dear, I would dearly love to hear your version of last night's drama.'

Christie asked if she would like the abridged version, or the full description of what she had seen.

Margaret said she'd start with what Christie had seen happen. Christie told her, leaving out her opinion that Gina had engineered the dramatic end to the evening.

When she'd finished, Margaret's immediate response was that the evil woman had planned the whole thing. 'She knew how important the painting was to you and decided to have some fun. Oh, and I bet my boy was at her side, waving the smelling salts under her nasty, pointy little nose.'

'I'm afraid so. But I left immediately after he ran to her side, I just couldn't watch. I was sick to my stomach at seeing her lying there by my ruined picture.' She paused. 'Jane managed to restore it. She worked all night. You would never know — well, *Ian* will never know, and that's what is important.'

'Mmm, but she managed to spoil your gift, didn't she? Take the simple delight out of the giving.'

'Oh well. At least, thanks to Jane's hard work, I do have the picture restored and reframed.' Christie went on to explain what she planned to say to Tom when she next spoke to him.

'All for the best, my dear. I'd do the same. He'd be horrified if he thought we believed that his precious Gina had faked her "collapse". Yes, you're doing the right thing.'

They agreed that Margaret and Tom would be at The Mulberries by seven o'clock and said their goodbyes.

As it turned out, Tom rang her later that morning. Christie had been so concerned about what he would think of her that she had totally overlooked the fact that, involved with Gina as he was, he hadn't even noticed her leave. He didn't even know she had gone until later.

She listened to his apologies with a mixture of relief, irritation and injured pride.

'I wanted her to go to hospital,' he was saying, 'but she'd have none of it. If Gina makes up her mind up about something, you're wasting your breath arguing with her. She seems all right now, I'm glad to say. She had Delphi with her when I left. She'd cooked her a dinner and taken it over, although whether Gina eats it or not is another matter.'

Christie let him talk on. Finally, he confirmed that he and his mother would be with her by seven, and that they were both looking forward to the evening.

She hung up feeling a trifle miffed. She had worried all morning about what to say to him and he hadn't even given her a thought. Honestly! She determined that for the remainder of her stay she'd let all these people get on with their lives. She was thirty-three, for goodness' sake, a sensible adult with an average IQ and — usually — a fairly balanced view of the world. Surely, she could manage to mind her own business?

CHAPTER EIGHTEEN

'Our Christie's entertaining again,' exclaimed Liz, pushing her phone back into her pocket. 'She's got a bigger social circle than us.'

'Nice to see, though,' said Matt. 'Didn't you tell me she had a pretty rough love life when she was a bit younger?'

Liz nodded. 'Oh, yes, two bites at the cherry and both turned out to be bitter fruit. One was married but had omitted to mention it to Christie, and the other was a real tosser. I had his number the first moment I saw him, but poor Christie was head over heels in love with him. That was painful, not just for her but for the people closest to her, me included, having to watch her be taken for a ride by a scheming scumbag. But fate has a way of sorting things sometimes. He married this woman who was reported to be loaded. It turned out she was a bigger con artist than he was. She had sod all and took him for every penny he had. True justice.' Her amusement faded. 'Oh, Matt, I'd so love to see Christie with a really nice partner. But she was so hurt, especially the last time, that it will take one helluva special person to make her trust anyone again.'

'What about that friend of yours from the bookshop? He's a nice bloke, unattached, they'd have lots of interests in common and he's passably good-looking, isn't he?' Matt raised an eyebrow. 'If you like the studious type, and I'd have thought that might appeal to Christie.'

'Well, I don't intend to start matchmaking, Matthew Ballard. I was only passing a comment.' She smiled. 'Although I think they'd make a great pair. Trouble is he's hankering after someone else.'

'Idiot,' muttered Matt.

'As it happens, I think you're absolutely spot on there. Anyway, we should be concentrating on work, not rearranging the love lives of our relatives and friends.'

'I suppose I'd better give Charley a ring and update her. Not that there's nearly as much as I'd hoped for.' He stretched. 'I had such high hopes when we realised that there was another party involved, but chasing up leads four years after the event is pretty well impossible.'

'Isn't it just,' said Liz. 'Just our luck that the florist we believe delivered those flowers had gone bankrupt and the owner had moved away.'

'Even so, this mystery person exists. That poor kid Sandy wouldn't be in the state she's in if he didn't. There has to be some way of tracing those threats without bringing the police into Sandy and Tony's lives.' He sighed. 'I've told Bryn that we have an informant who confirms the existence of a secret admirer, but also told him that our snout knows no more than that and would deny everything if questioned.'

'Did he accept that?' asked Liz.

'Because it came from us, yes. He knows we wouldn't try to hide info for the sake of getting a collar. And he's been down a few blind alleys of his own in his time.' He looked at Liz. 'So, what have you got planned for the rest of today?'

'I'm going to take a few hours out, Matt, if that's okay?' Liz said. 'Christie's chat was full of her social calendar, but I know Christie. Something's bothering her. I thought I'd call by and have a coffee with her. A problem shared and all that.'

'Sure,' he said. 'Good idea. She's still very upset over Auden's illness, maybe that's it. And she'll be pretty well cut adrift when her job finishes. I expect she'd like someone to discuss it all with.'

'That's what I thought. I'll ring her and—' She stopped. 'What?'

'I wonder . . .'

'Come on, Matt. Out with it.'

'I've been so wrapped up in our mystery man that I forgot something that came to me when we were with Christie last,' Matt said. 'It might interest her for her research.'

'Yes, yes. And?'

He stood up. 'I need to go up in the attic. If it still exists, I know exactly where it will be.'

Leaving a baffled Liz staring after him, he hurried out.

While she made coffee, Matt waded through records of his family history, trying not to get sidetracked by faded photographs and childhood mementos. Then Liz heard a "Gotcha!"

More rustles and thumps, and Matt was back downstairs, brushing strands of yellow loft lagging from his trousers. He handed Liz an old, faded scrapbook.

'I remember my father reading to me from this when I was a kid. The idea was to frighten me off the marsh.' Seeing the book suddenly brought back all his childhood fears.

Liz leafed through it, growing increasingly excited. 'This is exactly what Christie is researching. Who put it together?'

'My grandparents — my grandfather in particular. He was keen on history and had a very enquiring mind. My dad always said I took after him. He would have been pleased with my choice of career.'

The scrapbook contained accounts of local stories, going back years. His grandad had taken them from real events as well as folktales and rewritten them as children's stories. Each tale was preceded by a poem with the same general theme, some famous and others whose origins were more obscure.

'This is fascinating,' Liz said, now completely engrossed. 'Listen to this. It's about two brothers living on the marsh and it's all written in local dialect. They are looking at clouds and your grandad has written—'

'"Look tha'! If ya squint a bit ya can see a boggart in that one!"'

'"What a' load a' kelter! It looks nuthin' like a boggart,"' Liz chimed in. 'And this line here. A girl says, "Stop ya chitterin'! Ya sound like a load a' sparrers!"'

He closed his eyes. 'I can remember that one almost word for word. It's about Charlie and Georgie and Dickie and Maggie . . .'

She laughed. 'This is brilliant. Christie will be over the moon when she sees it. Can I take it when I visit?'

'Of course. It's no good stuck up there in the attic. I'll have it back when she's finished with it, but there's no rush. She might like to show her boss, if he makes it back to work okay.'

Liz rang Christie, who sounded pleased she was coming. 'I'll be off now, Matt. We can chat while she gets the meal ready for tonight.' She kissed him. 'Thank you for searching out this marvellous book, sweetheart. It will cheer her up better than anything.'

* * *

Christie turned the pages, her eyes shining. 'This is amazing! I can't wait for Auden to be well enough to see it. Would Matt mind if I get it copied?'

Liz told her that she could keep it as long as she wanted and was welcome to copy it. 'I've only skimmed through it, but it seems to really capture what the old folk felt about the marsh and the superstitions that surrounded it.'

'It's going to be so useful, Liz.' She ran a hand over the cover. 'Oh, look. It's called *The Marshlight Mysteries*, I like that. It sounds familiar somehow, but I can't think why.' She smiled at Liz. 'Yet again, your Matt has come up trumps.'

Liz smiled. 'Now, Miss McFerran, two things. I'm a great sous-chef, so what can I do to help you with your preparations for tonight? Prepare vegetables maybe? Plus, I have a feeling there's something bugging you, and it's not how to make a pavlova. Like to tell?'

179

Christie thought of all the years they'd known each other, and the floodgates opened. She told Liz about the animosity she felt toward Gina Spearman and her spiteful games.

'And you really think she deliberately tried to destroy your painting?' Liz shook her head. 'That's monstrous!'

'Know what, Liz? I think she's disturbed. No one in their right mind acts like she does.'

'Steer clear, dear friend. Avoid her like the plague.'

'I'd love to. But the people I most like are all enmeshed by the black widow spider — Tom, Delphi and Jane — and I'd hate to lose them. The only one not caught in her web is Ian, and he says the same as you.'

'Tricky . . .' Liz stopped slicing vegetables and stared down at them, unseeing. 'I see your problem. I suppose the best you can do is try to see them when she's not around. Like you *are* doing really, by inviting them here.'

The conversation moved on to other things, finally returning to the scrapbook. 'I can't wait to read it. I'll go through it tonight after everyone's gone home. It's the perfect way to tie up the research. I've been thinking that I should add some oral history, but this will be much more suitable. What better than the words of someone from an earlier generation?'

Liz's visit left Christie feeling a good deal easier. She had needed to talk to someone, and on top of that she now had this wonderful manuscript produced by Matt's grandfather.

She glanced at her watch. Time to get ready.

* * *

An hour later, dinner was all prepared and bubbling away in the kitchen, and the table was laid for four. Christie was in a state of mild trepidation. She hadn't made a "proper" dinner for donkey's years and had been glad of the assistance of her "sous-chef."

Ian was the first to arrive. She would give him the picture later. It should have been a special moment but as it was, well, she just hoped he liked it.

She sat him down in the chair looking out over the garden. While he sipped at a small, dry sherry, she took another look at the table arrangement. She had discovered some "best" china, patterned with green hops and gold leaf. A search had revealed a damask tablecloth and some assorted silverware. Earlier, she had pulled a few blossoms from the bouquet that still sat forlornly on the floor of the laundry room and set them in four individual sherry schooners which she stood beside each place setting. The result, with the addition of some crystal wine glasses and green and gold serviettes, was rather splendid.

Ian was standing in the doorway. 'Very nice! And I see you've found the family Royal Worcester.'

She must have looked concerned because he beamed with delight and said he was pleased to see it being used again. Then the doorbell rang, and Ian opened the door to a smiling Margaret and Tom laden with various packages.

'I told Mother she was overdoing it, but she insisted.'

He placed two bottles of wine, a box of mint chocolates, a frozen ice cream dessert and a bottle of a cream liqueur that Christie had never seen before on the wooden draining board.

'Where's your freezer? This is about to defrost on me, and don't worry about the Irish Cream. Mother discovered it on one of her many trips to Ireland and brought back a case or two. Everyone gets one at some point and it's your turn now.' He grinned. 'And don't be fooled by its sweetness, it's lethal!'

He put the dessert and wine away and sighed loudly. 'Getting Mother out to a dinner party is like organising an army manoeuvre!' They laughed. In the sitting room, the old lady was busy giving Ian an account of the history of The Mulberries. Christie asked them all to be seated. She put Tom in charge of the wine and went to the kitchen to serve. She was just putting the final garnish on the starters when she heard the sound of somebody's ringtone. Moments later, Tom appeared at the kitchen door. His face was drawn and anxious.

'Christie, I'm so very sorry about this. It's Gina, she's collapsed again. Delphi is with her but she's distraught. I have to go. You do understand, don't you?'

Oh, she understood all right. Mustering a smile, she said, 'Yes, of course you must go. Your mother will be fine with me and Ian. I'll run her home later or call a cab, but don't worry, she'll be all right.'

With apologies to his mother and the reverend, Tom hurried away.

'That cunning, conniving bitch! Sorry, Ian, but it has to be said.' Margaret was almost purple with rage.

'Ah, would this be the one driving Christie here to drink?' Ian sounded mildly amused.

'Who else?' gasped Margaret, almost beside herself with rage. Christie handed her a glass of wine. Margaret took it with a hand that trembled and sipped it gratefully. 'That woman will be the death of me.'

Christie went to fetch the dinner while Margaret launched into a recital of Gina's latest malicious acts. Ian listened, all amusement having drained from his expression.

When Christie returned with the food, he was asking Tom's mother if she really thought that Gina would fake an illness in order to disrupt Tom's evening.

'Oh yes,' said Margaret, her mouth set. 'And it won't be the first time either.'

Christie flashed the old lady a warning look. She didn't want Ian to know about what had happened to his gift. Margaret nodded.

Ian gave Margaret the advice he had given her: keep Gina at a distance. Christie said it was impossible for Tom to avoid her, since their three lives — Tom, Delphi, Jane — had become so intertwined with her own.

In that case, Ian said, they might have to learn to live with her.

They finished their first course and Christie was pleased when both her guests had second helpings of the main. She left a plate aside for Tom, not knowing why she'd done it.

Her guests asked for a break before tackling the dessert, and Christie decided it would be a good time to give Ian his painting.

Overcome with embarrassment, she mumbled her appreciation of Ian's generosity in allowing her to stay in this lovely cottage, and went to retrieve the picture, which she propped up on the sofa.

He stared at it in silence, then said, 'Evelyn's garden! Oh, how wonderful! Whenever was this painted? Christie, it's beautiful! Is it really for me? I couldn't possibly accept such a costly gift. There was no need, no need at all. You are most welcome to stay here. Oh, but look at the way the light filters through the roses!'

While Ian praised it enthusiastically, Christie saw something else in the picture, its scars and blemishes. Above all, she saw the expression Gina Spearman had worn as she lay crushing the beautiful thing. Christie hoped never to see it again.

They made their way back to the table. With a soft tap on the door, Tom entered. He looked defeated, unhappy. Rueful. 'False alarm. I don't suppose there's anything left?'

Christie hustled him into the kitchen before his mother could launch into another diatribe — directed either at the evil Gina or her son. As she passed Ian, she whispered to him to please calm Margaret down.

Tom was hurt. There was no need to discuss it further. She handed him his plate of food and he said he'd risk a glass of wine — 'I need it.' He didn't explain.

As Tom ate, Ian showed him the painting, singing its praises.

Margaret, meanwhile, insisted they have the pavlova, as the frozen dish would keep in the freezer. As they ate, Christie and Ian endeavoured to keep up a flow of cheerful banter. It was hard work but seemed to pay off.

Later, Tom joined Christie in the kitchen while she made coffee. 'Oh God, Christie. Why do I always jump whenever she clicks her fingers?'

'What happened?' she asked quietly.

'I really have no idea.' He pushed his glasses up onto the bridge of his nose. 'When I got to Tadema House, Delphi was still there; she met me at the door in floods of tears. I went in and found Gina, right as ninepence, having a go at Delphi for overreacting. She said she'd just been taking a nap but Delphi had panicked, thinking she had passed out again. Basically, she told us both to bugger off and leave her alone. I really hate her when she gets in these terrible moods but,' he looked with sudden interest at his shoes, 'then I get worried about her. She doesn't mean to hurt us, she hates herself for it afterwards, but it's very difficult to deal with. I want to help but I know that anything I say will be wrong. Then Mother starts on about her, or she doesn't say anything, which is even worse because I know what she's thinking. Mother doesn't understand. Gina is a very complicated person. She had a terrible childhood that has made her mistrustful of people and independent to the point of reclusiveness. And of course, she's an academic. She gets impatient with us plebs. We're not exactly in her league, Delphi and I.'

Christie wanted to shake him, to tell this poor, sad man that he and Delphi were better human beings than Gina could ever be. But she knew she'd be wasting her breath.

While they drank their coffee, Ian told Tom and his mother about their trip to Sly Fen and the strange lights they had seen. That evening seemed so long ago now. She had been eagerly carrying out her research for Auden, and now he was dreadfully ill, and she was more or less unemployed.

Margaret had seen the lights many times but could offer no explanation. Tom had always thought they must be a natural phenomenon, but he failed to provide an explanation for why they moved away from the watcher. 'When I was a kid, you never let me go out on the marsh, did you, Mum?'

'It's not a good place for children. Some of the mothers would let their young ones go out cockling or collecting samphire but I valued your life too much. I wasn't going to lose you to the tides.'

'I don't recall any of my schoolmates drowning,' Tom said somewhat petulantly.

'Then you won't remember young Donald Fyson, will you?

'Donnie? Surely Donnie died of an illness. Pneumonia, wasn't it?'

'He was pulled off the marsh more dead than alive,' said Margaret. 'The pneumonia set in after a day or so and then he was gone. Then there was Annie — I forget her surname, oh yes, Annie Grimes.'

'Annie went mad, Mum. They took her to that big sanatorium outside Lincoln. She didn't drown.'

'Annie was collecting samphire for her mother. A mist came down and she was lost out on the marsh. When they found her, she was raving about lights and monsters. Poor little thing never recovered. She died in that mental home, you know.'

'I never knew that,' admitted Tom.

'As I said, the marsh is no place for children.'

Ian added, 'It's no place for adults either, unless, like Dominic, you know it really well.'

'But let's not forget he nearly came undone as well,' Christie said, 'when we were all out there.' She would never forget his near miss with the jack-o'-lantern. She wanted to tell them about the scrapbook, but for some reason kept it to herself. Maybe she wanted to read it first. They had more coffee, then Tom said that he and his mother had better make a move.

Rather than waste Gina's flowers, Christie sent the old lady off with the remains of her bouquet, not mentioning where they had come from, and they drove off down the lane.

Ian got his coat and his precious painting and prepared to walk back to his temporary home with the Campions. As she had drunk next to nothing, she offered to drive him, but he said he'd welcome the fresh air. Before he left, he asked if she was free the following night. The Campions had asked him to eat with them and they wondered if she'd like to come too.

'And come early, I'd like to have a talk with you. I'm a bit too tired tonight and I need to get my thoughts in order first. The effect this Gina woman is having on you all is most disconcerting, it really is.'

Too right. She said she'd meet him there at six thirty.

He hugged her tightly, saying she had no idea how happy the painting had made him. Now he would always have a piece of his beloved sister with him. It would hang in pride of place in his London home.

His eyes brimming, he turned and walked slowly down the lane.

Christie left the dishes and went straight to bed, praying for a night without dreams. She couldn't stop her mind from returning to the events of that evening, particularly Gina's summons to poor Tom. She wanted so badly to get this dreadful woman out of her life, but her influence persisted, like a vigorously growing creeper that uses another plant for support, eventually strangling the life out of its hapless host.

CHAPTER NINETEEN

Christie awoke late with a headache like that of a rugby player after a night's celebration rather than a quiet meal with a vicar and an elderly lady. She'd drunk hardly anything, so why the pounding head?

She had a hot shower and felt a little better, until memories of the evening began to seep back into her mind. Tom's abrupt departure and return led her thoughts to the odd blend of personalities all circling Gina. Tom, at once effervescent and bookish. Blonde Delphi, not bookish at all but warm and likeable. Fey Jane Waterhouse, floating at the periphery and much put-upon.

How to describe this woman, the person they all loved and feared? A sudden image rose into Christie's mind: Gina as the hub of a wheel. Speared and bleeding on the ends of the spokes were the tiny figures of Tom, Delphi and Jane. And what of her? Was she too impaled on a spoke, encircling the hub? Was she another plaything? Just how much power did Gina have over her?

She had certainly pulled off a masterful move with the painting. It had been waved in front of her, just out of her reach and then snatched from her, destroyed before her very eyes and finally returned to her, ostensibly restored but flawed in ways only she could see.

She played Tom with consummate skill, relaxing the strings and allowing her puppet to approach Christie then tightening them again, whisking him away only to restore him to her, crushed like the painting, her pleasure in him ruined.

And poor Delphi. Dangling her dream in front of her and using it to drive a wedge between her and her husband.

The painting of Tadema House, cruelly rejected then accepted — only because Christie had wanted it.

Now in a thoroughly bad mood, Christie stomped down the stairs, made tea and had some breakfast. Having cleared away the debris of the previous night's meal, she pulled off the tablecloth to put it in the wash. Underneath, and resting on the table, she found a piece of folded paper with her name scribbled on it as if in haste. She opened it:

Forgive me, but I have to talk to someone. Please ring me when Tom is at work. I am very worried for his safety. Margaret.

Christie stared at the note, glanced at the clock and went to the telephone. It rang and rang. She tried again ten minutes later but no one picked up. Why couldn't Margaret have just asked without anyone overhearing? And what did she mean about Tom's "safety?" It was an odd word to use.

Her head throbbing, she tried Margaret's number a third time. When she answered, Margaret sounded close to tears. 'I'm sorry about the cloak-and-dagger bit. It was that fiasco with Gina; her causing my Tom to go rushing off on a wild goose chase, yet again. It was the straw that broke the camel's back, Christie. I wanted to talk to you then, but I was terrified that he'd see me whispering to you, so I left you a note. When we got home last night I went straight to my room. Tom followed me in and ordered me to say what was on my mind. He can't stand it when I go all silent on him. I was well aware of that, but I was afraid that if I did speak, he would jump down my throat.'

'Go on,' said Christie gently.

'Well . . .' There was a noise as she fumbled with the receiver. 'I suppose I said a bit too much. By then I was so angry that I let him have it with both barrels. I wish I'd kept my mouth shut. Oh, Christie, he stormed out of the house. I haven't heard from him since.'

She could hardly believe they were talking about the Tom she knew. How could he have left the old lady alone all night and upset, and not even rung her this morning? He adored his mother. What on earth had happened to make him behave so callously?

'Have you spoken to the Reading Room, Margaret?'

'Yes. They told me he's taken a day off.'

'Was Gina there?' Christie asked.

'It was her that told me,' Margaret said.

'Did she say anything else?'

'Not a thing, but I bet he was with her last night.'

'Margaret, do you know where Tadema House is?'

'Oh yes. You can't miss it. The signpost at the entrance still reads "Marshlight Farm," its original name. You drive into the village and go past the church. It's some way out, set back on the right-hand side of the road, hidden in some great high conifers and rhododendrons. Why do you ask?'

She was asking because she had a notion of driving over and checking whether Tom's blue Peugeot was parked outside. If it was, she intended to give Margaret's son a piece of her mind. 'Oh, maybe I'll just see if he's there, make sure he's okay, I guess. Have you got food for today, Margaret? I can easily bring something for you if you're stuck.'

'Thank you, my dear, but I'm fine. I'm not actually very hungry.'

Christie could imagine. She was about to ask Margaret what she meant by Tom's "safety" when she heard her crying, so she murmured some comforting words, ending the call when Margaret sounded more like herself again.

She debated whether to ask Ian to go with her. If Tom wasn't at Tadema House, she would value his opinion on what to do next. In the end, she decided to go alone.

The driveway was empty.

She left her vehicle by the church and walked up the lane to have a closer look at the place. Tadema House was certainly imposing, but surely much too big for a woman on her own.

Keeping to the grass to muffle her footsteps, she made her way to the front door, wondering if she should ring the bell. Instead, she found a path that led round to the rear gardens, a block of stables and a garage.

The blue Peugeot was parked in front of the garage doors. So Tom was there after all. Now what to do? Her earlier intention of marching up to the front door and giving him a piece of her mind evaporated. She stood, hesitant, staring at the car.

'I wondered if Mother would send you.'

'God! Tom! You frightened the life out of me!' Christie clutched at her chest. Sudden shocks did little for her damaged heart valve.

'Sorry, are you all right? Come in. I'll get you a drink of water. I didn't think about your illness, I'm really sorry.'

She followed him into the house. 'How did you know I was here?'

'CCTV. Gina has a state-of-the-art security system. She doesn't like intruders on her property. The grounds here run down to the marsh, and it's pretty remote for someone who spends a lot of time at work and away from the house.'

Christie had never been called an intruder before and some of her anger returned. 'I wouldn't be here at all if Margaret wasn't so upset. How could you leave her alone like that, Tom, immediately after a blazing row? Oh, and she didn't send me either. I rang *her*, as it happens.'

She took the glass from him and sat down on a kitchen chair. The steel and black leather went with the table, which had a thick smoky glass surface.

Tom seemed both ashamed and hostile. 'You've no idea what my mother can be like, Christie. I'm thirty-four, I want a life of my own. I don't need to be treated like a teenager anymore.' He kicked against the curved steel leg of the table. 'I think perhaps I made a mistake in having her live with me. Gina says it rarely works and I think she's probably right.'

Gina says. Christie pictured shattering dear Gina into shards, just like a glass tabletop. 'Tom. You and your mother get on better than any mother and son I know. She loves you to bits and you love her, don't deny it! It's not staying out at night, I'm sure you've done that dozens of times, it was how you did it. Look, you've hit a rough patch. It happens, but you'll get over it, just don't hurt her like this. She's worried sick about you.'

He had the good grace to look remorseful. He stood up and paced the room, his hands pushed deep in his pockets and his shoulders slouched.

'What happened last night?' she asked.

'I suppose I was hurt by Gina's behaviour towards Delphi and me. I was angry at myself and I took it out on Mother. She refused to speak all the way home, giving me her tight-lipped silent treatment, and stomped off to bed. I flipped, she flew back at me and I finished up storming out of the house and driving off.'

'Did you come straight here?'

'No. Actually, I was on my way back to you, again!' He scratched with great concentration at a speck of coffee on the marble counter. Still intent on removing it, he said, 'I, er, well I thought you might get the wrong idea, so I went to the shop instead. I let myself in and was surprised to find Gina there. She said she couldn't face being alone at Tadema House after she'd upset Delphi and me and she was going to sleep on the couch in the office. Anyway, she insisted I follow her here and stay the night. She said I was much too upset to go home. She convinced me that it was best for both me and Mother if I cooled down a bit before I tell her she can't expect to rule my life completely.'

The bitch. 'So why didn't you ring this morning?'

'Oh, Gina told me to take a day off, get some rest. She said she'd call Mother for me as soon as she got to work. I was just getting ready to go home when you arrived.'

'Gina did speak to your mother, but it was Margaret who phoned the shop, Tom, and Gina omitted to say where you were.'

'Oh. Oh, well, I guess she thought I needed a bit more time. Maybe they were busy, and she never got around to it. I'm sure she had her reasons.'

Oh yes, I'm sure she did. 'Please go home, Tom. Your mother's devastated. She's only thinking of you and your well-being, you know.'

'I know.' Hearing the irritation in his voice, she decided not to push it further. 'This is a fabulous house, isn't it? A bit on the large size for one, I'd have thought?'

'Mmm. Gina'd always loved it so when her parents died and it came onto the market, she sold the family home and bought it.'

'Just like that, eh?'

'Just like that.'

'Wealthy lady.'

'She's a shrewd businesswoman. The Reading Room isn't her only business, you know. She has other very successful enterprises that bring in a healthy income.'

She stifled her retort, saying merely that she should be going.

Some of the old Tom showed in the sheepish grin he gave her. 'I've behaved rather badly, haven't I? Thanks for talking to Mum. I'll get back to her now.' He seemed to think for a second. 'Want a quick tour of Spearman Towers before you go?'

Afraid the mistress of the house might return at any moment and find her there, she reluctantly refused. 'I'll ring Margaret and tell her to kill the fatted calf, shall I? That you'll be home in about an hour's time?'

'Yeah, something like that. I'm not sure what got into me, Christie. Mother has never annoyed me in the past, but these days I feel I could throttle her sometimes. Then, of course, I feel guilty. Perhaps I need a holiday.'

'That sounds like an excellent idea. Why don't you think seriously about it? It may be just what you need.'

'You could be right. Thanks for coming to find me. I'm sorry. The more I think about it the more I realise what an arsehole I've been.'

'Go on home now. I'll speak to you soon.'

She gave him a hug. He clung to her like a child seeking solace.

She drove home, pensive. If only there were some way she could remove Tom from Gina's influence. He was a different person when he wasn't under her spell; a caring man, someone she'd like to spend more time with.

Back in The Mulberries, she rang his mother. The line almost pulsed with Margaret's relief. Christie hoped she wouldn't lay into her son again. He was obviously still on edge. It was going to take a lot of work on the part of both. And with Gina Spearman hovering in the wings, would the task prove too much for them?

* * *

'Hello, Sarge!' DC Bryn Owen's voice crackled as the signal on his mobile came and went. 'Are you free for a quick visit? I thought I might call in for a cuppa and a quick update on the case, if that's all right. I'm not far away.'

'We're both here, Bryn, come on over,' said Liz.

'See you in ten.'

Liz called up the stairs, 'Visitor on his way, Matt.'

'Coming!'

Liz was working at her laptop on the kitchen table, trawling through newspaper coverage from the time of the murder, along with social media posts and true crime chat forums. She had wasted hours on Duncan Hartland's anti-police campaign, which consisted largely of rants, none of them quite abusive enough to get the site blocked. Freedom of speech, Liz supposed. People had a right to their personal opinions.

She filled the kettle for tea. It would be nice to see Bryn again. She'd spoken to him on the phone a few times but hadn't seen him in person for some time. They had been a tight-knit team, back in the day.

She had never told Matt, but being back on her old stamping ground and seeing all her friends still doing the job that had been her life for so long had pained her terribly. Given her injuries, there was no way back, so she'd had to face the truth and learn to live with it. She and Matt were both alike in mourning the loss of the job they loved, but she'd learned to accept that some things can't be changed. As to Matt, she wasn't sure.

Bryn arrived just as the tea was ready. Somewhat to her surprise, he hugged her affectionately. 'It's been too long, Sarge. You're looking good, though.'

'How's tricks with you, Bryn?' she asked.

'Pretty okay, thanks. Guess who's doing his sergeant's exams?' He gave a little bow.

'About bloody time!' Matt exclaimed from the doorway. 'I've been telling you for ages to get your finger out and move up the ladder.'

'Well done,' Liz said warmly. 'You'll sail through.'

When they'd finished catching up, Bryn crossed his arms across his chest. 'So, any further with the mystery man in Lindsay's case?'

Liz shook her head. 'No, I'm sorry to say. But we're both convinced that Paul Redman is right. From little things our contacts have been saying, we're pretty sure there was someone else sniffing around her.'

'Whoever it was turned her head, Bryn,' Matt said. 'Why else would she ditch the man she was planning to marry? Trouble is, it's hard to prove it after all this time. Anyway, Lindsay's sister Paula will be back tomorrow, which might give us a better understanding of our police-hater, Duncan

Hartland. We've been told that he was obsessed with Paula, which makes us wonder about him.'

'Meanwhile, have you got anything for us?' asked Liz hopefully. 'I know we aren't supposed to be privy to what's being said at the nick, but still.'

'Not much.' Bryn gave her a wry smile. 'Although I don't remember being told I can't pass on anything of interest. The DCI must have forgotten to mention that bit, so if anything turns up that might help you, you'll hear about it. Anything specific you're looking at?'

'Lindsay's last day,' Matt replied sombrely. 'We want to try to establish a timeline of her movements. Sometime during that day, she either saw or spoke to the person who killed her.'

'Hmmm. As far as I can recall it's very sketchy, but I'll message you what was logged back then.' Bryn looked pensive. 'The more time that goes by, the harder it gets to check or trace anything. I hate old cases.'

Matt shrugged. 'True, they are challenging. But some people remember a lot more than you'd think.'

'Then let's hope you find someone with a bloody good memory.' Bryn stood up. 'Ah well, better get back to the station. Thanks for the tea. Great to see you again, Liz. I'll be in touch later today.'

Liz watched Matt and Bryn walk to his car. If only she had access to all the official police databases that she'd had in the past. She missed the PNC in particular. Then she reminded herself that she and Matt had managed to track down Sandy Giles using good old police footwork. They actually knew more than Bryn did about the mystery man who had threatened Sandy. Not that they could share that with their colleagues in the police. Sandy and her brother had sworn that if they involved the cops they'd either deny everything or do a runner. No, they had to keep digging in the hope that Sandy might just recall some other small detail which would lead them to the killer.

CHAPTER TWENTY

Christie was sitting in the garden finishing a snack lunch when she saw a car draw up. At first, she thought it was someone for her, but then realised that it was her neighbours arriving home.

In the bungalow next door lived a retired couple who had "downsized," moving from their family house in town to be rid of two flights of stairs and a leaking roof. Bill and Lynne were friendly but not intrusive, so she was surprised to see them coming round to the back garden.

'Oh, look! It's still as lovely as when Evie was here. You're doing a good job, me duck.'

Christie liked the Lincolnshire way of calling everyone "duck," pronounced to rhyme with "book." Either that or "mate," with the elongated "aa."

'Thank you. How are you both?'

'Fine. We've come to see if you'd like to pop in for a drop of sherry with us this evening. No reason, just being neighbours an' all.'

Remembering that she was supposed to be eating with the Campions and Ian, she asked if they could make it the following day.

'No trouble, duck. We'll see you then. About seven? Give y'a chance to have ya supper, like.'

She wished she were still researching for Auden. She had a feeling that Bill and Lynne would have some good yarns for her.

She accompanied them to the front of the cottage, where Lynne paused, her hand on the gate. 'Oh, before I forget, duck, don't be minding old Katie. She's our cat. Evie used to feed her for us if we went away. She often sits in your porch. Evie put a cushion there for her. She's too old to chase birds or mice now, so she's no trouble, but sling her back through the fence if she gets in ya way.'

Christie had noticed that the indentation had deepened but she had yet to meet the owner of the furry bottom that made it. As if to make a point, an ancient and overweight tabby sauntered casually in through the shrubs and jumped, surprisingly lightly considering its bulk, onto the bench. It emitted a satisfying deep purr when she tickled its ears.

Lunch over, she decided to drive into the town to buy Pip and Dominic some flowers to take to dinner that evening. Considering their trade, wine would probably be superfluous, and she didn't want to arrive empty-handed.

Half an hour later, while she stood examining the florist's displays, she remembered the enormous bouquet Gina had sent. When she calculated what she was spending on a modest one, she realised that Gina had probably parted with about fifty pounds for hers. God, the lengths she was prepared to go to, just to further her game plan.

The florist having said it would take ten minutes or so to arrange her bunch, she left for a short wander around the shops. On her way out, she saw a pretty, straight-sided crystal vase with three single blooms and some foliage in it. It would look good on Jane's desk and make a perfect thank you for her hard work on restoring Ian's picture. She took it straight to Herring Lane.

The gallery was busy. Jane was talking to some potential buyers and Gary was on the phone. Christie stood the vase on the desk and had a look at the paintings while she waited. After the visitors had left, Jane approached and greeted her warmly.

Christie indicated the vase. 'Just a little thank you for all you did the other night.'

Jane seemed pleased with the gift. She looked tired and there were dark circles under her eyes.

Christie asked her if the open evening had been lucrative — she didn't like to say "a success" after that evening's denouement.

Jane said she had done very well. She had sold several paintings and had been commissioned to paint a series of waterscapes for the new country club.

So Gina had her uses after all.

'Gary will be holding the fort for a while. I need some time just to concentrate on painting. Plus, I'm hoping for a break. I haven't had a holiday in years.' She sighed. 'My last picture . . . I wasn't pleased with it at all. I need some fresh stimulus — different surroundings, brighter colours. Southern skies, perhaps. Foreign ones. I don't know.'

'Have you got anything planned?'

'Not exactly. Gina mentioned something, but I'm not sure if it's definite.'

Christie couldn't help herself. 'Good grief!' she blurted out, 'Not another holiday! She went somewhere tropical not so long ago, then there's her trip to Greece with Delphi and now somewhere else with you. It's a wonder she finds time to work at all!'

Her remark had been intended as humorous, but a strange look swept across Jane's face, something like disbelief. Hurt? Christie realised she'd put not just her foot in it but her leg, right up to the knee.

Jane's laugh was pitched too high. 'Last year she went away four times, all to exotic locations. She has the money. She has no need to work at all if she doesn't want to, so why not?'

'I'd probably do the same,' Christie said, horribly uncomfortable. She looked at her watch and said she really should dash.

Jane's relief was palpable.

Outside, the hot sun struck Christie's already burning face. What was it with these people? Whatever she happened to refer to seemed to have a hidden agenda behind it, some drama or secret she wasn't privy to. Roll on the evening, and the company of uncomplicated people.

* * *

Christie made her way to the B&B beneath a clear, blue sky. The sunny weather improved her mood considerably. She was still discomfited by her conversation with Jane, but she pushed it to the back of her mind. She was getting tired of having to stop and think every time she opened her mouth.

She found Ian sitting outside. 'Welcome! What a splendid evening. I thought we might sit in the garden for a while.'

Seeing him after a few days' absence, she was again struck by how handsome he was. No wonder, then, that despite being in his late seventies, he still turned heads — Margaret Parrish's among them.

They wandered round to the back garden and sat on a kissing seat under an arbour of cascading scarlet and pink roses. 'So, Reverend, you may begin your interrogation. I'm ready.'

'It's not exactly an interrogation, you know. You make me sound like an inquisitor. I have a little story for you first.' He leaned back and crossed his legs. 'In the years when I was visiting my sister, I was often in the company of Margaret Parrish. I have always been, um, how can I put it, "attracted" to her. She's kind, funny, good company. In other words, Christie, if my life had been other than what it was, I may have . . . Oh dear, I'm not doing very well, am I?' He looked at her helplessly.

She laughed and said he'd explained perfectly, smiling at the thought of Margaret's reaction to what he'd just said.

He looked relieved. 'Well, the thing is, one of the things that always struck me about Margaret was her extraordinary relationship with her son. All my life I have been working with families, happy and otherwise, and Margaret and her boy had something no other family I've met had. But now . . .' He sighed. 'Christie, if they don't address the rift that is developing between them, they'll finish up hating each other. Really hating someone takes a lot of strong emotion. It's the other side of the coin from love. Tom and Margaret might very well be tossing a coin that could land on the wrong side.'

'I've sensed it myself, Ian. I know exactly what you're saying.' She went on to tell him about the previous night.

'He actually went off and left her after an argument, not even saying where he was going? That's not in his nature. He knows her difficulty in getting about, and he's not an unkind soul. He wouldn't do such a thing, surely?'

'But he did. With the encouragement of his dear employer. It was Gina who talked him into staying out all night and who told him not to contact his mother. I don't know what sort of power she has over him, Ian, but her hold is very strong.' She went on to tell the reverend about her odd conversation with Jane.

'She obviously didn't know about the Greek adventure with Delphi, did she? What's the betting that it's the same holiday?' he said.

'What, you think she's invited both Jane and Delphi?'

'Probably. Playing one off against the other and most likely your friend Tom as well. Has he mentioned needing a holiday recently?' Ian glanced at her. 'Oh dear.'

'What on earth is she playing at? What is her problem? Whatever is she trying to prove?' Christie was enraged.

'Nothing, my dear. She is simply playing. The game is everything.'

She gaped at him, trying to understand.

He continued. 'Look at you, Christie. She has you climbing the walls already, and you hardly know her. How long have you been here? In the space of weeks, days even, she has had a greater impact on you than anyone else you've ever met.'

'But . . .'

'Admit it. The sad thing is that under normal circumstances she wouldn't be bothering with you at all. All you would have seen was a polite and efficient businessperson, nothing more. You're not a game-player so you wouldn't have given her devices the time of day. You would have been no fun at all. But due to your involvement with her innocent playmates, you too became fair game. Actually, you've probably spiced up a bit of a boring contest. Think of it, Christie. Sweet, frothy Delphi? The slight and artistic Jane? Mummy's boy Tom? Are these the kind of opponents Gina Spearman would choose if she could? No. It's been slim pickings in Fenfleet until you came along. I'm sorry to say this, but I think you might be rather more fun for our Gina than you would have liked.'

Glancing at her face and the horror written all over it, Ian took her hand. 'Perhaps you should view it as a compliment.'

'You have got to be joking.'

His loud guffaw dissipated a little of her tension. 'Goodness me, my dear! As far as Gina is concerned, you are probably the best thing that has walked through her shop door in years.'

Her appalled look gave rise to more laughter, which eventually had her laughing too, though she had no idea why.

Ian raised an eyebrow. 'So perhaps we should employ a stratagem of our own.'

She protested. 'No games, Ian, please. We'd be the same as her in that case.'

'Ah, but what if we were better? Then we might just be able to release her imprisoned pawns and restore them to their proper places on the board.' He gave her a long look. 'Why should she get away with messing up their lives?'

'Is this the man who told me to avoid the vexations of the spirit, to keep her out of my life and let only nurturing souls close to me? Doesn't sound very Christian to me.'

'I've had a change of heart. I don't like to see my friends made use of. "Fight the good fight" may be a better motto than "turn the other cheek."' He smiled angelically.

'You old devil!'

'Not so much of the "old" if you please, young lady. Now, as I see it, you have four options. One, you go back to Scarborough, at once. Two, you remain here, finish your holiday and ignore them all, have nothing to do with any of them. Three, try to reason with them, make them see sense, abandon Gina and believe in you, and four, fight back. From the sidelines, of course. Beat her at her own game. Then let her be the one to let them go. What do you think?'

'But how? How can I possibly beat her at her own game? I wouldn't know where to begin.'

'Honestly, can they be any worse off than they are already?'

Christie had no answer to that.

* * *

The food and the company were perfect, and the conversation lasted well into the night. But in the background, Christie kept hearing Ian asking why Gina should get away with ruining people's lives.

She could no longer dispute the fact that she was totally obsessed by Gina Spearman. Ian was right. It was time to make a decision and act on it. If it had not been for her feeling for The Mulberries, she would have packed up days ago and gone back to Yorkshire. But now she knew that wasn't going to happen. She was in too deep.

There was nothing else for it, she would have to be a match for Gina Spearman.

Dom escorted Christie back to The Mulberries, and she marched along, full of high purpose. It never occurred to her that perhaps her friends didn't want saving.

CHAPTER TWENTY-ONE

The following morning, Christie was barely out of the shower when the phone started ringing.

Liz was the first to call, checking to see how she was faring on her own and how the new friends she'd been so anxious about were doing. Christie said she was happy in Evelyn's cottage, but her friends were continuing to be a worry. All at once she heard herself say, 'I suppose I couldn't ask you to do a little bit of ferreting for me, could I? Say no if you're too busy but since it's your line of work . . . if you have a few spare minutes?'

Liz chuckled. 'I know what you're about to ask, cousin dearest. You want to know more about your "evil genius," don't you?'

Christie laughed in her turn. 'Got it in one.'

'Leave it with me. Our investigation seems to have ground to a halt, so I'll be happy to have something to occupy my idle moments. Tell me what you already know about her and I'll try to see what I can find.'

What Christie knew turned out to be very little. She hung up wondering why she'd asked, but at the same time glad that she had.

While she was having breakfast, her phone rang again. This time it was Richard. 'He's so much better, Christie. If you want to come up next week, he'd love you to visit.'

She told him she'd be there without fail. They chatted away, both relieved that Auden was making some progress. Christie asked him if she could bring him anything in the way of food from the vegetable capital of England, but Richard said he was fine, living on takeaways and ready meals. 'At least I haven't sunk to using the hospital cafeteria yet. I tried it once and, oh my dear, never again! The food they give Auden isn't too bad, but I do sneak him in some treats — you know, a little smoked salmon and some of that game pie from the village delicatessen that he loves so much. Oh, and the odd Belgian chocolate.'

Cheered by the news from Richard, she finished her breakfast then remembered her promise to call on Margaret that day, to see how she was. She decided to ring Ian and arrange a time.

When he answered, Ian sounded tired and low-spirited. He'd had a sleepless night and now felt drained. 'I think it's all catching up with me, Christie. I know my faith should be a solace, and of course it is. But I'm only human. Like anyone who loses the person closest to them, I'm heartbroken. I miss her. I miss her so much that my heart literally aches.'

Christie was terribly sad for him. There was nothing she could say that wouldn't sound trite. She suggested that perhaps he should forgo today's visit to Margaret.

'Thank you, my dear,' he said. 'I'll just have a quiet morning here. But perhaps you'd go? What she said about being afraid for Tom's safety worried me. I mean, he's not actually in mortal danger, as far as we know, so it's a strange thing to say.'

'I'll go shortly,' Christie said. 'I won't ring first. I'll call you this afternoon and tell you what she says.'

* * *

Christie arrived in Friary Terrace in under half an hour.

'Oh, my dear! I'm so pleased you came.' Margaret welcomed her inside.

'I thought I might be able to scrounge a cuppa.' Christie noticed new worry lines on Margaret's face. She appeared to be as exhausted as Ian had confessed to being. However, she did seem relieved that she'd come.

'Come on in. You haven't seen my rooms yet, have you?'

She led Christie through to her "snug." 'We share the main part of the house but also have our private spaces. So necessary, don't you think?'

Decorated in shades of pastel, Margaret's rooms were given over to a vast collection of photographs. The walls were festooned with pictures of Tom, from a babe in nappies to a recent black-and-white portrait obviously taken at the Reading Rooms. Tom on a tricycle, Tom in his pram, Tom in cricket whites, Tom gallantly rowing his father in a heavy old-fashioned boat. Tom toasting an unseen host with a fluted glass, Tom in his "library," with a copy of Giger's *Necronomicon II* open on his lap.

On closer inspection, she saw that not all the pictures were of Tom. There was one of Margaret's husband, a couple of Margaret herself, and a few of people Christie didn't know.

She heard Margaret call to her from the kitchen, and Christie went to help her carry in the tea. 'Sorry. The china would end up in a million pieces if I tried to carry that tray. I can cope with a single mug, although more often than not there is less tea in it than when I started out on my journey. Damned arthritis!'

They drank their tea in companionable silence for a few minutes.

'Now, I expect you're wondering what on earth I was on about in that note I left you. I know it was a melodramatic way to put it, but I really do fear for Tom. Perhaps I should have said "sanity" rather than "safety."' She raised her twisted arthritic hand to her forehead.

'Tom's father was a lovely man, so kind and gentle. Tom resembles him more than he does me. But there was a weakness in his bloodline.' She stared for a long moment at the photograph of the fair-haired man. 'I'm telling you this in confidence, Christie. Even Tom doesn't know the truth about his father.'

Christie's heart grew heavy with dread. What was Margaret about to tell her and did she want the weight of this secret?

'William had an important position and was well-liked and respected in government circles, so when he had a break-down, it was hushed up and he was quietly spirited away to a private hospital. Though he was given the best professional treatment, the night staff were careless. Six weeks into his stay there, my darling William hanged himself from a light fitting in the hospital storeroom.'

Christie made a small sound.

'It was a long time ago, my dear. Tom was only ten at the time, an impressionable and sensitive child. He worshipped the ground his father stood on. He . . . I never had the heart to tell him the full story. I told him that William had collapsed while travelling abroad and had fallen into a coma from which he never regained consciousness. His body lay in a Chapel of Rest in Fenfleet, and we said good-bye to him there, just Tom and I. Tom didn't attend the funeral.'

'Didn't he ask any questions about his father's death?'

'Oh yes, but William often went away for months on end, so his absence was nothing unusual for Tom,' Margaret replied.

'You said a breakdown, Margaret. May I ask what happened?'

The old lady blew her nose. 'I've never spoken of it before, but I suppose it doesn't matter now. His depart-ment basically paid me to forget the whole episode.' She snorted. 'As if I could! Anyway, William was admitted to the private hospital under another name. He became plain William Brown. It took weeks of negotiation to even get him cremated under his own name. I had to let "things" die down, as they put it.'

She paused and let out a long sigh.

'Well, William had been acting a little out of character for a while. It was nothing major, and I put it down to overwork and stress. If we had known more about his own father's illness, we — that is, the doctors and I — would probably have recognised the signs but we didn't. William's parents were long deceased. Then, one day William reacted badly to an incident that occurred in his office. It had to do with another member of staff whom William suspected of perpetrating a number of wrongdoings. This woman was a particularly unpleasant character and had been making life difficult for William's secretary. William couldn't prove anything against her. When she wrongly accused his aide of committing a breach of security, William confronted her. My sweet, gentle husband drove a paperknife into the woman's eye, blinding her, and immediately tried to turn it on himself. He was overpowered before he could injure himself, but from that moment on, he never stopped trying. Luckily, his department had taken note of his allegations and she was already under scrutiny. She was quietly and permanently removed from the service.' Margaret had been staring into the distance while she spoke. Now she faced Christie. 'So now you know why I sometimes overreact where Tom's concerned. I watch him like a hawk. I failed to see the telltale symptoms in my poor William, but I won't make the same mistake with Tom. That is why I'm living here. My arthritis is bad, but I could have managed perfectly well. I wanted to be with him for *his* sake, not mine.'

Christie was flabbergasted. After a while, she said, 'But he won't necessarily suffer from whatever affected his father, will he? It could skip a generation, or it could have only affected William and his father.'

'Of course, and Tom has shown no indications whatsoever of being at risk. When I was asked to "forget" what had happened, I imposed one or two conditions of my own.

One was to speak to the psychiatrist who had been treating William. Like you, he said there was only a slight chance that Tom would be affected. He said that there was usually a trigger which precipitated such a breakdown. He also said I must not tell Tom that his father and grandfather had committed suicide. He firmly believed that when told of a hereditary condition, some people actually develop it themselves. As in, "it runs in the family, so I'll get it too." A kind of fatalism, I suppose. So I followed his advice and kept Tom in the dark. Now this.'

'Surely you don't think his attraction to Gina could be the spark you've been fearing all these years, do you?'

'Not in itself. I'm sure he is strong enough to weather a case of unrequited love. No, there is something about Gina that frightens me. She is so unpredictable, which could be very unsettling for Tom. You've seen for yourself how she blows hot and cold. One day he is flavour of the month, the next she can't be bothered to give him the time of day. Suppose she allows him to get close to her and then dumps him? Well, that might push him over the limit, don't you think?'

Christie remembered the trip to Peterborough, culminating in his abrupt dismissal and the humiliating offer of money for the train fare home.

They sat in silence. Christie felt way out of her depth. If only Ian had been here with her, he was such a wise man. 'Margaret,' she said, 'how would you feel if I told Ian about this? If you say no, then that's fine, but he might be able to help.'

Margaret looked at her hands, readjusted her glasses. 'What harm can it do? But please — I know he's not a Catholic priest but ask him to treat what you say like a confession. Tom must never know about his father.'

Christie agreed. She recalled what Ian had said about his feelings for Margaret. But that too had been confidential.

She was about to leave when Tom arrived. He often popped home in his lunch break, to check on his mother or get away from the shop for half an hour. He seemed less than pleased to see her there, almost as if she'd betrayed him in some way. Or had she imagined it?

She smiled brightly and said she'd called by to deliver a message for Margaret from Ian. When he seemed less than convinced, she explained that the vicar was resting today after a sleepless night.

It sounded lame even to her, and she made her excuses, saying she intended to spend the afternoon spring cleaning The Mulberries.

This did raise a smile. Most people on holiday, he said, didn't use it up spring cleaning. He went on to say that he hoped she could tear herself away from the Hoover on Tuesday evening, as Gina was giving a dinner party at Tadema House, and she was invited.

Taken unawares, she didn't know what to say, until she caught sight of Margaret behind him, nodding furiously.

Okay, she would watch Margaret's son for her. 'Well, of course. Thank you, I'd love to come.' The words nearly choked her. 'I can have the official tour of Spearman Towers then, can't I?'

As she drove home — yes, The Mulberries was now home to her — she went over all she had to say to Ian. There certainly was a lot. But uppermost in her mind was the surprise invitation to dinner at Gina's home. It was certainly not a simple request, that was for sure. Gina always had an agenda.

In her surprise, she hadn't even asked Tom who else would be there. 'Oh my God!' she groaned. 'What on earth have I let myself in for?'

Just before she got to the cottage, she swung into the parking area in front of Stone House. There she found a dishevelled Pip struggling with a hosepipe and a dripping wet and woeful-looking Jessie.

'Cow muck! She had a wonderful time on the sea bank rolling in it. You should smell the Land Rover. Ripe, to say the least.'

'The joys of owning a dog, huh?' Christie laughed.

Shaking herself, Jessie slunk away to the summer house.

'Come on in, Christie. Fancy a coffee? I was just going to make one for myself.'

Christie accepted and followed her into the kitchen.

'I called by to ask you to pass on a message to Ian when you see him, if that's okay?'

'Certainly. Poor man, he looked ghastly at breakfast. He said that he'd wanted to go into town with you but was too exhausted. Did you go on your own?'

'Yes, I had a cup of tea with Margaret Parrish.'

'Oh, I wish I'd known. I've got some runner beans and some fresh tomatoes for her. Not to worry, Dom will be going in tomorrow anyway. We often drop by with some veggies from the garden. She says they taste so much better when they are grown with love.'

They chatted for a while about nothing in particular. Christie found it wonderfully restoring after the intense conversations she'd had of late. Pip said she'd get Ian to call her when he finally surfaced, and Christie left her preparing the evening meal.

* * *

Ian turned up at around three that afternoon. By then, Christie was busy cleaning, surrounded by various detergents, the vacuum cleaner and a mop and bucket.

'My dear girl! You're supposed to be on holiday, not skivvying.'

Christie laughed and brushed some dust from her jeans. 'It's weird. When it comes to cleaning my house in Scarborough, I have to force myself to do it, but here it's almost a pleasure.'

They sat down at the kitchen table. 'Evie always said that she enjoyed housework here. It must be the cottage, it likes to be cared for, so it repays you with a feeling of satisfaction.'

She gazed around the place. 'It does feel a bit like that.' She looked back at her friend. 'Now, are you less tired? You do seem much more like your old self.'

'I went back to bed and I slept for hours. It's something I never do normally, but I obviously needed it. Now I feel quite restored, thank you for asking. So, what news?'

Christie hardly knew where to begin. It took her a full half hour to tell him about Margaret's secret, and Tom's invitation to Tadema House.

'My goodness! You know, I always thought that Evelyn knew something about William and the way he died. And if Margaret told you, she may well have told Evie, since she was her best friend. It's a lot to carry alone. Did the doctors give this condition a name?'

She shook her head. 'Not that I know of. Margaret called it a weakness, a breakdown.'

'A "weakness." How very Victorian of her. I'm sure it's a recognised psychiatric disorder. I'm not sure that she's done the right thing by keeping Tom in the dark about it. Conditions that were untreatable years ago can be managed easily these days with the correct medications. The boy should know the family history — it's his right. What if he were experiencing problems? The doctors would have nothing to go on — I mean, Margaret won't be around forever, watching his every move.'

Catching Christie's worried frown, he gave her a reassuring pat on the hand. 'It's all right, I have no intention of breaking the confidence, I'm just voicing my thoughts out loud. What do *you* think?'

Christie had once had a friend who was convinced that she would die in her thirties because her mother had, and she told Ian the story. "She believed that she had every illness imaginable, and I'm sure it was the constant anxiety that actually did kill her, at thirty-nine."

'I'm sure that can happen, but I just feel that as an adult, he should be fully aware of the illness that killed his father and grandfather. As I said, medical science has made giant steps since then. I wish I knew what it was they suffered from.'

When conversation turned to Christie's forthcoming dinner party, his eyes assumed their usual twinkle. 'So, Miss

Spearman has invited you to join in the game, formally this time, and you have accepted.'

She didn't like the sound of that at all. 'I can always opt out. It was just Margaret nodding frantically at me that made me say yes. I can always change my mind.'

'Don't do that. If you can manage to stay in control and are careful, then I think you should go. You may learn a lot about Gina — and the others, for that matter.'

'But I'm not sure that I can be. Self-controlled, that is. You know how she affects me.'

Ian chuckled. 'Just pretend you're on a fact-finding mission. Listen and watch and remember all you can. Endeavour not to get too involved in what's being said or drawn into any arguments. Just be polite, detached, and hurry back and report to me.'

'Can't I just plead a headache and stay at home?'

Ian chuckled. 'Come on, you're used to researching things, so make her a case study and enjoy a delicious meal at the same time. You can bet your bottom dollar that Gina only serves the best.'

It appeared that between Margaret and Ian, Christie had no choice in the matter. 'Okay, but why has she invited me?'

'I think that will only become apparent when you are there. Sorry to disappoint you, but there could be a dozen different reasons for the party. It depends on what stage of the game she is at. It's a shame you don't know who the other guests are. Tell me as soon as you find out, won't you?'

She grimaced. 'You'll be the first to know, I promise.'

'Well, I had better be getting back. I've a lot to think about. Oh, and Pip said you are welcome to come for dinner if you don't feel like cooking tonight.'

Christie was obliged to refuse. She had already prepared an enormous fresh crab salad that had to be eaten today.

As she waved him off down the lane, she was interested to see a car draw up alongside his. He and the occupant exchanged a few words before whoever it was revved the engine and sped towards her. The car drew up and the bulky frame of Denis, Delphi's husband, fought his way out of the dented front door. Concern was writ large on his face, tinged with anger.

'I'm sorry,' he said, his voice gruff, 'but she come 'ere before, so I thought maybe you'd 'ave seen 'er?'

'Delphi?' Christie enquired. Who else?

He nodded.

'You'd better come in. Did you two have another row?'

The big man stood in the doorway and looked down at his boots.

'Don't worry about them, come inside and sit down.'

He perched on the edge of the sofa like an overgrown schoolboy caught out in some misdemeanour.

'Okay, Denis, now what's happened?'

'Don't rightly know, miss. We seems to be falling apart of late.'

'The holiday?' she asked tentatively.

'I put me foot down on that, I'm afraid. I've nearly got enough saved to take 'er away meself, so she won't be going without. No, she just seems to pick on me all the time, miss. Can't do nowt right. An' she's always runnin' after that bloody boss of 'ers. Says she's not well, so my Del's runnin' up to that big posh 'ouse all the time wi' grub for 'er. She were out till midnight last Saturday. Midnight! All cause of bleedin' Gina Spearman!'

'And this time?'

'Lord knows! I went to pick 'er up from work, an' they said she were gone early. No message, no idea where she'd gone. She's doin' me 'ead in, miss.'

'How long has she been like this?' As if she didn't know.

'About six months, but she's gettin' worse. It started when she got the job at that bookshop. At first, when she started bein' critical, I thought it was just all those toffs, but now, well,' he gave a hopeless shrug, 'I can see us splittin' up, miss.' There was no mistaking the tear in his eye. So he wasn't an academic, but so what? The big man truly loved Delphi, and her actions were tearing them apart.

'Perhaps she had a good reason for leaving early, Denis. Why not go home? She's probably there now, waiting for you. I don't think she will, but if she does come here, I'll send her home to you.'

Denis looked perfectly miserable. He sighed, then admitted there was little else he could do. Chasing around the countryside seemed rather pointless when he thought about it.

As an afterthought, Christie said he could, of course, try Tadema House.

'Oh, she wouldn't be there today. The girls at the shop told me Gina'd gone to Lincoln to see a printer or summat. I'm sorry, miss. It's probly me, goin' off 'alf-cocked. Mebbe I didn't listen to what she were sayin'. P'raps she has taken 'erself off shoppin' or the like. I'd better get home. Sorry to have bothered you, and thanks f'listening.'

He left Christie with yet another worry. There was no doubt in her mind that Delphi's disappearance had something to do with Gina's games. And once again — by design or accident — it had landed on her doorstep.

CHAPTER TWENTY-TWO

Liz had embarked on her new topic of research — the life and times of Gina Spearman. She had begun to wonder about Spearman herself. Christie had reacted to this woman so strongly, which just wasn't like her. Christie was one of the most calmly amiable people she'd ever met, so there had to be something behind it. Perhaps it was time she had a proper look at Ms Spearman, in the flesh. Wasn't she in need of a nice new crime thriller? She resolved to call in at the bookshop when she next went into Fenfleet.

So far, all the information she'd found on the internet had concerned business awards or related accolades. Gina certainly had a good head for enterprise. She seemed to have fingers in several different pies other than the book trade, though it appeared that the Reading Room was the project she spent most time on.

Munching a chocolate biscuit, Liz had a look at the Companies House website. According to their listing, Gina Spearman's bookshop was a huge financial success. Liz let out a low whistle. *And I thought small independent shops were all going under.* On the same site she found another of her several enterprises, a small import business, and that too was thriving.

Okay, thought Liz, we know about the businesses, let's see what we can find out about Gina herself. Liz was good at that.

Thirty minutes and several chocolate biscuits later, Liz had discovered next to nothing. The most comprehensive information came from a short biography that Gina herself had provided after being awarded the prestigious "small business of the year" prize. This provided a detailed account of her university education and her achievements, but the only personal element was that she was an only child and had made her own way up the ladder to success.

Liz needed more to go on, including the names of Gina's parents, before she could delve deeper. Every damned result she turned up had something to do with books or business. Every picture showed her at a formal occasion, usually relating to one or the other of those awards. After yet another cheesy image of Gina, champagne glass in hand, standing with the chairman of Fenfleet Council, she closed her laptop. And reached for the biscuit tin.

She sat back, frowning. Liz had spent her whole career delving into people's lives, every corner, down to the smallest detail. Her interest had been sparked and now she needed to know what made Gina Spearman tick. She had taken this on as a diversion, something to do during a brief interlude in the Lindsay Harrison case, and to help her cousin. But now it was becoming something more, and she was experiencing the first tickle of the old sensation she used to get when a suspect started to become of major concern. But why Gina Spearman? This was a successful businesswoman, not some scummy criminal.

She stood on a chair to put the biscuits out of reach. She was caught now, needed to do some proper detecting, more than just a flip through social media. Liz practically rubbed her hands together in glee.

* * *

At the end of the afternoon, Christie received a call from Tom, asking if she was still coming to the dinner on Tuesday.

'Gina said seven for seven thirty. Dress code, smart casual.' He laughed. 'But you can ignore the smart bit. Gina rarely dresses up — she hates all that. Jane always dresses the same wherever she goes. Those long flowy thingies always make me think I should be wearing flares, a flowery shirt and matching kipper tie.'

This made Christie chuckle. What a thought! Plus, Tom had just given her an opportunity to find out who'd be there. 'Oh good, Jane is going. Anyone else I know?'

'Delphi, who will probably turn up looking like a Barbie doll. Her "Ken" has been invited too but I've a feeling he'll probably give it a miss.'

You bet he will.

'Gina said she's also invited one of her old university tutors who is in the neighbourhood at present. That's about it, I think.'

'Great, Tom. I'm looking forward to it.'

'Me too. Gina is a fabulous cook.'

'Goodness, is there no end to her talents?' *Oh, why did I say that?* 'I'm joking,' she said quickly. 'I'm not surprised, though. She seems to be good at whatever she sets her mind to.'

She would have to do better than that if she were to make it through the dinner party without incident. So much for being detached.

'I'm hoping Tuesday evening will give you a chance to see the real Gina, the caring and generous one,' said Tom, sounding terribly earnest. 'It's unfortunate that you've only seen her bad side, so I'm hoping you'll leave the party with a very different view of her.'

She tried to excuse herself, saying she really must go now, but Tom was in full flow and didn't hear.

'I feel so sorry for her, Christie. Even though my dad died young, I had a happy childhood. Gina's parents were terrible to her. There was no actual physical abuse, well, not that I know of, but she underwent terrible mental torture. She was treated abominably. She said that on one occasion, she was made to sit in a cupboard all evening while her parents hosted a reception. She said that when she was finally let out, she couldn't even stand up. To this day, she's frightened of the dark. She was constantly told she was ignorant and stupid, so she determined to make something of herself. And she has, and I really admire her for it.' He finally drew breath. 'Sorry. I'm going on, I know, but it's easy to get the wrong impression of her and I think you have.'

'I've got to admit that hearing the way she spoke to both you and Delphi at the shop didn't do a lot to make me like her. That's quite understandable, Tom, isn't it?'

'I guess. But believe me, Christie, there's a lot more to Gina than that. Just keep an open mind. I think you'll see a different person.'

She said her mind would be a blank canvas. She didn't say that what was painted on it would be up to Gina.

Christie had her supper, wondering if she could get out of going next door for a sherry. Unable to think of a single excuse, she tidied herself up and tramped around to the little bungalow.

She was ushered in like royalty, which made her feel horribly guilty for having not wanted to go. She soon discovered that "sherry" was an extremely broad concept, meaning every drink under the sun. She had been right about the wealth of stories Bill and Lynne had to tell and tried to commit as much to memory as possible. As it turned out, she didn't leave until nearly ten, having spent a thoroughly enjoyable evening.

She had only just got back when there was a knock at the door, and she heard Bill call out that he'd forgotten to tell her something. He warned her that they were going to be harvesting one of the fields that night, so she shouldn't be frightened if she heard the machines or saw the lights out over the fields. If you didn't know, they could give you a bit of a scare.

As he turned to leave, he stopped. 'Oh, you've got one of my niece's paintings!' Jane was his brother's girl and 'a right talented lass at that'.

Christie had had no idea that their surname was Waterhouse, and it came as quite a surprise to find out that they were related.

The lights travelling up and down the dark fields were indeed eerie. Christie peered out of the window and watched the great harvesters lumber up and down. If Bill hadn't warned her, she might well have been a little frightened by it. As it was, the rumble of engines filled her dreams.

* * *

Oh shit! I've got nothing to wear. It was Tuesday morning and Christie sat up in bed, recalling that she'd planned to sort out something suitable the day before, but never got around to it. After reminding herself this was supposed to be a holiday, she'd spent all of Sunday and most of Monday working in the garden, and just enjoying being at The Mulberries.

Now she needed to get her brain into gear. Christie wanted to make a good impression. But more than this, she wanted it to seem as if she considered the evening worthy of dressing with special care for. She was catching on.

She laid out almost her entire wardrobe on the bed, picking up this and that and discarding it. Finally, she put everything back in the cupboard and hunted for her credit card.

By ten o'clock, she was at the checkout counter of the big department store in the High Street with an armful of new clothes. She was, she realised, starting to get in the mood.

She had toyed with the idea of buying new shoes, instead blowing the money on a bottle of the most expensive perfume she'd ever owned. She took her acquisitions home, hung them up and spent the rest of the day back in the garden.

It was time to take a bath. For a time, years ago, she had practised meditation. Now, to calm herself, she tried again. And failed. She was far too excited.

She dried herself off and lay for a while on Evelyn's bed, admiring the tapestry. Suddenly, a thought occurred to her that had absolutely nothing to do with the forthcoming dinner. If and when he decided to sell, she would ask Ian Hardy if she could buy The Mulberries. She knew that this was Auden's last book, so she would be free to sell her Scarborough house and move to the Fens. Though small, the cottage suited her needs perfectly. It was no great distance to travel for her cardiology check-ups, indeed they might refer her to a local hospital, and she had no other ties.

As the thought took hold, it was all she could do not to grab her phone and ring Ian right away. No. She'd get tonight over with first, then put the offer to him. Once the Yorkshire house was sold, she would have enough money, along with her savings, to keep her going for quite some time, and with her few investments, possibly indefinitely.

She had no clue what The Mulberries was worth, but she knew Ian would be fair. House prices here were low compared to Scarborough. Her town house would easily buy this cottage and then some. Her heart raced with excitement. This could be her home.

Having come up with the idea, she could think of nothing else. Then she started to wonder if Ian had made other arrangements. He might have — after all, she was just a temporary caretaker. The joy and excitement that had taken wing crash-landed in a fluttery heap, a dying bird. She was hopelessly in love with The Mulberries and wasn't sure how she would bear its loss.

She told herself that if she was meant to live here, she would, and that was that. "*Believe that what is needed will be given.*"

Christie put on her new clothes and prepared for the coming evening. She stood in front of the mirror, slightly surprised at her reflection, all the while repeating to herself, 'Dear, sweet Ian. Please sell me Evelyn's cottage.'

She had booked the village's single taxi for six forty-five. She could easily have driven herself but thought a drink or two might make the evening a bit more bearable. She asked the driver to return for her at 10.30, and he said she could always ring if she decided to change the time.

At seven o'clock precisely, Christie was at the door of Tadema House, nervous but determined to make Ian proud of her.

Delphi answered with a smile her eyes did not reflect. She apologised for Denis, saying he'd had no need to bother her. She had been a bit late leaving work, that was all. It was no problem, Christie said, and Delphi led the way to the lounge.

Tom and Jane were already there. Tom kissed her cheeks. 'You made it.'

Jane, reclining on an enormous cream sofa, indicated for Christie to join her. 'Gina is still busy in the kitchen, she's been there most of the afternoon apparently, along with her assistant, our Delphi. She'll be out soon.'

Christie noted the disparities. Delphi had said she was at work, Denis said Gina was in Grantham and Jane thought they were both here. She pushed the thought aside, concentrating on appearing relaxed.

Tom, having apparently decided against flares and kipper tie, was in smart, stone-coloured chinos, a deep blue shirt and navy and beige suede loafers.

Delphi, still wearing a fixed smile, said, 'I'd better go and help.' She disappeared, presumably in the direction of the kitchen.

When Jane asked how Christie was faring at The Mulberries, she was tempted to tell her about her idea. She pushed that thought aside too, knowing she had to speak with Ian first. She said only that she was really happy there and would be sorry to leave it when the time came.

Jane said she understood what she meant. She had almost felt a presence there, guiding her hand as she made her painting of the garden. Thinking of The Mulberries' peaceful atmosphere, Christie looked around her. Tadema House was indeed fabulous, a showplace, like something out of *Homes and Gardens*. But it felt cold, somehow, empty, despite the expensive furnishings.

It was fitted throughout with thick cream carpet, the kind that makes you want to walk on it barefoot. The lounge walls were covered in what looked like a rich, textured silk. They were hung with large Pre-Raphaelite reproductions — not originals, surely? One was cleverly lit and carefully protected from the light. There was a small, printed card in a simple black frame next to it. It was not a picture she recognised, but she probably wouldn't, not being keen on the Pre-Raphaelites. Christie looked closer. This one definitely was the real thing.

The doorbell sounded and Tom went to answer it.

A tall woman strode in and gripped Christie's hand, making her wince.

'Dr Naomi Smythe,' she said, emphasising the "Doctor."

Her interpretation of "smart casual" was interesting. She appeared to be wearing a giant onesie that reminded Christie of an enormous Andy Pandy outfit, thankfully without the funny hat. Only Jane seemed totally unaware of how extraordinary this woman looked. She asked Naomi where she was based and they learned she was at Keble College, Oxford, lecturing on the History of Art. She was staying in Lincoln for a few days and had bumped into Gina purely by chance. She went on to heap praise on her former student, while Christie sat, nodding sagely.

Gina appeared in the doorway. She was wearing a black polo neck sweater and black jeans, and a long black-and-white check apron. 'Hello, everyone. My apologies for not meeting you at the door. Dinner won't be long.' She looked around. 'Thomas, you're shirking your duties. Some music, please, and Naomi doesn't have a drink.'

He opened his mouth, then closed it and picked up a remote. A moment later the gentle sound of Mozart drifted into the room.

Christie didn't have a drink either but said nothing.

Jane was sipping a gin and tonic. Christie and Naomi both chose Tío Pepe. After about ten minutes, a flustered-looking Delphi scurried in and asked them all to go through to the dining room. This was another elegant and soulless room. Neither the flower arrangements nor the flickering candles gave it any warmth.

Delphi disappeared and returned with an enormous tray laden with plates of food. Christie had brought wine with her, but this was nowhere in sight. Beside the table stood four tall ice buckets, each containing a bottle of champagne.

After they had seated themselves, Gina appeared, pushing a hand through her hair in her characteristic nervous gesture. She seated herself at the head of the table and asked them to help themselves to champagne. 'Drink as much as you like. The refrigerator is full of the stuff and nobody is counting.' She introduced the starters. 'There is a homemade pâté — my own recipe, I can recommend it. Or sautéed chicken livers, bacon and avocado served on a bed of warm salad leaves, or melon with aged port.'

The presentation was faultless. Christie thought of her simple fare, the odd flowers in drinks glasses and the dining table that, with both its leaves out, dwarfed the sitting room at The Mulberries. Then she recalled the warmth of that humble cottage. She knew which she preferred.

She chose the wilted salad, which was the best she'd ever tasted. Remembering Ian's advice, she said so.

Gina dismissed the comment, but Christie saw a hard glint in her eye that told another story.

A few sips of champagne told her she'd made the right decision in taking a taxi. A few more sips, and she began to relax and enjoy Naomi's entertaining stories of university life. Tom seemed reflective, almost mournful, and Christie knew he yearned to be able to say "my college," "my house," "my subject." But there was nothing she could say.

Then Delphi, all unawares, came to his assistance. Naomi mentioned Keble's past alumni, and Delphi looked at Tom in appeal. He smiled at her and said softly that alumni were former pupils or students. She gave him a grin of thanks, while Naomi apologised for using the term in non-academic company. It kind of included Tom in that higher echelon.

Gina drew a breath, obviously about to utter some cutting remark, so Christie suddenly said, 'That painting, the one in the alcove in the lounge. I was meaning to ask you about it.'

'Oh, that.' Gina's tone was cold. 'Not one of his best, I'm afraid. You probably realised it's a Strudwick.'

Christie's blank expression gave her away.

'Ah, not someone you're familiar with, I see,' Gina said.

Jane came to her help. 'I'm not surprised you don't know him, Christie. You'd have to be a real Pre-Raphaelite buff to recognise that particular painting.'

Naomi said, 'Interesting chap, all the same. He was a studio assistant to Burne-Jones, and you can really see his influence when you look at the women's dreamy faces. And, Gina, I don't agree with you that it's not one of his best. It's a very fine piece. You are lucky to have discovered it. I hope you are well insured?'

So it was an original.

Gina looked at their empty plates and then at Delphi, who leaped to her feet as if a starting pistol had been fired. Without a word, she cleared away all the dishes, went to the kitchen and stood uncomfortably in the doorway, no doubt awaiting further orders.

Gina and Delphi then brought in the main course, a lobster that was similar to a Thermidor but with a different flavour. It was served with tiny new potatoes, fresh local asparagus spears, sugar snap peas and an interesting side dish of shrimp and rice in a fresh herb dressing.

They had all begun the meal, which was delicious, when Gina flung down her fork. 'For heaven's sake, Delphi! I said lightly salt the rice, not bloody preserve it in the damned stuff. You've ruined it! Don't eat the shrimp, folks. My assistant here obviously thought you wouldn't mind being up all night drinking water.'

Delphi blushed to the roots of her hair. Her embarrassment was painful to witness.

'But, Gina, I'm sure I only put in what you told me.'

'Will you please just throw it away. It's like brine!'

Christie had already tasted a small forkful and thought it delicious, and certainly not over-salted. Should she speak out? Only Naomi declared that she wasn't a lover of rice, so she hadn't tried it. With a silent apology to Delphi, Christie kept her mouth shut.

Before she could change her mind, the offending dish was whisked away. It had apparently been worth the cost of the shrimp to make Delphi look foolish.

Delphi had returned from the kitchen and was toying with her lobster when Gina reached across and patted her arm. 'I'm sorry, sweetie. I shouldn't have barked at you like that. It wasn't your fault. It is hard to get that delicate balance between the herbs and the salt. I should have done it myself.'

For an hour they ate and drank copiously, and to Christie's surprise, no one else came under attack. Naomi asked about her research. She knew the "jack-o'-lantern" painting and was able to give Christie a little more of its history.

'It seems to have disappeared. It was sold by Sotheby's back in the eighties to an anonymous buyer. Hughes did some very sinister illustrations, you know, for children's stories. Typical of the era, of course. Fairy tales were very grim and frightening back then.'

Tom reminded them that "Ring a Ring o' Roses" was about the Black Death, which set off another conversation.

The meal over, they retired to the lounge for coffee. Gina instructed Tom to make it, saying she would treat the other guests to a tour of Tadema House.

They wandered from room to room. It was a beautiful old property and well-looked-after. Many of the original fittings were still in situ. But every room gave Christie the same feeling that she was visiting a stately home, or a film set. Unlived in. Certainly, plenty of money had been thrown at it, but no love.

They returned to ground level and went through the hi-tech kitchen to a conservatory. This was a long, glass-covered area that ran right along one outside wall. In one corner was a huge purple flowering bougainvillea and, suspended from the highest point, an old-fashioned clothes airer that let down on a pulley. There was some rather nice cane furniture and a table supporting several rather sad and dry pot plants. It had a stone floor with a scattering of woven mats. Gina said she generally used it to do the ironing in or dry off washing.

Christie was just considering what she would have done with it had it been hers when she saw a look of dismay on Jane's face. She followed her gaze and saw the beautiful painting of Tadema House, hung crookedly on a masonry nail on the roughly distempered brickwork.

So this was Gina's purpose in bringing them to the sunroom. It was Jane's turn.

Gina smiled. 'Oh, don't make anything out of that. It's only there while I find a home for it. It's difficult to place when all the others are oils and it's such a different style.' She lowered her head and raised her eyes in an attempt at coyness. 'I did tell you it wasn't really my thing, didn't I, Janey? No offence, but I'm just not sure where it will go yet.'

Jane managed a weak smile and added quietly that the strong light through the glass would ruin it if it were left there too long.

'Oh, I'll find a home for it somewhere,' Gina said dismissively. 'Now, let's see what Thomas Maxfield Parrish has managed to do with my special blend of ground coffee, shall we?'

Christie thought he had done a superb job with her "special" coffee, but Gina sipped it and pulled a face. Christie was still thinking about the painting in the sun lounge. She had assumed it had been hung there to get at Jane; now she realised it was more likely to get at her. Not only could she not have it, but it was to be neglected and slowly ruined.

By this stage, Christie was so incensed she kept her mouth shut from then on. Gina, meanwhile, was suddenly the life and soul of the party. She amused her friends with anecdotes of life in the shop, she involved them and drew them in. She touched hands and ruffled hair affectionately. She praised them and vowed they were the best friends ever.

And they fell for it. Every one of them.

At ten o'clock, Gina slipped her arm through Tom's and asked him to help her brew more coffee. Delphi was busily explaining the story of her unusual name to Naomi, while Christie sat quietly with Jane.

She told her how devastated she was at seeing the painting out in the sun lounge. Jane made light of it, saying she was sure Gina would move it soon and if she didn't, well, it was hers to do what she liked with. She could hang it in the coal-shed if she so wished.

Noting the edge to Jane's voice, Christie dropped the subject. Another point to Gina. Christie sat in silence, hoping her cab would be early.

Naomi was staying the night while Delphi, Jane and Tom were going to share a taxi back to town. Christie said they could share hers, but Delphi wanted to stay and help tidy up. Tom said he would wait for her — Denis was working a night shift and he had promised to see Delphi home safely. That made Christie wonder how things were going in that semi in Fenfleet. Since she had at least twenty minutes to go before she could make her escape, she accepted another coffee.

'So, who'd like a walk to help the dinner go down?' Gina said, and waited for a response.

'Through the village?' Tom asked.

'No. If we go out at the back of the property, we can cut across to the sea bank. We could look for some of Christie's ghost lights, or at least chase burning marsh gas.'

'But it's pitch black out there tonight, we'd kill ourselves,' exclaimed Tom.

'I have storm lanterns and torches and I know the way.'

Christie said her taxi was about to come, so she'd have to forgo the adventure.

'What do you have to get home for? Cancel the cab. I'll pay it off when it gets here, and you can stay over. There's plenty of room.'

'Oh, do come, Christie.' Delphi bounced around like a child.

'I really don't think it's such a good idea. The marsh isn't safe, especially at night,' Christie said.

Gina gave her a withering look.

Naomi came to her rescue, saying that she had no sensible shoes, and her feet were so big that nothing of Gina's would fit her.

Gina threw up her hands. 'All right, but I insist we go another night. We'll go a-dancing on the Fens!' She twirled, grabbed Tom, and swung him around.

Everyone laughed, even Christie, though hers was purely out of relief. She had just heard the doorbell.

They all stood around while she thanked Gina for a splendid meal. She asked again if she could give anyone a lift, but they all said they'd stay on.

She sank into the back seat of the taxi and closed her eyes. She couldn't wait to get back to the peace and quiet of the cottage. Though the evening hadn't been the total disaster she had expected, the strain of walking on eggshells for four hours had exhausted her. At least she had managed to keep her mouth shut. Ian would be pleased with her.

She paid the cab, thanked him several times for being so punctual, at which he looked somewhat bemused, and hurried inside. She went straight to bed and immediately fell into a deep and dreamless sleep, waking only once to close a window. A storm had broken.

CHAPTER TWENTY-THREE

After breakfast, Christie went to see Ian at Stone House. He was keen to hear about her evening and listened attentively. When she mentioned the fine food and vintage champagne, he remarked that he'd dine with the Devil himself to get that sort of treatment.

When she had ended her story, he said, 'I think the presence of the university lecturer was no coincidence. I'm sure she was invited for Tom's sake, to remind him of having missed out on an academic career.' He paused, thinking. 'I have no idea why she should belittle Delphi so much, unless it's just to beat her down in order to pick her up again, to show everyone the extent of the control she has over her.'

Christie agreed: Delphi was like the whipped dog that licks the hand that beats it.

'The picture, of course, was a double-handed blow to both you and Jane. But there is one thing I don't understand, and that's why she tried to get you all to go out onto the fen. I don't know that area very well, but there is a well-known trail, Brown Water Fen Walk, or something like that, behind her land. It's fine in the daylight, but at night it would have been treacherous. Plus, for heaven's sake, you'd all been drinking.'

'It could have been to make me look silly. I'd told them about my earlier trip to Sly Fen and the lights that we saw. I really don't know.' Since she didn't believe that Gina would deliberately try to kill them all, Christie could come up with no suggestion.

Ian's expression was still thoughtful. 'I think what was most enlightening about the whole evening is the fact that none of them wanted to leave when you offered them the chance. They stayed with her, when any one of them could have left in your taxi.'

She remembered them standing on the steps at Tadema House, clustered around Gina as if posing for a group photograph. She saw again the look that Gina had given her as she turned to leave. The flash of triumph before the friendly smile and the wave, as she turned and led her entourage inside.

It came to her that the whole evening had been staged to show her who was in charge. Gina pulled the strings, not Christie.

Ian agreed. 'But don't be discouraged. You can't expect them to see through her just like that. She has been slowly brainwashing them for ages — stories of her dreadful childhood, plying them with gifts, allowing them to spend time in one of the richest houses in the area. They might not like the tempers and the tantrums, but they believe them to be part of her complex personality. They put up with them because she is, they think, misunderstood, damaged by her wicked parents. Good at heart and highly intelligent. Oh, and they truly believe that she needs them. Most of all they *want* her to need them. It's all extremely unhealthy, but understandable. Take it slowly, Christie. Work on them, get them to trust you. Then you have to find ways to let Gina let herself down, show them her true colours.' He paused. 'I hope you're planning to stay around for a while. This can't be rushed — you saw that from Jane's reaction to you over the painting.'

Christie saw her opportunity and jumped at it. She offered to purchase The Mulberries. Then she waited, her chest tight with anticipation.

Ian sat in silence for what felt like hours, his face impassive. Then the corners of his mouth lifted. 'Some of the younger choirboys have an expression that I rather like. Whenever they come across a coincidence they say "spooky." So, Miss McFerran, "spooky." I had been planning to leave this until you went back to Scarborough, but this morning I rang a local estate agent to get a valuation. They were going to visit as soon as you'd left. So you see, I had already been planning to put it up for sale.'

'So would you consider letting *me* purchase it?' Her voice shook slightly.

'I would be delighted.'

Her heart sang.

'It would be perfect for two reasons,' Ian said. 'One, I couldn't ask for anyone better to have living in my sister's beloved home, and second, because I'm planning to return to London.'

The singing stopped.

'As you know, I retired some time ago, but I am still needed in my former parish. I've been wallowing in my grief for too long. I have to let Evelyn go, and that means her precious cottage as well. I'll be with her again before long and in the meantime, I must get on with my own life.'

Christie didn't know what to say. She was both ecstatic and desolate at the same time. She would have The Mulberries but lose her friend and his wise counsel.

'If I could make just one request,' Ian asked. 'The tapestry. It has been in my family forever, but I can't take it to London. For one thing, the room would be diminished without it and besides, there's nowhere to put it at my home. So, would you mind making provision that should you predecease me, the heirloom comes back to me?'

'Ian, I would leave the entire house to you. I have no family, there's no one to inherit my property, so I would be happy for you to have it back.'

He shook his head and laughed. 'Just the tapestry, honestly. You have no idea what your future holds. If you buy The Mulberries, it's yours forever, to do whatever you want with.' He heaved a sigh of satisfaction. 'If you just trust in whatever spiritual being is right for you, the world can be a wonderful place. Evelyn loved that house more than anything else in the world, and I know it's going to the right person.'

Christie took his wrinkled hands in hers. 'Thank you.'

* * *

'Guess what!'

Matt looked up at Liz, who was just pushing her phone back into her pocket. 'I know. You've solved the case.'

She laughed. 'I wish. But listen, Matt. Our Christie is moving here. She's buying Evelyn's old cottage!'

Her news didn't come as much of a surprise to Matt. Christie had clearly fallen for the Fens, but the speed of her decision was a bit unexpected. He smiled at Liz. 'So you'll have your childhood playmate here for good. That's wonderful.' He meant it. He had worried that Liz had lost most of her friends since they'd retired because they had all been work colleagues. He'd feared she would be lonely and cut off if anything were to happen to him.

'Oh, its brilliant news, isn't it? We're the first people she's told. Ian agreed to it earlier this morning. An estate agent is going to value it tomorrow, then Ian's agreed to a private sale.' She beamed at him. 'And he'll await payment until she sells her Scarborough house. What a great situation to be in.'

'Oh, that house in Yorkshire should walk off the books,' Matt said. 'It's in a great location and she's kept it in good condition even though she's hardly been there in the last few years.'

'She's already contacted a local agent, and she'll be going back up there in a day or so to set the wheels in motion and see Auden at the same time. I think this could all go through very quickly. Then she can start afresh here.' Liz flopped onto a kitchen chair.

'Am I picking up a hint of something negative?' Matt said.

'No-oo.' She sighed. 'Well, not exactly. It's just, oh . . .'

'From the beginning, as we coppers say.'

'Okay, Officer Ballard. And don't dismiss this as fanciful, all right?'

He raised his hands in surrender. 'Just tell me.'

'Christie has become really fond of some of the people here — in a very short space of time, I mean. She's quite involved with them, possibly more involved than she intended. I know it sounds a bit, well, petty really, but it seems that three of them are being influenced by Tom's boss, the owner of the Reading Room. The woman, Gina Spearman, is a very successful local businesswoman. The thing is, Christie is really worried that this woman's influence is spoiling their relationships with the people closest to them, as in the likes of Tom's mum, Margaret Parrish.' She pulled a face. 'Christie really dislikes this Gina woman. She's got it into her head that she's a dangerous game-player and I'm afraid she'll try to stop her in some way.'

'Well, if it's Gina Spearman, she should step well back,' Matt said. 'I've had a few dealings with that lady in the past, and she has a lot of clout in the local business community and the town council. I'd think twice before I got involved with her, I really would.'

'You know her?'

'Not as in *know* her, but I've seen her in action in a couple of disputes concerning Fenfleet Council and local policing.' At the time, Matt had put Spearman down as the academic called in to put the country bumpkins back in their place.

'Did you like her?'

'I never got close enough to form an opinion, but from what I saw, she wasn't my kind of person. Why?'

Liz looked thoughtful. 'Christie asked me if I knew anything about her and I realised that I didn't, so I did a bit of checking up. She bothers me, Matt. And it bothers me even more that Christie has taken such a strong dislike to her. I know my Christie and that never happens, she's the eternal peacemaker. So if she's picked up on something in Gina Spearman, I very much doubt that she's wrong about it.'

'So now you're anxious that if she moves here permanently, fur will fly?'

'I think it's going to happen anyway, sweetheart, but if she's living here, she has nowhere to run.'

'Bit dramatic, surely?' said Matt, with a half laugh. Then he saw Liz's expression. 'So what do you suggest? Tell her to think carefully before moving?'

There was a long pause, then Liz said, 'No, but I'd like to know more about Gina Spearman. Can you afford for me to take a couple of days away from the Lindsay Harrison case, to dig around a bit?'

'All I'd say is tread warily, my love. From what I've seen, hers is not a foot you want to stamp on. She's got clout and she's loaded.'

Liz looked relieved. 'Thanks, Matt, and I'm not going to question her or anything, just do some background research.' Suddenly, she said, 'Oh.'

'What?'

'Something just occurred to me.' Liz went and fetched her laptop. After searching for a few minutes, she looked up at him. 'Just coincidence, I'm sure, but one of Spearman's minor investments is an interest in Rowantrees, the garden centre where Lindsay Harrison worked.'

Matt wondered why her name hadn't come up when they were investigating the place.

Liz took her phone from her pocket. 'I'm ringing Sandy Giles. I'm sure she won't mind talking to me since she doesn't work there anymore.'

Matt left her talking to the brother, Tony, and went to fetch his file on the Harrison case. A lot of people with connections to Rowantrees had been interviewed during the original investigation, but he had never seen Gina Spearman's name crop up.

When he returned, she was sitting at the kitchen table looking extremely perplexed.

'Dare I ask?' Matt said.

'Something I never realised before. Lindsay Harrison worked at Rowantrees all right, but she didn't just work in the plant section. Apparently, she was also part-time in one of the outlets there.'

'Which outlet?'

'The bookshop. Like most big garden centres, they have a section that sells books and cards, and the owner of the franchise is — guess who — Gina Spearman. Sandy helped her out if Lindsay got busy and her section, which was pottery, china and gifts, was quiet. That's how they became friends. It was also how she kept those flowers and gifts secret from the others, because generally she was on her own in her little book department.' Liz leaned forward. 'And get this. It wasn't widely known, but there was a general belief that the anonymous benefactor who put up the offer of a reward for information leading to the capture of Lindsay's killer was Gina Spearman.'

Matt now understood Liz's confusion. 'How much was that for?'

'Fifteen thousand pounds. Quite a significant amount, wouldn't you say?'

Matt got on the phone to DCI Charley Anders.

'Sorry, Matt,' Charley said. 'That one's a dead end. The transaction was made through a solicitor who was adamant that his client remain anonymous. What I do know is that the offer is still open and will stay that way until we have a conviction.'

Matt ended the call and sat staring into space. 'So, let's say it's Gina — after all, she's wealthy enough. She must have thought an awful lot of a part-time sales assistant to pledge that kind of money.'

'Or have some other agenda, but don't ask me what. It just doesn't sound quite right, does it?' Liz murmured. 'But we don't even have proof that it's actually her.'

'Okay, Liz, do your sleuthing, but be careful what you tell Christie. We can't have her taking up a fight that she'll never win. And now we have a vague connection between Lindsay and Gina, I don't want Christie muddying the waters for us either. This is probably nothing at all, but if Gina Spearman was never interviewed first time around, we might need to have a word with her ourselves.'

Liz nodded and stood up. 'Time to get to work.'

* * *

Christie spent the rest of the day largely on the phone. She rang her solicitor and told him of her plans, and he gave her the name of a reputable estate agent. She rang the company and their valuer said that though he didn't want to raise her hopes, he had a client waiting for a similar type of property in that very location. If the Scarborough house turned out to be suitable, then the sale could be quick, painless and quite lucrative.

Ian's agent was to value The Mulberries early the following morning, which suited her perfectly. It was fortunate that she'd recently cleaned it so thoroughly. She'd already contacted Richard to tell him to expect her the day after tomorrow, so all that was left was to tell her new friends. She wondered what their reaction would be. Her initial thought was to dash into town before everything closed and give them the news, but common sense saved her the trip. She'd get the formalities over first, then when all was underway, she'd tell them.

As it was, she settled for a pleasant evening alone with a snack supper and a glass of wine and made plans for all the things she'd like to do when the cottage became hers. As she settled down to sleep, she realised she had been too busy to even think about Gina. How wonderful that was.

CHAPTER TWENTY-FOUR

The following morning the estate agent, a plump young man called Darren, was moving from room to room at The Mulberries, measuring up and asking questions. Christie let him assume that she was showing him around in the Reverend Hardy's absence.

Darren chatted incessantly. 'It's full of character, but it is very small. One-bedroom cottages in a rural location aren't exactly bestsellers. A single bedroom would do for an elderly person, except those stairs rather rule that out. The older generation prefer bungalows. And single people, well, the size of the garden could put them off and finding work up here is not easy, so, although it's lovely and full of charm, I can see this sitting on our books for a while.' He made copious notes and raved about the bathroom. 'Really unusual to find an old cottage with so many original fittings as well as a top-of-the-range bath and shower room! I'm sure the right buyer would be over the moon, it's just the problem of finding that special person.'

You're looking at her, sunshine. She pitied poor Ian, having to go through all this just to get a valuation.

At long last, he closed his briefcase, handed her back the empty coffee mug and said he would be ringing the reverend later in the day. He thanked her for her time and roared off down the lane in his flashy Toyota.

After he'd gone, Christie felt suddenly deflated, although she wasn't sure why. She was left with a whole day to fill and wasn't sure how. Well, she needed fuel for her trip, so she might as well go into Fenfleet, top up with petrol, grab a few supplies for the next day's journey and do the rounds of her friends.

It didn't quite go to plan.

At the gallery, Gary informed her that Jane was out painting in a corner of some cornfield. Tom had been sent to collect a valuable order from a book wholesaler in Peterborough and Gina, thanks be to God, was with the accountant all day.

That left Delphi and Margaret. She climbed the stairs to the café and was welcomed like a long-lost sister. Delphi poured drinks and handed over her apron to an older lady with a lilac rinse. 'Lily, I'm on my break, okay.'

The lady smiled, revealing a magnificent set of gleaming white false teeth.

Delphi stifled a snigger. 'Ee, but they frighten the life out of me,' she whispered. 'They're two sizes too big, I'm sure.' She looked happy, relaxed. 'I'm so glad you called by. It was a smashin' meal the other evenin', wasn't it? Except for me ruining Gina's rice. Silly me.'

Christie was tempted to tell her that she thought it had tasted fine, but Delphi was rattling on. 'I deserved the telling off, fancy being so daft! Those shrimps must've cost a fortune and I messed it up. I wonder about myself sometimes, Christie. I don't know why Gina puts up with me, I really don't. I must drive her nuts.'

Tempted to throttle her, Christie settled for praise. She pointed out her good points and said she thought Gina was lucky to have her. In her opinion, there had been no need to be so rude in front of the guests.

Delphi seemed bent on stirring her coffee. 'You don't know her, Christie,' she murmured. 'Not like I do.'

Suddenly, Christie was sick to the teeth of being told that she didn't know Gina Spearman. 'Okay, Delphi, tell me

about her. Why do I seem to see a different person to you?'
She hadn't meant to sound so harsh, but of course, Delphi
was used to being spoken to that way.

'She had a really difficult time when she was young, poor
thing. I mean, I didn't have much, but at least me mam and
dad didn't knock me about. I know she has a temper, but
it's just because she cares about me. Sometimes I think she
cares more than Denis, just differently, you know. An' she's
so good to all us staff. Do you know, last Christmas, she
bought us all a turkey! A right biggun, an' all. And we had
all sorts of special goodies — chocolates, dates an' that, and
fancy Christmas crackers from a posh shop in London, plus
a big bonus. Then there's the holiday . . .'

Christie said she thought Denis had put his foot down
where that was concerned.

'She really wants me to go, says I deserve it. I do, too.'

'What about Denis, Delphi? I thought he was taking
you.'

Delphi pouted. 'But I want to go to Greece. Den can
only afford Majorca. He doesn't understand.'

'So you'd go without him?'

'He says he'll go back to his mother's if I do.'

Christie noted that Delphi hadn't said she wouldn't go.

'Oh, Christie! It's the dream of a lifetime! You'd think
he'd put me first, wouldn't you?'

It was like hearing an echo of Gina's words. After a
while, she said, 'Why don't you put aside the money Denis
has saved towards a holiday in Greece next year? Then you
can visit your dream place together.'

'Denis knows sweet FA about the ancient Greeks! It'd
bore him to tears. Now Gina, she's clever, she'd be able to
tell me all the stories, and the history and stuff. Don't get
me wrong. I love my Denis, but you have to make a stand
sometimes, don't you? Do something for yourself.'

Christie knew she wasn't going to win this one. Delphi
had no idea what could actually happen to her marriage if she
continued to chase this pipe dream, and the only person she

appeared to be listening to was Gina. If they didn't watch out, the holiday was going to cause a serious rift between this previously happy couple. Her question was why. What reason would Gina have to split them up, make them both unhappy?

She changed the subject. She was seriously considering giving up on trying to help her friends. It was a thankless task. If she couldn't win over Delphi, what chance would she have of persuading Tom or Jane? She might just as well let them all get on with it. Surely Tom had more sense than to let his dear mother get hurt? And Jane had real talent, she could get by on her own merit. She didn't need Gina Spearman. If she needed help with her finances, she should get an accountant or a financial advisor. Couldn't she see that Gina was belittling her work solely to hold her back? Jane's work was inspired. But her self-confidence was being undermined by her "good friend". Some friend!

As Delphi chatted away about the dinner party, Christie took stock of her position. She was hoping to start a new life here and wanted it to be peaceful and contented. All this aggravation was, as Ian had said, "a vexation to the spirit." Did she really want that?

She smiled warmly at Delphi. 'Do what you think is right. Just remember that Denis loves you and you're hurting him by always putting Gina first. That's how it looks from the outside, anyway.'

'Oh, he'll get over it. It's not as if I'm going off with another bloke, is it? As my mam'd say, "He'll come round wi' the rattle o' the bucket!"'

Her naivete amazed Christie. From the brief exchange she'd had with Denis, she had got the idea that his emotions ran deep. Though he'd had little schooling, he understood what was important in life, and he took his marriage very seriously. He would never forgive Delphi if she betrayed him by rejecting his hard-earned holiday in the sun in favour of a jaunt with a rich bitch.

But what the hell? That was their business. Time for Christie McFerran to butt out. She had plenty to occupy herself with. After all, she had a house to sell. Without mentioning her plans, she told Delphi to give her love to Tom when he got back, and then she left.

She opted out of visiting Margaret too. She would ring her when she'd had a word with Ian. Margaret would be pleased she was moving into the area, but perhaps she should cool off her visits a bit. Much as she liked them both, Christie couldn't be her son's keeper. It was all becoming too messy. She hadn't asked for the old lady's dark secret to be loaded onto her shoulders. She wasn't that strong.

Ian would be disappointed in her, but he was leaving anyway. Surely he wouldn't expect her to fight on alone?

Then there was Tom. If he was going to pay heed to the song of the siren, there was little she could do to stop him following her into the deep. She would be around to help pick up the pieces when Gina got fed up and spat him out, but that was all she could offer right now.

As she walked back through the town, the church spire caught her eye. She had been in once with Ian to light a candle for Evelyn. This time, she was alone. She went to the box of candles in the side chapel and bought three — one each for Tom, Jane and Delphi, consigning their care to Ian's greater Protector. She had taken on a task she could never finish and should never have begun. Now she was opting out. Ian would have to forgive her, as would Margaret. She was not up to the fight.

Leaving the church, she felt better. It wouldn't be easy to stand aside. She knew there would be times when she would be tempted to interfere again in Gina's games, but she would just have to learn to turn away. Once Gina realised that Christie was no longer playing, she would let her go, an expendable pawn.

She decided to go directly to Stone House and see Ian. With luck, he'd have a price for her, and she'd know where she stood with the house.

Ian sat outside under a big green umbrella, nursing an orange juice and reading what looked like a financial report. His face lit up when he saw her.

'Thank heavens! I was getting quite out of my depth with this. Why can't solicitors and accountants write in English?' He threw the papers down and sat back. 'Well, I've had a quote on the cottage. The estate agent rang about half an hour ago. They think between seventy-six and seventy-eight.'

Christie's mouth fell open.

Head tilted, he asked what she'd thought the property was worth. She said a house like that in Scarborough would go for over twice that amount.

Ian laughed. 'You could buy a three-bedroom semi-detached for that in this part of the country!'

'You mean The Mulberries is worth under eighty thousand pounds?' Christie was staggered. A neighbour of hers in Scarborough had got nearly two hundred thousand for his three-bedroom town house. Ian said that houses in a town like Scarborough were probably like gold dust.

'If you're happy with seventy-six, that's fine by me — along with the tapestry.'

She nodded dumbly, wondering what she'd be offered for her Scarborough house.

Ian said he was going to leave it for a day or two before telling his agent that The Mulberries was going to be sold under private sale, as he felt a little guilty about not putting it on their books.

Knowing how volatile the market could be, she asked Ian if he would be able to wait until she sold her house, should things not go as planned. He said he was in no hurry at all. When the sale in Scarborough was finally agreed, he would instruct his solicitor and she could go ahead with the purchase. 'I'm arranging a small get-together on Saturday,' he added 'You will be back from your trip by then, won't you?'

She nodded. 'Hopefully by about midday, if everything goes well.'

'Excellent. Weather permitting, an al fresco supper here at seven. I will be leaving on Monday morning, back to the Smoke.'

She felt a pang of sorrow. She would miss the Reverend Ian Hardy a great deal.

'Don't look so sad, my dear. I shall pay regular visits. Pip's cooking is far too good, and I shall require an occasional "fix" of her beef Wellington with fresh local vegetables.' He sighed. 'Which brings me back to this.' He picked up the report. 'My accountant urgently requires my thoughts on this rather boring document. I had better press on, or I will be late for my dinner and that would never do. Will you forgive me?'

Christie decided against telling him she was opting out of Gina's game. She'd leave it until he was about to go. She said she must be off, as she had to get her things ready for an early morning start. She gave him a hug and thanked him again for allowing her to buy the cottage. Then she drove around the green and down the lane towards home.

As she parked, she saw Bill and Lynne waving to her from their garden. They had erected a dark green striped gazebo and were placing their garden furniture under it. 'Fancy a sherry, duck?'

Knowing they were soon to be her "real" neighbours, she parked and joined them.

'This is rather splendid,' she said, admiring the awning.

'We love the garden, me duck, but we can't take the sun like we used to. This should give us a bit a' shade.'

Bill went in to get the drinks and Christie sat in a big padded reclining chair and chatted to Lynne. She told her not to be concerned if she didn't see her around over the weekend, as she was going back to Scarborough on a flying visit.

'I bet you'll be glad to see your own home, won't you? 'Olidays are all very nice, but there's nowt like ya own place, is there?'

She decided she could safely tell them of her plans. After all, she would soon be here permanently. She waited until Bill returned, then told them they were soon to have a full-time next-door neighbour but to please keep it under their hats until everything had been finalised.

The couple seemed genuinely delighted. They had been a bit concerned as to what might happen to the cottage. So much farmland was being sold off to property developers that they had been dreading someone building a housing estate in Evelyn's garden. 'Do you know, duck? They put up ten on old Jake Penrose's bit a' land just outside Fenfleet. The 'ouses was that close together they could clean each other's winders if they leaned far enough out.'

How lucky she was. Not only was she buying a lovely old property, but she had wonderful neighbours to go with it.

They chatted on for a while until it was time for Christie to leave and get her packing done.

After a makeshift supper, she rang Liz and gave her her travel plans, promising to ring and let her know that she had arrived safely. She sat for a while in the old chair looking out over the garden and sipped a glass of wine.

'To us!' she said, and raised her glass to the cottage.

In response she heard a whisper, very faint. Her rational mind put it down to a draught from the chimney, but in her heart, she knew it was Evelyn, lifting an ethereal glass in return.

* * *

Unlike Christie, Liz and Matt were far from happy with their day.

It seemed that Gina Spearman, well-known local businesswoman, had no personal life. Liz had resorted to making a visit to Sandy Giles.

'I asked her what Lindsay had said about her boss at the bookshop. Apparently, she was a hard but generous taskmaster. Sandy said she also knew her, although not well, and that she herself wouldn't want to work for her. A moody cow, she said, and you never knew which way the wind was blowing with her. Lindsay, who used to read a lot and loved long words, had called her "capricious," a word Sandy said she had to look up on Google. But Lindsay wouldn't hear a thing said against her. She reckoned she was "awesome," and couldn't do enough for her. All very reminiscent of what Christie says about Tom and Delphi.'

'Well, I've had a long talk with Bryn,' said Matt. 'He went through the original reports and couldn't find a single mention of Gina. They had her boss down as a man named Ernie Carter from the garden plants section who, apparently, was pretty cut up about the girl's death. He said she was a real grafter, worked all hours and was very conscientious. Nothing came up about her part-time work in the books section.' He ate a forkful of fish. 'So, after that, I went to Rowantrees and talked to Ernie myself. Nice bloke. An older guy, well past retirement age but he's too good to let go. What he doesn't know about plants isn't worth knowing. When I asked about the bookshop, he said a lot of the staff worked part-time in other sections to earn a bit more money, but she'd never mentioned where she did her extra hours and he didn't ask. She was good with plants and that's all he cared about.'

'You'd think he'd have seen her there.' Liz frowned.

'He's an old-style plant man, Liz. He told me he preferred the days when they only sold quality plants and compost and proper gardening materials. He said he hadn't got time for all that rubbish, and he never sets foot in what he calls the "arty-farty" section.'

Liz chewed ruminatively. 'None of this adds up, does it? A part-time assistant in a book outlet — oh, and by the way, Gina used the garden centre outlet to get rid of whatever didn't sell in the Reading Room, plus bargain editions she picked up from end-of-line and clearance suppliers. Anyway, as I was saying, why would the girl have thought her "awesome?" She spent most of her time in a different area altogether, and Gina only turned up once a week to check the stock and generally shout at the staff.' She finished her portion of their fish and chip supper and sat back. 'She couldn't possibly have put up a reward of fifteen grand for a kid she hardly knew.'

'But that's the belief at Rowantrees.' Matt laid down his knife and fork. 'Ernie suggested I talk to one of the checkout girls who had been with the company forever. She confirmed — sorry, *thought* that Lindsay might have known Gina from outside the garden centre. She said she'd seen Gina pick her up a couple of times after work and they'd drive off together.'

Liz stared at him. 'She never mentioned this before?'

'Why should she? No one even knew about Gina in the first investigation, so her name never came up. They were focused on her ex-boyfriend and then, later, this "mystery man."'

'We need to talk to Gina Spearman, don't we, Matt?'

He nodded. 'And I suggest we go tomorrow morning. Christie will be well out of the way by then, heading north.'

Liz cleared away the supper dishes, still wondering. The fact that this woman who so disturbed her cousin had turned up in an old murder enquiry made her acutely uneasy. Was Gina temperamental but good at heart, sufficiently so that she would pledge a lot of money to find the killer of someone she supposedly hardly knew? Or was she something much darker?

CHAPTER TWENTY-FIVE

After an uneventful journey, Christie arrived in Scarborough earlier than expected. She pulled into the drive and sat looking at the house, feeling faintly guilty. It had been in her family for generations, and she hoped her forebears would understand.

Inside, everything was as it always had been, but she felt as if she were looking at an old photograph. This place was a memory, somewhere from her past. Already she was thinking of The Mulberries as home.

She had decided to take very little with her. Ian was selling his sister's home complete with all its fittings and furnishings. She would take nothing from here other than personal belongings.

At ten, Betty Chambers, her next-door neighbour, rang the bell. Christie had called the night before and told her she was coming. They hugged and Christie handed over her present, an exquisite Chinese-style ceramic pot cover with a huge potted hibiscus to go in it. Betty was a houseplant fanatic.

'I've told you before, Christie, there's no need. Keeping an eye on the place for you gives me something to do. But what a wonderful colour! It'll go perfectly on my sideboard.'

Christie felt guilty all over again. But there was nothing for it, she would have to tell Betty about her impending move forthwith. The estate agent would be arriving at eleven.

Betty turned out to be surprisingly stoic about it. She was in her early eighties and for a while now had been considering moving to a retirement complex. 'This could be just the push I need, dear. I'm even tempted to let your young man have a look at my place while he's here. Only yesterday, the Glades sent me another brochure asking if I would like to be put on their waiting list. It's pricey, but really nice. They have a cafeteria if you don't want to cook for yourself, a games room, wonderful gardens and it's near the sea front. I've got no one to leave my money to, my love, so why not enjoy it?'

Christie agreed wholeheartedly and with a great deal of secret relief. She said she would tell the agent when he arrived. He would at least be able make an appointment with Betty to view her house.

Betty went off to "tidy up a bit," in case he fancied a quick look round.

After she'd gone, Christie packed two large suitcases with clothes and her favourite books. The more she took now, the less she'd have to worry about when she made the final move.

The estate agent turned out to be a clone, an exact replica of Darren, the agent from Fenfleet. He measured up and mentioned the usual "well-appointed" and "much sought-after area." He told her straight away that she should be looking for something in the region of one hundred and eighty to two hundred thousand — more if she wanted to hold out for a higher price. In other words, after all the fees had been paid, she would make well over a hundred thousand. This represented her freedom. Her life from now on could be very pleasant indeed.

She told him to go ahead. She wanted to make a quick sale, so if he had any offers, he should let her know. He admitted that he already had a client that might be interested and would suggest he view it as soon as possible. She filled in all his documents without even bothering to check the company's percentage, gave him a spare set of keys and shook his hand. He said he would contact her on her mobile to let her know what his client thought. She directed him to Betty Chambers's house, and he thanked her for the possible extra business. And it was done.

She loaded the car, ready to set off as soon as possible. She was still trying to get her head around the prospect of making a large sum of money out of doing something she really wanted to do. Richard had told her she could go to Auden's place whenever she wanted and he would be there waiting for her.

Christie stood in the road and looked up at her old home, silently thanking it for sheltering her over so many years. She arrived at Betty's just as the agent was leaving, saying he would be back to do a proper estimate later.

She wished Betty good luck with her sale. Betty said she would continue to send the post on. She gave her an affectionate hug and said she would ring if she had any news. Christie promised to do the same. Everything was falling into place. Even her concerns about her dear old neighbour had come to nothing. She drove away without a backward glance.

* * *

Tom Parrish was pleased and surprised to see both Liz and Matt walk into the Reading Room, but rather less happy when they said they needed to talk to his boss.

'Well, er, she's been tied up on the phone for most of the morning. She specifically asked not to be disturbed.'

Matt noticed the trepidation with which Tom eyed the closed door. 'Sorry, mate, but it's important.'

Tom sighed, grimaced and said, 'Okay. Wish me luck.'

'If it helps, tell her we want to ask her about Lindsay Harrison,' Matt added.

A few moments later, Tom emerged from the office. Saying nothing, he held the door open for them and closed it behind them.

'Forgive the mess. You wouldn't believe how much paperwork it takes to keep the wheels of commerce turning.' Gina pushed a pile of files to one side of the desk and smiled at each of them in a slightly distracted way. 'Sit, please. I can't say this hallowed office has ever received a detective chief inspector and a detective sergeant before, even if you are both retired.' The smile widened, and she shook their hands. 'Gina Spearman. I'm pleased to meet you.'

'Well, you seem to know who we are, so maybe I should tell you why we're here.'

'Thomas said Lindsay Harrison.' Ignoring Liz, she fastened her gaze on Matt. 'Don't tell me the police have finally found the animal who killed her.'

'Sadly, not yet, Ms Spearman. But they're not giving up,' Matt said.

'And they're so desperate they're relying on private detectives to do their work for them.' She broke into a smile. 'I'm joking. Although it's no joking matter, I know. How can I help you?'

'We are just doing some groundwork, Ms Spearman, and talk—'

She held up a hand. 'It's Gina, Matt. Much simpler, less of a mouthful. You were saying?'

'We're talking to anyone who knew her, going over what they recall, to see if anything new has transpired. You weren't interviewed at the time, but we've recently been informed that she actually worked for you and that you knew her well.'

Gina sighed. 'Yes, she did a bit of part-time work at the outlet, cash-in-hand, I'm afraid. She wasn't on the books.' She ran her hand through her hair. 'I did it as a favour to her, poor kid. I felt sorry for her.'

'Why?' asked Liz.

'She was bright and very intelligent for a local working-class girl. Her family didn't help her much and she was desperate to make it to university. I saw her potential and tried to help.' She shrugged. 'That's all.'

'Can you explain why you never came forward?' asked Liz.

'I'm not desperately sure that these are the kind of questions that civilians should be asking. Or am I being paranoid?' She regarded Liz coolly.

'You don't have to answer any questions at all, Gina,' Matt said. 'But as you clearly cared about her, we hoped you'd want to help us. We are trying to build up a better picture, both of Lindsay herself and what happened.'

'I can tell you a little about Lindsay herself, but as to what happened, I wasn't there at all that week, which is why I never spoke to the police. I knew nothing until I was told about it. You see, I am an excellent businesswoman and highly intelligent — I'm not blowing my own trumpet, just stating a fact — but I am not strong emotionally. I did not take the news well, I'm afraid.' She stared down at her desktop. 'The thought of the life of that pretty, bright young woman being extinguished before it had hardly begun . . . it devastated me for quite some time.'

'And because of that, you offered a reward for any information that would assist in bringing the killer to justice?' Liz's voice was soft, understanding.

Nicely dropped in, thought Matt.

Gina Spearman finally raised her gaze. 'Me? Oh no. I have no idea who pledged that reward, although bless them for their kindness. Sorry, I can't help you there.'

They asked a few more questions about Lindsay herself, and then the shutters came down. They wouldn't be getting any more from Gina today. Matt glanced at Liz, thanked Gina for talking to them and stood up. 'We'll leave you to your work. I think we'll go and get ourselves some tea in your café before we leave.'

'Tell them there's no charge. Your drinks are on me, and whatever you want to eat. I'm sorry I couldn't be of more help.'

The door closed behind them. Not quite a slam, but not far off either.

They sat upstairs with two coffees and two custard doughnuts.

'Oh my!' breathed Liz.

'I dread to ask what you thought.' Matt pulled a face. 'Did you notice her wrist?'

Liz nodded. 'As she held out her hand to shake mine. A faint scar, straight across the inside of the wrist. Couldn't have been an accident, could it? Not in that position.'

'Maybe she really is emotionally weak. I'm telling you, if that wasn't a suicide attempt, I'll go to the police ball dressed as Shirley Bassey and sing Big Spender.'

Liz snorted. 'Now that's something I'd pay good money to see!'

Matt sipped his coffee. 'Seriously, what was your take on the lady?'

'Woah! Complex. Very. Totally disingenuous. Those cruel barbs supposedly intended to be humorous. I'd dearly love to know what her real reason was for making a friend of Lindsay.'

'Me too,' he said. 'And what was that about her parents not helping her? From everything I've read, they spoiled her rotten.'

'And desperate to go to university? Her mate never mentioned anything about that. As I recall Sandy Giles said that prior to her break-up with Paul, all she talked about was settling down and getting married, nothing about uni,' Liz said.

Matt wished he still carried a warrant card. It would have allowed him to lean so much harder on Gina Spearman.

'Now I'm beginning to understand why Christie can't bear her. Tom was bricking it when he knew he had to go and interrupt her, wasn't he? And I could be wrong — maybe she doesn't really know it herself — but I think Christie is very fond indeed of Tom. If I'm right, it would smart to see Madam-I'm-So-Intelligent talking to him like he's a bag of shit!' Liz was beginning to grow angry herself.

'I wouldn't like to get on her wrong side, that's for sure,' said Matt.

'And yet they all, including Tom, think the sun shines out of her arse,' muttered Liz. 'He's a smart man, so why does he let her treat him like a doormat? I think that's what gets to Christie more than anything.'

'Well she *is* extremely clever. She's an expert manipulator and she knows exactly how to play them. Its mind games, Liz. Plain and simple.'

'So what kind of game was she playing with Lindsay Harrison?' asked Liz. 'Was that what got her killed?'

Though he didn't say so, Matt was wondering exactly the same thing.

CHAPTER TWENTY-SIX

Christie was on her way to see Richard. Later, they were to go to visit Auden in hospital. She drove to Auden's bungalow with a new sense of purpose. She rather liked the feeling.

Auden's home nestled, hidden almost out of sight, in a wedge-shaped piece of land on a bend in the lane that led to the beach. The garden fell sharply away from the house, giving an uninterrupted view of the sea. People often called it a waste for a blind man to own a house with such a breathtaking view, but Auden swore that he could only write by the sea. The smell of salt, the sound of the waves endlessly pounding, the caress of the sea mists on his bare arms brought him alive, inspired him to work. He had a summer house built like a log cabin at the bottom of the garden, where he spent his days with Richard, dictating his novels. There was a pool, a sauna and a jacuzzi, and a cleverly designed terrace laid out with raised beds planted with perfumed flowers and herbs. The interior of the bungalow was open-plan, designed with its blind owner in mind.

As she pulled into the drive, Christie saw Richard waving from the kitchen window. He ran out, kissed her on both cheeks and took her bag. He had insisted she stay the night after her visit to Auden, and leave the following morning. She hadn't relished driving both ways in a single day but hadn't wanted to go to her house either, so spending the night at Auden's suited her perfectly.

Lunch was laid out ready. Christie, who had completely forgotten to eat, was famished.

As they ate, Richard filled her in on Auden's progress. 'He is desperate to finish the book. So much so that he wants me to take some of his recording equipment into the hospital for him. I'm not sure that it's a good idea — fine while I am around, but, well, after all, the dear man is blind. Anything could go missing and he'd be none the wiser, would he?'

'Perhaps you could leave him with a hand-held recorder. They cost next to nothing and at least he could dictate some of his ideas for you to transcribe later.' Auden liked to record his thoughts as soon as they came into his head. He often said that his best work had never been committed to paper because by the time he had located his recorder, he'd forgotten what he wanted to say.

'Yes, I thought that too. I bought him a cheap one in the town this morning, as it happens.'

'He must be a lot better, Richard, if he feels he can continue with the novel.'

'I think it's the thought of finishing it that is keeping him going. By the way, he's really looking forward to your visit. We can go whenever you're ready. There are no set visiting hours.'

Richard drove, to give her a break from driving. She had found a flowering white gardenia in a garden centre before she left, and its perfume filled the car.

'He will just *adore* that, dear heart! Gardenias and jasmine are his absolute favourites. Um . . .' Richard paused. There was clearly something bothering him. 'Christie? Would you do something for me?'

'Of course.'

'Since he went into the coma, I've spent practically every moment with him, so I'm not exactly objective anymore, but I think he has a problem with his memory.' Richard practically blurted this out. 'Would you keep an eye on him and tell me if you notice any signs yourself? The doctor more or less insists I'm imagining it, but I'm not so sure.'

She assured him that she would. She could see why Richard was so worried. Auden Meeres's books were known for their convoluted plots and last-minute twists. If he was having memory problems, the consequences for his work didn't bear thinking about.

When Christie gave him the gardenia, Auden stroked the waxy, creamy-white petals, tears trickling down his face. He apologised, saying the illness had left him rather emotional, and he tended to cry easily. He ran his hand over her face and declared that the Lincolnshire winds had roughened her skin, and they joked that she'd finish up with cheeks like a warthog's bottom. For about an hour, she sat on his bed and held his hand while they talked.

As soon as Richard went off to get some drinks, Auden tightened his grip. 'Before he returns, I must ask you something.'

She looked at him anxiously.

'I am going to suggest something to our Richard. Tell me if you think I'm doing the right thing.'

Now she was really concerned.

'I don't wish to cause undue alarm, but I fear something isn't quite right in my brain since the operation.'

She drew in a breath to speak but he held up his hand.

'Hear me out, girl. This is my last book, and it means everything to me. I'm almost certain that I will not live to finish it, so I am going to ask Richard to complete it for me. I have the story outline, the basic plot, and he knows the way I write better than anyone. He is more than capable, don't you think? I would instruct my publisher to print it under both our names and Richard would get the royalties and the accolades. It would be a little thank you for all the help he has given me. What do you think?'

Christie said it was a wonderful gesture. In her opinion, Richard was indeed perfectly able to do it. She asked him what he thought was wrong with his brain.

'Haven't a clue, my dear. But I don't want to worry Richard any more than he is already, poor lamb.' He turned his unseeing eyes in her direction. 'I am very aware of how Richard feels, Christie. I assume you are as well?'

She nodded, forgetting that Auden couldn't see her.

But he'd obviously sensed it, or maybe he was just certain of her response. 'I thought so. I have no relatives to speak of, so he will inherit everything. I have never been able to, ah, reciprocate, but I do care about him. It is the least I can do. He has dedicated almost his whole life to looking after me. No one has a right to expect loyalty like that. I have been a very lucky man.'

Richard came in with coffee. 'So, what have you two been discussing in my absence?' He tried to sound cheerful but worry shone through his voice like a torch beam through tissue paper.

'Oh, this and that, dear boy. This and that.'

Christie experienced an overpowering sense of déjà vu. She was no longer in the hospital but sitting with an old lady as she poured out her dark secrets. Suddenly, she wanted to be back in her tiny cottage. She ached for her sitting room, Jane's painting of the Fens, the open fire and the view out into the garden. She had had enough of being the listener.

Auden was saying, 'Your work on both the Cornish wreckers and the will-o'-the-wisp has been excellent, my dear. I could feel the sea mist drenching my clothes and smell the eerie stink of the marshes. I believe I have all the research I need, certainly enough to get us to a satisfactory ending.'

'I have one more offering, something you'll appreciate.' Christie had brought Matt's grandfather's handwritten accounts of past victims of the marsh, and the mysterious jack-o'-lantern. She placed it in front of him and gave him a summary of the contents.

Auden ran his hands over the old paper, as if trying to extract its tales by touch. 'My God, I can smell the age on it. This is splendid, Christie!'

'I've made you a copy, as Matt would like it back.'

'Of course, of course,' breathed Auden. 'But just to touch the original manuscript is priceless. Read me a few lines, please.'

She opened the scrapbook and turned to a story about a young girl who had fallen and injured her ankle and was trying to get off the marsh before nightfall. Christie took a breath and read:

"Lizzie was a tough child all right, but the tales of the evils that met on the marsh in the dead of night were starting to run through her head. She did not believe in the black dog — Hairy Jack, they called it, a dreadful phantom that haunted lonely places. She didn't believe in the shag-foal either, the demon donkey with flaming eyes. That was surely a joke, wasn't it? And she didn't believe in the bogles, the goblins of green mist. In fact, she did not believe in any of those malevolent and tricksy spirits of the Fens. But it was hard not to be frightened of the night itself, and she did believe in the Lantern Man."

Auden heaved a contented sigh. 'And she met with a terrible end?'

'She did,' said Christie. 'As do all the victims in these stories. The book is beautifully produced, with an etching on the front and a few appropriate lines from Shakespeare about goblins.'

He smiled. 'This wonderful find is the *pièce de résistance*. It has spurred me on. You really are a treasure, dear Christie. But I fear we are going to lose you. Is that right? Richard tells me you're planning to settle in that big flat county. And before you say anything, I completely understand why. My very first novel was conceived beneath those big skies. The Fens were where it all began, and it has always had a place in my heart.'

So that was why it was so special to him. She told him about The Mulberries, her tiny piece of the past. He wished her well. Then, to her amazement, he said that although her work had ostensibly finished, he would like to pay her a retainer fee, a small monthly figure, just in case either he or Richard should require an additional detail. Christie assured him that she would be happy to help for no recompense at all.

But he wouldn't hear of it, and so the deal was agreed. Auden leaned back, suddenly pale, and announced he was unbelievably tired. He was asleep before they'd even left the room.

'This happens.' Sadly, Richard looked across at the sleeping figure. 'We must let him rest. I'll come back later, just to see if he needs anything for the night. The nurses are great but, oh, you know, I feel better if I check on him.'

She did know.

They ate a simple, delicious fish dinner in a restaurant near Auden's house. Remembering Auden's insistence that Richard should not worry, she told him that he had shown no signs of memory problems while she was there, although he had mixed up some of his words once or twice. This made him a little happier.

Later, Richard drove back to the hospital for half an hour while Christie sat out in the summer house and endeavoured to rest her overtaxed brain. She would have loved to take a dip in the pool, but it was sadly neglected, with leaves and assorted debris drifting on the surface. Cleaning the pool had been at the bottom of poor Richard's list of priorities.

When he returned, they sat looking out over the sea with a bottle of Chardonnay and a bowl of rice crackers between them. They remained there until the ocean was invisible in the dark.

She left at nine the next morning, promising to return soon. She hugged Richard and made him promise to call her if he needed some support.

As the landscape changed, and the gentle green woodlands gave way to acres of potatoes and cabbage, Christie felt a heaviness descend on her.

She was now in possession of two weighty secrets. The one concerning Tom's father would probably remain that way, but the secret of Auden's failing brain and Richard's inheritance would eventually be common knowledge. Christie swore that if she ever had a secret of her own, she would take it with her to the grave.

CHAPTER TWENTY-SEVEN

At around six thirty, Christie was making her way to Stone House. She passed the fields of broad beans, which were turning dark, the leaves curling and beginning to fall. There would soon be a different harvest in those acres. Christie hoped it wouldn't be onions.

Pip had laid out a simple buffet in the private gardens, away from the other guests. Dominic was turning the meat on the barbeque, and a mix of delicious aromas was beginning to fill the evening air.

Pip handed her a tall glass of sparkling wine. 'This is one aspect of the culinary arts my husband excels in. And don't even try to ask him how he makes that sauce. It's a closely held secret.'

Ian hurried over and asked her to join him for a few moments. They strolled to the far end of the patio. 'Have you told anyone yet, other than your cousin? It's just that I had a very odd call earlier this morning, about the cottage.'

Christie shook her head, then remembered her neighbours. 'But I specifically asked them not to say anything until the sale had been finalised. I'm certain they wouldn't gossip. Other than them, absolutely no one, and anyway, I've been in Yorkshire.'

'How very strange.'

'So what did they say?' she asked, suddenly anxious.

'Well, basically my dear, you've been gazumped. Well, you would have been, had I not turned the offer down.'

'Who by?' she exclaimed.

'I suspect property developers. The estate agent said he had been instructed to offer the seller ten thousand pounds more than the asking price. They said the anonymous buyer was most eager to purchase the property.' Ian looked at her anxious face and smiled. 'Don't worry. I thanked them for their trouble but told them that the cottage would not be going on the market after all. The agent was a bit miffed but said he would hold onto the details in case my private sale fell through. Weird, though, isn't it? I haven't told a soul, and it wasn't even on the estate agents' website.'

'Ian, I could afford more, you know. I could even match your anonymous buyer's offer if it would help.'

'No, my dear,' he said. 'I certainly don't need more money. My sister and I both led simple lives and we saved a fair bit over the years. But I do thank you for the offer. It's sweet of you, and I appreciate it. Now, perhaps we should return to the others and tell them our news before they think we are planning to elope!'

All the guests had now arrived, including Tom and Margaret.

Their news was met with cries of approval. Tom gave her a peck on the cheek. 'Great news, Christie. It's a super cottage, I know you'll be happy there.' But there was a distinct lack of enthusiasm in his tone. Margaret, on the other hand, was utterly delighted.

Pip and Dominic clapped her on the back, crying, 'Welcome! Welcome!' in unison.

Ian looked on, smiling.

They ate and drank well into the evening. Ian spent a long time chatting with Margaret. Once more, Christie thought they would have made a good couple.

At the end of the evening, she accompanied Tom and his mother to their car. Ian said he would see her before he left, and not to worry about the anonymous buyer who was trying to gazump her.

Margaret asked what he meant, and Christie told her about the mysterious offer.

Tom shook his head, looking baffled. 'Ten grand is one hell of a lot of money, especially around here. I wonder what is so special about The Mulberries?'

As she approached the house, she saw that there was still a light coming from the next-door garden. It was Bill and Lynne, happily reclining beneath their new gazebo, drinks in hand. The now familiar call of 'fancy a sherry?' floated across the garden.

She declined the drink but wandered over to say goodnight.

'Glad we've seen ya, ma duck! We wanted ta let ya know that this old fool here told our niece about ya movin' in an' all. Hope it's not a problem?' Lynne looked at her anxiously. 'A few drinks in 'im an' 'e'll talk the hind legs off a donkey, that 'e will! Afore I knew it, he's goin' on about how lucky we are not to be 'avin' an estate in our back garden!'

Christie said it was no problem at all, she'd told a few people by now.

With a stern glance at her husband, Lynne observed that you couldn't take him anywhere.

Inside, Christie fell, fully clothed, onto the bed. Home! Well, nearly. If it had been anyone but Ian she would have either lost her dream or a large sum of money. She wondered who this prospective buyer could be. And — as Tom had said — what for? What was so special about this place? It had to be a property developer, who else? Especially when you took the size of the garden into account, and the way it extended into the farmland next door. There was a good chance the farmer was selling off a parcel of his land, and The Mulberries obtruded into his fields. Naturally, the developers would want that as well. It made sense. Bill and Lynne had mentioned developers when she'd told them she was moving in. That would explain their insistence on remaining anonymous — they'd know they wouldn't be welcome.

She hoped they weren't planning to build on the farmland next door. Perhaps she should have checked.

She drifted off to dreams of JCBs rumbling down her idyllic country lane and lorries loaded with building materials thundering past the cottage, shaking the roof tiles and covering Evelyn's garden with a lethal film of cement dust.

A noise woke her sometime in the early hours. It was still dark. She lay, rigid, listening, wondering what she should do.

It was a rhythmic, hammering sound, like someone banging urgently on the front door. She crept out of bed and peered out of the window, down to the front path. Lit by a full moon, it was empty. She couldn't see right into the porch, but that appeared to be empty as well.

The noise began again, and then she realised that it was a shutter, broken loose from its clasp and banging against the wall of the cottage. She went through to the bathroom, pushed up the sash window and re-attached the shutter. At least it hadn't broken, it had just come unhooked.

It was nearly a quarter to two. The drinks of the previous evening had given her a thirst and she went down to the kitchen to make tea, which she took back upstairs with her.

Wide awake now, the questions began again. What if she was wrong about the housing development? Perhaps it was someone who really did want the house, maybe for personal reasons. It could be an old family property that had been sold on, then someone, generations later, wanted it back in the family again. Or maybe a keen gardener? The garden was very special, almost worthy of being open to the public.

Or maybe it was someone who didn't want her to have it.

She blinked, seeing again Gina's face when she had fallen and damaged the painting. Surely not! "He's gone and told our niece," Lynne had said. Jane could well have told Gina. How long would it take to ring round the local estate agents and ask who was carrying the property?

What a hateful thing to do. Her head pounded. She heard Ian say that the game was everything. Gina wouldn't need a reason. She just wanted to give Christie McFerran the fright of a lifetime. She picked up her tea and drank deeply. Surely even Gina would not be that evil?

Please God, let me be wrong.

* * *

Matt lay awake, waiting for dawn. He'd been uneasy all night, had tossed, turned and slept only fitfully. This unpleasant habit stemmed from his time in the force. When some case troubled him, he struggled to let it go long enough to sleep properly. Tonight, he kept reliving their chat with Gina Spearman, and every time he went over it the more certain he became that they were dealing with someone either very disturbed or very dangerous, maybe both.

'Talk to me,' said a sleepy voice beside him. 'There's no need to tell me *who* is on your mind.'

'I'm so sorry, I've woken you up. Go back to sleep.'

'I dreamed about her.' Liz turned and nestled in beside him. 'It wasn't a sweet dream.'

'I can believe it.' He held her close. 'Hopefully, we'll get something back from Bryn this morning. He's going to run a full background check on her — you know, the data we can't access anymore.' He sighed. 'I have an awful premonition that this is going to turn out badly.'

He felt Liz draw in a breath. 'And my Christie is far too close to it. I'm going to ring her this morning and tell her to stop trying to rescue her buddies and steer well clear. She'd be better occupied saving her runner beans from blackfly right now.'

'She'd be a damned sight safer, that's for sure.' He kissed her forehead. 'Well, if anyone can make her listen, it will be you, sweetheart.'

'I'll give it my best shot.'

They lay together in silence for a while, then Matt said, 'Don't get me wrong, I love Christie and I know how close you two are, but sometimes she gets a bit overemotional. It kind of wears me down.'

'I've never seen her quite as intense as this,' Liz said. 'I'm beginning to wonder if moving to the Fens is such a good idea after all, especially considering the people she's got herself involved with.'

Matt shook his head. 'You need to rein that girl in fast, especially given our interest in Gina Spearman.'

'No pressure there, then,' sighed Liz rather miserably. 'I just hope she'll listen.'

* * *

After a sleepless night, Christie was fit for nothing and mad as hell. She burned the toast, threw it in the bin and hunted for some cereal. She realised too late that the milk was off and had already doused her cornflakes with it. At that point she decided to do nothing that involved the use of sharp knives or hazardous equipment.

She made more toast and crunched it angrily. As she hated black tea and disliked coffee early in the morning, she found a carton of orange juice and while opening it, managed to squirt a good third of it up the kitchen wall before knocking the rest into the sink. She salvaged enough for a small glass and sat wondering miserably what else was going to go wrong that day.

She managed to take a shower without disaster and decided that checking out property developers couldn't do too much damage.

A search of the Planning Applications section of Fenfleet Town Council's website showed nothing specific for her area. She was used to research, and soon found a link that was more explicit. It seemed that only two areas within the village limits had been granted permission for construction. One was right up near the roundabout at the entrance to the main A-road, a good mile away, and the other was already underway on the Fenfleet Road. Other than a request to put up a large new dry-food store in the local animal feeds supplier, there was nothing else being considered at present.

Christie then chanced a phone call to Lynne next door and asked her if, to her knowledge, the farmer who owned the land surrounding her cottage had ever sold off sections of his land before. Lynne said absolutely not. She was sure that the land was family-owned and according to them, the boundaries had remained the same for nearly a hundred years.

Christie thanked her and ended the call, trying to remain calm. She could still be wrong about Gina. There could be a bona fide buyer who truly wanted The Mulberries for a perfectly good reason.

'And if you believe that, you'll believe anything,' she muttered.

She pulled out her mobile and rang Ian. She told him of her suspicions, and he agreed that she could be right about Gina, but as he was leaving the next day, perhaps it would be better to ignore the whole thing. He sounded weary and admitted that he was regretting asking her to take up arms without his support. She should remember that he was selling the property to her, no matter what obstacles anyone else attempted to put in the way.

'I would be incensed too if I were in your position, but I caution you to be very, very sure of your facts if you decide to confront her. It could be a big mistake.'

'While I was on my way back from Yorkshire, I decided to walk away and let them all get on with it. I really meant it too, until this offer for The Mulberries came up.'

'I understand, Christie, I really do, but my advice would be to rise above it. Evelyn's cottage will be yours come what may, so you'll have won. Let that woman go and ruin some- one else's life while you enjoy your own.'

Christie asked him why he'd had this change of heart. 'What happened to "fight the good fight," Ian? You really believed we shouldn't let her get away with making people's lives a misery.'

He told her to call by later so they could talk properly. He just had to pack, make a few calls and then he'd be free. 'And I'd like to see you before I go. We've made a lasting friendship, and I need to know you are all right before I head off.'

'I'd like that,' she said. 'Is mid-afternoon okay? I thought I'd make a few discreet enquiries with the estate agent. I've checked online and they do open on Sundays. It's just to clear my mind, in case I've got it all completely wrong. Then I can tell you what transpires.'

'Christie, just do not, under any circumstances, confront Gina without speaking to me first,' Ian said. 'I'll explain later, but I made an unforgivable mistake in encouraging you to play her damned game. Just forget it, please.'

Christie promised not to do anything rash. She called the estate agent, and in her best London accent asked to speak to the representative who was dealing with the Reverend Ian Hardy's property, The Mulberries.

A young woman came on the line and said that Darren was not in the office today, but could she help.

Perfect. Christie said she was checking to see if her secretary had on her behalf put an offer in for The Mulberries. She could hear a keyboard clicking as the woman began typing.

After a short pause, she informed Christie that it appeared from the records that the Reverend Hardy had accepted a private offer and the property was now officially off the market.

Christie feigned disappointment and asked if they still had the details of her offer. There was more clicking, and then the woman said that they did. A lady had rung and put in an anonymous bid of ten thousand over the asking price, whatever that was. She had said she would ring again when they'd spoken to the vendor. Christie said that if the vendor had committed himself to a private sale, she would not be pursuing the matter further, and to please disregard any further calls, as she had dealt with it personally.

She hung up. So it was a woman who had made the offer. Just as she'd expected. She picked up her mobile and rang Jane Waterhouse's number.

To her surprise Gary answered, and for a moment she was thrown. 'It's all right, I just called in to pick up some things and have a coffee with Jane. She's going to be working in her studio for the rest of the day. I'll get her for you.'

Having exchanged greetings with her, Christie said she was sorry to have been upstaged, so to speak, by Bill and Lynne regarding her news.

'Oh, Christie, I'm really pleased you're buying the cottage, and my aunt and uncle are chuffed to bits with the prospect of having a "single lady" next door.'

They laughed at that and Christie said there wasn't much chance of that situation altering in the foreseeable future. 'My lovely friend Ian is returning to his London home tomorrow. We had a bit of a leaving party for him last night and I told Tom and his mother, but I've not yet had time to tell Gina.'

There was a pause. 'Actually, Christie, I think I may have already mentioned it to her. We spoke on the phone not long after Uncle Bill told me the news and I'm sure I told her then.'

Christie looked down and noticed that she was clenching and unclenching her left hand. 'Oh well, that's good, it'll save me the bother. Er, I've had a thought, Jane. Now I'm actually going to live here, and since I've given Ian your amazing picture of the garden, would you consider doing me a painting of The Mulberries — the cottage and the garden?'

'I would absolutely love to, Christie! It would be my pleasure. That place is quite magical. I assume there's no great rush, is there?'

'None at all,' Christie said.

'That's great then. I have to complete this set of paintings for the new country club. You remember the big commission Gina arranged for me? I've done one already and I'm well into the second, so as soon as they're finished, I'll ring you, okay?'

Christie was now left in little doubt about who had tried to forestall her purchase.

She walked out into the sunshine, breathing deeply, her head reeling. She meandered slowly around the garden, touching a leaf here and a petal there, allowed a tendril from a passion flower to wrap itself gently around her finger, desperate to calm her growing anger.

Still seething after ten minutes of this, Christie knew that her seven-year temper-loss cycle had come round again, and there would be no stopping it. She stormed through the house, grabbing car keys, handbag and phone, slammed the door, locked it and drove off towards the town and the Reading Room.

CHAPTER TWENTY-EIGHT

Halfway to Fenfleet, Christie pulled into a lay-by and stopped. What was she thinking? It was Sunday. The Reading Room was closed. She pulled out her mobile and saw she had two missed calls from Liz. She desperately wanted to talk to her, but it would have to wait. Right now, she had far more pressing business.

She swung the car around and now headed for Tadema House. Conscious of her state of mind, she drove fast but not recklessly. Soon she found herself standing at the door of Tadema House with no idea how she'd got there.

As soon as Gina opened the door, Christie screamed at her, 'How dare you!' Looking bemused, Gina invited her to come in, no doubt to keep the rest of the village from hearing.

Literally beside herself, Christie was unable to stop. All the hurt she felt for her friends and the way they had been treated by this woman forced its way to the surface and spewed out like lava from a volcano. She shouted on until she ran out of steam, though she was no calmer. She was, however, starting to realise the mistake she'd made in coming here like this. Throughout the whole onslaught, Gina had remained perfectly calm, flatly denying her accusations.

After a short silence, she said, 'Very well. Perhaps you'd like to show me some proof of my alleged, er, crimes.'

She said nothing, for of course, she had none. Oh, dear God, she had been all kinds of fool. She had played directly into Gina's hands.

Gina regarded her. Her pale blue eyes registered contempt, and also disappointment. They said she had expected better of Christie, a little more intelligence. Then her expression altered. She had no doubt decided to get what amusement she could out of Christie's discomfort.

She offered her a drink, told her to sit, saying that she was obviously terribly upset over what had happened, and rightly so. But it wasn't her. Whatever would she want with that little cottage when she had this? She waved a hand at the soulless living room.

Ignoring her offer of a drink, Christie made for the door, where she turned and said, 'But surely the game is everything.'

Gina regarded her with interest. She blinked slowly and then bared her even white teeth in a malevolent smile. 'Then prove it, Christie. If you can.'

Somehow, Christie stopped herself from running, and walked back to her car with as much dignity as she could muster.

Her driving on the return journey was appalling. She made it to Stone House and Ian, and practically fell into his arms.

Sobbing with anger, frustration and annoyance, she poured out her story while he listened, making sympathetic noises. He went and fetched a glass of brandy, which she drank.

'I don't know what got into me, I really don't. I promised I wouldn't confront her, yet I couldn't stop myself.'

'It sounds like the red mist to me,' he said with a rueful smile. 'And people have murdered when they see that. At least she is still with us.' He paused. 'She is, isn't she?'

Christie was finally forced to smile. Yes, Gina was alive and well when she left her.

He wasn't angry, Ian said, just sorry she'd been pushed that far. He told her he had been awake half the night, consumed with guilt for asking her to fight for their friends knowing he wouldn't be there to support her.

'We were wrong to interfere, my dear, even if our intentions were good. Good intentions have a way of backfiring sometimes.'

Christie nodded, determined, this time, to walk away. She finished her brandy and switched her phone back on. She had two messages, one from Liz urging her to call and the other, surprisingly, from Scarborough. 'Ms McFerran. Please ring immediately. House sold, subject to your approval. Clive.'

She handed the phone to Ian.

'That's more like it!' he said, giving her a hug. 'I'll ring my solicitor first thing in the morning. And would you mind if I came around after supper this evening so I can have a last look at The Mulberries before I leave?'

'I'll have your sherry poured and ready,' she said.

Back at the cottage, she made a coffee and took it up to the bedroom. Unused to drinking during the day and exhausted after her encounter with Gina, she kicked off her shoes and lay down on the bed. Remembering Liz's message, she sent a rather vague text saying she was tied up with calls about the house sales and would ring later that day. Her sore eyes began to close, and she lost herself to sleep.

Just like the night before, the same noise of banging dragged her from the depths. She got up and hurried to the bathroom to reattach the shutter and found it still firmly hooked, but the sound continued.

Still barefoot, she went downstairs to the front door. She opened it to find a furious Tom.

He moved towards her, causing her to back away into the lounge. 'What the hell are you doing, Christie? Have you any idea of the trouble you're causing with your constant interfering?' He was pacing the room like a caged animal.

She opened her mouth to speak but, much as she had done at Tadema House, he continued with his verbal assault.

'You don't know what you've done, do you? Gina is in a terrible state and it's all your fault! As if she would want this poky little cottage!'

'Hold on a minute! She was fine when I left her, it was me that was upset.'

'Oh really.'

'Yes. Really. It's true I shouted at her, but I still believe what I said. And Gina Spearman was as cool as a cucumber when I left Tadema House.'

'Well, she wasn't when I found her an hour ago. She was as drunk as I've ever seen anyone, really ill. Gina doesn't drink and she had put away more than half a bottle of malt whisky. It's a wonder she's still alive. I'd still be with her now if I hadn't been so bloody angry. I left Delphi looking after her.'

Christie was bewildered.

'We opened our homes to you, and this is how you repay us. For some reason, you've embarked on a one-woman vendetta against Gina, and I'd like to know why. You don't even bloody know her!'

Christie became fascinated by the small veins that were standing out on Tom's temples, pulsating very slightly.

'What is your problem? You saw her have a go at us a couple of times, at the shop. So what? It happens at work. If we're not upset about it, I'd very much like to know why the hell you should be!'

This could not go unanswered. 'Because she treats you and Delphi like servants and she relegates Jane, who is a brilliant artist, to the category of amateur Sunday dabbler.'

'Hasn't it ever occurred to you that we like to help her? God, Delphi adores Gina. She'd do anything for her.'

'Why? The woman is doing nothing but causing a rift between Delphi and her husband.'

'Well, I'll tell you. The wonderful Denis has been ill-treating Delphi, but the poor girl is too frightened to admit it. Far from causing a rift, Gina's helping her through it.'

Christie didn't believe that for a minute and said so.

'People are not always what they seem, are they, Christie? You should know that. He keeps her short of money, then he goes off up the pub at every available opportunity. And he hits her.'

'Has Delphi told you that, Tom? Did you hear it from her, or from Gina?'

'She told Gina in the strictest confidence. I wouldn't dream of asking her about it and upsetting her further.'

Christie groaned. Maybe she should try another tack.

'She ruined my painting, my gift for Ian. You have to admit that.'

'And she had it repaired and reframed. What more do you expect? She blacked out, Christie. Plain and simple. She has an eating disorder, or didn't you notice at the dinner party? Were you too involved in looking for points to score? Didn't you see how little she ate? Don't you know about anorexia? Don't your precious Auden's books have real-life problems in them, or do you just research the weird and the fanciful?' He paused to draw breath. 'You upset Jane too, making her think that Gina didn't want her painting. Were you too busy shouting at her earlier to notice where she's hung it? It's in the main hall, in pride of place. Or did you conveniently miss that minor detail?'

He was right. It had barely registered at the time, but yes, when she thought of it, the painting had been hung on the wall facing the entrance. Very clever. She bit her lip. 'Okay,' she said, 'so what about all the holidays? Or is it just the one and she's playing you off against each other? Delphi thinks she's going to Greece, but Jane believes she's going away too, and what about you, Tom? Has she offered you a nice break yet?'

He laughed mirthlessly. 'You really do have the wrong end of the stick. If it weren't so hurtful it'd be farcical. She wants to take Delphi away in order to build her up for what she may have to face when she returns — a split with Denis. It's something Delphi has always dreamed of. Denis has had long enough to take her himself, but he's too fond of the bevvies, it seems. And as for Jane and me, Gina has arranged for me to accompany Jane on a painting holiday in Tuscany, all expenses paid. Just the two of us. Is that the way your bully would treat her friends?'

My God, she had every avenue covered. 'Come on, Tom. Even your mother doesn't trust her.'

There was a long silence. Tom flopped down heavily onto the sofa.

'Oh, why didn't I realise before? You've been fed all this garbage by her. Mother and her creepy pal, the vicar.' He ran his fingers through his hair in the mannerism Gina always used. 'So that's it. They've used you and you've fallen for it.'

'Tom! That is preposterous. Your mother simply loves you and doesn't want to see you hurt or taken for a ride, that's all.'

'Wrong! She's a jealous and selfish old woman who has had her own way for far too long, that's what she is. If anyone treats me like a servant, it's her. Cook, chauffeur, housemaid, lackey, no wonder she doesn't want me to have a life of my own.' He was almost in tears.

'Tom, it's not like that. She really is afraid for you.'

Another sardonic laugh. Christie thought of what his mother had said about his father's illness and the trigger that could set it off.

'What about your dear, sweet friend the reverend, eh? I'll bet he has been geeing you on as well. They're thick as thieves, Margaret and Ian. Am I right? I am, aren't I? Hasn't he encouraged you to put the boot in, on my dear mother's behalf? Well, hasn't he?'

For the first time since she'd met Gina in the Reading Room, Christie doubted herself. What if she *was* wrong? She had no answer for Tom.

Tom now looked like a man who has run a long, hard race. He was out of breath, drained. He got slowly to his feet, like an elderly man.

'I'm sorry for you, Christie. Delphi told me you've been unlucky in love. You're jealous, aren't you? Bitter and jealous. But worse than that, you've allowed yourself to be used.'

As she watched him walk away, she thought Tom made a rather good knight in shining armour.

It was just a pity that he was Gina Spearman's.

* * *

When Ian arrived an hour later, Christie said nothing about her visitor. She now doubted not only herself but everyone else. She needed to think clearly, but her clamouring mind would give her no respite.

Ian's gaze was full of nothing but kindliness and sympathy, but the drop of poison Tom had injected was having its effect. Christie couldn't meet his eyes.

She tried desperately to pull her tattered wits together. This man was her friend. She was buying his dear sister's cottage, for God's sake! Then she heard the voice of the estate agent. "I can see this sitting on our books . . . not exactly bestsellers. Only one bedroom . . .'

"Thick as thieves." Could it have been Margaret who rang the estate agent with the anonymous offer?

Ian commented on how tired she looked. He drank his sherry, toasted The Mulberries and its new owner, gave her his home number and said she should ring him whenever she wanted. He rose to leave, saying he would miss her. 'One more thing, Christie. I hope you will be free of your game-playing adversary but,' he seemed to be weighing something up, 'I wasn't sure if I should give you this but if she comes after you again, you may find it useful.'

He took a folded sheet of paper from his trouser pocket and handed it to her. It was an address in Louth in the Lincolnshire Wolds.

She looked at him, uncomprehending.

'It could be your trump card. She tells everyone her parents are dead, that she was abused by them, stories that all vary slightly if you listen closely.' He suddenly looked old and tired. 'Don't ask how I came by this. It's the address of the care home Gina's mother was placed in six years ago, just before Gina sold up the family home and bought Tadema House.' He hugged her and wished her well, saying he would do all he could to make the house sale go smoothly.

Christie hugged him back, her mind a whirlpool of conflicting beliefs into which Ian had just tossed a stone.

CHAPTER TWENTY-NINE

'Something's not right with our Christie. She doesn't want to talk to me. I'm going over there, Matt.' Liz stood up and fetched her car keys.

'I'll come with you.' Matt laid down the sheaf of papers he had just printed off.

'No offence, oh love of my life, but maybe this needs girl-talk.' Standing behind him, she put her arms around him, nibbled his ear and kissed his neck. 'I hate to leave you, but needs must and all that.'

'Then you go careful and ring me if anything is wrong. Please.'

His caring expression filled her with love for him. 'I promise.'

At The Mulberries, she got out of her car and heard Christie call out, 'Over here. I'm in the garden.'

Liz went in through the gate and found her cousin sitting on a bench seat that faced towards the orchard, a large memo pad and a pen in her hand. 'I should have phoned. I'm sorry.'

'Yes, you should, you ratbag! I've been worried sick about you.' Liz bent down and hugged Christie, then flopped onto the bench. Christie looked terrible. 'So, what was so important that you could ignore your loving cousin?'

'I hardly know where to start.'

'To repeat Matt's favourite phrase, "From the beginning, please."'

'It's a mess, Liz. I've cocked the whole thing up, and now I don't know what to believe anymore.' She stared at her notebook. 'I'm trying to set down the pros and cons of what, if anything, to do, where to go and who to trust.'

'Oh, wow! Heady stuff.' Liz put her arm around Christie's shoulders. 'It's not something to be undertaken alone either. Good thing I came.'

'Yes, I'm glad you did,' Christie said in a small voice.

For an hour, as the sun began to drop lower and finally disappear over the horizon, Christie told her everything that had happened since she got back from Scarborough.

Liz listened, not as a friend and relative but as a police detective. As far as she could see, Christie had five options: 'One. Put a hold on the sale of your house and return to Yorkshire to rethink. Two. Go ahead with the sale and either purchase The Mulberries or look for somewhere else. Three. Cease to have anything more to do with Tom and the others and find new friends. Four. Apologise to Tom — tell him you were wrong and that you'll stay out of everyone's affairs from now on and try to build bridges. Five. Try to find proof of Gina's game-playing. How does that seem to you?'

'Much the same as I'd been thinking. But it's not that simple, Liz.' Christie looked close to tears. 'In my heart of hearts, I believe that Gina really is evil. If you'd seen the way she looked at me when she told me to prove what I'd accused her of. It was really scary and horribly intimidating. But then some of the things Tom said honestly made me wonder if I'd been wrong about her. Now, well, I'm so screwed up I don't trust my judgement anymore.'

'Okay, let's treat this like one of my investigations, or one of your research projects and, as it's turning chilly out here, I suggest we go inside, okay, cuz?'

Inside, over several hot drinks and half a packet of biscuits, they continued to debate.

'It's the inconsistencies in Gina's stories that worry me,' Liz finally said. 'According to you, Tom said that as a child she had been mentally tortured by her parents but not physically abused, then Delphi said that her parents actually knocked her around. And I don't like the way she confides in her "friends," giving them deeply personal and secret information about each other and telling them never to mention it, as it was divulged in confidence. That stinks!'

'Like telling Tom that Denis is a violent drinker. That surely can't be right. He loves Delphi, I'm sure of it.' Christie sighed. 'But as Tom said, who knows what goes on behind closed doors.'

'I've seen plenty of that with domestic violence cases,' admitted Liz. 'But you know when you talk to the people. You can almost smell their fear. I've only met Delphi a few times and I'd swear she's no battered wife.' She leaned forward. It was time to move this on. 'Okay, McFerran, I'm going to tell you something now, so pin back your ears, listen hard and I want to hear your gut feeling on what I'm going to ask you when I've finished. No emotional crap now, use your gut, your basic instinct. Understand?'

Christie nodded.

'Yesterday, Matt and I interviewed Gina Spearman at the bookshop. It concerned her possible involvement with a young woman who was murdered four years ago and whose killer never caught.'

Christie mouthed an "Oh," but she said nothing.

'We left the Reading Room both of us with very bad vibes about that woman. Matt passed her name onto the DC who is working the case with his DCI. It's only for a background check. We had some facts back earlier today and are expecting a lot more very soon.' She looked at Christie. 'Can I see the address that Ian Hardy gave you?'

Christie took the sheet of paper from the back of her notebook and passed it to Liz.

She stared at it. Louth wasn't that far away, probably three-quarters of an hour's drive.

'Well, our searches have come up with a death certificate for Gina's father and, although she says her mother is also dead, so far no record has been found.' She looked up at Christie. 'I came here to tell you to have nothing more to do with Gina Spearman, but seeing this address, I think it could give you the answers you need in order to move on. Tomorrow, you and I will take a little drive out to Louth. That should bring us both a little more clarity.'

Christie looked more like her old self. 'Yes, we'll do that. But what was the question that you wanted to ask me, Liz?'

'Gut feeling, remember? What do you really think of Gina Spearman? Emotional wreck? Suffers anorexia and various other mental health problems because of an abusive childhood? Or scheming, devious manipulator who enjoys playing games with other people's lives?'

'The latter, without a doubt.'

'And Tom, Delphi and Jane? What of them?'

'Hopelessly reliant on her. Controlled. Unable to see the truth, even when those that love them are involved.'

Liz beamed at her cousin. 'There! You've got to the essence of it. And at the very least our trip tomorrow should give us absolute proof that Gina's a liar. I'll see you at ten o'clock. I'll ring ahead and talk to whoever runs this home, then we can plan how we're going to tackle this woman without causing trouble for anyone, including us. Gina's mother was called Alice, Bryn says.'

Liz left Christie looking a lot less troubled than when she had found her.

Back home, she gave Matt the whole story.

'What a bloody mess!' groaned Matt. 'Poor Christie had so many dreams for this place and it looks as though this dreadful woman is going to poison the whole thing. Hell, she really needs taking down, doesn't she?'

'But it needs to be done properly, my darling, not by someone like Christie. The problem is that unless we can find actual proof connecting Gina to Lindsay's death, we can do sod all. She's committed no crime that we know of. In fact, as

281

I'm damned sure it was her that put up that reward, all she's done is be a stalwart of the community. On the surface, she was trying to help a promising girl move on in life.'

'Ugh, pass me the sick bucket,' muttered Matt. He reached out and took Liz's hand. 'You take care tomorrow and tread very warily with this lady in the care home. It's a very strange situation and until you get a lot more information about who she really is and why she's there, you could be skating on thin ice with the management of the place.'

'I'll be careful, never fear. You know, my darling, the one thing that keeps eating away at me is how Tom suddenly threw the blame for everything at his mother. I've known Margaret and Tom for years, and their lovely mother-son relationship was genuine and deeply felt. I'm afraid that wonderful boss of his may be deliberately causing a rift there.'

'To what purpose?' It was nearly midnight, and Matt locked the doors and put the lights out. 'Because she had a crap childhood herself?'

'I have no idea and, after my two-and-a-half hour session with Christie, my brain has turned to mush. I need sleep!'

* * *

The following morning, Christie dressed with a little more care than usual. She wasn't sure exactly what excuse Liz was going to come up with for trying to visit a perfect stranger, but it might be a good idea to look smart.

At breakfast, she was surprised at how hungry she was. It had to be Liz's calming influence. One thing that she knew she had to do before they went was ring Margaret.

She timed it for after Tom would have left for work, then took a deep breath and picked up the phone.

Margaret's voice was shaky and when she realised who was speaking, she burst into uncontrollable sobbing. After several minutes of trying to get some sense out of her, Christie decided that, Tom be damned, as soon as they returned from Louth, she would go and talk to her in person. She told her so, but the old lady regained her voice and told her not to. She was afraid of Tom calling home for something and finding her there.

'I'm afraid I'm not his favourite person at present, Christie dear. He's given up even pretending to be civil to me.' She blew her nose. 'He told me, in great detail, exactly what he had said to you and he accused me of plotting with Ian to make use of you in order to ruin his friendship with Gina. Can you believe such rubbish? And from my son! Even so, I wondered if you would believe him and not wish to speak to me again, that you might even hate me.'

Christie assured her that that was not the case, although she admitted she had been shaken by his outpouring and confused by some of the so-called facts he presented her with. But she most certainly didn't hate her. In fact, she was more worried for Margaret than she had been for herself.

Margaret shed more tears. 'My son has hurt me, Christie, but I know he has been lured away from me by a clever and unscrupulous woman. Yes, I am sad he has proved to be so weak. I'd have thought he would have seen through her by now. I know he will one day. I just hope that day won't come too late. Until then, I suppose I'll have to endure his silences and his rudeness.' With a catch in her voice, she said, 'When someone you love is acting out of character like that it really hurts. They're no longer the person you knew and loved, and you just want that kind and loving person back again. It's horrible!'

Christie said she really felt for her and, if it helped, she wanted her to know that she wasn't going to give up trying to find a way to show Gina up for what she really was.

Margaret sounded dubious. 'Don't get me wrong, my dear, but I don't think you are any match for her. If you go playing with her foolish fire, you could get badly burned.'

At the words "foolish fire," the will-o'-the-Wisp, the jack-o'-lantern, the *ignis fatuus* came to Christie's mind, and she was reminded of what they did. They lured poor innocent souls from the path and into the mire. She suddenly saw

Tom as one of those innocent souls, faithfully following the duplicitous light and wandering from safety — into what? Where was she planning on leading him? Christie felt light-headed. 'That is exactly what she is, isn't she, Margaret? She is the hobby lantern.'

'Oh yes, my dear. This woman's no puckish, elfin child, full of mischievous fun. She's no playful spirit, content to lead her human prey into some embarrassing situation so as to laugh at him. I have lived all my life on the Fens, Christie. I've seen my share of strange sights, but every time I see Gina Spearman, I see a cold blue corpse candle glowing above her head.'

Christie shuddered.

'Fanciful, I know, but that's what I see. Sadly, my son doesn't. He gives flesh to the bones of her lies. He sees only what he wants to.'

'I'll do what I can, Margaret, even if I'm no match for her. I have to try.' Margaret's words had only convinced Christie that she must not give up trying to stop her. 'Did Tom ever say much about Gina, as in did he ever tell you anything about her that could help me find out about her history?'

Margaret let out a loud exclamation and gave a harsh laugh. 'Did he! In his early days at the bookshop, he only had one topic of conversation — the fabulous Gina. Well, for some reason I stored away quite a few snippets of information, like a squirrel hoarding nuts.' She laughed again. 'Let me see. Her father, Adrian Spearman, was from Yorkshire and her mother from here in Lincolnshire, from a place named Huttoft, a village on the coast up near Sutton-on-Sea. The family home was a Georgian house near Spalding. Not to Gina's taste, it seemed, as she sold it as soon as her parents died.'

So, it seemed Ian had kept his secret from his friend. Margaret did not know that Gina's mother was alive and living in a care home in Louth.

Margaret thought that the mother was called Annie or possibly Alice. She had been in her sixties when she passed away. The father had been much older than his wife, about a fifteen-year gap, she thought.

'When did they die?' Christie asked.

'Let's see. Well, the father had been dead for a good few years when Tom went to the Reading Room and the mother died the year he started there, so four years ago in August.'

Christie glanced at the clock. Liz would be here at any moment. She thanked Margaret for all her help and told her to keep her chin up, not to give up on Tom and to ring her whenever she wanted, day or night.

'You take care, *great* care, my dear. I'll help you in any way I can. Just don't for one single moment forget who you are dealing with.'

That I won't, thought Christie grimly and, as Liz's car pulled up outside, she also remembered her promise to Liz to steer clear of Gina. She exhaled. One day at a time. She'd see what this visit produced and revise her future strategy after that. Most importantly, Gina must not be allowed to continue to destroy other people's lives.

CHAPTER THIRTY

'Brilliant!' Liz exclaimed on hearing what Margaret had said about Gina's parents. 'That fits with what I got from Bryn and what I told the care home. I decided to say nothing about being a private detective and said instead that you were researching a book on local history. I'm your secretary, by the way, Lizzie Wright, and your name is Ruth Coleman. I thought it best not to use our real names, just in case. You believe oral history to be an important form of historical record and get lots of wonderful stories from the elderly.'

Christie laughed. 'Well, that's not far from the truth. Did they agree?'

'The owner, who's called Leonard Sands, was initially suspicious but it didn't take long to win him round. I told him a friend who had been visiting another resident had recognised Alice and wondered if she might help you with your research for your new book. He seemed to have no problem with that. He said that since Alice never gets any visitors, it would be nice for her to share reminiscences or memories of her old home in Huttoft. He said she can be a bit difficult sometimes and he daren't leave us alone with her. She's not dangerous but she can be a bit off-putting if she has one of her turns.' Liz pulled out onto the main road. 'He said she looks a lot older than her years, so I chanced asking what her problem was. He said it was the same as all the other residents — the Joan of Arc home provides care for stroke victims.'

* * *

Miss Coleman and Miss Wright had no problem locating Joan of Arc Court. It was a purpose-built home, a single-storey building, fairly modern but with a slightly unkempt air about it. It was not what Christie had expected.

Liz announced their arrival to see Mrs Spearman. The door made a howling noise and she pushed it forward.

The hall smelled of boiled cabbage. A middle-aged woman with startling orange hair bustled out to greet them. 'Hello, dearies. Len is just checking that Alice is ready for your visit. This is quite a red-letter day for her, so we have to make sure she has her best bib and tucker on.'

Christie tried hard not to stare at the shock of flaming hair. 'Alice doesn't have many visitors, then?'

'I've been here four years, dear, and you're the first I've seen.'

'How come?' asked Liz. 'She is not very old. Doesn't she have any sons or daughters?'

The woman looked grim.

'Ah. Leonard obviously hasn't had time to speak to you about her, has he? Listen, if you're going to talk to her, on no account must you mention her daughter. It upsets her so much she gets ill. I'm sure Leonard will explain this before you go in, but it is important, dearies. We don't want her to have a turn, do we?'

They shook their heads and promised to say nothing. 'Poor Alice,' said Liz compassionately. 'Did her daughter die, then? Is that why talking about her makes her so upset?'

'Heavens, no!'

They waited for more and as Leonard hadn't yet put in an appearance, Molly, as she called herself, took them into her office and pointed to two plastic chairs.

287

'This is just between us, all right?' She leaned forward at her desk, her ample bosom resting heavily on a well-read copy of *Hello* magazine, and lowered her voice to a whisper. 'Alice rambles sometimes, but on other occasions she's quite coherent. When she first came here, she would kick off something alarming about the girl — shout and swear; they often do, bless them, it's the frustration, you know. But anyway, reading between the lines, I think the daughter was a real handful as a child. Not just a bit wayward, but serious bad news. I think Alice and her hubby finished up taking her to all sorts of doctors and clinics, you know the sort I mean.' She pointed a finger at her temple. 'It seems there was an incident that— Oh, Len! It's the writer ladies come for their visit. I've just been telling them not to mention the daughter.' Molly smiled apologetically and left them with a tall beanpole of a man in ill-fitting grey trousers.

He shook their hands and led them back out into the cabbagey hallway.

'She's as ready as she'll ever be, ladies. I don't know that you will get much from her today, but I can't deny her the opportunity to have guests and a little moment of fame, can I?'

The man had a weary, patient smile.

If the worn carpet and scratched paintwork were anything to go by, running the Joan of Arc care home must be quite a struggle. Christie thanked him for allowing them to see Alice and tried, unsuccessfully, to steer the conversation back to the daughter.

'Just no talk about family members, okay? Stick to her own childhood and recollections of Huttoft. Here we are, then.'

He opened the door to a small, airless room.

'Sorry, it's a bit hot in here. Alice doesn't like the window open, I'm afraid.'

Alice Spearman sat in a winged armchair. Her hair was pulled back severely from her face, in a sort of grey, wispy French plait. It wasn't a professional job, but it looked freshly washed. She suspected the plait to be the handiwork of Leonard Sands, or the flame-haired Molly. Alice sat hunched and twisted in the old chair, which made her look as if she were hiding something away. One arm was supported by a narrow webbing sling and one leg rested on a footstool at an odd angle. Even though one side of her face drooped slightly, Alice gave them a beaming smile.

'Here we are, my love. It's the two lovely ladies I told you about. They've come to talk to you about Huttoft.'

Feeling like a total fraud, Christie smiled warmly at Alice.

'Leonard, please don't address me as if I have Alzheimer's. You've told me about Miss Coleman and Miss Wright's visit, and I am very pleased to make their acquaintance.'

She noticed that Liz looked as surprised as her. What had she expected? A drooling vegetable? Anyway, certainly not this well-mannered lady who was asking them in an educated voice to please take a seat. Her voice was clear, she hardly slurred at all and when she looked at her more closely, Christie could see where Gina got those ice-blue eyes.

There could be no doubt that Alice was Gina's mother.

'So, you want to know about Huttoft. What sort of book are you compiling, my dear?'

Leonard sat opposite them. His eyes did not leave Alice.

Christie rattled off the story that she and Liz had concocted on their way here, using Google to check out Huttoft. She mentioned the petrified forest of ancient trees that was very occasionally visible at low tide, and asked whether Alice had any recollection about a strange tradition of celebrating "Clerk Thursday" after Ash Wednesday, which apparently caused havoc, with the local kids not attending school. Alice listened, nodding sagely.

She recalled Clerk Thursday with a laugh and was halfway through a tale of her schooldays when suddenly her voice faltered. Her cheek twitched slightly, and one eye developed a slight spasm. She continued to talk, but no longer about her childhood. She seemed to be having a conversation with someone, and about a different subject altogether.

Leonard reached across, gently stroked her hand and spoke to her in a soft, almost cajoling tone. She looked at

Christie with a strange expression, then suddenly reverted to her Huttoft childhood.

If she had been doing genuine research, she would have found little useful information. They soon began making polite noises about having to leave. Alice looked from one to the other of them, then fixed her gaze on "Ms Coleman." 'Who did you say you were, dear?'

Christie reminded her.

She smiled, said goodbye and thanked them for visiting her. 'Long journey home, have you?'

Christie replied that it wasn't too far, only to Fenfleet, forgetting that that was where Gina lived.

Alice's eyes narrowed to hostile slits. The atmosphere in the overheated room became distinctly chill. Leonard Sands all but shoved them out of the door and slammed it behind them. Out in the hall, they heard her screaming.

'*She* sent them! Sent them to gloat over me! To see if I'm still alive! Well, I am! And I hope they do tell her! I won't give her the satisfaction of dying!' There were other words, now muffled and garbled, and they heard Leonard talking to her, calming her and trying to reassure her.

'Hellfire,' murmured Liz. 'I didn't expect that!'

Christie felt quite sick. 'We'd better go back to the office and wait for him, although heaven knows how we are going to explain this.'

Eventually, Leonard returned and took up his seat. 'I'm so sorry about that,' he said. 'I should have known something would set her off.'

Liz hastily assured him that it was they who should be apologising.

This happened all the time, he said, some chance word would send her into a fit of rage. He offered them a coffee before they left, and they accepted with alacrity.

As they waited for Leonard to bring their drinks, Liz said, 'We've come this far, we might as well go for broke and ask Leonard about the daughter. He can only clam up on us.'

Soon, he was back with cups and saucers, plus a small plate of shortbread biscuits.

He sighed and took a biscuit. 'It's very disturbing when that happens, especially if you aren't used to it. We think the stroke exacerbated some old nervous problems. You just wish you could do more for them. Our resources here are pretty stretched but my staff are the salt of the earth. We do our best.'

'I can see that,' said Christie. 'And it must be difficult with residents like Alice.'

'Oh, she isn't the worst, bless her! We have a few who really shouldn't be here but it's their home now. You can't move them on, it'd kill them.'

To bring the conversation back to Alice, Liz asked bluntly, 'What happened between Alice and her daughter to make her react like that? Or was it just the stroke?'

Leonard said that Alice was not at all confused about her daughter. 'After Alice's husband died, the daughter took advantage of her mother's ill health to use her power of attorney to defraud her of all her money.'

Christie's horror must have shown on her face.

'I know. It sounds impossible, doesn't it?' he said.

'How did she finish up here?' she asked.

'She was left at the casualty department of the local hospital.'

'What? Dumped?'

'That's right.' He shrugged.

The implications were huge. If Gina could do that to her own mother, what could she do to someone like Tom? Or the innocent Delphi? Or even Jane, so talented, but with no confidence in herself? 'Couldn't anything have been done?'

'There was no one to fight for her. To begin with, we didn't even know who she was. The stroke was a bad one and she didn't receive medical attention quickly enough to be given tPA to break down the blood clot. Her speech took a long time to come back, and any mention of her daughter so disturbed her that we had to put her health and well-being

291

first. If we had introduced the daughter back into her life, it would have sent her over the edge. And to be honest, even if she got the money back and went to some posh care establishment, do you think they would look after her any better than us?'

Christie thought of the freshly washed hair and the way he had held her hands and talked her down after her outburst and agreed. He might not have plush carpets and fancy fittings but as he'd said, he was doing his best, and he truly cared.

'Alice has also hinted at cruelty, both mental and physical. Her own mother!' He shuddered. 'Personally, I wouldn't let her anywhere near our Alice. The woman should rot in hell for what she did.' He coughed. 'Sorry.'

Liz said they were right behind him there. Just how much, he wasn't to know.

They finished their drinks and thanked him profusely. He shouldn't be concerned, they wouldn't be bothering him or Alice again, and they were sincerely sorry for upsetting her.

On her way out, Christie promised herself that if she ever came into money, she would send Leonard Sands and his team a big fat cheque.

CHAPTER THIRTY-ONE

Liz dropped Christie off at The Mulberries with the instruction not to do anything until she heard from her. She needed to consult with Matt.

Matt was horrified when she told him what Gina Spearman had done. 'It's beyond belief. How could she do such a thing to anyone, let alone her own mother?'

'The trouble is, we have no actual proof that it really was Gina who abandoned her at the hospital.'

'Well, you certainly won't find any CCTV evidence from that long ago. All you have is the word of a disturbed and unstable woman, who you tell me is so confused that she cannot even sustain a conversation.' He gave Liz a rueful smile. 'To be honest, without a DNA test you don't even know if this woman really is Alice Spearman.'

Liz shook her head. 'Oh, I know. It's her all right. They look alike and she turns up at the hospital just when Gina says her mother died. But as you say, I haven't got a shred of bloody evidence.'

'Did you hear anything else that might give you something concrete to work on?' he asked.

She nodded slowly. 'Maybe. This will take some investigating and as PIs we can't go through the official channels

— doctors and the like. Bryn could, I suppose, if we manage to get some definite link between Gina and Lindsay. We were told that Gina was a problem child, as in seriously disturbed, and went to various doctors and clinics for treatment. It sounds as though this story about her abusive parents is a crock of shit. That is something definite, if we can just get confirmation.'

'I don't mean to be a prophet of doom, Liz, but all you'd be proving is that she's a liar and that's not a crime.' Matt grinned. 'If it was, most of the population would be banged up.'

He was right. Nevertheless, every new piece of information added to her understanding of Gina. Piece by piece, she was building up a picture of a cunning, callous liar — and a liar on that scale was dangerous. The more lies she uncovered, the less she trusted Gina's word on anything, including her relationship with Lindsay Harrison. But she needed more.

Then the seed of a new idea began to take root in her mind. It would cost her, but at this stage she was willing to part with some of her money.

'What have you got lined up for this afternoon, Matt?' she asked.

He groaned. 'I said I'd meet Paul Redman. He rang while you were out. He seems to think he's got another lead. It'll turn out to be as useful as an inflatable anchor, I'm sure, but I have to look at it. Then I need to tie up with Bryn again. He texted me just before you got back and said he'd got a couple of other bits of information on Gina. But he'll be tied up until after three.'

'Are you all right flying solo on those?' Liz said. 'I'm going into town this afternoon. I suddenly have an overwhelming desire to look at watercolour paintings.' She smiled angelically. 'You know that wall in the dining room? Well, it looks sort of empty, and I've been wondering what would go there. A watercolour featuring the Fenlands would be perfect.'

'Sounds a rather expensive way of getting to talk to the artist.' Matt raised an eyebrow.

'Sort of. But hey, I don't get out much. I reckon it's time I blew some of my hard-earned cash.' She kissed his cheek and gathered up her things. 'Good luck with our Paul.'

'And good luck with Leonardo.'

The gallery was empty when she walked in. A young man emerged from an office at the rear and greeted her with a smile. 'Just browsing? You're most welcome to take a look around.'

She returned the smile. 'No, actually I was wondering if Jane Waterhouse was in today.'

'She's in her studio.' He pointed his thumb ceilingward. 'Is it important? Only she's working on a commission.' The smile widened. 'I'm Gary, her number one, maybe I can help?'

'Hello, Gary. My cousin, Christie McFerran, told me about this place. Actually, she suggested I talk to Jane about a painting for my dining room.' She looked at him hopefully.

'Oh, Christie sent you. Then I'm sure Jane will happily come and have a word. Do have a look around and I'll go and talk to her.'

While she waited, Liz wandered around, interested to see the work that her cousin admired so much. She soon saw that Christie had been right in her assessment. Jane was indeed remarkably talented.

'You must be Liz.' Jane Waterhouse seemed to materialise out of nowhere. 'Christie told me how kind you've been and what great friends you are. I'm Jane. It's a pleasure to meet you.'

Liz immediately took to this woman with the other-worldly air and floating, gossamer clothes. She praised her work. 'There's a blank wall in my dining room and Christie suggested I talk to you about something suitable to hang there.'

Jane asked about light, décor and what kind of art she was looking for.

Liz said that living so close to the marsh, she would really like something sort of misty that rendered its atmosphere. As the room was decorated in a neutral shade, she thought most colours would work.

'I adore the one that Christie has in The Mulberries.'

'Ah, well, maybe I do have something . . . Can you give me a few minutes to go back up to the studio? I have an unfinished painting there that I was working on just before I had a big commission come in. In fact, why don't you come up with me? If it would suit, I could finish it fairly quickly.'

Liz followed her up two flights of stairs and stepped into a long room with huge, slanted skylight windows. It was lined with shelves bearing trays and racks of paints, brushes, cleaning materials and stacks of different supports, from board to paper. She was at present working on a large and striking landscape that closely resembled Tanners Fen. 'This is marvellous, Jane!' Liz exclaimed. 'You could almost walk right into it.'

'I'm not sure I've done justice to the water — although this is exactly as I saw it when I visited the place.'

To her untrained eye, Liz said, it was perfect. Even though Liz knew very little about art, Jane seemed relieved to hear her opinion. *She must be very insecure*, Liz thought, *to take note of what I have to say*. Perhaps, despite the impressive studio and gallery, she had no idea how good she really was.

'This is it. As I say, it's unfinished, but I think you can get an idea of the atmosphere of the place.' She picked up a large sheet of thick textured paper and stood it on an easel. 'It was to be the sister picture to the one that Christie kindly purchased. It has similar tones and that misty kind of evening feel to it, don't you think?'

Liz agreed. It would be perfect. 'This is exactly what I envisaged. When you have time, please finish it for me, but there's no hurry. Do your commissions first.'

'I've promised to paint The Mulberries for Christie when I've finished it,' said Jane. 'But I'll get yours in first, since it's almost complete.'

She spoke warmly of Christie, so Liz assumed she was unaware of the falling out between Christie and Tom. She supposed it was because she'd been working all hours on the commission. Liz decided to ask what she'd come here to find out.

'This has been an absolute delight, coming in here and seeing all your beautiful work. It's really lifted my spirits.'

'I'm glad to hear it.' Jane smiled.

'I've had a rough few days, to be honest. I'm on my way to Greenborough to see a friend who's been admitted to hospital, all very sad.'

Jane looked at her enquiringly. 'Is she ill? Had an accident?'

'Neither, actually.' Liz assumed an expression of abject misery. 'Sadly, the silly girl tried to kill herself.'

'Oh no! How awful,' Jane exclaimed. 'Was it something she'd attempted before?'

'No way! That's why I can't get my head around it. She's one of those people who you think has her whole life under control. Brilliant job, no money worries. I just don't understand how someone so, well, so *together* and apparently well-balanced could do such a thing.'

'I know exactly what you mean,' Jane said. 'A close friend of mine attempted to take her own life, and she's one of the most intelligent and clever businesswomen you could ever meet. I was astounded and terribly upset. To make it worse, if that's possible, it happened right here when she was staying with me. If I hadn't heard something and gone into the guest room, she might have bled to death. It was horrible.'

'She didn't cut her wrists?' said Liz. 'God, that's what my friend did, only in the bath.' She had seen a few of those in the force, and it wasn't an easy way to die. 'Still, she's in good hands now. They have an excellent psychiatric unit at Greenborough. I'm just hoping it's a one-off, you know, things just got too much for her for some reason. Is your friend okay now?'

'Yes, although she is still very troubled. She finally opened up to me, and I believe that helped. The damage stems from a terrible childhood.' She gave a deep sigh. 'Mind you, I wouldn't be surprised if it happened again. She is desperately insecure, although, like your friend, people who don't know her never get to see the real person. Only her close friends see her vulnerability.'

'You never quite know what's going on in people's heads, do you?' Liz said, and glanced at her watch. 'Oh dear, I have to go. Can I leave you a deposit on that amazing picture?'

But Jane said she should come and see it when it was finished and, if she still liked it, they'd talk about a suitable frame and she could pay then. 'Love to Christie,' she said in parting, 'Hope to see her again soon.'

Liz hurried back to her car and sat behind the wheel, staring at nothing. There was little doubt as to who Jane was talking about. Christie had said that Gina stayed over regularly. That and the description of her as a clever, intelligent businesswoman, coupled with the scar Liz had seen on her wrist, made it pretty damned certain.

She thought back to what she had learned of attempted suicides while she was in uniform. A genuine attempt was usually successful. It was carried out when the person was alone or out of reach and couldn't be stopped, like jumpers. A cry for help was a different matter, as was someone desperate for attention, or a few cases she'd come across of a person who was trying to make someone close to them feel guilty, as in "This is all your fault. Look what you made me do."

Well, Liz knew which category Gina fitted into, and it certainly wasn't a genuine attempt. She wondered where to go next. Should she go straight home? Call in on Christie? They had said they would talk through Christie's options again after they had investigated the care home. And Christie bothered her. Liz loved her to bits, but she was much too susceptible. They both hated injustice and the thought of Gina using her power of attorney to get her hands on the family money, then dumping her desperately ill mother, might well send her into another fit of rage. After all, she'd seen the red mist once before. Liz started the car. Perhaps it was time to give her cousin a little reminder about backing off.

Liz found Christie chatting to her next-door neighbour, which was a relief. At least she hadn't driven off to Tadema House with a chainsaw in the boot.

Christie introduced them, and as soon as she heard that Bill and Lynne were related to Jane, Liz told them she'd just been to the gallery. 'She's so talented! Christie was right, she's wasted here in the muddy Fens.'

'We've told her, time an' again, duck,' Lynne said. 'Kept on at her till we're blue in the face. Such talent, and here she is, stuck in the bloody — 'scuse my French — village hall, teaching a load of bored housewives how to paint daisies. Wasted. Totally wasted.' Lynne shook her head and then looked at them, her eyes wide. 'Why don't you two ladies have a word with her, me ducks? She'd listen to you.'

With a doubtful glance at Christie, Liz said they'd give it a try.

'She had the chance once, you know. A city gent bought one of her pictures — "Spring Morning" it was called. I can see it now, lovely it was, all dewy with primroses and moss and that. Well, this man bought it for a friend's birthday and a few days after, she had a call from the friend. She offered our Jane a space in a posh gallery in Oxford.'

Christie asked what had happened.

'Don't rightly know, me duck. One minute she was over the moon, practically bought her train ticket, next she was right down in the dumps. Said she wasn't good enough. Refused the offer and stayed here.'

A sneaking suspicion was creeping into Liz's brain. 'Was that long ago?'

Lynne paused to think. 'About eighteen months, I suppose. Yes, I remember she was having a bit of a tough time making ends meet. Her uncle and I offered her a bit a' money to tide her over, but I think that snobby friend a' hers must a' helped her out. One of these 'ere cash injections you reads about. We never 'eard no more about the Oxford Gallery, or 'er money troubles.'

Yet another unprovable item for her list of the lies, deceit and manipulations of Gina Spearman.

They left Lynne and went inside.

'So, you bought one of Jane's pictures?' said Christie, grinning at her. 'Sudden interest in art, was it? Or did you just want to get a look at Jane Waterhouse?'

'Bit of both,' Liz admitted, smiling. 'Hey, but you'll love it! It's a work in progress and it was intended to be the sister picture to yours, which I thought very appropriate, don't you?'

Christie agreed and offered coffee or tea.

Over their drinks, they discussed what they had discovered in Louth. Liz asked Christie if it had influenced the decision she'd made.

'I'm staying right here, no matter what. I love this cottage. You and Matt aren't far away, and I refuse to let that evil woman drive me away.'

Although she welcomed the thought of Christie being close by, Liz wasn't all that happy with the steely edge to her voice. 'I'm thrilled you want to stay, honestly, but please, don't let Gina drag you back into the web she's spun. Like I said, the police are sniffing around her, so you shouldn't interfere. I'm starting to believe she's truly unbalanced — not just controlling and power-mad but dangerously psychotic.' She swallowed hard. 'I couldn't bear it if you got hurt — well, more than you have been already.'

Christie leaned across the table and took her hand. 'Oh, I know exactly what she is, dear Liz. My mind is now crystal clear, not clouded by emotion as it was before.'

Liz had never seen her gentle, sensitive cousin look so cold and determined. It scared her.

Christie released her hand. 'I spoke to Margaret earlier. She's in bits, Liz. I don't know how I could ever have doubted her, but it did serve one purpose. I can now see exactly how the others have been slowly and insidiously groomed to become reliant on her and swallow all her malicious lies.' She stared into her coffee. 'I truly believe that if

Tom doesn't wake up and see her for what she is, it will kill Margaret. And maybe that's the intention. After all, we know Gina Spearman doesn't hold mothers in particularly high regard, don't we?'

'Well, I can't deny that,' said Liz, 'but I do have a suggestion that may help to keep you from falling back into her clutches.' It was worth a try. 'Come back to Cannon Farm and stay with us for a while. Step right away until the dust settles and the police finish investigating her. It'll mean I'll be there to nail you to the floor if the red mist descends again.' From Christie's expression she knew the offer would be declined, but Liz persisted. 'The estate agents all contact you on your mobile, so it won't hold up the sale of the house. Do say yes.'

Christie said it was a very kind offer, but . . .

Liz drove home half an hour later, certain that Christie had a plan in her head. And she wasn't sharing it with her cousin.

CHAPTER THIRTY-TWO

Seated at the kitchen table, the only sounds Christie heard were the clock ticking and the wheels turning inside her head. Ian had given her a trump card in the form of Alice. Her problem was how to use it. She couldn't tell Margaret, who would certainly tell her son and then the rift between them would be irreparable.

She certainly couldn't tell Tom. Jane would bring down the shutters and retreat into her shell. That left just one person.

'Gina,' she breathed. In some way she had known this as soon as she set eyes on Alice. And however much she searched her mind for someone to lighten her burden, help her choose another path, there was no one.

This would be her final attempt to give three friends their lives back.

Blackmail. A simple enough strategy. *Leave them alone and I'll leave you alone. If you interfere in their lives one further time, I will take them all to the Joan of Arc home to meet your supposedly dead mother. I will introduce them to the man who has cared for her for the past four years.* Gina had driven the wedge between Delphi and Denis, so she could damn well repair the damage, and mend the rift between Tom and his mother. As for Jane, she could give her back her self-esteem and allow her to proudly be the gifted artist that she really was.

Christie noticed that it was growing dark. She stepped out into a wet nightscape. At some point during her deliberations, it must have rained. Like a ghost, a barn owl drifted silently over the hedge, startling her. It turned its round, flat face to hers and soared away, crossing in front of the full moon.

The night had stolen the colours but made amends by filling the air with perfume. It felt like a message.

She sat on the wooden seat, unmindful of the damp. Perhaps, after all, there was someone to help her carry this burden. As she thought this, a shower of rose petals fell from a high branch, raining grey confetti on her shoulders.

An unseen friend. She sat with her friend until sleep threatened to overtake her.

* * *

Matt thought that this time Paul really had hit on a possible witness, someone who might have been in the premises the night Lindsay was murdered. The downside was that she was away on holiday and couldn't be contacted for several days. It was frustrating, but really, after four years, what did a few days matter?

Now he and Liz lay in bed, once again talking about the woman who seemed to occupy most of Liz's waking thoughts — Gina Spearman.

'You can't force Christie to come here,' Matt said for the umpteenth time. 'You are just going to have to keep a close eye on her and try to keep her from doing anything stupid.' He turned and looked at her. 'If it were anyone else but Christie, I'd just tell her to back off and leave it at that. They're adults, after all, so let them fight their own battles. But I know how you feel about her, and I've seen for myself how nasty that Gina woman can be. She really does appear to have them all by the short and curlies, although it beats me why.'

'Christie says she's a game-player who moves people around like chess pieces.' She snuggled in closer to him. 'I think she's right.'

'And Mother got checkmated.' It was such a shame. Liz had been so happy when Christie arrived like a breath of fresh air. But now . . .

'Christie's got something in that head of hers, I know it. I can't stop worrying about her and what she might do.'

Matt drew her towards him. 'I'm afraid you'll have to just take it day by day. If things go tits up again, all you can do is be there to pick up the pieces. Not the best solution, but unless Bryn, or even we, can find something solid on Spearman, it's all I've got to offer.' He looked at her. 'Except . . . I could go and have a word with Christie if you like? Use a bit of "good cop, bad cop."'

'Would you, Matt?' she said sleepily. 'It might be what she needs. She and I are too close — we are like sisters, and they never take each other's advice. A stern warning from a big bad DCI might be just what is needed.'

'That's settled, then. I'll call by tomorrow morning.'

* * *

Christie awoke filled with a quiet determination. She would go back to Tadema House and confront Gina Spearman, and she would do it today. There was no point in putting it off. Her shock and anger at the way Gina had treated her mother would serve to fuel her resolution. There was no second shot at this.

She would go early, before Gina left for work. By eight o'clock she was ready to leave. As she took her car keys from the shelf by the door, she saw something glitter in a crevice at the back. She pulled the shelf out a centimetre or two, and a fine gold chain fell through the gap and onto the floor. It was a crucifix. It had a symbol engraved into the centre, too small to make out clearly but she thought it could be the initial "E." It was warm to the touch. She felt compelled to put it on.

She clipped it around her neck and, feeling it still warm against her skin, Christie picked up the keys and left.

At eight thirty, she pulled into the drive of Tadema House, rang the bell and stood back. She heard the sound of approaching footsteps and gently touched the crucifix.

Gina was dressed for work and holding a mug of coffee. Silent, she stood aside, and Christie walked in.

They went through to the lounge, where Gina stood in the bay window, her back to Christie. A hazy sun lit the lawns and the marsh beyond. With the mist still drifting lazily across the grass, the scene resembled one of Jane Waterhouse's paintings.

She offered Christie neither a seat nor coffee. Christie wanted neither. She had come to deliver her message and then leave. Christie couldn't help comparing the opulence of Gina's country house with the worn carpet and washed-out curtains in Alice's room at the Joan of Arc.

Gina turned to face her. In the morning light, the pale blue of her eyes had faded almost to white, and she stared at her like a blind woman. To avoid those eyes, Christie moved closer and stood at her side.

She spoke in a voice not her own. 'I have come to ask you to bring the game to a close. Three people are suffering because of it, and their loved ones with them. It is time it was finished. You have made your point, Gina. You can do whatever you want with them, they are no match for you. Why not let them go now? Leave them to get on with their lives.'

Gina stood impassive as a marble statue, with those same blind eyes.

Christie recalled Margaret's words about seeing a corpse candle above her. She now understood what she meant. There was indeed something deathly about her as she stood, silent and unmoving.

'Please, Gina. You've won. Let your prisoners go.'

Slowly, Gina withdrew her gaze from the window and focused those wintry eyes on her.

'I have no idea what you're talking about, Christie.'

'Yes, you have. You know exactly what I am talking about.'

Gina took a long, deep breath. 'If that was the case, and I'm not saying it was, what makes you so sure of my victory? How do you know what stakes I am playing for?'

'You have got them wrapped around your little finger. They jump to your every command. What more could you want? You've already caused havoc in a marriage, a family unit and a mind.'

'Perhaps they have more to give. Perhaps their sacrifices haven't been, how shall we say, complete enough. Hypothetically, of course.'

Christie struggled to remain composed. 'You really are something, aren't you? You won't be happy until you've drained every ounce of life out of them, will you? Then, no doubt, you'll blow the empty husks away.'

Gina snorted. 'How poetic.'

'Ah, but how true.'

Gina's tone turned dismissive. 'I'm tiring of this, Christie. I don't know what really brought you here, but I suggest you say whatever it is, stop whining about your dull, feeble little friends, and go. I have a business to run.'

'And more lives to ruin,' Christie retorted.

Her eyes narrowed. In that moment, she looked exactly like her mother.

'Spit it out. You wouldn't have come here waving your self-righteous banner and threatening me if there wasn't something you're dying to tell me.'

'I'll ask you one more time. If you think they're dull and feeble, why not move on to more deserving opponents? Leave them alone, Gina.'

'Between you and me, dear Christie, I'm nowhere near my final move. You are welcome to stay around and watch if you wish. It shouldn't take much longer.'

Christie had hoped not to have to play her final card. Now she saw that Gina would never give up. All at once, Christie understood. Gina's three musketeers all possessed something she would never have. Tom, a loving mother; Delphi, a loving relationship. Jane had real talent. Gina was deeply jealous.

Chilled to the marrow, Christie played her card. 'By the way, I met your mother yesterday.'

Gina's mouth dropped open.

Seconds passed. Then she hissed, 'My mother is dead!'

'Oh. Not according to her,' Christie said.

'Get out!'

But unlike last time, Christie did not run. She turned on her. 'Let them go, Gina, give them their lives back or I'll take them visiting.'

'You fool! They will never believe you over me!'

'Try me.' Christie grabbed Gina by her shirt front and brought her face close to hers. 'I swear to God, Gina, if you don't put things right, I will put them all in my car and take them to meet Alice.' She shoved her roughly back against the wall and strode out.

As she opened her car door to get in, she heard her scream, 'She's dead! My mother is dead, bitch, do you hear me? Dead!'

About a mile from home, Christie's heart began to race. She pulled into a lay-by and waited for the palpitations to stop. But they continued, her breath coming in short and painful gasps. She sat for a full fifteen minutes before she felt able to drive. She needed to get home, where she had some tablets that would help.

As she looked in her rear-view mirror, she saw Delphi's beat-up old car turning into the lane leading to Tadema House.

Christie wanted to follow Delphi, forestall her, but the pains were returning. She had no choice, she had to get back to The Mulberries.

Somehow, she made it and climbed gingerly up the stairs to the bathroom, where she kept her pills. She took one and, holding onto walls and furniture, felt her way to bed.

* * *

307

Christie slept for eight hours. She awoke, disorientated and weak, to the sound of someone banging on the door. The clock said six thirty.

'Coo-ee! Hello! Are ya all right, me duck?'

The palpitations had gone, so she staggered downstairs and opened the door to a worried-looking Lynne. Her neighbour said that she'd seen her return early in the morning, looking "right poorly," and noticed that the curtains had been drawn all day. When Christie still hadn't appeared by teatime, she'd decided to risk being a "nosey parker" and come to check on her.

'Ya give us a right turn, by no mistake. Ya do still look peaky, duck. Shall I call the doctor for ya?'

She assured her neighbour that she got these attacks sometimes, and today's had been a bad one. However, sleep and a pill had sorted it out and she felt much better.

Lynne pursed her lips doubtfully and urged her to get some food inside her. 'Ya'll feel better for it, dearie.'

Christie suddenly realised that she was starving.

'Tell ya what, dearie. Ya get ya self together and come over to the bungalow. I've got a plate a' dinner ready for ya. I said to my Bill, that lass'll need something inside her if she's not up ta cookin'.'

Christie could have hugged her. The last thing she wanted to do was prepare a meal.

She thanked her gratefully. Lynne said not to rush, it was ready when she was.

First, she rang Liz and told her she'd had bad palpitations but was okay now. Her neighbour was going to feed her, bless her heart. She omitted to mention the visit that had precipitated the attack.

Half an hour later, she was finishing a plateful of home-made steak and kidney pie, runner beans from the garden, new potatoes and mushy peas. She was sure she'd never tasted anything so good.

Lynne was just persuading Christie to try some steamed treacle pudding and custard when Jane walked in.

'Hello, love.' Lynne hugged her niece affectionately. 'You know our neighbour, Christie, don't you?'

Jane said of course she did. She smiled. Christie was one of her best customers.

So Gina had evidently not spoken to her yet.

Jane looked at Christie curiously, probably wondering what she was doing in her aunt and uncle's house and devouring their food. Christie told her she'd been a bit under the weather and her aunt had kindly taken pity on her.

'You can always rely on Auntie Lynne, she's a born carer. You should have seen her when I was a child. Talk about cosseted. It's a wonder I'm not totally spoiled.'

'Ready when you are, me duck!' Bill was standing by the door with a jacket over his arm.

'Must go. See you soon.' Jane glided over to her uncle and slid her arm through his. 'Your carriage awaits!'

'Silly bugger! Let's be off, then.'

Lynne wished them a nice evening and smiled after them affectionately. 'Every other Thursday, Jane takes ma Bill over to a little place just outside Fenfleet for an evening out with his old workmates. She leaves him at the pub and goes on to take an art class at the village hall. Then she picks him up later and brings him home. He loves it. He gets to have a few drinks with his cronies and doesn't have to worry about driving, and I get an evening to maself.'

This solved a minor mystery: Christie had been told that Jane taught watercolour painting but hadn't known where.

Christie assured Lynne that she and Liz would do their utmost to make Jane understand just how much talent she really had. She thanked her for the meal and said she would leave her to her peaceful evening.

Shortly after eight, a car drew up outside The Mulberries, and with a sinking heart she recognised Tom's Peugeot. The sleep and the food had helped a lot, but she was still exhausted after her clash with Gina and the heart tremors. She wasn't ready for another confrontation.

Christie stood beside the fireplace, wearily anticipating the coming hammering on the door.

The gentle tap surprised her. Perhaps it hadn't been a Peugeot? She opened the door and saw that indeed it had.

Politely, Tom asked if he could come in. He said he wasn't going to harangue her again, but he needed to talk to her.

Cautiously, she invited him in and gestured towards the sofa. He refused a drink and perched on the edge of his seat. A silence ensued.

After he had carefully examined each of his fingernails, he began. 'Gina didn't come in to work today.'

Christie swallowed hard.

'Delphi went to pick her up for work this morning as her car is in for a service. She said that when she got there, Gina looked really ill. Another migraine.'

Christie waited.

'At lunchtime she rang the shop and asked me to drive over to Tadema House with some stronger painkillers. She looked terrible, Christie. She told me it wasn't just the migraine. She was very upset after another discussion with you.'

Still, she said nothing.

'She asked me to speak to you on her behalf. She wants me to tell you things she finds too painful to say herself.'

She felt her anger return but managed to hold it in check. What fable had Gina invented this time?

He seemed to be taking his mission extremely seriously. He was calm, showing none of the rage of his last visit.

'She told me I was wrong to be so angry with you the other night, it wasn't your fault. You have been misled and have made some incorrect assumptions because of that. It appears to you that we are being hurt and taken for a ride, so naturally you want to protect your new friends. You like the place enough to want to move here, so you want to be happy and have people you get on with around you.'

She was beginning to feel sick.

'But you really do have a wrong understanding of Gina.' In the gesture she had initially found so endearing, he pushed his glasses further up the bridge of his nose. 'She told me to give you a message. She said not to question her about it yet, she would tell me when she was ready. She said you are wrong about the discovery you made. She knows how it must look to you, but it's not true. When she is strong enough, she will try to explain it to you.'

Like hell she will, Christie thought, but merely nodded.

'She has asked me to tell you the truth about her childhood—'

Christie held up her hand. 'Tom, spare me, will you? I've heard this before.'

'Please, Christie, let me finish.'

She shook her head in exasperation, but he continued.

'Her parents hated her. No matter how hard she tried, they made her feel like she was a big disappointment to them. She was ill-treated, mentally, throughout her early years. She loathed her home and her parents. The only reason she wanted to go to university was to get away from them. She studied and studied, passed her exams and got a place at Keble. She moved into halls of residence, then into a tiny bedsit, and never went back home. She says you may not understand, as you probably come from a happy home with loving parents.'

More sob stories about her cruel upbringing. Somehow, Christie managed not to utter a retort.

Tom stared miserably at his shoes. 'Basically, she has asked you to give her more time. She says she'd like to talk to you again, explain a bit better than she did this morning. In her way, she is saying sorry, Christie. Sorry that you've got drawn into something that is not what it seems.'

There followed a long pause.

Needing to get away from him for a while, Christie said she'd make them a hot drink. She boiled water and put coffee into two mugs. Why had Gina sent Tom to her with this load of old flannel? What was she playing at now?

She stirred the drinks slowly. Was it because she wanted Christie to be aware of how brainwashed he was? But she knew that already. She went to the fridge for milk. Something wasn't right here. The message had said nothing, certainly nothing new. So why send him?

They drank their coffee in silence. She remembered the comfortable silence on the night she went to dinner with him and his mother. She recalled his lopsided grin and his enthusiasm and was filled with a sense of loss. 'Are you going back to Tadema House tonight?'

'No, Delphi is with her. I'll probably ring her when I get home. Gina said not to go back tonight but to call round in the morning before work.'

She shivered.

'What's wrong? Is it your heart? You're as white as a sheet!'

She had no idea why, but a suspicion had just come into her head.

Jane was away at her fortnightly art class. Tom had been sent to see her with his meaningless message and then home. Denis worked the twilight shift on a Thursday night. Unconsciously, she touched the crucifix around her neck. It felt hot, almost burning.

So Delphi was alone with Gina. She had no idea why that thought should bother her so much. Delphi often spent hours alone with her.

Tom looked quite frightened. But he couldn't be half as frightened as she was.

'Tom,' she said in a whisper, 'please do something for me. Ring Delphi.'

'But why?'

'Please, just ring her. For me.' Surely, Gina wasn't so deranged that she would demand the final sacrifice?

He stood staring at her, looking bewildered, but he did as she asked and dialled. After a while, he turned to her. 'That's odd. There's no answer.'

CHAPTER THIRTY-THREE

The fear that her friend might be in danger overcame Delphi's old fear of the approaching night on the marsh. She had always been uneasy in dark places and this was a very dark place, but Delphi was even more scared for Gina.

Why did Christie ever have to come to Fenfleet? Gina had had her temper tantrums in the past, but things had never been as bad as this. Poor Gina had told her all the awful things that Christie had said to her and the wicked lies she had been spreading around about her and her Denis. How he hit her. How he drank away their savings. How could she? Yes, he was mad at her about the holiday, but hit her? He would sooner stick his hand in boiling oil. And drink? He had one drink at night after his shift finished and a couple of pints if they went to the local together. Not exactly the behaviour of a raging alcoholic.

She got to the end of the row of dark trees that surrounded the Tadema House grounds. Where on earth had Gina gone?

The night clouds were practically covering the sky now and she could barely make out the footpath to the marsh. At least she had thought to grab a torch when she dashed off after her sobbing friend. She peered this way and that into the gloom. The path ran both ways. To the left, it wound its way back to the lane on the far side of the village. To the right, it curved in a loop to the sea bank and the marsh.

Gina had told her that she often walked on the sea bank after dark. It was one of her favourite places. She knew the paths well and would sometimes walk out into the desolate marsh and sit for a while to think. So it had to be that way.

She turned on the torch and followed its weak beam down the right-hand path.

Damn Christie! And to think she'd been fool enough to like her. She had talked to her as if she really wanted to be her friend, listened while Delphi confided in her. Yeah, and talked behind her back.

Delphi winced. Why hadn't she thought to put on proper shoes? The stones and flints on the path were jabbing through the soles of her canvas casuals as if they were made of tissue paper. If only her Denis were here. He would find Gina and lead them both safely home.

The dull torchlight showed up something pale, lying on the path ahead. She knelt and picked up a white linen handkerchief. In the corner was a motif embroidered with the initials "GS". She pushed it into her pocket. At least she now knew that Gina had come this way.

When she finally reached the sea bank, night had fallen. She began to call her friend's name over and over. A night bird screeched. She called again. The breeze rustled through the grass. Oh, which way had Gina gone? She had been distraught, running out of the house sobbing and shouting, and cursing Christie McFerran for destroying her friendships with her interfering and her lies. It had hurt Delphi to see her in such distress. She knew how sensitive and fragile Gina really was.

At that moment, Delphi hated Christie with a vengeance. Tears of frustration coursing down her cheeks, she ran this way and that, calling out Gina's name. She needed help up here. She couldn't find her alone.

Oh, why was she so stupid? She had remembered to bring a torch but had forgotten to pick up her mobile phone.

Then she saw it! A faint light, out on the marsh. Gina had said she liked to sit out here and think. It had to be her. She yelled at the top of her voice, but no reply came.

Heartened, she directed her torch beam onto what seemed to be the clearest route to the light. The ground was pitted with the hoof-prints of cattle so she knew it must be safe to venture a bit further. She also knew that the tides came in fast, faster than she could run on the uneven terrain. But that was all right because Gina knew the tide times and she was there on the fen, breaking her heart over that callous bitch, Christie, so they would both be safe for a while.

The path was getting really difficult to follow and much wetter. But the light was still ahead of her. Not far now. She called to her friend again, but still there was no reply, nothing but the increasing sound of the wind in her ears.

Her torch flickered. She shook the thing, and the beam resumed its feeble job.

The light before her was only about fifty yards away now. It danced, flared and dimmed, then flared again. Stumbling towards it, calling out Gina's name, Delphi was plunged into darkness. She shook the torch frantically, but nothing happened. She shook it harder, crying in desperation, screaming at it to work again.

A weak ray trickled from the dying batteries, just enough to get her to her friend before it expired forever.

Delphi reached the light and stood, uncomprehending. At her feet was a rusty old storm lantern, carefully placed on a couple of old bits of rotten wood on top of a grassy mound. Inside the glass was a household candle, the kind you kept in case of a power cut. It was burned down to the last half-inch.

The useless torch, heavy in her hand, dropped with a soft splash onto the thin film of water that now covered the ground. She didn't understand.

Delphi stood, frozen to the spot, as realisation crept slowly over her. Gina wasn't here and she never had been. Suddenly, she noticed that her feet were wet. Water was trickling fast over her ankles.

She grabbed the lantern and tried to retrace her footsteps. But she had no idea which way she had come. And now a thick band of cloud hung over the fen. There was no moon. Not even a star to make a wish on.

When the water reached above her knees, she could no longer walk. She was too tired to fight the incoming tide. She recalled Gina running away, supposedly in paroxysms of tears. So why had her hankie, so carelessly dropped, been bone-dry and freshly ironed and folded?

She wondered if she would be able to swim. But the current dragged her this way and that. She no longer knew which way led to the sea bank and which to the Wash. Not that it mattered now.

She wasn't frightened anymore. She had no more fight left in her. It was all over. Her last feeling was one of terrible sadness. Now she would never be able to say sorry to Denis. Now she would never see Greece.

Above her there was a break in the cloud. A single star shone brightly.

Delphi made her wish and dived into the clear blue Aegean Sea.

* * *

Christie and Tom arrived at Tadema House to find the door open and the house empty. Delphi's car stood in the drive, its engine cold. Her purse, car keys, two packets of paper tissues and her mobile phone were on the kitchen work surface. They searched the grounds and found no sign of either woman. Tom phoned Gina's mobile, but it was switched off. He called Delphi's home number and heard her crackly answerphone message.

Tom drove into the village, called at the local pub and returned with no news. Meanwhile, Christie had searched the house and outbuildings and now stood staring down the pathway to the marsh. She knew what had happened. The moment they arrived and found them missing, she had known that somehow Gina had lured Delphi onto the marsh. She stood and strained her eyes into the pitch dark. As always, Christie had no proof.

She walked back to the house, to be told that Gina still wasn't answering her phone. Tom called the police and Christie called Matt and Liz.

The moment Liz arrived, she took Christie aside, while Matt spoke to Tom. 'Tell me everything, Christie, leave nothing out,' Liz said urgently. 'I won't be angry. If you don't, I can't help you.'

Christie told her the whole story, including her threat to take the others to Gina's mother. 'I'm so sorry, Liz, I just couldn't stop myself. If anything's happened to Delphi, and I know it has, it's all my fault.'

'Shut up, idiot, it's Gina's fault, all of it! Maybe you hastened the outcome, but with or without you, it was always going to happen with a psychopath like her.' She exhaled loudly. 'So where is she now?'

'I've no idea, but you can bet your bottom dollar that she'll waltz in and do an Oscar-worthy performance of panicking about her dear friend's whereabouts. I'm dreading it.'

'Just hold your tongue. Say nothing to her, Christie.' Liz gripped her wrist tightly. 'Not a word. I mean it.'

The police arrived first, two uniformed officers that Liz and Matt knew well. Between Tom and herself, they told PC Debbie Hume and PC Jack Fleet, who Christie had already met, what they knew, which was precious little.

'So the door was unlocked when you got here?' asked Jack Fleet.

'The back door was wide open, Officer,' said Tom. 'And the house was empty. No Gina and no Delphi.'

'The worrying thing was that all of Delphi's things, including her phone, were still on the kitchen counter.' Christie was fighting back tears.

After listening to what they had to say, the two officers, accompanied by Matt, took some powerful torches from their car and walked down to the marsh path.

'They'll scan the area with those high-powered lamps, but they daren't go too far in the dark.' Liz had slipped her arm through Christie's. 'If she's not found, or doesn't come home, they'll have a whole station-full of officers out here at first light.'

Christie shook her head. 'They won't find her, Liz. I don't know what she's done, or how she's done it, but Gina Spearman is behind this.'

Liz said nothing.

The small search party weren't away long.

'It's impossible. The tide's well in and it's black as pitch up there.' Jack sounded despondent. 'Not a cat's chance in hell of finding anything tonight.'

'We've rung it in as a suspicious incident,' Debbie added. 'The skipper is organising a team to be here at first light.'

Matt threw a worried glance at Liz and Christie. 'It doesn't look good. Why take off leaving the door wide open and all your things here?'

Before anyone could answer, Gina Spearman arrived back. She appeared surprised to see a police car in her drive, and a group of anxious people huddled outside her door. She demanded to know what had happened.

PC Jack Fleet told her and immediately she fell into Tom's arms. She didn't understand, she said. She'd been upset and depressed, so she had gone off for a long walk to clear her mind. 'But I swear that Delphi knew what I was doing! She said she'd leave me alone for a while to think.' She looked from one to the other, wide-eyed. 'Delphi said she'd wait up for me. I left her watching TV, so where has she gone?'

As Gina talked to the police, she kept running her hand through her spiky hair and gesturing wildly, begging them to find her dear, dear friend.

Christie felt sick.

Liz squeezed her arm, a reminder to keep quiet.

Jack Fleet rang Denis at the factory and broke the news that his wife was missing. Denis said that rather than go to

Tadema House, he would go home and wait for her there. Jack arranged for an officer to accompany him.

It was almost two in the morning when they gave up. The police were of the opinion that Delphi had gone to look for her friend on the marsh and lost her way. The tide came in fast, and she must have got cut off from the sea bank.

Gina added that a torch that usually stood on the kitchen windowsill was missing, which seemed to confirm it. Delphi had panicked, grabbed a torch and run out into the night. The outlook was bleak.

'We'll take you home,' said Matt to Christie. 'And I mean *our* home. No arguments. You're in no state to be left alone.'

She was too tired to even try arguing.

Of course, Tom didn't want to leave Gina and said he'd stay with her.

As they drove away, Christie stared blankly out the window. 'I keep thinking that if only I'd realised that something was wrong an hour earlier, Delphi would still be alive.'

'We don't know that she's dead yet, Christie,' said Matt. 'There may be a chance . . .'

But Christie knew otherwise. She kept hearing Gina say that her little friends hadn't suffered enough, they had more to give. Somehow, Gina had masterminded this whole thing. But would she be able to prove it?

She was glad to be back in the kitchen at Tanners Fen, with Liz and Matt close by. While they sat nursing hot drinks, Liz took the opportunity to put Christie's mind at rest over one important thing. 'We believe what you say about Gina Spearman, Christie. We're on your side, so don't be afraid to speak out. Matt here is working with our colleague Bryn to dig into her past. He's managed to find a few more pieces to add to the puzzle.'

'Oh?'

'Molly at the care home was right when she said Gina was a serious problem child. She was taken to various clinics by what everyone said were loving, desperately worried and exhausted parents. She moved between schools but remained a disruptive influence. Bryn traced a former school classmate who described her as spiteful, self-centred, egotistical and grossly overdramatic, especially regarding her supposed illnesses. Headaches were always migraines, or even symptoms of a brain tumour. And there were several threats of suicide, which were all so much hot air.'

'But she made it to university,' Christie said. 'I met one of her old tutors and she was full of praise for her.'

Matt leaned forward. 'No one has ever denied her intelligence, Christie. She was way ahead of her peers, her parents too, for that matter. Part of her problem was blamed on the fact that she was just bored.'

'At university,' Liz added, 'she finally found her intellectual equals, became friends with tutors who recognised her extraordinary abilities, and she began to learn how to use others in order to get what she wanted from them.'

'She studied psychology as part of her course, a subject she apparently found exceedingly interesting,' Matt added.

'Yet she also excelled at art history? Bit of an odd combination,' Christie mused.

'One of her fellow students said that Gina identified with the romantics, especially the Pre-Raphaelites.'

'And that's as far as we got,' said Matt, 'before all this blew up.' He yawned. 'It tells us one thing, though, and that's what lies she has told to her "friends". Abused? No. In fact, it may have been the other way around, especially regarding her mother.'

Christie had suddenly heard enough and said she was ready for bed.

Liz told her she'd popped a hot-water bottle in her bed to air it.

As Christie lay trying to stop her brain from churning, she was glad of that bottle, and she hugged it close. She needed the comfort, something to hold.

CHAPTER THIRTY-FOUR

The tide returned Delphi two days later, her body spotted by a fishing boat heading into the tidal river towards the Greenborough docks. She had been washed into a muddy drainage outlet and caught up in tangle of old mooring ropes.

When Denis heard the news, he collapsed. Delphi's parents, both already in bad health, were overwhelmed by the loss of their happy-go-lucky daughter, and her father had to be hospitalised.

On hearing of Denis's obviously sincere devastation, Tom seemed to set aside his suspicion — planted in him by Gina — that the man had ill-treated his wife, and went to offer his support. He was with Denis when the police called, and at once volunteered to go with him to identify her.

He told Christie later that he had been horribly shocked at the state of her body. It looked to him as if she'd been attacked or even murdered, but the pathologist explained that it was natural for a body to exhibit signs of harm in a case of drowning. When a person drowns, they always go face down. Their head and extremities hanging downwards can then receive cuts and abrasions from rocks or from being dragged along the bottom of the sea or riverbed. The pathologist had explained it all. And besides, they'd found weed and sandy soil particles in her lungs, which indicated that she had indeed drowned and not been murdered and then thrown in the water.

Christie spent the days before the funeral alternating between guilt and an all-consuming need to find proof that Delphi's death had not been an accident, even though everything pointed to that being the case.

After two days with Liz and Matt, she returned home. She spoke regularly with Ian, who offered to come and support her, but although their phone calls were a great comfort to her, right then all she wanted was to be alone. She told him about her visit to Louth with Liz, and meeting Alice Spearman and Leonard Sands. He said that he had never met Alice himself and had discovered her existence purely by chance. His sister had paid a visit to an elderly stroke patient living in the Joan of Arc home, a woman she had once nursed. As she was leaving, she saw Alice Spearman, who was being wheeled down to the dining room, and recognised her at once. Evelyn had met Alice many years previously, when she had been working on an orthopaedic ward and Alice had been admitted with a badly broken leg. She hadn't realised at the time that Alice's daughter was telling the world that her mother was dead — she would probably have considered it none of her business anyway. She did, however, mention it to her brother. Later, when Margaret Parrish had spoken out so vehemently against Gina, Ian had made a few discreet enquiries via an old friend in the Louth clergy. He had kept the information to himself, realising that Margaret, who would do anything to save her son from Gina's clutches, probably wouldn't be safe with such knowledge. It wasn't until he was about to return to London that he decided to give the address to Christie.

Christie took to walking the sea bank for hours at a time, in all weathers. Sometimes it was so hot that she nearly passed out. At other times wind or rain nearly drove her from the footpath.

The marshes had lost their magic for Christie, but they alone held the answer to what had happened to Delphi. Day after day, they drew her back to sit on the damp grass and stare into the bleak, empty vista. She had no idea what she hoped to find out there. Perhaps she was simply running away. She couldn't face anyone at the moment, only Liz and Matt and even them in small doses. The desolation of the marsh reflected her state of mind perfectly. As she searched the wilderness for clues as to what had happened, so she searched her soul for a solution.

Gina had stuck rigidly to the story that Delphi had been safe and well and settling down to watch a film when she went out for her walk. She said she must have been away for longer than she'd intended, and Delphi had gone out to meet her. Gina had no idea why she had taken the marsh path, although she admitted she'd often told her how much she loved that particular walk. She swore that on that night she had told Delphi she was going to walk through the village. Throughout, her manner was one of horror and disbelief over what had happened and, quite cleverly, Christie thought, she assumed the blame for not returning earlier. Jane and Tom were quick to insist that she was in no way responsible for the death, that she couldn't have known what Delphi would do.

But Christie had no doubt that Gina was to blame. And something else was quietly eating at her.

Because of the nature of the death, an inquest had been opened, then adjourned while evidence was collected. Little had been found, and the coroner was soon able to confirm the cause of death.

Christie had sat with Matt and Liz at the back of the room and listened to the statements of the police and the forensic reports. There had to be something, anything that might introduce an element of doubt as to the manner of Delphi's death. But there was nothing. The verdict was accidental death by drowning. Matt had said there was no other option. It was inevitable.

The one tiny thing that had stayed with her, something no one attached any importance to, was a small item found on the body. In pocket of her trousers was a folded handkerchief with the initials "GS" in one corner. The fabric would once have been white. Gina had confirmed that it was hers and that she had loaned it to Delphi earlier in the day when her hay fever had flared up. At the time it meant nothing to Christie, but later, as she was driving home, a question arose. If Gina had loaned Delphi the hankie, why had she not used it? You generally only begged a hankie if you were desperate to blow your nose or wipe away tears, and Gina had stated that her hay fever was bad. She recalled Delphi once complaining that she was going through paper tissues "like there was no tomorrow." She had made a comment about leaving tissues in the wash. Christie then recalled Delphi's car keys, purse, mobile phone and two packets of tissues, left on the counter at Tadema House. So why borrow that hankie?

Hardly vital evidence, she supposed, but still it worried away at her. She could make nothing of it, and it led her to no conclusions. But she couldn't forget it.

* * *

'Do you think I should go to the funeral tomorrow?' Matt peered dubiously into his wardrobe.

Liz shrugged. 'I'm not sure, sweetheart. I hardly knew the girl myself, and I'm only going to support Christie. With all the high emotion funerals tend to generate, I'm a bit worried about what might happen between her and Gina.'

Matt had been thinking along exactly the same lines. 'I'd hate her to turn on Christie, but equally Christie could lose it with Gina. If I went, it would be solely to keep an eye open for trouble.'

'I'll be doing that, never fear.' Liz chuckled. 'It's all right. I can see your dread at the thought of having to buy a new suit. It's written all over your face.'

He patted his stomach. 'I'm just a little concerned that all this contented good living might have affected my waistline. Only a tad, mind.' He pulled a face. 'And I hate funerals. I've seen far too many for my liking.'

'Leave me to go, then. I won't have time to feel maudlin, I'll be too busy keeping an eye on those two.'

Greatly relieved, Matt gave her kiss and thanked her.

Liz was lying on the bed, taking a few moments to relax. She tried to do this on afternoons when they weren't too busy, just to make sure not to overtire herself and bring on one of those damned headaches.

Matt lay down beside her. They held hands and stared up at the ceiling. 'Bryn has hit a brick wall concerning Gina's past, and her connection to Lindsay is too tenuous for him to spend any more time and resources on,' he said after a while. 'But I can't get it out of my head that that woman hasn't finished yet.'

Liz murmured in agreement. 'Since Christie told us what terrible things Gina was "hypothetically" proposing, I can't help fearing for Tom and Jane. Common sense dictates that she wouldn't dare hurt them now. Being connected to one "accidental" death is feasible, but another? A third? Far too risky.'

'Unless she finds a way to shift the blame onto someone else?' It was an ominous thought, but given her previous machinations, it was possible.

'Christie?' Liz shivered.

'Who else?'

'But if Gina did orchestrate the death of Delphi, it would have constituted her last act, her supreme moment. Wouldn't it? Surely, that would be checkmate.'

Matt wasn't convinced. Two players remained. What did she have planned for them before the denouement? 'You know, I've been thinking about some old case histories involving serial killers and trying to compare some of their actions to those of Gina. I hate to say this, but I don't think our Christie has heard the last of Gina Spearman.' He turned his head to stare into Liz's eyes. 'I suspect at some point she will want to make Christie fully aware of exactly what she has done.'

'What? Admit it to her? Surely not.'

'She will need Christie to know exactly how clever and dangerous she really is. By mentioning the mother, Christie pulled a punch on her that struck home. But Gina knows that Christie is no match for her; she's too soft, doesn't have the killer instinct.' He paused. 'And if that happens, what will Christie's reaction be?'

'I dread to even think.' She groaned. 'Should we warn her?'

'I think we're damned if we do and damned if don't, but my gut instinct says no. Well, not yet anyway. Get the funeral over first and then we'll think again.'

They lay for a while in silence, each lost in thought. Then Liz said, 'With all this upset recently I forgot to ask you about that woman Paul Redman told you about. You said she was on holiday. When's she due back?'

'Tomorrow, so if I'm not going to the funeral, I'll get off early and see her. Her name is Penny Moon and she's a lay preacher with the Fenfleet Methodist Church.' Matt propped himself up on his elbow. 'I know it's probably the kiss of death, but I've got high hopes for this one, darling. Paul reckons this lady might have seen something but never really appreciated its significance, which is why she didn't come forward at the time. He's practically been living at that garden centre, begging all and sundry to help him. A few of the members of staff, those who knew Lindsay Harrison, have formed a kind of support group for him.' Matt chuckled. 'They feel sorry for Paul and are trying to help him. It was one of them who recalled Penny and something she once said about Lindsay.'

'And what about our police-hating media troll, Duncan Hartland? I haven't heard too much about him recently,' Liz said.

'Probably because he got himself mugged last week. He's been somewhat quieter than usual.' Matt frowned. 'I reckon he upped his game regarding Paula Harrison.'

'Oh. And someone finally warned him off?'

'Looks that way. The upside is that the vitriol seems to have gone out of his social media posts and Bryn says they're no longer looking at him as a suspect for Lindsay's murder.

They think he really started all that media stuff to look good in Paula's eyes, so the heat is off a bit for Charley Anders.'

Liz turned and gave him a long look. 'But not for you, is it, babe? You want to find who killed that girl, don't you?'

'I do,' he breathed. 'I need to know that we are still . . . how can I put it? Still "of service," if you get my meaning. Able to make a difference.'

'To still serve.'

'Yes, Liz, that's it! Still serve the public, like we swore to do, even if we don't have warrant cards or uniforms anymore.'

She snuggled in closer to him. 'You'll always do that, my darling, it's in your blood.'

'Bless you.' He kissed the top of her head. But he still needed to prove it, if only for his own satisfaction.

* * *

Christie had already laid out her clothes ready for the funeral the following morning. She didn't want to be panicking over what to wear at the last minute. Now she was at a loose end, so she decided to take a walk to Stone House and call on Pip and Dominic. She hadn't seen much of them since Ian left, and she missed their company.

She found Pip, as usual, in her kitchen, up to her elbows in flour. 'Hey, Christie! Come on in.' She nodded towards a stool. 'You don't mind if I carry on with this, do you?'

Christie sat down and watched.

'I hear you and Tom fell out. Naughty, naughty!' said Pip, mischievously.

Christie was startled.

Pip smiled, 'Oh, don't worry, you get to hear everything in a job like this. I can't even remember who mentioned it. Someone just commented on it in passing.'

'I'm just amazed to be a topic of conversation,' Christie said.

Pip laughed. 'You obviously haven't lived in a village before, have you? People have already got you and Tom Parrish married off.'

Christie stared. 'I'd have thought they'd have paired him up with his boss, not me.'

'Oh no. You are much more interesting. You're the enigmatic stranger who works for a famous author. And let's face it, most people round here regard Gina Spearman with considerable distrust.'

'I suppose you only have to upset one or two people for the whole village to take against you.'

'Correct. Margaret Parrish is well-liked, and she doesn't have a good word to say about her. And Denis hates her. He reckons if poor Delphi hadn't been running around after Gina Spearman, she'd still be here today. On the other hand, the woman does a lot for local charities, runs several respected retail establishments and to all intents and purposes is a pillar of the community. She'll always have supporters as well as enemies.' She cocked her head at Christie. 'No guesses as to which team you'll join. Gina's not exactly your favourite person, is she?'

Christie said nothing. Other than Ian, Liz and Matt, no one knew of her suspicions regarding Gina.

Changing the subject, Pip asked how Auden was getting on. His condition was slowly improving, Christie said. The frightening episodes that had led them to fear the worst had lessened, and he and Richard were now working on finishing his book.

'And you, Christie? Any plans for the future?' Pip kept her eyes on her pastry.

'I have no idea,' Christie said flatly. 'Everything started so brilliantly and now, what with Delphi dying and Tom so angry, the shine has gone off it all.'

'But you and he are still talking, aren't you?' said Pip. 'Life does that. It has a nasty habit of turning things upside down, but then it throws open new doors.' She smiled at Christie. 'Bridges can be built, you know. Don't give up on Tom.'

'I never did,' said Christie sadly. 'He gave up on me.'

'Under orders from Gruppenfuhrer Spearman, no doubt.' Pip's loud laugh sent a cloud of flour flying up in the air. 'Oh, Christie! When the guest house is quiet, I leave Dom in charge and help out down at the local pub, and believe me, nothing gets past a barmaid! Half of my customers can see the way she has her little marionettes dancing with a twitch of her wrist. It's happened before, you know, a long while back, and, believe me, people in small villages have long memories.' Her smile faded. 'Hang on in there. One day he'll see sense, or maybe someone will cut the strings, then he'll need someone to put him together again. If you think he's worth it, and personally I do, then stick it out, girl!'

Later, Christie walked back to The Mulberries with renewed optimism. How fortunate that she'd gone to see Pip.

CHAPTER THIRTY-FIVE

Considering that Liz had little close connection with the deceased, the funeral of Delphi Seaton was one of the grimmest she'd ever attended. An air of shock seemed to hang over the entire congregation like a pall. The service itself featured no poems, songs or spoken remembrances, and even the hymns were intoned with little energy. The eulogy depressed rather than lifted the spirits.

Liz spent her time close to Christie, watching the attendees. She kept her closest eye on Gina Spearman, whose crocodile tears were a masterful piece of theatre. There was no doubt in her mind that they were a performance.

More interesting was the behaviour of Christie herself. She seemed to take in everything but register nothing. Throughout the entire ceremony, she kept her gaze fixed on Gina. Liz found something very disturbing in that gaze.

Denis had to leave immediately after the service, saying he wouldn't be able to bear the interment. A relative, who looked as if he could be a brother, followed him out and drove him away. As Delphi's parents weren't there either, it remained to her friends, workmates and neighbours to lay her to rest. Before he left, Denis handed Tom a single red rose and asked him to place it on the coffin for him, so it was Tom who assumed position at the head of the grave.

Gina joined him. She clung to his arm, sobbing, apparently stricken by the loss of her friend. Liz felt sickened, so it wasn't hard to guess at Christie's reaction to the performance. Liz noticed Jane Waterhouse, looking like a wraith herself, a diaphanous black shadow hovering behind Tom and Gina.

Tom was silent, his face drawn and haggard. On two occasions, Liz saw his gaze wander to Christie, and she thought his look contained a kind of helpless bewilderment. She saw Christie meet that gaze with one of intense sadness, but whether this was for Delphi, or Tom himself, Liz had no idea.

They left as the first handful of soft brown soil landed on the coffin. It seemed that no one had the heart to return to Denis's home afterwards. They sat in the car and watched everyone drift silently away.

After a while, Christie turned to her and said, 'How did she do it?'

'Do what?' Liz asked.

'Stand by that grave and feign desolation, all the time knowing what really happened to Delphi. When she probably stood on the sea bank and watched her die.'

Christie's tears flowed freely now. 'I hope she wasn't fed too many lies about me, Liz,' she gasped between sobs. 'I truly liked her, and I'd hoped that when I moved here permanently, we could have got to know each other better and become good friends.'

Liz squeezed her hand.

'I let her down, Liz. Oh, I'm under no illusions. Gina would have gone ahead with her plan whether I'd confronted her or not, but I speeded everything up — you said that yourself the other day. I was the catalyst. Now poor Delphi's gone, who will be next?'

Liz wanted to reassure her that Gina would never dare attempt another "accident" but recalled Matt's words and kept quiet.

'I've been tempted to tell Tom and Jane of my fears,' said Christie, 'and to hell with the consequences.' She sighed shakily. 'Then I realised how useless that would be. They would close ranks around her, and I would never be able to help them.'

Liz agreed. She started the car. 'We need a drink, my friend. Your place or mine?'

Christie gave her a weak smile. 'Can we go home to The Mulberries, please? Even if that means you can only have one drink?'

'I'll survive.' Liz looked at her steadily. 'You're sure you'll be okay on your own?'

She nodded. 'It's over now.' She pointed to the graveyard. 'Time to move forward.'

Liz pulled away, hoping fervently that Gina would let her friend do just that.

* * *

After waving her cousin off, Christie hurried upstairs and tore off her funeral attire, pulled on a baggy sweatshirt and a pair of old jeans and immediately felt better.

She was tempted to have another drink, but reminding herself of how early it was, opted for a walk around the garden, to breathe in some fresh air. She should ring Ian to let him know that she was okay, but she needed a few moments' quiet first.

She sat on the bench and held her face to the warm sun. At least there had been no arguments, which was something to be thankful for, although there had been a moment when she had been tempted to push Gina into the grave.

She got up and went inside. The cottage looked perfect bathed in sunlight. Hopefully, it wouldn't be too long before Jane could capture it in paint.

Next door's cat was curled up in the porch and a late-flowering climber had burst into glorious bloom over the old slates on the porch roof. It was an idyllic scene.

A scene whose peace was shattered when she found Gina waiting by her front door.

Further down the lane, tucked just out of sight behind the hedge, was the blue Peugeot. There was no sign of Tom.

'He's not here,' Gina said calmly. 'He dropped me back home, then I borrowed his car.'

'What's wrong with yours?' Christie asked.

'No idea. I'm not mechanically minded.'

Christie would have put money on the fact that her car was fine. It had only been in for a service the day that Delphi died. So why did she want to maroon Tom at Tadema House while she came here? 'What do you want, Gina?'

'Aren't you going to ask me in?'

'No. Say what you have to and go.'

'What about your neighbours? Jane's aunt and uncle, I believe.'

But Lynne and Bill had gone to Gibraltar Point for the day. 'You heard me, Gina. Spit it out or go.'

'Have it your way, Christie. Just a word of advice. You mentioned taking my friends to Louth. Well, I suggest you reconsider. You see, I know something about Tom's family history, and that of his father in particular. It would be awful if Tom were to find out about this little skeleton in the cupboard, don't you think? It could be *so* damaging.'

Christie couldn't speak. She hated this woman with all her heart. So this was to be Tom's fate. But how the hell had she found out about him?

Gina laughed coldly. 'I see you know the story. I thought dear Margaret might have confided in you, but I wasn't sure. You were her bright, shining hero, come to save her son from the wicked Gina. Shame you weren't quite up to it. Anyway, I'll leave you to consider carefully what you decide to do about Louth. I suggest you forget that you ever went there, unless you want your bookish little friend to learn a few nasty truths about Daddy.'

'You vicious, murdering cow!'

'Dear me! What a temper she has. And I suggest you start showing me some respect from now on.' Her voice became menacing. 'I'd think very carefully about Tom before you open your mouth. In fact, *if* you can sell this archaic hovel, I would do it now. You're no longer welcome here.'

Christie was beginning to shake with rage and frustration. But Gina had more.

'Remember, Christie, there is nothing — hear me, *nothing* — that can connect me with Delphi's tragic death. But don't forget what happened to her. Despite what they say, lightning can strike twice.' Her face was a mask of pure evil. Christie knew then that she had killed Delphi, just as if she had taken a gun and shot her. And she would do the same to anyone else who got in her way.

The sun had gone, and a fine misty rain was falling. Christie stood by her front door shaking like a leaf in the wind. Seeing those cold, cold eyes, she knew that telling Tom about his father's madness and his possible congenital connection would be a positive delight to her opponent. 'How did you know about his father?' Christie croaked.

'I've always known. That's why I hunted him down and took him on. Retribution, you see. I had an aunt who worked for the government. She was a highly intelligent woman and the only one of my hateful family to care about me. She understood me, may even have loved me, but she was taken away from me before she could let me see it. She was blinded, you see,' she paused, 'by Thomas's father. She killed herself not long afterwards.'

'So you came looking for Tom. To make him suffer for it, even though he doesn't even know what happened.' Christie felt sick. 'And Jane? What has she ever done to you?'

She smiled wickedly. 'Jane has done nothing. She has all the talent I aspire to but never possessed. And she has that wonderful name. I've always hated Spearman. Jane is an amusement, that's all. I love to toy with her affections. Time to go, Christie. So nice to talk to you. Do bear in mind what I've said. Oh, and good luck with the sale of the cottage.'

Christie stood and watched the blue Peugeot roar down the lane.

Moving slowly, she went inside and closed the door behind her. Her hands shook so much that the brandy bottle rattled against the edge of the glass.

She sat down and tried to come to terms with the significance of Gina's words. How had she, who was no game-player, staked her all on the spin of a wheel? In entering into the game, setting out like some foolish Don Quixote on her stupid, misguided crusade, she had all but caused the death of Delphi, and then lost everything. Her home, her friends and the chance of a new life.

Christie broke down and cried.

* * *

Tom Parrish paced the big, opulent lounge. He guessed where Gina had gone and had a bad feeling about it. He hoped there would be no more trouble. It was starting to wear him down, and now he had another thing on his mind.

On their return from the funeral, he had commented on how badly Denis had been affected by Delphi's death. To his utter shock, Gina had laughed in his face. 'My dear Thomas, you are so delightfully naive. Don't you recognise guilt when you see it? Darling, he's eaten up with it! Granted, giving you that rose was a nice touch. But Thomas, really. The grief was all for show. Oh, poor Denis, too grief-stricken to watch her put into the ground.' She laughed again. 'A charade, that's all it was.'

Gina didn't know that he'd spent time with Denis, and he hadn't mentioned that he had accompanied him to the mortuary either. He might be naive, but Tom knew real grief when he saw it, and Denis was in pieces. Why on earth would Gina not see it too?

The phone rang. He answered it, thinking it might be Gina, though his mobile signal was crap out here by the marsh.

A bright young voice said, 'Ah, hello there, this is Shelly from Bonfield's estate agents in Fenfleet.' It vaguely registered that Christie had mentioned Bonfield's when Ian Hardy was having Evelyn's cottage valued. He opened his mouth to speak, but the girl was in full flow. 'Please forgive me for using your private number but knowing that you were so interested in purchasing The Mulberries,' she gave a little laugh, 'as in offering well over the asking price, we wanted you to know that we have a delightful little farmer's cottage just come onto the books. It's almost the same as—'

Tom lowered the phone back into its cradle and stared at it. So it *had* been Gina who had tried to gazump Christie's purchase of The Mulberries! So what else had she done? He felt as if someone had sucker punched him. He closed his eyes, feeling sick. He had been the fool of all fools! He thought about his mother, then Christie. Oh my God, had Gina gone to see Christie? Was that why he was stuck here?

The anger started to well up in him. Or was he stuck? He went to where she kept her car keys, grabbed them and ran out to the garage. Her car started first time. The bitch! This was all a set-up. Then he heard an engine he recognised and bolted back inside again.

As Gina got out of the car, he ran up to her. 'So glad you're back. Got to dash, just remembered something important.' He took his keys, kissed her cheek, then, almost pushing her out of the way, leaped into his car.

'Thomas! Come back here right now! I need to talk to you! Stop!'

He ignored her. He should probably have done that a long time ago. Now he needed to get to Christie.

* * *

When Jane Waterhouse arrived back at the gallery, Gary handed her a letter. She took it and smiled weakly at him. 'Would you make me a coffee, my angel? A really strong one?'

Gary gave her a little hug. 'Oh dear. Grim, was it?'

She shook her head.

'Then go upstairs and change. I'll have coffee and choccy biscuits ready when you come down.'

She did as she was told and, seeing the letter in her hand, tore open the envelope. A while ago, Jane had submitted a painting called "Fenland Twilight", probably the best water-colour she'd ever made, for the Royal Academy Summer Exhibition. To her amazement, she'd been shortlisted. They had emailed asking her to deliver the original painting to the Royal Academy for the final round. She was planning to take it over the following week.

Jane read the letter eagerly, then frowned. She didn't understand. It didn't make any kind of sense. She didn't have a secretary, so how could he or she have possibly contacted them and said she was withdrawing?

In a state of utter confusion, she went back downstairs to Gary. 'Have you ever called yourself my secretary?'

'What?' Gary laughed. 'Certainly not. Assistant, right-hand man, friend, confidante, tea-maker, skivvy, cleaner, general dogsbody and gofer, yes, but secretary, no.'

She handed him the letter.

'It's a mistake. They've muddled you up with someone else, haven't they? Ring them. Do it now!' He pushed the letter back into her hand.

She did. There was no mistake. She had been removed from the list. The woman on the phone was sorry, but her instructions had been quite clear. Ms Waterhouse could not be reinstated at this stage, the finalists had all been selected. Perhaps she'd like to submit again next year.

She looked bleakly at Gary. 'I don't understand.' Then she saw something in his face that worried her. 'Do you know anything about this, Gary?'

'No, no, nothing, but I think I know who's behind it. It's the same person who talked you out of taking up that space in the Oxford Gallery.' He looked at her with compassion. 'I've never had the courage to mention this before. She keeps you down, Jane Waterhouse! She's jealous of your talent. Sorry, I know she's your friend, but it had to be said.'

She took her coffee up to the studio and flung it at "Fenland Twilight", wishing it were Gina Spearman's face.

CHAPTER THIRTY-SIX

'We need to get to The Mulberries! Now, Matt. Come on!'
Liz threw his car keys at him and grabbed her bag. 'I'll lock
up, you start the car, I'll explain on the way.'

Matt had barely got in from talking to Penny Moon and
had a lot to tell Liz, but he did as he was told. This sounded
serious.

Minutes later, they were speeding towards Christie's
village.

'You were right, Matt. Christie did have a visitor.' Liz
was staring ahead through the windscreen. 'Can't this thing
go any faster?'

'Not unless you want us landing upside down in a ditch.
And I assume you mean Gina?'

'She terrified Christie and more or less admitted responsibility for Delphi's death, *and* she's threatened Tom as well.'
Liz swallowed. 'But the biggest thing, Matt, is the reason
behind Gina's attempts to destroy Tom's happy home and
possibly his life. Christie wants you to make sure the police
know of this because it can be verified.'

Matt accelerated. Gina could have made a big mistake
in admitting to something like that. And if she realised it, she
could very well go back and silence Christie. They were just

over fifteen minutes away now, and Matt prayed it wouldn't be fifteen minutes too long.

* * *

Recalling what Gina had said about Tom's father and suddenly realising how it could be used against Gina had galvanised Christie into action. She had just phoned Matt and Liz when she heard another knock at the door. She froze. Matt and Liz couldn't possibly get here so soon after her call, and Lynne and Bill were out for the day.

Terrified, she picked up a knife from the kitchen counter. She moved to the door, pulled it open and jumped back, knife in hand.

'My God! I hope you're in the middle of cooking and not re-enacting the shower scene from *Psycho*,' said Jane Waterhouse.

Christie dropped the knife and gave Jane a hug. 'I'm so sorry! I thought . . . Forget it. Come in.'

Even in her current state of panic, she noticed that Jane was even paler than usual, and despite her humorous comment, looked terribly worried and upset. 'Whatever's the matter, Jane?'

Before she could answer, they heard the sound of an engine screaming to a halt outside and her fear returned tenfold when she saw the blue Peugeot.

As Tom tumbled out, she eyed the car warily in case Gina might be lurking inside.

He stood at the door, looking confused, until Christie realised he was unsure of a welcome. He waited, frozen in time, with the thin, driving rain plastering his thick dark hair to his head and sending droplets running down his anguished face.

Christie opened her arms wide.

He fell against her, sobbing like a frightened child, saying again and again that he was sorry. He held an arm out to Jane and the three of them came together in a hug, like survivors of some terrible catastrophe.

After a while, they went into the lounge and sat close together, while Christie tried to make sense of what they were both saying. How had it all changed so fast? She closed her eyes. When she opened them, she felt clearer and more positive than she had in months.

'Listen. Any minute, my cousin Liz and Matt Ballard will be arriving. You aren't aware of this, but the police are looking at Gina as a possible murder suspect, but I'll tell you about that later. Does Gina realise that either of you have had a change of heart?'

Jane shook her head. 'I've only talked to Gary. It was him made me realise what she's been doing all this time. I haven't spoken to her at all since the funeral.'

'And I just said I'd forgotten something desperately important and drove off. She'll think I'm acting weird, but she doesn't know about the phone call.'

'Then let it stay that way. It won't be easy, but you have to keep her thinking that nothing has changed. Then we'll all go to Tadema House together and have it out with her. If we stick together, she won't have a chance to work on any of us. Individually, well, I don't need to tell you what she's capable of.'

'She came here earlier, didn't she?' said Tom anxiously.

Christie nodded. 'She threatened me. She told me to move away, or my friends would suffer like Delphi did.'

Jane gave a little gasp and Tom swallowed loudly.

After a while, Tom said, 'What do we tell Liz and Matt?'

'Everything, except our proposed visit to Gina. We'll tell them about that after the event, okay?'

First, of course, Tom had to be told the truth about his beloved father's illness and the tragedy that had occurred because of it. It would be heartbreaking for him, but in her head, she heard Ian saying that the boy should be told, that it was only fair, and what if he were ever ill himself? He had a right to know the truth. And far better to be told by a friend who truly cared for him than someone consumed by hatred.

Jane and Tom nodded. Tom said, 'I'd better ring Gina and try to explain my sudden exit. I'll have to apologise, or she'll get suspicious.'

Christie agreed. 'Do it now, before the others get here. We need to keep her believing that nothing has changed until she finds us on her doorstep.'

Tom stood up. 'I'll do it in the car, just in case the others arrive.'

He left. 'I can't believe I . . .' Jane's eyes filled with tears. 'I've been so blind, for so long! How did it happen?'

After a few minutes, Tom came back in. 'I think she believed me. I said the pharmacy had texted me just before the funeral, asking me to collect some urgent medication for Mother and then with all the upset, I forgot. When I realised, I panicked. She asked me if I'd go over for supper tonight as she didn't want to be alone and, in her words, is "feeling so distraught about poor, dear Delphi." I said I would and asked if I could bring Jane.' He stared at each of them. 'If we don't do this soon, I could lose my nerve. What about you?'

They nodded. Both Christie and Jane felt as he did.

Outside, a car drew up. 'That will be Liz and Matt,' Christie said.

She hurried out to meet them. She had to tell them that Tom must be kept unaware of Gina's threat until she could break the news to him when they were alone.

Matt nodded. 'We get the picture. I'm guessing this dark secret that Gina wants retribution for is something pretty serious.'

She shook her head. 'It's going to be devastating for Tom, but Gina's left me no option.'

Matt and Liz were in "police" mode, firing questions at them as if they were back in the interview room. It helped. They made it real, solid. This was no fantasy, no game.

As the clock ticked on, many more incidents came to light. Tom and Jane went over all the times Gina had used them, played on their emotions. By now, they were looking wrung out. Liz glanced at Matt, who nodded.

'I think you've probably had enough for today,' he said. 'Especially on top of a funeral. You've all been most candid, and we really appreciate what you've told us.'

'It's been hard for you, we know,' added Liz softly. 'But we're just so relieved that you can now see her for what she really is. At last, she's beginning to make mistakes, and thank God you've still retained enough strength of will to recognise them.'

'I'm sure we don't have to tell you to keep well away from her from now on,' Matt said. 'We'll be passing on what you've told us to DCI Charlotte Anders of the Fenland Constabulary, expressing our deepest concerns about Gina Spearman. We'll tell you exactly why at a later date. Meanwhile, avoid her like the plague.'

They all nodded.

'Will you be all right?' Liz asked. 'Threats like that can be quite frightening. If you'd like to stay the night with us, our house is open to you all.'

Tom smiled at her. 'I have Mother to consider, Liz, and there's a lot of bridges to start rebuilding where she's concerned, but I really appreciate your offer. Bless you, both of you.'

Christie said, 'And I thought that Jane could stay on here for a while. We can give each other some moral support.'

'I'd like that a lot,' Jane said.

Matt stood up. 'Well, that's all sorted. Liz and I have a lot to discuss, arrangements to make. Ring us if anything else occurs to you, or you just need to chat, okay?'

He and Liz left.

For a while they sat in silence, until Christie said, 'We need to act tonight. It's the right thing to do. We don't have much time before either Matt or the police — probably both — pay a call on Tadema House. I appreciate Matt's warning, but this is our problem, and we must sort it out ourselves.' She looked at her friends with compassion. 'This will be the most difficult thing you've ever had to do, but it will give you your lives back.'

343

'Shall we discuss our strategy?' said Tom. 'We only have one chance at this, so we have to get it right. And whatever the outcome, it has to be our final meeting with Gina. I, for one, never want to see her again.'

His look was angry, resolute. Christie wondered how he was going to feel when he knew the truth.

Jane said that it might seem a small and rather selfish thing to others, but the way Gina had ruined her chance at the Summer Exhibition had been the final straw. 'How quickly love can turn to hate,' she added. 'I need to get back to the gallery. Poor Gary will be worried sick about me by now. I really need to thank him for making me see sense. So, what are our plans for tonight?'

They would keep it simple. Tom and Jane would arrive together, as if for supper, with Christie lying on the back seat of Tom's car, so she would not be seen on the CCTV. Tom and Jane would ring the doorbell, and Christie would slip out of the car and stand with them. When Gina opened the door, she would find all three of them.

Having arranged a time to meet, Jane returned to Fenfleet, and Tom and Christie were alone. Her first impulse was to tell him the whole story there and then. But it wasn't her secret to share, was it? It was Margaret's. But how to do it? Christie sat beside Tom and took his hand. 'Tom. There is something Gina told me that I haven't mentioned to the others because it's personal to you and your mother.'

He looked confused and a little fearful. 'What do you mean?'

'I want you to trust me, Tom. It's very important that this story is told while you and Margaret are together. I'm asking you to let me go home with you now. I promise to explain everything.'

He began to protest, and then stopped, his eyes searching her face. 'I'm not going to like this, am I?'

She squeezed his hand. 'No. I can't lie, it will be hard on you, but you won't be alone and that's what counts.' She stood up. 'I'll follow you in my car. Go home, Tom. I'll be there shortly afterwards. I have a couple of things to do, then I'll be right behind you.'

As Tom drove away, Christie made a call to Margaret.

* * *

Matt and Liz drove directly to Fenfleet police station and parked in the visitor's car park. It still hurt that Matt couldn't flash his warrant card and drive through the automatic gate into his own parking space.

Charley Anders held her office door open. 'Shall I call Bryn in to hear this?'

Matt said yes, and she rang the CID room. A few moments later, Bryn appeared and closed the door behind him.

Matt and Liz told their former colleagues that Gina had gathered a small group of people around her, manipulating them and controlling their lives. One of this group was now dead and the others were under threat. 'We know that this kind of psychological abuse isn't considered a criminal act — she hasn't broken any laws, and nothing has been proven against her. But we thought it important that you know what this woman is capable of,' Matt concluded.

'You say that Christie McFerran knows something about Gina Spearman that could link her to a crime?' asked Charley.

'She'll give us all the details later,' Liz said. 'It relates to a past event involving Tom Parrish's late father and his mother, Margaret.'

'Tom from the bookshop?' asked Charley.

'Yes. Do you know him?' asked Matt.

'Absolutely.' She grinned at him. 'I love a good murder mystery. I thought I might try to write one myself one day, but somehow I doubt that the language police officers really use would appeal to readers of cosy crime.'

'There's nothing bloody cosy about crime,' said Matt. 'We should know.'

'There's nothing cosy about Gina Spearman either,' added Bryn Owen. 'Okay, I've nothing concrete to connect her to Lindsay Harrison's death, but she's hanging around that case like a bad smell. I've been going into her background, from her schooldays onward, and her history shows a wicked woman in the guise of an academic and generous public-spirited figure.'

'Well, Christie McFerran would agree with the wicked bit,' said Liz darkly. 'We've no proof, as we said, but Gina all but came straight out with it, saying Delphi Seaton's death was no accident and Christie wouldn't want "lightning to strike twice."'

'Hmmm. That does sound wicked,' Charley said.

'I've got something else for you, Bryn. It might be what you're looking for.' Matt handed him a slip of paper with a name, phone number and address written on it. 'Penny Moon. She worked at Rowantrees and was there on the night Lindsay died. I saw her this morning, and she's prepared to talk to you. Right now, she'll be at the Methodist Church.'

Bryn took the memo. 'And did she see anything?'

'Oh yes, although at the time she didn't put two and two together. She saw two women arguing. Penny used to be in charge of the computer system that operated all the tills at the garden centre. At the time, she was trying to sort a glitch that was threatening to lock out the master till just as they were cashing up, so she didn't pay too much attention. Plus, it was past closing time and people were streaming out.'

'Why didn't she come forward at the time?' asked Bryn.

'She didn't make the connection. She didn't actually know Lindsay personally — most of the time Penny worked behind a computer in an office — but she did recognise one of the two women as the owner of the retail book outlet.'

'Gina Spearman,' murmured Bryn. 'But she swore she wasn't there that day!'

'She did,' Matt smiled smugly. 'She lied. The question is, why? Go and talk to Penny Moon. And if I were you, I'd get hold of all the CCTV tapes that Saltern-le-Fen would have seized and copied at the time of the initial investigation. Penny can tell you where she saw them, and you can take it from there.'

Bryn looked hopefully at his DCI, who nodded. He jumped up. 'Thanks, Matt. If there's any legal way we can get this woman off the streets, I'll find it!'

CHAPTER THIRTY-SEVEN

Knowing that Margaret hadn't wanted Tom to be told about his father, Christie called her. 'Margaret, if you want your son back, he must be told about the family history, and it's better coming from us than someone like Gina, who you can be sure will find the cruellest possible way to tell him.' When she added Ian Hardy's thoughts, Margaret was finally convinced.

Christie parked up opposite the Courtyard. She had no idea how Tom would react to the revelation. She hoped he would understand Margaret's reasons for remaining silent all these years. As she approached the door, she wondered if Matt and Liz used to feel like this when they had to deliver bad news.

The hour that followed was charged with emotion. Margaret handled it much better than Christie had expected. After all, it was far from easy for her.

Tom, realising that his behaviour since meeting Gina had often verged on the cruel, said that it was a lot to get his head around, but he did appreciate being told the truth. He even accepted with stoicism the news that it could be a hereditary problem. But he found Gina's actions incomprehensible.

His voice shook. 'And Gina told you that she'd actually looked for me? With the specific intention of wrecking my family and destroying my mother and the relationship we've had since my childhood? She hates us that much?'

'Oh, she knows how to hate all right,' said Margaret. 'It's love she has no capacity for.'

'She's twisted!' exclaimed Tom, 'And to think that I . . .' He put his head in his hands. 'Oh my God! I felt sorry for her! I was trying to help her, and I've hurt the people I love most in the process. What an utter fool I've been! She always said I was naive, well, she was bloody right.'

'It's not your fault, Tom,' Christie said, trying not to linger on the way he'd said "people." 'She's been planning this for years. It's a game to her, only it's real people being moved from here to there and then disposed of. We have to be thankful that she's finally shown her true colours before it was too late for you and Jane.'

'And you too, my dear,' added Margaret. 'The difference is, you came into the game much further down the line and saw through her immediately. She had already spent years grooming my son. It started so insidiously that back then no one, including me, realised it was happening.' She gave Christie a long look. 'Be careful, Christie. She could turn all her venom on you. After all, you've marched in and stolen her little playmates. More worrying than that is the fact that in daring to tell my son about his father, you've stolen her trump card. She will probably hate you for that.'

At Margaret's words, icy fingers skittered down her spine. It was true, but she'd come too far now to turn back. She just had to hope that the police would come up with something that at the very least scared Gina off.

When Margaret went out to the toilet, Christie took the opportunity to ask Tom if he was still up for tonight.

'Oh yes! Don't worry, I've already pushed my dad to the back of my mind. I'll deal with it later, when I'm able to think it through and talk about it properly with Mum. First, we have to rid ourselves of this . . . this disease that's blighted our lives. When that's done, I'll grieve for my father properly.'

'How will Margaret take the news that we intend to go back to Tadema House tonight?' she asked tentatively.

'With trepidation.' Margaret stood in the doorway. 'But I believe I'd do the same. If I were younger and more agile, I'd go with you.' She smiled at them both. 'Look after each other, that's all I ask.'

Tom would collect Jane and they'd be at The Mulberries by six thirty that evening. They would do as planned, confront Gina and leave her with a threat of their own, to leave them all alone once and for all.

She got up to leave, but Tom held her back. 'I'm not sure how to say this, Christie, but thank you. Thank you for not giving up on me. Most people would have long before now, and no one would blame them for it. I've been a real arsehole. I've no right to ask this, but do you think you can ever forgive me for how I've treated you?'

'You were an arsehole!' She smiled. 'But there's nothing to forgive, honestly. You've been a victim of a twisted mind, and you don't need people heaping blame on your shoulders when none of it was your fault.' She kissed his cheek. 'We are friends, Tom. We'll make a fresh start, okay? And I'll see you at six thirty.'

* * *

'Oh.' Gina looked mildly amused to see the three of them. 'Should I set another place for dinner?' Her gaze travelled from one to the other. 'Maybe not.' She stepped aside, holding the door open. 'You'd better come in.' She turned to walk ahead of them, but they remained where they were.

Gina gave a theatrical sigh and shook her head sadly. She looked from Tom to Jane. 'Don't tell me you've been listening to this one's ramblings?' She gave Christie a dismissive glance. 'A complete stranger, and an irritating and interfering one at that. I expected better of you two.' She looked reprovingly at them as if they were two naughty children.

Christie couldn't help but admire Gina's composure. She prayed that neither of the others would crack as the master manipulator got to work in earnest.

'Oh, for heaven's sake! Come on in, all of you, we'll have a drink and talk this through.' Her smile faded when no one made a move to follow her.

'We aren't coming in, Gina,' said Tom. His voice rang out, surprisingly strong. 'We've come to make things perfectly clear.' His eyes on hers, he said, 'It's over. We now know exactly what kind of game you've been playing and what kind of woman you are. Do not dare contact any of us ever again, understand?'

For a moment, Gina's face twisted with rage, immediately followed by hurt and disappointment. 'Thomas! How can you possibly say that? You've been my dearest friend. Haven't I looked after you, showered you with gifts and attention . . . ?' She drew in a shaky breath, then slowly moved her gaze to Jane. 'You too? Another one who bites the hand that feeds her.'

'Cut it out, Gina, it won't wash anymore.'

Tom's derisory tone hit home. 'You despicable and ungrateful pair! After all I've done for you. Especially you, Jane Waterhouse. You're a joke, you really are. Useless at business, a financial washout, you would have sunk without trace if I hadn't been there to bail you out. You think you're running a classy art gallery? Hah! A shambles more like.'

'Jane has more talent in her little finger than you have in your whole body,' said Christie.

'Oh yes,' Gina hissed. 'Her namby-pamby pictures. I almost forgot.'

Gina turned, ran into the hall, lifted the painting of Tadema House from the wall and smashed it with all her force against a hall table. Glass shards and splinters of frame flew everywhere. 'That's what I think of Jane's talent!'

Christie was horrified, but Jane said calmly, 'Well done. You saved me the trouble. That was to have been my parting gesture.' Then she laughed, the chuckle of a happy child. 'Oh, and despite all your efforts, I do know how good my work is.'

Gina stood amid the debris, a trickle of blood running down her right hand, and turned her attention to Christie. 'You, you snake in the grass, seem to have forgotten one important detail.' She raised an eyebrow. 'Something that maybe you should have considered before you engineered this little farce.'

'Forget it, Gina. I know,' said Tom.

There was a long silence. In the distance, Christie thought she heard the wind sighing and the tide lapping onto the marsh. A dead girl's whisper of gratitude.

'I'm warning you!' Gina screamed. 'You'll be sorry, all of you. You think you've won, but it's far from over, you wait and see. You'll all live to regret this!'

Tom put his arm round his two friends' shoulders and led them away. They heard a door slam and the sound of breaking glass. No one looked back.

CHAPTER THIRTY-EIGHT

A few days later, at eight fifteen in the morning, Matt was just pouring his second cup of tea when his phone rang.

'Matt, there's something you need to see,' DCI Anders said. 'How soon can you get here?'

He glanced at the time on his phone. 'Twenty minutes, Charley.'

'Then leave now, please.' She hung up.

'Liz! Grab what you need. We've had a call-out.'

* * *

Charley Anders closed her office door. 'It's Gina Spearman.'

'Again? What trouble has she caused this time?' groaned Matt.

'She's dead.'

'What?' Liz exclaimed. 'How?'

'Hanged herself. Perfect timing, as it turned out. Bryn Owen had not only managed to find proof that she had been with Lindsay Harrison immediately before she was murdered, but that it was Gina who sent all those gifts in the weeks before her death. Turned out the "man" in the car was

Gina. In the dark car park, it was easy to see the short hair, the jacket, and make assumptions.'

'Gina killed her?' Matt whistled softly.

'A little more legwork is required to establish final proof, but it's almost certain.' Charley looked from one to the other. 'Do you guys know of anything that might have pushed her over the edge? You did mention something about this alleged manipulation thing coming to a head.'

They told her everything Christie had said about their visit, including her threat to make them sorry.

'Mmm. So, coupled with the fact that you'd told her we were upping the ante on Lindsay's murder investigation, she decided to opt out.' She leaned back in her chair and frowned. 'She'd attempted suicide before, hadn't she?'

'On more than one occasion, as far as we know, but none of them were genuine,' Liz said. 'She always timed it so that she'd be found, or the injury she inflicted on herself wasn't quite severe enough to actually kill her.'

'Well, this morning's attempt certainly succeeded, although her cleaning lady was due to arrive less than twenty minutes later.' She glanced at a memo. 'Mrs Sharkey. Local woman, has her own key, always arrives at seven thirty, and does two hours every weekday.' Charley stood up. 'I'm going over there now. Want to tag along? After all, you've been a big part of this.'

They followed her out.

On the way there, Liz said, 'I just want to make sure she really is dead. A whole load of people will be free to lead their own lives if she's no longer around to torment them.'

'I'd like to say that's a little harsh,' said Matt, 'but I'm afraid I agree.'

The scene at the house was, as they expected, a hive of activity. Police cars, vans, forensic vehicles all parked haphazardly outside the entrance. A possible murder suspect was dead. Every avenue had to be covered, even if it seemed clear that this was a case of suicide.

The hall and staircase had been covered in protective plastic, and they donned the usual disposable forensic suits, masks and shoe protectors. It all made Matt ache with nostalgia.

'Well, well! My old friends! This makes turning out to this miserable fen at this time of day worthwhile after all. So, they finally admitted that they couldn't do without you, eh? How are you both?' Professor Rory Wilkinson, Home Office pathologist, beamed at them happily.

They chatted for a while, and then Charley asked how he was getting on with the deceased.

'Getting on fine, thank you, dear heart, though she doesn't say much. She was hanging on the upstairs landing. We've taken her down and bagged her, but not removed her yet. At first glance, it appears ridiculously clear-cut. Loft hatch left dropped down. Strong wooden pole placed across the aperture. Soft rope with a rather unprofessional noose attached. Sturdy, two-tread step-stool found kicked over beneath the corpse. And, finally, the angle of the ligature marks on the neck are angled with the higher part towards the knot, so definitely a hanging, not a manual strangulation. Pretty textbook, although I would have expected something so determined to have been carried out in a locked room and at a time when no one was expected, wouldn't you?' He raised an eyebrow. 'Still, we can't have it all ways, can we? A troubled mind often doesn't think of everything.'

'Was there a note?' asked Liz.

'Oh my! Was there. A right tale of perfidy! Treacherous and traitorous unfaithful black hearts that have cut her to the quick. She has named and shamed the guilty parties and cursed herself for selflessly showing them nothing but generosity and love.' He wiped away imaginary tears. 'It's worthy of a place in the literary pantheon.' Rory shrugged. 'Basically, chaps, she's well pissed off with her mates and blames them entirely for her topping herself.'

Matt smiled at Liz. 'Still the same old hopeless case, but I miss him.' He turned to Charley. 'When the SOCOs have finished here, could Liz and I have a little look around? I know it's not exactly protocol.'

'We're going to be here forever, Matt. You know how it goes, checking through the house and all her things. Don't forget, we have Lindsay Harrison firmly on our minds, not just a sudden death. I have no objection to your presence here, just keep it low profile.' She raised an eyebrow. 'And should you notice anything that you think needs to be called to our attention . . .'

'Of course.' Matt grinned.

They found Bryn Owen upstairs. He looked pleased to see them. 'Hello, boss. Morning, Sarge. This is a turn-up for the books, isn't it? Just when I was looking forward to a nice little chat with her too. Practically had the old handcuffs out. Such a pity.'

Matt smiled. 'Rotten trick, I agree. But in truth, lad, you've been spared. That woman would have played so many games with you that you wouldn't have known which way was up. Consider it a blessing.'

'Oh, well, if you put it like that. I'll just have to settle for proving her guilty posthumously.'

Matt asked Bryn if he had been up in the attic.

'Yes, boss. Luckily there are two hatches — it's a big, long loft up there, and quite unlike any I've ever been in. It's empty! No junk, no bits of old furniture, no history, no Christmas decorations, nothing. Forensics have already checked for prints around the hatch and so on. Wanna take a look?'

Matt said he would. Liz declined, saying she'd take a walk around the house.

They used the second hatch in one of the bedrooms. The loft was massive, part-boarded and, as Bryn had said, pretty well empty. Matt noticed the usual water tanks and a lot of TV aerial equipment, loft lagging and a few lengths of thin timber, but other than that, it was devoid of all the clutter people usually stuff into their attics.

'SOCO said he only found one set of prints on the cover and the hatch surround, boss,' said Bryn. 'The prof is right — clear-cut.'

They went back downstairs. Matt wandered around the big farmhouse, wondering why one person should want to live here alone. He came across Liz in the main bedroom.

'I was trying to get a feel for this woman from her belongings, but it's characterless, Matt. There's nothing here with any soul. It's just possessions or carefully placed show-piece items.'

Liz watched two uniformed constables who were methodically going through drawers and cupboards.

'I'm just going to take a look outside,' said Matt. 'Won't be long.'

'What for?' Liz asked. 'Can't be much there.'

'No reason, just want to poke around.' There was a reason, though. Something was making him uneasy, but he had no idea what.

In one of two double garages, he found something that set alarm bells ringing, but still, the whole picture wasn't clear. He stared down at a large compactor sack full of something heavy, which on closer inspection turned out to be damp soil. It had been tied tightly at the top and rested on a sack barrow. Next to it were two more lengths of broken wood, the same kind as he had seen in the attic. He leaned against the wall and thought hard. Either he was getting fanciful in his old age, or . . . Matt breathed out. Well, what?

'Matt.'

He turned and saw Liz walking towards him, white-faced. She carried an evidence bag and handed it to him. 'Found in the back of Gina's underwear drawer. There is also a bag of clothing in the wardrobe that would neither suit nor fit our dead woman.'

Through the plastic he saw a scarf printed with dozens of brilliant rainbows, all overlapping each other. He looked at Liz, baffled.

Liz opened the photo gallery on her phone and selected a picture. It was a photograph of Frances Morton's sister, Amy Roberts. The butterfly girl.

He looked closer, then Liz zoomed in on the scarf around her neck. Multicoloured rainbows.

'Frances gave it to us. It was the most recent photo she had of her sister before she disappeared.'

He closed his eyes and rubbed at his temples. 'Surely not?'

'This woman, this Gina Spearman, was pure poison. Thank God she's dead!'

Liz looked about as disgusted as he had ever seen her. He squeezed her shoulder gently. 'Better show that to DCI Anders, don't you think?'

'With pleasure.'

She turned to go. 'There's something else,' he said.

She waited, head to one side. 'Yes?'

'No. Sorry. Let me think on it. You go and see Charley. I'll be with you shortly.'

Alone again, Matt tried to lift the sack of damp earth in an attempt to gauge its weight. Then he picked up two of the pieces of broken timber and stared at them. It was possible.

He stood very still, his mind buzzing. He should be running after Liz to find Charley Anders. Instead, he remained standing in place. This could wait until they were home again.

Two hours later, a mud-splattered Kia Picanto drew up outside Tadema House. Matt watched as Liz ran across to the man and woman who stepped out and hugged them both. 'Frances! Jason! We can't be sure, and we're not a hundred per cent certain what this means exactly, but the police need you to look at some clothing for them. Can you do that?'

Frances reached for her husband's hand. 'Of course. I have to know what happened to my sister. I'll do whatever you ask.'

On the dining room table lay the bright, multicoloured outfit — the long shimmery skirt, the gypsy blouse, the fuchsia strappy sandals and the rainbow scarf, all carefully protected in evidence bags.

Seeing them, Frances broke down and turned her face to Jason. So they knew who the clothes belonged to. The next question that formed in Matt's mind was, where was the girl who wore them?

* * *

They did not get home until early afternoon. Liz hurriedly threw some sandwiches together and Matt poured them a scotch. It was far too early, but Matt needed it and he guessed that when he told her his thoughts, Liz would too.

'Okay, Matt. Tell us what's eating away at you.' She gave him a long look. 'And I gather I'm going to need this, right?' She pointed at the glass.

He took a deep breath. 'Consider this. Gina Spearman was hugely self-important. She had an ego the size of Antarctica, never admitted to being wrong about anything, was massively overdramatic and loved to control people. Correct?'

'Correct,' Liz said.

'She had made other attempts at suicide, all believed to be only attention-seeking. We know this for a fact.' He paused. 'So, Liz, is she really the type to kill herself?'

Liz frowned. 'Go on.'

'Now, this time she decides to really scare her little puppets. She wants to make them feel extremely guilty. So she decides on a hanging. But things need to be very carefully planned and quite a bit of experimenting done to get her "gallows" right. She weighs herself, then fills a large sack of soil to the same weight, drags it upstairs on a sack barrow and rigs up a gallows, using the open loft hatch.'

'Exactly as we saw it,' said Liz.

'Not quite, my love. She used a length of weak timber that she knew would snap when she dropped. She tested it several times with the soil in the bag. It broke every time. The broken wood was left out in the garage, with the sack of soil and the sack barrow.'

Liz reached for the scotch.

'Gina set the whole thing up for herself, in the knowledge that the worst she'd get was some bruises, a sore throat and a bit of chafing from the rope. She decided to wait until a short time before her cleaner was due to arrive, who would find her, lying on the floor, gasping and choking. She was also careful to leave the front door unlocked, just in case Mrs Sharkey had forgotten her key. At around 7.10 a.m., she jumped. To her death.'

He could see Liz running through what they had seen on the landing, then she said, 'Someone replaced the weak timber with a strong wooden pole!'

He nodded slowly and sank another big mouthful of scotch. 'Yep. The original timber was left lying on the loft lagging in the eaves after the stronger one had been put in place. Murder, Liz, plain and simple.'

Liz stared at him, then closed her eyes tightly, 'But, Matt, that means . . .' she faltered. 'Oh my God!'

'Exactly. Our prime suspects are Tom Parrish, Jane Waterhouse and, I'm afraid to say, Christie McFerran.'

'Oh fuck!'

'Nicely put. Of course, there's no reason it had to be one of them — hell, she made so many enemies in her life. I mean, I'm sure if Lindsay's boyfriend Paul had found out about her, he'd have done it with a smile on his face. Then there's Delphi's husband for sure. But do you now see why I've kept this to myself?'

'Oh Lord! What do we do?'

Matt reached across the table and took both her hands in his. 'I'm going to make a suggestion and I don't want you to answer immediately. Just think on it, for as long as you like, but take this into consideration at the same time. Charley Anders got Superintendent Ruth Crooke at Saltern-le-Fen to loan her their drone and a pilot. Just before we left Tadema House, they reported that there was an overgrown paddock at the far end of the grounds, quite close to the marsh path.

From the air, they pinpointed three rectangular areas of new growth. The term they used was "areas of soil and vegetation disturbance indicating fresh clandestine graves." He tightened his grip. 'Given a little longer, I would have put money on the fact that your Christie would have made it four.'

'And your suggestion?'

'For now, forget what I saw. Forget what I've just told you. They're more interested in pinning Lindsay Harrison's murder on her and, when they start digging up the paddock — well! There'll be a media-fest. The whole country, maybe the world, will be asking what went on at Tadema House.'

'No one else noticed that wood in the attic?' asked Liz.

'Bryn didn't make anything of it, and I doubt it would have meant anything to the SOCOs. As soon as our Rory mentioned the ligature marks being consistent with a hanging and that there was no fingerprint evidence other than hers, I think they all switched off.' He released her hands. 'They might just go over everything later and come to a conclusion, who knows?'

'But we would be covering up a murder, wouldn't we?' Liz, very pale now, sipped at her scotch.

'I'll do whatever you want, Liz. But, please, let's put off making that decision until we've both had a chance to really think it through.'

She nodded, then summoned a smile. 'On the plus side, this could be a three-in-one result, couldn't it? But it'll be so sad if one of those clandestine graves turns out to be that of Amy Roberts.'

It would be, Matt knew. From what her sister had said, Amy had met someone she didn't want to talk about, who had changed her whole personality. Who else but Gina Spearman? And the other two graves? Time alone would tell, but he was sure they were good people, possibly naive or easily influenced, who had had the misfortune to cross paths with a woman who was evil to the core.

EPILOGUE

One year later

Jane Waterhouse rented another, bigger gallery, close to Market Square. She regularly exhibited around the country and one prestigious art gallery, just off the King's Road in London, kept a minimum of three of her landscapes on permanent display. She was soon hailed as an exciting emerging talent.

Gary remained her right-hand man, added the title of financial advisor to his list of positions and, along with Jonathan, his accountant partner, took Jane out of the red and well into the black. He also managed to work another small miracle in the aftermath of Gina Spearman's death by contacting the Royal Academy and explaining that Jane had been targeted by someone bitterly jealous of her work. He told them that her exquisite watercolour had been purposely damaged, although he omitted to say that Jane had done it herself, and begged them to restore her place on the shortlist with a work of equal merit. He sent in a digital image which ensured her a position among the exhibitors. So Jane got to deliver her picture to the Royal Academy. It didn't win a prize but, with 4000 entrants, that was hardly a surprise.

More importantly, it marked a turning point in restoring her shattered confidence.

* * *

Tom and his mother Margaret made some big changes too. It was something of a gamble, but after several months of negotiations and juggling of finances, they bought the Reading Room. They completely renovated it, stripping the place of all reminders of its former owner, including her old office, which had been the scene of so many of her cruel tantrums. Tom took considerable satisfaction in the knowledge that in the process of extending the café, it became the ladies' toilet.

Margaret was happier than she could ever remember, and now felt well enough to help out behind the till for a few hours a day. Even when she wasn't working, she would spend her days sitting in the reading section, her head in a book, or chatting to the customers, or perhaps going out for afternoon tea with her companion, the Reverend Ian Hardy, who these days seemed to spend almost as much time in Fenfleet as he did in London.

* * *

Christie's dear friend, Auden Meeres, passed away just weeks after his final book, *Marshlight*, was finished. After the funeral, she went back up to Scarborough and stayed with Richard for a fortnight, to help him sort out and catalogue Auden's legacy and generally provide a shoulder to cry on.

A few days before she was due to return home to The Mulberries, he took her out to dinner, saying he had a surprise for her. As they ate, he told her that Auden had given him a rather unusual gift, a challenge that could benefit both of them. 'My dear,' he had said, full of excitement, 'some time ago, Auden had ideas for three books he had planned to write and then set aside. He gave me the full synopses. Everything is there! Plot, characters and storylines. He asked me to write them for him, as a kind of memorial. He says he knows I am capable of doing it, his publisher is happy for me to go ahead, and I have to admit that we have worked so closely in the past that I really believe I can do it!' She had been delighted for him and assured him that he was more than able to rise to the challenge. Then he had added, 'And I need a researcher, Christie. Well, not *a* researcher, I need *Auden's* researcher. He always said that his books would never have been as good if he hadn't had your amazing descriptions to work on. I want to work just as he did. Will you do it? He's left a considerable sum for your salary, and the location for the first book is Paris.'

She accepted at once. Paris! Lynne and Bill had offered to look after The Mulberries while she was away, and she was now free as a bird. Well, sort of. She and Tom saw a lot of each other these days, and she had an idea that when these three books were completed, and Tom's new business was running smoothly, it might be time to settle down. They had had one holiday together, in Greece. Their friend had never made it, so they went for her, visiting Mount Parnassus and the town of Delphi, and all the other places she had so much wanted to see. It seemed like the right thing to do.

* * *

On the last Friday of every month Jane, Tom and Christie made sure to spend some time together. If the weather was fine, they went to the sea bank at Sly Fen with a small bunch of flowers for Delphi. If the weather was too bad, they met at Christie's home. The disastrous and life-changing happenings of the year before had brought them together, and they wanted to remain close. They knew things about Gina Spearman that no one else could know. It was their secret, and it would stay that way.

* * *

The police proved beyond all doubt that Gina Spearman had murdered Lindsay Harrison, Amy Roberts and two other unidentified young women. Delphi's death was attributed to her, but of course that could never be proven.

Liz and Matt followed the progress of the case closely. Regarding that desperately important decision they had to make, well, they are still thinking.

THE END

APPENDIX

The Marshlight Mysteries

by

James Alfred Ballard

Tales from accounts of true happenings on that desolate area of Sly Fen

Up and down, up and down;
I will lead them up and down;
I am fear'd in field and town;
Goblin, lead them up and down.
—William Shakespeare

STORY ONE: LIZZIE

The day was bright, we tarried long,
Listening to the skylark's song.
Now twilight comes, and with it, fear,
We know we cannot linger here.

But night falls fast, the owl takes flight,
And now we pray for blessed light.
And there it is! A lantern's glow!
Rejoice! It isn't far to go!

We run, we cry, "You've come at last!"
Then we stop, and stand, aghast,
The light has gone, there is no guide,
No lamp, no stars, just a surging tide.

Laughter sighs on the breath of a breeze,
"These two were caught with too much ease!"
Blue flames dance and chuckle with glee,
As our bodies are dragged out into the sea.
—Anon

Her ankle throbbed mercilessly. The simple journey back from Old Bessie's cottage was taking longer than she could have dreamed.

She had collected the potion that her father had ordered to help his condition and was making her way home to him when she turned her foot on the uneven, damp ground. If only Alfred had been home in time to collect it. He always made the trips to Bessie's, especially later in the day when the light was failing. The old woman's cottage was in a perilous place surrounded by bog and unhealthy ground. How she had ever lived so long was a miracle in young Lizzie's eyes.

She knew the way well enough, and she knew where not to tread. It was just that the pain in her foot was making clear thinking impossible and she had to keep stopping to rest. Making sure that the pot of vile-smelling ointment with the cloth covering it was safe in her basket, the little girl sat on a grassy hummock and wondered if she had broken the ankle. She pulled her thick stocking down and saw, in the last weak rays of the sun, a dark stain right around the heel from ankle bone to ankle bone. The flesh was taut, swollen, and in the dwindling light, looked stretched and shiny. She was not a silly child — the only daughter of a fen eelman, she was tough enough, but as the evening fell, she decided that 'if 'twere a sprain, it were a baddun, but most like, it were broke.'

She moved on slowly. When Alfred got back, he would surely come out and meet her. She suspected the pony was lame again and her brother was having to walk back from town, and it was a long way on foot.

There was a sound to her right, a squeal, and she turned in time to see an owl rise up from the marsh, a tiny dark creature in its talons. The shadows were deepening, and the night sounds were beginning.

Lizzie was a tough child but the tales of the evils that ran loose on the marsh in the dead of night were starting to run through her head. She did not believe in the black dog — Hairy Jack, they called it, a dreadful phantom that haunted lonely places. She didn't believe in the shag-foal either, the demon donkey with flaming eyes, that was surely just a joke, wasn't it? And she didn't believe in the bogles, the goblins of green mist. In fact, she did not believe in any of the malevolent and tricksy spirits of the Fens. But it was hard not to be frightened of the night itself, and she did believe in the Lantern Man.

Since she was a babe, she had seen the fairy light out on the marshes. The tiny flickering flames that danced across the boggy ground. Her clever brother told her it was marsh gas. So why did it move away when you approached it?

Oh, how much farther? Tears were coursing silently down the soft, chilled skin of her cheek. The foot was hurting more and more, it was nearly impossible to even hobble. She swallowed hard. Alfred sometimes took a shortcut. It saved about a half a mile but ran hazardously close to the brackish waters of the marsh itself and was prone to flooding at high tide. She was sure the tide was out now, and decided that if no one had come for her by the time she reached the rough track to the back of their cottage, she would risk Alfred's hazardous route.

To a child with agonising ankle pain, that half a mile less to walk seemed worth the risk.

She finally reached the fork in the path. It was almost dark. The shadows from the night clouds were deep and menacing. Suddenly, from the direction of her home, she saw the bright bobbing light of a lantern.

'Alfred!' Her brother had come for her. Glory be! She would never sleep late on a Sunday again, never miss another service as long as she lived. Amen!

She made her way painfully towards her beloved brother. He, too, had chosen the lower path and the lantern light was clearer now. She called out to him, but a stiff breeze was blowing in off the Wash, and her piping voice was lost in its sinister whisperings.

Thank God for her brother! She hobbled faster towards the warm golden light of the bobbing lamp. Once, she tripped and fell, then struggled valiantly to her feet, panicking for a moment that she had lost her bearings and that her dear sibling would not see her. No, he was still there. Not far now.

Then it was gone. And the firm ground beneath her feet had taken on an insidious spongy feeling. The basket fell to the ground, the stinking ointment staining the cloth around it.

She turned abruptly, and her injured foot was suddenly relieved of the pressure of the hard path as it sank into the mire. A grim thought passed through her mind as her tired body was overtaken by the murky waters. Her brother had been wrong. It was not marsh gas. It was the Lantern Man.

STORY TWO: ARCHIE

See him flicker, see him flare,
See him dance in the cold night air.

See him glimmer, see him glare,
See him lead you who knows where?

See him laugh, see him smile.
Is it fun, or is it guile?

Does he tease? Or does he play,
Or does he steal your life away?
—Anon

'Jesus! Riley, what the 'ell do we do now? 'E's as drunk as
David's sow! And last I 'eard, 'e were 'eading for Sly Fen!'

'Well, we gotta get 'im. But if we're not back at camp
by curfew, we'll all be in the glass 'ouse by dawn! Come on,
we'll pinch a couple of bikes from the back of the pub and
get after 'im. We'll have 'em back before throwing-out time.
No one'll know, so long's we get a move on.'

They were no more than nineteen, their drunken mate
even less than that. They had all taken a fair few drinks, but

Archie had really pushed the boat out. The sergeant would have them all on report if they did not find the young soldier and get him back to his hut, and quick. Pedalling as fast as their strong legs would allow along the ruts and holes of the narrow path, Riley and Bill searched for their comrade.

'Where is the silly sod?' Bill jumped off his bike and stared across the farmland. The evening was gathering around them and the shadows lengthening.

'I dunno where the bugger is, but when I gits me 'ands on 'im, 'e's gonna wish 'e'd never set eyes on that barmaid! Showin' off, that's what 'e was doin', just cause she was eyeable. An' now look! If we can't find 'im, we are all gonna be in the bloody cart.' Bill swung his leg over the crossbar and rode off again.

'Dacker down a bit. I can't keep pace wi' ya! I think they put this bike's saddle on arse fost!'

'Shut ya tatie-trap and ride. It'll be dark soon. Archie! Archie! Where are ya? Ya God-damned nowter!'

At the end of the track was the high, dark mound of the sea bank. Both young men dreaded the thought that the drunken Archie had made it over the top and onto the marshes, but neither voiced his fear. They abandoned their bikes at the base of the slope and scrambled up on hands and knees. They were hit by a chill wind as they straightened up and gazed over miles and miles of desolate fen.

'Oh God! Riley, how we gonna find him out 'ere?'

Nothing moved but the dark night clouds that seemed to be racing towards them. All they could hear was the occasional bird call, and their own shouts were blown back into their worried faces as the wind whipped in from the estuary.

'Maybe we should go back to camp and get 'elp. We'll never find the silly beggar on our own.'

'Too late, Bill. Look at th' sky.'

It was almost dark, and a ripple of fear threaded its way from one lad to the other. There were no indications as to which path the young private had taken. In fact, it was nigh on impossible to make out a path at all. The wet and soggy ground seemed to be nothing but a mass of wet, grassy hummocks and mud. They stood, helpless, staring out over the fen, when suddenly they both saw a light, and about a hundred yards from it was the meandering and inebriated form of Archie.

'Thank God! Let's get 'im!'

The two lads picked their way uncertainly through the mire, towards the soldier. But he was steadily moving away from them. They yelled and screamed at him, but to no avail.

'Why isn't the person with the lamp leading him back to the sea bank?'

Bill was confused, but Riley was frightened. He didn't think it was a person. He had lived down here in the south of the county all his life. Bill was from the North, up Louth way. He'd know of the old tales but would not have seen the lights on the fen before. Wouldn't know the local stories. 'Don't look at the lights, Bill! Just watch Archie. We have to get him to hear us and turn round. He has his eyes on the hobby lantern and if we don't stop him, he'll follow it into the water!'

'I don't understand!'

'Just keep shouting! And don't take your eyes off 'im.'

The strange light weaved ahead of the young soldier. It was as if he had no ears to hear or eyes to see. He simply followed the light onward, wherever it led.

For ten minutes, they floundered on after their friend. Their voices became hoarse, and there were salty tears in their eyes. Then, suddenly, Archie was gone, and the bobbing, dancing light became just a hazy glow that flared for a minute, then disappeared. They could barely see anything, and the wind was now tearing at their hair with something like venom in its grip.

As Riley touched Bill's arm, they both knew they had lost the fight. It was time to save their own necks. The young fen man had taken careful stock of an outcrop of stunted trees on the sea bank. He was using them as a guide to retrace their footsteps. Bill clung to the rough weave of his uniform jacket and stumbled after him.

The sea bank was close, as Riley urged his failing friend on. 'Only a few more yards, Bill! Keep goin', we're nearly there!'

For a moment, the wind dropped, and Riley realised that the grip on his blouse had slackened. He heard his friend's soft voice whisper in his ear, 'It's back.'

The soldier's blood turned to ice, cracking through his frozen veins. He turned slowly, to see what looked like two cold, silvery-blue eyes regarding him. Or were they flames? They changed colour to a soft aquamarine and swayed gently to and fro. He was hypnotised.

Almost. 'Don't look! Bill! Look away!'

But his comrade's eyes were fixed on the lights, and he was slowly, almost imperceptibly, moving away from Riley.

Riley was a tough lad, and he decided he had no time to lose. He swung a solid punch at Bill's chin and knocked him to the ground. Half carrying, half dragging him, he pulled his soldier friend the last hundred yards to safety. As he sank beside Bill on the path, he heard the sound of hissing emanating from the marsh, and with a final flare of evil light, the will-o'-the-wisp was no more. The young warrior cried then, because he knew that eighteen-year-old Archie had joined the foolish fire on the Fens. Archie, too, was no more.

STORY THREE: LUCY

Remember me when I am gone away,
Gone far away into the silent land.
—Christina Georgina Rossetti

Lucy North was the youngest of three sisters, each of whom was imbued with great determination and single-mindedness.

From a very early age, Hannah, the eldest, had made it perfectly clear that she wanted a "career." She had worked hard at her education, and now taught in a prestigious academy for young ladies in Switzerland.

Elspeth had determined to marry well. Her ideal husband was chosen, wooed and bewitched by her charm, and of course, her ability to manage a household and balance the housekeeping with the skill of a genius.

Lucy, however, had another passion. It was the end of the nineteenth century, and London was alight with the fire of the English art movement. She begged her father to accompany her to exhibition after exhibition, while she drank in the works of Millais, Rossetti and Holman Hunt. Her dream was to submit a painting to the Royal Academy. Women were now painting and receiving accolades for their work, and she too sought to have her name in the art reviews.

In 1882, chaperoned by her long-suffering parent, she visited the newly opened Marianne North Gallery at the Royal Botanic Gardens at Kew. She was astounded. They entered a naturally lit gallery that resembled a Greek temple with high clerestory windows casting, that day, shafts of sunlight onto hundreds of botanical studies. The 832 paintings had simply taken her breath away. Even her father, a down-to-earth and somewhat phlegmatic man, had been captivated by the vibrant colours and exotic splendour of the fruits of the extraordinary Miss North's world travels.

From that day onward, Lucy determined to find her own forte. She experimented with colour and light. She studied the work of artists she admired, as well as those she didn't, seeking her particular niche, the genre she would shine in.

She began to travel, in search of landscapes to memorialize, to fix on canvas. It was beyond her family's means for her to tread in the footsteps of her venturesome and intrepid namesake. She would never see Borneo, Abyssinia or Ceylon, but she could be touched by the mist in the Scottish glens, climb the dizzy heights of the Cornish cliffs and swish in bare feet through the sweet meadow grass of the Cotswolds. Her talent was improving, month by month, painting by painting, and now, at her aunt's home in Lincolnshire, she believed that she had found her true métier.

She chose landscape, and was at her best in the wild places, the most lonely and inhospitable corners of her island home. She found she could capture a little of the sadness, the desolation, brief fragments of a melancholy moment, and deftly brush it onto, and into, her work. She had completed five canvasses during her stay in the East, and her father was sending for her the next day.

But before she returned to London, she had one remaining painting to complete, a dark and gloomy portrait of a young eel catcher, leaning into some brackish water and collecting his traps. She had a presentiment regarding this particular painting. This was to be the one that would change her life. It was, by far, the best she had ever done. Only the sky was uncompleted.

So there she sat at her wooden easel, precariously balanced on the soft, damp ground, gazing from her work to the horizon and back again. The boy who had modelled for the eel catcher had just left, promising to return for her in half an hour. He had made her promise not to move from the spot. His hastily spoken admonishments at her determination to remain on the fen at close of day were ignored in her desperation to finish the painting.

By the light of a lantern and what was left of the evening afterglow, she worked on frantically. A touch of indigo, a line of peach, a wash of sombre grey. There! Lucy took a deep breath and put her brushes down. She held up the lantern, shedding its rays on the canvas, and was satisfied. The painting was finished.

She sighed. The long exhalation was not out of place on the misty marsh. She felt as if the painting had drawn every scrap of energy from her, and she slumped forward on her webbing seat. She looked around her. In the blink of an eye, the twilight had turned to night. She doubted she had the strength to pack up her materials, close down the easel and bear her precious burden back to the house. The eel boy would be back soon, and she would pay him to carry her belongings out of this darksome fen.

Her relief at completing the scene had made her oblivious of the time. She sat for a little longer, waiting in the lamplight, then forced herself to pack away her paints and brushes. As she carefully began to lift her masterpiece from the easel, she saw his light moving swiftly across the boggy ground towards her. She put the heavy canvas back, deciding to leave it for her young friend to carry, and finished collecting up the tools of her trade.

She called out to him, but a light breeze wafted her greeting up into the night air. He was not far away now. She could see the glow of his lantern quite close to her, just beyond a dark cluster of scrubby bushes.

Taking her leather bag and folding seat, she moved towards him. He appeared to be a little further out than she had thought. She waved her lamp to and fro, and in answer, his light also bobbed backwards and forwards.

She was annoyed that he had not returned to the spot where he had left her. Her treasure still sat on the tripod — she could not leave it, yet she could not carry it. She hastened towards him, fearful, not for her life, but for the precious picture.

What was the matter with the stupid boy? Surely he was moving away from her? More in anger than in distress, she plunged forward, shouting the young man's name.

The light danced tantalisingly close, as she tried in vain to get her bearings and to drag her mud-sodden skirts from the mire. She fell, and felt deeper waters pull at her petticoats. She cast aside the seat and the bag, tried to haul herself up, but the weight of her heavy garments and high, leather boots drew her inexorably beneath the waters of the incoming tide.

Her last sight, as cold, peaty water filled her mouth, was the light, dancing joyously around her finest, and final, painting.

STORY FOUR: THE YOUNG SAILOR

Eternal Father, strong to save,
Whose arm doth bind the restless wave,
Who bidd'st the mighty ocean deep
Its own appointed limits keep;
O hear us when we cry to Thee
For those in peril on the sea.
—William Whiting

He was young. Too young to be onboard ship. But no one had given it a second thought, as he was strong and looked older than his years.

'Get that line, seaman! Afore it lashes yer t'death!'

The rope snaked past him. He slipped on the heaving, sea-soaked deck and reached frantically for a wooden upright to save himself from going overboard. He knew the line could cut him to the bone, even sever a limb. He waited, pushing his drenched locks from his eyes, then pounced on the rope and lashed it firmly.

This night was to have been his first ashore in many weeks. He may have been but a lad, but he aimed to partake in all the delights available to men from the sea. Now he wondered if he would ever see dry land again, let alone find solace in the arms of a beautiful woman.

One of the three lanterns was out on the poop deck, and the master had sent him aft to fix it. The storm showed no sign of abating and, as he fought his way to the stern along the treacherous deck, the ship plunged into a trough, and a great wall of water towered above him.

He flung himself through a hatch and prayed that the hull of the merchant ship would hold. Until tonight their voyage had been charmed, with good weather and no trouble from those cursed privateers. Then the storm had hit, only a few hours from port.

He staggered back up to the deck and thanked the Lord that they were still in one piece. Soon they would see the lights of the harbour.

It was hard to tell exactly where they were, they had been so badly torn from their course.

There was a cry from aloft.

The lights!

If they could only get a little closer to the shore, and the winds drop. He might then yet have his pleasures.

The captain brought the ship round and made for the welcome of the lights.

The first submerged obstacle tore into the keel and nigh on broke the ship's back. The mizzen mast snapped like matchwood and crashed past him onto the quarterdeck. The ship was dragged back and driven towards the shallows. A sandbank appeared from nowhere and tilted the wooden ship at an angle there was no recovering from.

It had happened in the twinkling of an eye. He had been sailing into port, the precious cargo safe and intact, now he clung to the spar, fighting for his life in the cold, dark waters.

Suddenly there was uncertain ground beneath his boots. It moved and dragged at his frozen feet, still tossing him this way and that, but he was ashore!

He threw himself onto the sand and saw his welcoming committee. Men, old and young, poachers and fishermen, women — beauties and hags — even children, standing in a line, staring as their bounty washed ashore.

Then he saw their faces. He had heard tales of the poor folk hereabouts, waiting for a wreck, seizing their chance to take a little of what the rich had. And it was a small step from waiting for the sea to deliver the bounty to helping it along with their lying lights and treacherous lanterns. He had heard they could strip a ship in one tide, even stooping to strip half-dead men of their clothing.

He spat saltwater from his lungs and reached out a bruised and bloody hand in appeal. Their manner was threatening, their eyes hungry.

His clothes would indeed be stripped from his body, but not by some voluptuous woman. No, he would be rendered naked in a much darker manner.

STORY FIVE: DICKIE

Collect your peat, your weeds, your eels,
Dance through the marsh on spring jack heels,
In the sea-washed home of goose and owl,
Of skylark, linnet and waterfowl.
Samphire Sister, the day is bright.

But eve'tide fall, keep the path through the fen
And believe not the lies of the Goblin men.
Ignore the call of the fairy fire
Or you'll follow their lights down into the mire.
Samphire Sister, beware the night.
—Anon

The children sat with their backs to the mossy wall.

'I'm bored.'

'Yer always bored, Georgie Moorcroft.'

'I'm not! I just hate the school holidays. It wouldna be so bad if me mam and dad could afford to take us away somewhere, but there's six of us.'

'There's six of us too, if ya count the baby. We never 'ad no holiday. Me, I've not even seen Skeggie, nor am I likely t', if me muther keeps having bairns!'

'Stop ya chitterin'. Ya sound like a load a sparrers!'

'All right, Maggie. 'Ave you got some better idea of what we can do?'

'We could go to see owd Carrie's new pups.'

'That owd beezum! Me muther'll gi' me a good slappin' if I go near 'er!'

The heat was making the children even more restless and fretful than usual. After a time, they decided it would be cooler up on the sea bank. Even when the haze rose from the burning cobbles in the village, up there a breeze blew off the Wash. The four youngsters made their way slowly, still picking and needling at each other.

Charlie Spanner was the first to the top. He stood on the grassy causeway, high up above the marsh, and held his arms out wide to try and catch the slightest rustle of air. Unlike Maggie, Dickie and Georgie, he loved the holidays. To the others, school was a respite, somewhere to go to get away from their families and the endless chores. Charlie lived alone with his father and elder brother. They'd been tight-knit since his mother died, and he resented sitting in the stuffy classroom when he could be helping his dad in the house or on the land. Even today, he had baked bread, cleaned the house and mucked out the chickens before he even dreamed of going out to find his friends.

They threw themselves down in the long grass, lay on their backs and watched the fluffy white clouds sail slowly across the sky. They looked for monsters and dragons in the drifting masses of what they called "hens scrattins".

'Look tha'! If ya squint a bit ya can see a boggart in that one!'

'What a load a kelter! It looks nuthin' like a boggart.'

''Ow d'ya know what a boggart looks like in the first place?'

'Cause I seen one!'

'Ya have not!'

'Have so! In Sly Fen.'

Charlie looked aghast. 'I'm not allowed on Sly Fen.'

'Nor am I, but I goes there. I collects the samphire and sells it t' owd Jessie. 'E's abless 'imself, but 'e still makes a bob or two out o' it from the cook up a' the Manor.'

'Maggie Midgley, yar a big ligger!'

'Doan' gainsay me! It's the truth, I'm tellin' ya. I'd taken Jessie a basketful, but 'e said the cook were doin' some picklin' an' needed more. It were nearly darklins, but 'e said 'e'd pay me double if I'd get it there 'n' then. So I went back to Sly Fen.'

The others had grown silent. Maggie had a reputation for feathering her own nest. She liked money and was pretty mean for an eight-year-old. She may well have gone back out on the promise of double pay for the aromatic marsh plant. They looked at her, wide-eyed, hanging on her every word.

'So, I'm going towards the nearest beds, not too far into the marsh, cause it's gettin' gloomy, an' I sees this light.' She stopped for effect.

'A hobby lantern?' Georgie looked frightened.

'No such thing.' Charlie was older and more worldly-wise. 'It's just burning marsh gas. Me dad calls it a "natural phenomena". Worrever that is!'

''Tweren't no marsh gas, Charlie Spanner. It were right strange. It bobbed about like a lantern on a pole, an' when I looked close, there were a boggart a'carryin' it! It were short and all hunched over, wiv a big, ugly, hairy head an' a hideous face, like a goblin!'

Georgie, the youngest, looked as if he were about to cry, and his friend, Dickie Wilson, put a reassuring arm around the lad. 'Yar frightenin' 'im, Maggie.'

'Good! Teach 'im not to go on the marsh, won't it? There agin, all you lot are too lily-livered to even go near the Fens at twilight!'

'We're not!' Dickie was putting up a good show of bravado. 'Me an' Charlie walked through the graveyard when it were night, didn't we, Charlie?'

'Aye, we sat on the Black Tomb an' all, and dared the ghosts to come and scare us! That's not lily-livered.'

The two boys folded their arms defiantly and looked at the diminutive, curly headed figure of Maggie Midgely, who sat cross-legged, smiling angelically at them.

'So, if ya so brave, you'll meet me at Sly Fen at ten tonight, will ya? Collect some samphire and prove ya not the scaredy cats I think ya are?'

'Me dad'll kill me!'

'See! What'd I tell ya! Scaredy cats!'

'No! I'll sneak out. I'll meet ya at ten. I'm no coward!' Dickie stood, in his most manly stance, above the girl and glared at her furiously.

Charlie felt sick. They had not really sat on the tomb. They had invented the story to look big in front of the girls. They'd got as far as the graveyard gates, heard a noise and run like frightened rabbits. Now Dickie was planning on going out on the fen at dark! And Dickie's father was a tyrant. If he found out the boy had sneaked out of the house after dark, he would kill him. 'Don't listen to her, Dickie! She's just tryin' to get ya in trouble! Think o' ya dad's temper! He'll gi' ya a right pastin'. It's not worth it!'

But Dickie wasn't to be called a coward. He marched away down the slope to the lane, calling back over his shoulder that he would see her that night. Sly Fen at ten o'clock, and Maggie had better be there!

At half past nine that night, Charlie Spanner confided in his older brother, Hugh, telling him of Maggie's dare, and Dickie's hot-headed promise to go out on the marsh. The older boy looked pensively at his sibling. He was sensible, nearly a man really, at thirteen.

'His father's a bastard, Charlie. He'd thrash the daylights out of him if he knew what he was up to.'

'I know. Do ya think maybe he would have come to his senses by now?'

Hugh shrugged. 'I doubt it. He's a stubborn one, is Dickie. I'll bet he's been stewin' on it ever since. 'E won't wanna let Maggie Midgely get one over on 'im! 'E'd never live it down.'

'Well, I'd better go out after 'im then. See that 'e's safe. Hugh, will ya cover for me with Dad?'

'No!'

Charlie looked downcast.

'I won't. But I will come with ya and get the silly sod back 'ome afore his dad misses 'im!'

Charlie punched his big brother on the arm in relief. He had not wanted to go out after Dickie, but a friend was a friend, even if he were dafter than a brush!

Their dad had gone to the next village for a meeting and would likely not be back before midnight. He had to cycle, and the meeting hall was way out the far side of Butterwick. He'd no doubt have a jar or two with his mates afterwards, and probably have to get off and push the bike round the narrow bendy bits in the lanes — it was preferable to falling in a ditch. They left him a note, just in case he came home early, and pulled on their boots. Armed with the hurricane lamp from the coal hole, some household candles and matches and a small bottle of their dad's home-made carrot whisky, the two brothers marched out into the purple evening.

It was just after ten when they reached the dark shadow of the sea bank. Sly Fen stretched out in front of them, a brown stretch of marshy land, interspersed by dank, black pools of water and a few scrubby, deformed trees. There was no sign of life. The brothers both hoped that the two rivals had seen sense and given up the dare.

A slight wind lifted Charlie's long, barley-coloured fringe. He heard a noise. He gripped his brother's arm. 'Listen!'

They stood stock-still and strained their ears to pick out what had not been dripping water, the night wind or a hungry owl.

'Over there! Damn it! It's Dickie! Look, 'e's right out there by that cattle trough!'

True enough, silhouetted against the darkening sky, Charlie could make out the outline of his schoolfriend. He stood on the wooden side of the cow's drinking trough and was waving frantically to someone a little to their left.

''E must be calling to Maggie. I can't see 'er from 'ere, but 'e's waving to someone all right!'

Some of the boy's words carried across the marsh, tossed about by the wind and thrown haphazardly towards the two brothers.

'So, who's the coward now? Come on, come out here and join me! Or are you afraid of the boggart?'

There was laughter, an eerie sound, not like their friend at all. But it had to be him, didn't it? They ran along the sea bank towards the spot where Maggie must be waiting. Hugh shouted to her, yelling at her not to go out on the marsh. But they could not see her anywhere.

Charlie called out furiously to Dickie, but the boy seemed oblivious to them.

'Oh, sweet Jesus!'

Charlie stared at his brother, then saw what had made the God-fearing boy utter an uncharacteristic blasphemy. A bluish light was bobbing and dancing in a meandering fashion, across the damp and boggy ground, in the direction of Dickie Wilson.

'She's going out to him! The little fool! The silly little fool! Maggie! Maggie! Dickie! Tell her to go back! The tide will be turning, for God's sake!'

But rather than send the girl with the lantern back to safety, an excited Dickie was calling her on, daring her, cajoling and encouraging her, deeper and deeper into the encroaching night.

'Charlie! Light the lamp! Quick!' Hugh urged.

He fumbled with the matches, dropping most of them into the soft ground. Finally, the wick glowed, he adjusted the wheel and a firm, bright flame filled the glass with a hiss, and brought their two terrified faces into stark relief.

'Hold it high! Make sure they can see it. And call out for all you're worth!'

Their shouts and screams made not one iota of difference. They could have been calling from a different planet.

Still the boy, now just a dark shadow, and the girl, but a swaying glow of light, moved towards each other.

'I have to go to them. I have to get them back!' Hugh's eyes were blazing as brightly as the hurricane lamp.

Charlie saw the spectres, the shapes that were his two friends, the blackened sky and the darksome fen. And in the lamplight, his beloved brother. 'No.' His voice was soft. He didn't implore, didn't demand or command. He merely said, 'I've lost a mother. Would you have me lose my only brother?'

Sly Fen fell silent. The wind fell too. The owl drifted away, silent, ghostly. Charlie felt his brother's arm about his slight shoulders. 'You are right, little brother. We didn't send them out there, so we will not die because of their foolishness.'

With a sigh, a breeze entwined its way around the boys. Above them, the first stars flickered into view.

'Sorry I'm late. Had trouble gettin' way from me mam.' The words, spoken with a slight sneer, nearly caused Charlie to drop the lamp.

'I see you've made it, Charlie Spanner, even if you 'ad to bring your big brother f' support. More than we can say for that wimp, Dickie Wilson!'

'Maggie! But we thought . . . But the light! You were out there! With Dickie!'

The child looked confused. In the beam of the rusty old hurricane lantern were two haunted and bewildered young faces. She stared, with the brothers, across the unbroken, Stygian nightscape of Sly Fen.

'What light?'

Thank you for reading this book.

If you enjoyed it please leave feedback on Amazon or Goodreads, and if there is anything we missed or you have a question about, then please get in touch. We appreciate you choosing our book.

Founded in 2014 in Shoreditch, London, we at Joffe Books pride ourselves on our history of innovative publishing. We were thrilled to be shortlisted for Independent Publisher of the Year at the British Book Awards.

www.joffebooks.com

We're very grateful to eagle-eyed readers who take the time to contact us. Please send any errors you find to corrections@joffebooks.com. We'll get them fixed ASAP.

Made in the USA
Monee, IL
21 July 2021

74069469R00229